the RUNAWAY *Pastor's Wife*

DIANE MOODY

Cover design by Hannah Schmitt

Front cover photo: © 101dalmatians | istockphoto.com
Front cover photo: © Adventure_Photo | istockphoto.com
Back cover photo: © strickke | istockphoto.com
Back cover photo: © Egorych | istockphoto.com

DEDICATION

From a former pastor's wife
to all those still living in the fish bowl, while—
teaching like Beth Moore,
reaching like Billy Graham,
nurturing like Mother Teresa,
parenting like Dr. Dobson,
informing like Oprah,
dressing like Princess Diana,
and of course,
playing the piano
(in a pinch)

ACKNOWLEDGMENTS

To Brandi Wilson, my pastor's wife, who makes it all look so
easy with three young boys and a rock star husband.
You're my hero!

To Debbie and Terry Capes, for your faithful
encouragement through all these years to complete this
book. Mission accomplished!

To Sally Wilson, my incredible writing buddy who keeps me
motivated and holds my feet to the Red Tree fire.
I couldn't do it without you!

And finally to Ken, my patient husband of thirty years
who believes in me far more than I'll ever believe in myself.
Thanks for making the journey such a cool ride.

Diane Moody

Prologue

Stillwater, Oklahoma
Seventeen years ago

I don't have a clue."

"He's your best friend—what do you mean you don't have a clue?"

"Correction. *You* are my best friend." Michael Dean leaned across the plaid-covered table to plant a pizza kiss on his girlfriend's lips.

"Michael!" Annie Franklin snatched a napkin to wipe her mouth.

"What?"

"Look at this," she flipped the napkin smeared with pizza sauce. "You can sweet talk me any day, but lose the grease first, okay?"

He watched his girlfriend, enjoying her reprimand. He drank in the sight of her long brown hair, curled and shining even in the dim candlelight of their favorite pizza dive. Her sparkling eyes, a rich shade of deep sable, danced as if hiding some delicious secret—eyes that never failed to mesmerize him.

And her smile . . . he could lose himself in that smile. Any time, any day. He reached for another slice of pizza, folded it in half, and took a huge bite. "You're beautiful when you get mad," he mumbled. "Did you know that?" He locked gazes with her as she finished wiping her mouth.

A reluctant smile spread across her face. "Stop changing the subject. Why is Grady so upset?"

He knew Annie wasn't afraid to plow through his evasiveness. After three and a half years together, she knew his every nuance. He could hide nothing from her. Inseparable since meeting the first week of their freshman year at Oklahoma State University, he enjoyed the honesty and openness between them—a trait he knew she cherished. And while they didn't always agree on every subject, there was nothing they wouldn't or couldn't discuss.

He took a long gulp from his frosted glass of root beer and wiped the foam off his mouth with the back of his hand. "He's ticked off at Coach for benching him the last five games. Can't say as I blame him."

"Me neither. You'd be climbing the dugout walls if it was you."

Michael cocked an eyebrow. "No kidding. I mean, think about it, Annie—it's our senior year. This is *it*. The stands are crawling with scouts, and there's Grady—parked on his keister. Look, I feel for him, but what am I supposed to do?"

Annie pushed her plate aside. "I'm sure it doesn't help that those same scouts are swarming all over *you*." She reached for his hand.

He lifted her hand to his lips. "Can I help it if I'm incredibly awesome?"

"Not to mention arrogant, cocky—" She pulled her hand back, grabbing a napkin to wipe off his pizza lip print.

"Seriously, I'm sorry it's happened to him, but at this point I can't carry him any more." Michael leaned back in the booth. "The stakes are too high. If I'm gonna go in the first or second round of the draft, I've got to concentrate on my own game. Grady's got to look out for himself."

"I know, but I hate to see him so depressed. Grady's like family to us. We can't just let him suffer. I wish there was—"

Wham!

A pile of textbooks slammed onto their table. "Hi guys! Oooh . . . pepperoni! My favorite! Scoot over, Annie." The spirited blond plopped down in the booth next to Annie, making herself at home. "Hey Brandon?" she yelled over her shoulder. "Bring me a plate and a Diet Coke, okay?" The waiter nodded his reply as she reached for a slice of pizza. "So what's going on?"

"Christine, nice of you to join us," Michael laughed. "Please—don't be shy. Have some pizza."

"Thanks, sweetie," she answered, missing his sarcasm. "Michael, what'd you get on that Business Finance exam?" She popped a piece of pepperoni into her mouth. "That one ate my lunch. I'll be lucky if I even passed it."

"I doubt that." He winked at Annie. "But I don't know what I got on it. I was out of town for a game and haven't checked the grade postings yet." He took another drink, watching his two favorite girls. Best friends since middle school, Annie and Christine Benson were as different as day and night but closer than sisters. Their friendship was something to behold. A genuine work of art.

"Whatever. Hey, Annie? Can I borrow your black dress?" Christine took a sip from Annie's glass. "I have a date tonight."

"The last time you wore it you got salsa on it and didn't bother to have it cleaned. Tell me one good reason I should loan it to you again."

"Because I'm your best friend? Because I know all your juicy little secrets?"

"You're reaching, girlfriend."

"Because my date has two extra tickets to see James Taylor next week?"

Michael slapped his open palms on the table. "Loan her the dress! Just make sure she hands over the tickets first. All right, Tumbleweed!" He stretched across the table to give Christine a playful kiss on the cheek.

"Stop it!" She pulled away. "You know I hate that stupid name. Grady says it all the time and it annoys me to death."

He ignored her as usual. "Hey, Annie. You 'n me and James Taylor. How about it?" His eyebrows danced as he crooned the opening lyrics of *Something in the Way She Moves*.

"Sing it, sweet baby James," Annie swooned.

Michael continued, his pitch perfect as he sang the familiar, romantic words of the song they'd long ago dubbed "their" song.

"That's real nice, but what's the big deal?" Christine

4

complained. "I was kind of disappointed Seth had these tickets. I'd rather see Springsteen. Or Michael Jackson. James Taylor is just too, I don't know, *sedate* for me."

Michael's serenade continued, the lyrics echoing in his glass when he took a sip of root beer. He wiped his mouth again. "Because James Taylor is a classic. He's the hands-down, all-time best singer-songwriter there is. You should feel blessed—your date has excellent taste in music. Just like us. We like the real deal, the main man, the true blue, Sweet Baby James. Don't we, Annie?" He reached for her hand across the table.

"We do, that we do." She smiled back at him with a wink. "Christine, the dress is yours. But this time, don't bring it back until you get it dry cleaned, got it? Tickets or no tickets."

"Sure. Whatever," Christine dismissed. "But while we're at it, there are more important things to discuss here. Like shoes. I need your black stilettos to go with the dress."

"Yes, Annie. She simply MUST have those stilettos." Michael batted his eyes, swishing his dangling wrist across the table. "Though personally, I'd prefer the strappy rhinestone sandals. But that's just me."

ᘏ

Annie flicked a packet of sugar, hitting him square on the nose. "Enough! I don't wear your cleats, sweet thing, so you stay away from my shoes. Got it?"

She gazed across the table at Michael who was still

laughing at his own joke. He rolled his head back, then finally caught his breath and leveled his eyes back toward her.

And there it was. That lopsided, boy-next-door grin that melted her every time. How could a smile say so much? As if every emotion in his body was expressed in that one simple gesture. Dimples as deep as the Grand Canyon set in a golden tan. Perfect white teeth. The sun-kissed highlights in his shaggy brown hair, still wet from his after-practice shower. Annie sighed, taking it all in. She rested her chin on her hand and lost herself in his warm brown eyes.

Oblivious to Christine or the other patrons of Hideaway Pizza, Annie felt a surge wash over her like she'd never known before. In that single moment, she knew without a shadow of doubt she would spend the rest of her life with this man who meant more to her than life itself.

I love you, she mouthed silently.

He winked again. *I love you more.*

Chapter 1

Tampa, Florida
Present day

Annie McGregor felt the heat of impatience creep up her neck as she clutched the steering wheel, the cell phone cradled against her shoulder. "Because I can't be there. I'm sorry, but you'll just have to manage without me."

"Well, calling Tuesday morning is rather short notice, don't you think?"

Annie bristled. "Fran, I know it's short notice. Something has come up and I simply can't make it to Bible study this morning." Glancing over her shoulder, she merged into the flow of traffic entering the Tampa International Airport, irritated at the obstinacy on the other end of the line. Didn't "assistant" mean you _assisted_ when necessary?

"What's wrong, Annie? You sound upset."

Fran's tone iced through her veins. "I'm not upset! But I don't think I should have to explain myself just because I can't be there. You'll do fine without me. Run the video then break them into their small groups. It's not that hard, Fran."

"Are you sick? Is one of the kids sick? Is it David? Is something wrong?"

Here we go again. All the questions. The constant prying. Why does everyone think they're entitled to know my every thought and action? Annie took a deep breath, willing herself to calm down. Fran wasn't a beast. She meant well. "Look Fran, I can't be there. Can we just leave it at that?" She cringed at the hypocritical tone of her own voice.

"Annie, what's gotten into you? You've been so irritable lately. And I don't mind telling you, I'm not the only one who thinks so."

"Fine. I'm irritable. I'm crabby. I'm obnoxious. So *sue* me."

She snapped the phone off and tossed it toward her purse in the passenger seat . Annie bit her lower lip to dam the flood of tears, desperate to keep her appearance intact until she walked through the door of Christine's cabin in Colorado. Catching her reflection in the rearview mirror, she was startled by the angry woman looking back at her. Tiny red lines laced roadmaps across tired brown eyes, normally warm and smiling. With her thick hair pulled back into a long pony tail, her face looked pale despite an earlier dash of make-up, her lips pinched in an absurd scowl. Disgusted, she muttered a growl and pressed her foot harder against the accelerator as she flew through the ribbons of traffic approaching the airport terminals.

Seated on the plane two hours later, Annie reached into her purse to turn off her cell phone. The special cell pocket was empty. She panicked, digging through the rest of her bag. Nothing. Mentally back-tracking her morning, her shoulders sagged in disbelief when she remembered tossing it toward her purse in the van, but apparently not *into* her purse. The tiny gadget was most likely resting between the passenger seat and door.

Great. Just great.

"Ladies and gentlemen, welcome aboard Delta Airlines Flight 1624 with non-stop service to Colorado Springs. The captain has been given clearance to depart from the terminal at this time, so we ask for your immediate attention to the flight attendant nearest you regarding our safety features."

Annie continued shaking her head, still livid at the blunder in her well-constructed plans. Then a thought occurred to her. Maybe leaving her cell phone behind wasn't a mistake after all. Maybe it was exactly what she needed to do.

Oblivious to the flight attendant's voice drifting through the crowded cabin, Annie looked out the window beside her as the aircraft backed away from the gate then rolled gently across the tarmac. Gates and hangars marched slowly by. She leaned over to look up at the sky, studying the ominous clouds overhead. *God, please hold the weather just a few more minutes until we can get up above the clouds. I can't bear to stay on the ground another minute.*

She realized she was doing it again. Her jaws ached from the constant clenching, a mindless habit she'd acquired over the last few months. She flexed her jaw, dropping her mouth open and shut, open and shut, working out the kinks.

Get a hold of yourself. It's a four-hour flight. That's all.

She closed her eyes, taking a deep breath. She couldn't believe she'd been so ugly to Fran on the phone.

What am I doing here?

Always, whenever the wave of hostility or anxiety began to threaten her composure, she reached for something to read. Earlier, while rushing through one of the airport gift shops, she picked up a copy of Grisham's latest bestseller. Trusting the author to give her the escape she desired, she reached for the book stuffed in her carry-on bag under the seat in front of her. Rummaging through the bag, she noticed the tapestry cover of her journal. Her heart began to hammer against her chest.

Not now. Not yet.

Finding the novel, she plopped it in her lap and flipped through the introductory pages to the first chapter. By the time the 737 screamed off the runway into the air, she'd read the first sentence four times. As the darkened sky swallowed the silver bird in flight, she slowly closed the book and exchanged it for the journal. Thankful for the empty seats beside her, she caressed the worn cover gently in her hands, tracing the rounded edges with the tip of her finger.

My life is pressed between the covers of this book.

For some reason, the realization hit her hard. For as long as she could remember, she had recorded the details of her life. Sometimes the entries stretched page after page as she relayed significant events. Others were brief—sometimes nothing more than a simple phrase or thought or a single lyric from a song that touched her. *But it's all here. The story of my life.*

Yet even now, as the plane's vapor surely trailed the expanding distance behind them, Annie knew what she must do. She swallowed hard and opened the journal.

I'm engaged! I can't believe it! The most wonderful man on the face of the earth wants to marry me! How can that be? It was so romantic—the way he proposed, surprising me below my balcony. Even the neighbors got in on the act. Yes, David McGregor, YES!! I will marry you!!! And I will follow you to the ends of the earth . . .

A slight smile tugged at her mouth, the memories rolling over her in a gentle wave. David had been such an unexpected joy in her life. Hard to believe they once lived such a fairy tale existence. She ignored the nagging swell of her heart rate, refusing to think beyond the entry. She continued revisiting the special moments of her life, occasionally skipping notes here and there, sometimes several pages at a time.

David's first Sunday as the new pastor of Tall Pines Community Church. We were so nervous! I got up early to make his favorite breakfast but he couldn't eat a bite. But he was AMAZING once he got to the pulpit. His voice was a little shaky at first, then he found his stride and spoke like he'd preached every single day of his life. I was so proud of him!

Her stomach muscles tensed. She remembered the glow of those early days of ministry, happier times now filtered through far too much resentment. *I was such a naive fool back then.*

She flipped through the pages, then paused to read the December 20th entry from just over sixteen years ago when a little guy named Max joined them quite unexpectedly.

We're parents! I can't believe it! It all happened so fast. I only wish we could've met his birth mother or at least find out why she picked us. Max is only 8 months old and absolutely adorable. Father, thank You for letting us be Mommy and Daddy to this little guy. He's the best Christmas gift—and first anniversary gift—we could ever ask for!

Annie could see the sparkling eyes and curly brown hair of the little boy who stole their hearts. Definitely a case of love at first sight. How was it possible this same bundle of joy was now driving? Shaving, no less!

She read on.

My back is killing me. I had 15 four-year-olds in Sunday school this morning and none of my helpers showed up. It never fails. How can they be so inconsiderate? It wouldn't be so bad except I can't get around very well right now. Baby Jeremy is due in three weeks, and I feel like a beached whale. Oh Lord, forgive me for being so frustrated with these folks. I'm sure they had their reasons.

"Would you like some lunch?"

Annie blinked out of her nostalgic cocoon as the flight attendant extended a small basket toward her. "Oh . . . yes, thank you." She slid the ribbon bookmark to her page in the journal, dropping down the tray table from the seat in front of her. She reached for her billfold, pulling out sufficient bills to pay for the meal.

She hadn't noticed the flurry of activity in the plane as passengers removed plastic wrapping from thick deli sandwiches, potato chips, and oversized sugar cookies. As if on cue, her stomach growled, reminding her she'd forgotten to eat breakfast that morning. She took a bite of the turkey and provolone sandwich, silently praying over her meal. Then, taking a deep breath, she gazed toward the panoramic view out her window.

Maybe it's all in my head. Maybe things really aren't as bad as they seem. If only I'd taken more time to stop and breathe once in awhile. If only I'd forced myself to take a few breaks along the way, go to the beach like I used to. Soak up the warm sunshine and feel the sand between my toes.

"Beverage?"

The friendly attendant had returned with a drink cart. "Yes, please. Mineral water with a twist of lemon?"

"Sure," the uniformed brunette answered, popping open a bottle and pouring it over ice in the small glass. She tucked a wedge of lemon on the rim and handed it to Annie.

Later, all remnants of her lunch removed, Annie retrieved her journal and opened it once again. She turned to the place she'd marked with the thin satin ribbon, working her jaw again. She skimmed through more of the entries, memories and details of a marriage and a family that somehow lost its way.

The night David arrived half an hour after Jessica's birth.

Even now, more than five years later, the resentment gripped a secret place in her heart. He'd apologized a thousand times. No, it wasn't his fault. Jessica had arrived two weeks early. There was no way he could have known when he left town for the convention. But by the time her contractions began, she knew he would never get back in time. She'd tried to be gracious and accept it, but somehow the apologies weren't enough. It was so much more. For the first time, as if in living color, she saw the literal reality of what their life had become.

The church owned David McGregor.

And he allowed them to do so.

Of course, he never had enough time to stop and ponder anything so close to home. They kept him much too busy. Annie still believed he was a good decent man who loved her and loved their children. So what had happened? How had David let it come to this? How had *she* let it come to this?

Annie had asked those questions more times than she could count. Rocking little Jessica, she would voice those concerns to David in cross whispers when he came home late at night. His response? A blank stare. Too tired to face a confrontation, he would nod his head, apologize, then shuffle off to bed. By morning, he would cling to her in bear hug embraces, grovel in more apologies, and make all kinds of desperate promises. But she knew things would stay the same. He would be sucked back into the relentless vacuum of his chosen profession.

She might as well be a single mom.

The thought sent a familiar grip circling her head. She reached for her bag and the migraine medication she lived on these days. The bitter pill melted under her tongue as she waited for relief. She tired of the beleaguered journey through the pages of her life, but she kept on. She was searching for something—anything that would help her find her way back. Anything that could give her a clue. Her body begged for a nap, but she picked up the book once more, passing months of entries as she neared the last few handwritten pages.

Last year's Mother & Daughter Banquet . . . As chairman of the annual event, Annie had barely seen her daughter and mother-in-law that night. Two bites into her salad, she was whisked away to attend to another emergency. It wasn't until the end of the banquet she spotted her disappointed daughter, still sitting at their table, stirring her cold potatoes in a pile of mush. Annie sat down beside her, stroking the long blond curls before pulling her into a hug. "I'm so sorry, sweetie. I didn't mean to desert you and Gran."

"That's okay, Mommy. It wasn't any fun anyway. Can we go home now?"

She could still feel the sting in her eyes at the honesty of Jessie's statement. All that work. All those months. But Jessie was absolutely right. It was no fun at all. It was a mother and daughter celebration, but *this* mother had spent only five minutes with her daughter. *Five minutes.* Suddenly, the truth pierced her heart: Jessica got crumbs that night—Annie's crumbs. The same kind of crumbs Annie got from David.

What goes around comes around.

Annie exhaled a hushed moan, rolling her neck to stretch out the kinks. *Enough of this.* But there was one page more she must read. She didn't want to read it. She had to. The words written there were still fresh, lettered only seven days ago.

Today, I drew a line in the sand. It is the line that divides all my yesterdays from all my tomorrows. I will no longer be who I have been. I am through with that life. I have to get away. I have to, or I will lose my mind. Tonight I made reservations for a flight to Colorado. I leave one week from today. I'm borrowing Christine's cabin while she's overseas right now. There I will figure out what I'm going to do. I will open my heart to God and ask for His help, but I will no longer remain as I am. Something happened today. And when it did, something snapped inside me. I needed David desperately. But he was gone. He always is. He was ministering to a hurting family in our church. They needed him. How typical. And how utterly ironic.

Annie slammed the book shut. She dropped her face into her trembling hands. *Oh God, no. Not here. Don't let me fall apart. Not yet.* She squeezed her eyes and pressed her lips together, steeling herself against another wave of emotion, this one trying desperately to pull her under.

High above the earth in a plane arcing over the Midwest, Annie knew she must come to grips with who she was and exactly what she was doing . . .

A pastor's wife, running away from home.

Chapter 2

Seminole, Florida

It never fails," Caroline McGregor mumbled. "The closer it is to school dismissal, the higher the chance for rain." She pulled her car into the long curling line of vehicles behind the school building. The afternoon downpour hastened windshield wipers into rhythmic frenzies, like so many metronomes all out of sync with one another.

Caroline put the car in park and relaxed. Absently running her hand through her thick white hair, she tucked renegade strands back into the loosely woven French braid. Realizing she'd forgotten to put on her lipstick, she dug in her purse for the tube then adjusted the rearview mirror to see herself. She didn't care much for mirrors. They seemed a necessary evil to anyone her age. The hazel eyes looking back at her seemed weary and strained, the crow's feet feathering from them more numerous than she remembered. She blew out an indifferent sigh and concentrated on applying the lipstick to her open lips. Tossing the lipstick back in her purse, she gladly shoved the mirror to its original position.

Peering out her side window, she could tell the storm was socked in for the rest of the day. Something was bothering her. She couldn't put her finger on it, but her soul was troubled. She glanced at the building impatiently. "C'mon, c'mon . . . ring the bell."

Tall Pines Christian School, a private school spanning kindergarten to twelfth grade, was an extension of the large metropolitan church for which it was named. Sharing the same sprawling campus in Seminole, Florida, both church and school boasted a growing membership in this middle-class area, a bedroom community on the Gulf coast sandwiched between Clearwater and St. Petersburg.

Routinely, the elementary wing of the school launched into the ritual known as *Rainy Day Procedure* on days such as this. A mass of teachers in yellow slickers huddled beneath oversized umbrellas, escorting each young scholar to his or her family car with Mom at the wheel. The cars advanced at a snail's pace but it was a small price to pay for curb service and staying out of the rain.

"Jessica and Jeremy McGregor, please," Caroline called out to the teacher on duty who approached her car. She heard the names of her grandchildren repeated on the battery-powered megaphone by the haggard teacher. In only a matter of moments she spotted her two grandchildren knotted under one of the umbrellas. They climbed into her car with a barrage of eager, breathless questions.

"Gran! We didn't know you were picking us up today! Where's Mom?"

"Can we go to PJ's, Gran?"

"Can we go to PJ's and then to *your* house?"

Always happy to see her grandkids, Caroline felt her apprehension ease. She laughed as she pulled out into traffic. "Whoa—slow down! I can only answer ten questions at a time. Put your seat belts on, then Jessica, you first."

"Where's Mommy? How come you're picking us up?" Jessica's head full of blond curls bounced with her animated questions. Her deep blue eyes sparkled with excited curiosity.

"Your mother called early this morning and asked me to pick you up today. She said she had some things to do and wasn't sure when she'd be back."

Jeremy, at the wise old age of eight, followed with another torrent of questions. "Will you take us to PJ's for a donut and some hot chocolate, Gran? We haven't been there in forever!"

Caroline glanced at the review mirror to peek at her youngest grandson. His light brown hair, shaggy in its usual disarray, covered his head like a dust mop. The stubborn cowlick atop his forehead stood at attention. She loved that cowlick, an inherited gift from her late husband. The resemblance sometimes took her breath away.

"In *forever?*" Caroline feigned dismay. "Why, I can't believe how cruel your parents are! I suppose I'll have to report them to the DEA."

Jessica wrinkled her face. "What's a DEA?"

"Donut-Eaters Anonymous. It's a non-profit support group for deprived children like you. A *huge* organization, in more ways than one, I might add."

"Ah, you made that up!" Jeremy countered. "There's no such thing . . . is there?"

"Okay, so you caught me. I confess. But I must admit this weather sure makes a hot cup of coffee sound good."

"All right!" Jeremy cheered.

"As long as we're back in plenty of time before Max gets home. I don't want him to come home to an empty house."

She stole a glance in the rearview mirror again just as Jessica rolled her eyes. "We *never* know when Max will get home so don't worry, Gran. We'll have lots and lots of time."

Caroline smiled at her granddaughter. To a five-year-old, a sixteen-year-old brother was nothing short of a constant aggravation. And while there were occasional, stolen moments when Jessie truly adored Max, she never hesitated to remind her parents and grandparents of any possible shortcomings she might discover.

"No kiddin', Gran," Jeremy added. "Max thinks he's so cool now that he can drive. What's the big deal about driving anyway?" Jeremy shook his head, rolling his eyes just as his sister had. "I mean, what difference does it make how you get somewhere—whether you drive or your mom or dad drives or your grandmother drives? It's only a car, for crying out loud."

"It may not seem like such a big deal now, but when you get to be Max's age, believe me—you'll be counting the days until you can get your license."

"Hey, Gran, speaking of coffee, can I have a cup of coffee too?" Jeremy asked, his voice sounding mysteriously deeper. Caroline laughed at the sudden change of subjects. Keeping up with these two was like following the moves of a ping pong ball in a championship tournament.

"You know, like the time you fixed me a cup at your house," he continued. "That was pretty cool—you 'n me discussing real important stuff over coffee."

She recalled the mug of mostly cream and sugar with only the slightest trace of coffee. "Yeah? Like what kind of 'stuff'?"

"Don't you remember? Stuff like what I wanted for Christmas, what kind of PlayStation games you needed to look for. Stuff like that."

"What a memory. Just like your father. Jeremy, you are truly a gigabyte brainchild. Well, I tell you what. You stick with hot chocolate today and we'll save the coffee for your next visit to my house. How about you, Jessica? What kind of donut are you going to have today?"

"PJ prob'ly won't have any left but I want a chocolate one with sprinkles."

"Jessie, you're so boring. You always get the same thing. Dull, dull, dull," Jeremy lectured, playfully dumping her backpack onto the floor of the car.

"You're such a creep!" Jessica chided, slugging her brother in the arm. "Gran, look what he did to my backpack!"

"C'mon, you two. Either get along or I'll head straight to the house sans donuts."

Jessica gathered her belongings. "Will Daddy be home for dinner tonight?"

"As a matter of fact he'll be home all night. Your mom said he doesn't have any meetings at church tonight, so he should be home in plenty of time for dinner."

Caroline pulled into the vacant parking lot. "Here we are. Looks like we might have PJ all to ourselves. Now watch the puddles, kids. Let's make a run for it!"

"Good-morning-how-you?"

PJ Ludwinski always greeted his customers the same way, with those same exact words, no matter what the time of day. The McGregor trio made their way through the glass door, their arrival announced cheerfully by the jangling bells on the door. An ancient radio was playing a rousing rendition of *Roll Out the Barrel*, to which the crusty Polish owner and sole employee danced a jig as he made his way to the counter. "Ah! My McGregors! Come in! Come in!"

The popular neighborhood donut shop was by no means fancy, but to Caroline's grandchildren, it was magical. Souvenirs from around the world hung from dusty rafters above, most of them gifts from faithful customers. Colorful piñatas, beer steins, a flock of artificial parrots, and too many hats to count. A Polaroid gallery of loyal customers covered the back wall. Toddlers with chocolate-smeared smiles. Construction workers in hard hats. Wrinkled senior citizens, many long since gone to the Donut Shop in the Sky.

Yes, PJ's boasted a rich legacy. Greasy, but rich.

On this late and rainy afternoon, Jessica hurried to grab a seat next to her grandmother along the counter. Jeremy busily spun himself around and around in circles on the vinyl-covered stool—never mind that he'd been told not to spin on his stool each and every time they came to PJ's.

"Jeremy, you stop dat spinning. You makin' me dizzy," the old man scolded, trying to sound stern, but they weren't fooled.

"Hi PJ. Wassup?"

"I'll wassup you," he teased, grabbing pastries from the display shelf. "Now—here we go," he announced, his sing-song cadence spawning the usual giggles as he delivered their standard order. "A chocolate sprinkle for Miss Jessica and a chocolate éclair for Mr. Jeremy. Now—what can I get da pretty grandmama?" he asked, hands planted firmly on his hips.

"PJ, I'd love a hot cup of coffee if it's fresh," she smiled, always amused by the comical eighty-year-old. PJ was like family to the McGregors. They had history.

"For you, I *make* it fresh! Five minutes—give me five minutes!" Off he dashed to brew a pot.

"Gran, can we do something special for Daddy since he'll be home tonight?" Jessie asked, her mouth already lined with sprinkles and chocolate icing. "I've been thinking. It seems like he could use a little happy about now. Don't you think?"

Caroline pushed a blonde curl off her granddaughter's

forehead. "Honey, I think that would be lovely. What did you have in mind?"

"I know! We could make him chocolate chip cookies! He loves those," Jeremy said, poking his finger into the éclair. Nibbling at the sides, he exposed the luscious creamy filling, obviously savoring every lick.

While the rain trailed rivulets down the storefront window, the plans continued over coffee and pastries until at last the threesome slid off their stools and headed for the door.

"Thanks for the treats, PJ," Caroline said, herding the kids into their raincoats. "And the coffee was wonderful—as it always is."

Before their old friend could reply, Jeremy interrupted again. "Hey, Gran, I know what would *really* make Dad happy—let's get him some of his favorite ice cream—Death by Chocolate!"

"Bye PJ!" Jessica waved as they headed to the door.

"Bye-bye-nice-day!"

Following her grandchildren, Caroline said good-bye to the old man as she held the door. Already wiping down the counter, he mumbled, "'Death by Chocolate'? What kind of kook names his ice cream Death by Chocolate?"

Caroline chuckled as the bell over the door jingled as if punctuating his question.

≈

Just after six-thirty, David McGregor turned into his shaded driveway at home. He pulled around to the back of the house, spotting his mother's car parked under the basketball hoop. The two-car garage was open, beckoning him like a familiar welcome sign to the home and family he loved. It was usually long after dark when he made this final trek home, and the house was always locked up for the night by then. He hoped the kids didn't have too much homework. It was his first evening off in weeks.

Pulling into his side of the garage he noticed his wife's van conspicuously absent. *Wouldn't you know it? I finally have a night home and Annie's out. Must be a committee meeting or something. Go figure. Oh Annie, I really need you tonight.*

"Daddy!"

His quiet thoughts were quickly overwhelmed by two rambunctious kids bursting through the door from the kitchen.

"Daddy, we helped Gran fix dinner and we made chocolate chi—"

"Jessie! It was supposed to be a surprise!" Jeremy scolded. "You're such a blabbermouth!" Brother and sister both leaped into their father's waiting arms as he dropped his briefcase and knelt beside his car. "Hi Jess! Hey there, slugger! Boy, is it good to see you guys. Can you believe it? A whole night at home all to ourselves! Where's Mom? Did she have a meeting?"

"Who knows, Dad," Jeremy answered. "She's been gone all afternoon. She had Gran pick us up 'cause she didn't know when she'd be back."

"How about Max? Is he home?"

"He's upstairs in his room. He just got home a few minutes ago. If you ask me, he's spending way too much time with that girlfriend of his, Dad."

David scratched his head, his expression exaggerated. "Funny thing—I don't remember asking you, but thanks for the information, Jeremy." He faked a punch to his son's stomach then grabbed him in a bear hug.

"Daaaaa-d!" shrieked Jeremy as he fought his father's tickling hands.

Jessie's eyes widened with delight. "Daddy, guess what? Gran took us to PJ's after school and I got sprinkles."

"You did? Now since when has my little angel liked sprinkles?" David asked as he hoisted up his daughter to ride on his back.

"Daddy! You know I *always* get sprinkles on my donuts."

"Oh, that's right—I just forgot. And I bet your big brother here got a chocolate éclair, am I right?" said father to daughter over his shoulder, their foreheads touching.

She cupped her free hand over his ear and whispered, "Yes, he *always* gets éclairs. Dull, dull, dull, don't you think?"

"Now, Jess, on that I must disagree. Jeremy is lots of things but dull is not one of them. Hey, did Gran cook dinner? What's that I smell?" he said, sniffing the air like an animated coon dog. "What's she got cooking in there?" His eyebrows danced up and down, immediately mimicked by his daughter.

As David, Jessie and Jeremy plowed through the

kitchen door, Caroline lifted a steaming dish from the oven. "Well, I suppose I could lie and tell you I've been cooking all day long, but it's a little hard to lie to my own son. Especially since he's a man of the cloth. And especially in front of his own children."

"What's a man of the cloth?" Jessie asked.

"A man who sells tablecloths door to door."

"Daaa—d," Jeremy rolled his eyes. "That's okay. We didn't really want to know anyway."

"It's just an odd little name for a minister," Caroline answered, shaking her head at the antics of her grown son. "And no, I have no idea how such an expression came to be."

"Hi, Mom," David smiled then kissed his mother on the cheek with a lingering hug. Looking into his mother's face was like looking in a mirror, David thought. They shared the same broad McGregor smile. A tinge of melancholy swept over him. Annie used to laugh when she described his lopsided grin as "deliciously mischievous." He hadn't heard her laughter in a long time. He pushed the thought away, studying his mother's kind face again. The shape of her eyes and her smile was identical to his, only the noses differed. David had the nose of all the McGregor men—"prominent," they liked to call it. His hair, once sandy blond, was now heavily peppered with the same white hair that adorned his mother's head.

Too many years in the ministry. He'd earned each and every one of those gray hairs.

Caroline stepped back and took a good look at her son as she slung the dish towel over her shoulder. "Mighty long hug for an old lady, David. You all right? You look exhausted."

"Oh, I'm fine, Mom. Really. Just never seems to be enough hours in the day to get it all done. That's all. Annie's going to be late tonight?"

Caroline finished setting the table. "Apparently so. She called this morning and asked if I could pick up the kids and come over until you got home. She didn't say how late she'd be. But she left dinner ready to put in the oven, so I expect she knew she'd be pretty late."

He felt his mother's eyes on him, no doubt surveying the weariness that seemed to constantly engulf him these days.

"David, go upstairs and get comfortable. Wash up and relax for a few minutes. Come on down when you're ready and we'll eat then. No rush."

"Mom, I'm forty-one years old," he laughed, "and you're still telling me what to do."

"You're right. Guilty as charged. A man never outgrows his need for his mother. Now just do what I tell you or dinner will get cold."

"Some things never change," he moaned for her benefit. He dragged himself up the stairs. Reaching the landing, he looked into Max's room, noticing his oldest son working at the computer on his desk.

"Hey, sport—how's it going?" he asked, knocking gently on the open door.

"Wait. Give me a sec. Let's see. You *look* like my father. You *sound* like my father, but hey," Max paused, glancing at his bedside alarm clock, "it's way too early for *my* dad to be home. So exactly who *are* you?"

"Very funny. Fact is, I actually have the entire evening home, thank you very much. I'm tempted to lock the doors so no one can leave. I want you guys all to myself tonight," David yawned as he sprawled across Max's bed. "Just wish your mother was home."

"I know. I'm kinda surprised she's not home yet. She's always home for dinner. Must have gotten delayed or something.

"So how's school going?" David asked, his eyelids heavy as his head sunk into Max's pillow.

"I got an A plus on my physics exam today. Not bad, eh?"

David sat up to give his son a high five. "That's great! Physics is brutal. You must have inherited your mother's knack for academic genius. I'm impressed! Good for you, Max."

"Yeah, well, you wouldn't believe how hard I studied for it. Totally out of character for me."

Smiling, David stood up and tousled his son's dark hair. "Totally *just* like you. I'm really proud of you."

"Is it time to eat yet? I'm starving."

"Pretty soon. I'm going to take a couple minutes to clean up and get comfortable." David was halfway to the master bedroom, already kicking off his shoes. He tossed his briefcase on the chair and sat down on the side of the bed. Pulling off his golf shirt, he fell back across the white comforter.

Don't shut your eyes or you'll be snoring with your next breath. He knew without question he could sleep for a month if given the chance. *I've got to start running again. Get back in shape. I'm not 101 . . . yet.*

Turning his head slightly to his left, he noticed an ivory envelope leaning against the pillow sham. He smiled lazily. *A note from Annie. It's been a long time.* He reached for the envelope and was surprised to find no trace of her familiar cologne.

"Daddy, will you play some Go Fish with me before dinner?" Jessie yelled up the stairs.

"I'll be down in a minute, pumpkin," David answered through a yawn as he opened the letter. His thoughts drifted back to other notes Annie had left him over the years.

Surprise!
The kids are spending the night at your parents,
We have 7:00 reservations at Giovanni's,
and I have you all to myself
for the next 24 glorious hours!

But his favorite had been the note he found tucked inside his briefcase one Friday morning several years ago. The poetry was corny, but the message was unforgettable.

Roses are red,
Violets are blue,
The Love Boat sails at seven,
AND I'M KIDNAPPING YOU!!!

Within moments, Annie had suddenly appeared, whisking him off on a cruise for seven of the most wonderful days and nights of his life. He could almost feel the sea breeze against his face as he began to read.

Dear David,

It's not like me to leave this note for you instead of explaining myself face to face. We were once able to talk about everything, good or bad. It was one of the first things that attracted me to you—your ability to be real and open and honest, straightforward. But I can't face you this time. Not that you could spare the time to listen anyway.

I have to get away for awhile. I'm on the verge of losing my mind and don't know what else to do. I've been hanging on by one tiny, single thread, and now the thread has unraveled.

By the time you read this I'll be on a plane. I will not tell you where I'm going because I don't want you coming after me. I've made all the necessary arrangements, and there is no reason for you to worry. I will call you when I'm ready to talk. Just pray for me.

I know Caroline will be anxious to help out with the kids, and it will be good for her to stay busy. The anniversary of your father's death is coming up, if you recall. She needs to be close to you and the kids right now.

I have no idea how long I'll be gone. I need time to sort everything out. There's a malignancy of bitterness and jealousy and even hatred toward the church that is devouring me. I blame the church, I blame you, and I blame God for taking you away from me and the kids, and I don't know what to do with all that. The guilt of that realization alone has almost destroyed me.

I don't even know who you are anymore. The man I married disappeared and I can't find him anywhere. As heartless as it may sound, I believe Caroline and I have much in common—we're <u>both</u> widows.

I can't live like this anymore, David. I can't and I won't.

I will leave it entirely up to you as what to tell Max, Jessie, Jeremy, Caroline, or anyone else.

I still love you, David McGregor. I just can't be with you right now.

Annie

Chapter 3

Houston, Texas

Come on . . . come on . . . come to papa, baby . . . all right!"

As the dimpled ball plunked into the cup on the eighteenth green, the tall, muscular golfer raised his arms in triumphant victory. "Yesss! Yes, yes, yesss!" His boisterous celebration echoed across the clear Texas sky as he strutted like a peacock, his putter held high like the scepter of a crowned king.

"Ah, get outta here, Dean! You call that skill?" his buddy teased. "You always were the luckiest son of a—"

"Now, now, Jimmy—don't go playing the bad sport on me. You know raw talent when you see it. And I'll wager, my man, that you've never witnessed finer golf anywhere than what you've witnessed here today, pro tour notwithstanding. Am I right?" Michael laughed, wrapping his free arm around his friend with a hearty grasp.

Jimmy Peterson shook his head in disbelief as he pulled off his leather glove. Stuffing it into his pocket, he continued the banter. "Yeah, you don't play so bad for an old man. In fact, you move pretty well for someone on the geriatric tour."

Michael cupped his hands over his heart, grimacing playfully through his broad smile. "Now you're getting personal. I'm deeply, deeply hurt. That's exactly what I'm talking about—you are the epitome of a sore loser. You better pull yourself together or the bouncer of this elite country club may have to kick your sorry butt out of here!"

"Are you kidding? This club *pays* me just to play here. I'm a draw for them," Jimmy answered with a swagger. "They figure celebrities like me will bring in membership by the droves. You play your cards right and they might even let *you* join one of these days."

Michael steered their cart to the clubhouse entrance then braked and slid out from behind the wheel. "Oh Jimmy, my man, you really are a pro, you know that? One hundred percent, Class A professional bull! As you recall I'm on the board of this prestigious club. Don't make me keep reminding you about that, son," he teased. "C'mon. Lunch is on me."

They made their way into the casual grill that overlooked the plush greens of the golf course at this exclusive Houston country club. Membership here was strictly a matter of having the right name, the right credentials, and of course, an adequate bank account. Both Michael and Jimmy had the name recognition to play these fairways any time.

A first round draft pick out of college, Michael played first base for the Houston Astros for a long and successful career before retiring to pursue other interests. When reality convinced him his pro ball days were nearing an end, he chose to go out in style while he still had the chance.

Early in his career with the Astros, Michael met and married Amelia Thomas, the socialite daughter of Elliot Thomas, United States congressman and Texas billionaire. The Thomas family had roots dating back to the earliest settlers of this rugged land and was known throughout the country.

Michael met Amelia at this same country club thirteen years ago. It was the off season and he had just finished eighteen holes of golf. The weather had been unusually windy and wet; not a particularly great day for golf. Stopping by the bar for something to warm him, he noticed the beautiful blond with long, gorgeous legs sitting at the bar. Never one to pass up a chance for some major league flirting, Michael made the usual small talk and had her laughing in record time. Her smile dazzled him, and he was struck by her obvious class. This was no Texas barfly.

His hunch was confirmed when the distinguished congressman appeared shortly, putting his hand gently on her shoulder. "Ready, dear?"

Amelia patted his hand. "Sure, Daddy. I was just visiting with—I'm sorry, I didn't catch your name?"

"Where are my manners?" he apologized, tilting his head slightly in embarrassment. "My name is Michael

Dean," he said, holding his hand out to her. "And you must be—well, of *course* you are Amelia Thomas." Turning to her father, he continued, "Congressman, it's an honor to meet you as well." He grasped Thomas's hand firmly, smiling warmly at father and daughter.

The expected recognition finally hit the statesman. "Of course! Michael Dean! I should have recognized you immediately. You play first base for our Astros!"

"Yes, sir, I sure do." Michael beamed.

The congressman continued, "Fine season last year, son. You made us proud. It's an honor to meet you, Mr. Dean."

Michael pulled his hand free. "Uh, yes sir, thank you sir, but the honor's all mine. I wouldn't want to seem forward, but if you could give me a few minutes to clean up, I'd be honored to buy you and your daughter a drink if you have the time?" Michael looked deeply into Amelia's soft green eyes shining beneath long, thick lashes.

Amelia stood up, "Well, Mr. Dean—"

"Michael. Please call me Michael."

Her smile widened at his familiarity. "Very well, *Michael.* We thank you for the offer and perhaps we'll meet again and take you up on it then. Unfortunately, Daddy and I have a dinner engagement with some rather important constituents. Otherwise, we'd be pleased to have a drink with you. Wouldn't we, Daddy?"

"We certainly would, honey. Michael, we'll take a rain check, except we want you to be our guest up at the house. I insist. How can we get in touch with you?"

Michael grabbed a cocktail napkin off the bar and borrowed the gold Cross pen that Mr. Thomas extended toward him. It was engraved, *Office of the United States House* of *Representatives*. He smiled at the congressman then scribbled his name and phone number and handed it to Amelia. "I'll look forward to hearing from you. Both. Anytime." He felt like a schoolboy meeting his prom date's dad for the first time. "It was a pleasure," he added, making a quick escape.

After a whirlwind, highly-publicized romance, Michael and Amelia were married in one of Houston's most memorable weddings. The marriage was a great fascination to Houstonians and sports fans alike.

For the groom, however, the fascination quickly wore off.

Amelia was as refined as she was beautiful. She was educated at an expensive private college in Texas where she belonged to the finest sorority while maintaining excellent grades. She continued to perform all the expected roles thrust upon her as a Houston debutante. When her mother died of cancer, Amelia assumed the position as her father's escort to the perfunctory galas in both Texas and Washington. She thrived in the spotlight, loving the excitement and glamour of politics.

She was also very much in love with her handsome husband, a baseball star and celebrity in his own right. The perfect fan, Amelia attended every game, sitting with the wives and families of the other players. When they kept a polite distance from her, she nonetheless made every attempt to be one of them. She and Michael hosted several barbecues at their estate for the players and their families. She made every possible effort to be the best wife to Michael and best daughter to Elliot.

Sure, she had grown more beautiful with each passing year, but in Michael's opinion she was still—well, *boring*. She was too beautiful, too proper, and much too refined. He realized his disappointment early in their relationship, but refused to believe it would ever be a serious problem for him. After all, this prize had come with unlimited opportunities and connections. What's a little boredom at home when you have the world at your fingertips?

Furthermore, Michael knew that "Daddy" was more than pleased with his son-in-law. He introduced Michael to people and situations most people only dream about. Then, only a year after the marriage, Elliot approached Michael with a proposition: he would set up his son-in-law in any business venture he wanted. He promised Michael he would make sure this business would always be a success. Michael knew enough about Elliot Thomas by that time to realize the potential of such an assurance. It was a win-win situation. A gold mine for the asking.

Thus began *The Sports Page*. Michael had given considerable thought to what kind of company he would create. After all, the inevitable age crunch would someday send him to the locker room for one last time. He began dreaming of a line of stores selling sports equipment and athletic wear for every conceivable sport. In addition, the stores would share facilities with the ultimate athletic club. Michael would use only state of the art equipment in his weight rooms, gyms, courts, and locker rooms. He would cultivate a clientele that would give the club status and class. This would be no sweat tank. The Sports Page would make history.

And that's exactly what it did. From that initial conversation with his father-in-law to the grand opening of his first facility, Michael personally oversaw every single detail to perfection. Even before the balloons deflated and the last of the confetti was swept away from the inaugural celebration, the empire of The Sports Page was well on its way. In only a few short years, while still continuing his career with the Astros, Michael witnessed his company's growth as it exploded across the country. The Page, as it was nicknamed, soon took residence in almost every major city in America. Michael was indeed an American success story. After his retirement from baseball, his picture was more likely to be found on the front page of *Fortune* magazine than *Sports Illustrated*. He had tasted the best of both worlds.

Yes, life had been good to Michael Dean.

Now, years later, playing a round of golf with his old friend Jimmy was a welcome change of pace. Their usual teasing had lifted his spirits considerably as it always did. Jimmy and Michael had been good friends for many years. While Michael quickly worked his way up through the farm teams, Jimmy had taken the sports broadcasting world by storm. Whenever their paths crossed, they headed for the nearest golf course.

Relaxing over his second beer, Michael sat back on the

barstool. Jimmy peered over his Diet Coke, casting a long hard look at his burly friend.

"If you don't mind me butting in—"

"I do, so don't."

Jimmy smiled. "Michael, what's eating you? What's going on? Buddy, you and I go way back. You may be able to pull off this carefree façade with everybody else, but I can read you like a book. What is it?"

Michael toyed with a salt shaker for a long time before answering. "I don't know, man. Got a lot on my mind, I guess. Didn't realize I was so transparent. I'll have to watch that." His smile was half-hearted at best.

"C'mon, Michael. What gives? You and the queen having problems?" Jimmy had never taken Michael and Amelia's marriage too seriously. He knew the *old* Michael Dean—the ball player with a girl in every city on the league schedule and then some.

Michael looked up and started to make another wise crack but stopped short. He spotted a familiar figure in a dark suit just over Jimmy's shoulder, standing at the entrance to the grill.

Jimmy, reacting to the change in Michael's demeanor, looked over his shoulder. "Friend of yours?"

Michael shifted uncomfortably. "No, just one of Elliot's stiffs. These guys drive me insane," he grumbled as he stood. "Listen, Jimmy, I gotta go. I'll give you a call in a couple of days." He patted his friend on his shoulder, "Good seein' you, man. Keep working on that swing," he mused, gesturing a practice swing of his own.

After quick instructions from Elliot's body guard, Michael made his way down the hall to the private conference room. He knocked softly then opened the wide polished door. "Michael. How nice of you to join me. Here, have a seat. Fix yourself a drink. You look awful."

Michael bypassed the open cabinet of liquor and took a seat across the broad table from Elliot Thomas. "Gee, thanks, Elliot. Nice to see you too."

The congressman continued writing on his leather-bound pad. "Hard to run a corporate business from the greens, isn't it? You getting tired of your career or just loafing off like the has-been jock you are?" The watery eyes of his father-in-law glanced up at him only briefly during his flippant attack.

"Come now, Elliot," Michael countered. "You know that even hard working CEOs are entitled to an occasional day off now and then. Why? Has your spy network been feeding you lies about me again? What's their method? Do they hide in the bathroom stalls and pick up tidbits of juicy gossip to pass along? Or have you got your hooks into the private day timer on my computer? Gee, I thought I'd covered all my bases. I must be slipping. Tsk tsk."

Elliot continued writing as if he hadn't heard a word. Then, quietly and methodically, he closed the valise, straightened his silk tie and folded his hands on the table.

"Michael, I see no reason why you and I can't have a civilized conversation. It appears to me as though we have a bit of a problem. Something that needs immediate attention."

"Oh yeah? It seems to me we have a number of problems. Which one did you want to address today?"

The congressman rolled his neck. "You're absolutely right. We do have a number of problems. Very serious problems. But today I want to discuss Amelia."

"Ah," Michael whispered as though hearing a well-kept secret. "Yes, Amelia. Why am I not surprised that dear ol' Dad wants to 'discuss' his perfect little girl with the evil son-in-law?"

"All right, cut the sarcasm. I've had just about enough."

"Good. That makes two of us. What do you propose we do about it?" Michael began swiveling his chair from side to side hoping to portray an air of indifference.

"I understand you have begun divorce proceedings."

Michael stopped cold. "You don't waste any time, do you? What, have you got my attorney's office bugged as well?"

Totally undaunted, Elliot responded. "Don't change the subject. I want some answers and I want them now."

Michael took a deep breath and slowly began rocking his chair again. He hated himself for allowing Elliot to get under his skin like this. He glared back at the congressman. "Yes, Elliot, I have begun divorce proceedings. Something I should have done years ago. But I'm still curious how you found out about it. I just spoke to Thad yesterday and I know he would never break our attorney/client confidentiality. I haven't even spoken to Amelia about it. So just exactly how did you find out?"

"It is entirely irrelevant to discuss how certain information makes its way to my attention. You should know by now that no one in public life can do much of anything without someone finding out. I've had you tailed from the day you and Amelia began dating."

Michael gasped before he could stop himself.

Elliot continued. "A man in my position cannot take chances. I had to make absolutely sure that you were of sufficient reputation before I could allow Amelia to become involved with you. Oh yes, I know you weren't exactly spotless. You had a number of affairs with a number of different women. That was no great surprise for a man like you—rugged good looks, athletic, a sports celebrity and all. We all know such indiscretions are a part of that lifestyle. But after a period of time finding you to be faithful to Amelia once you began seeing her, I was satisfied you would make a good husband for her.

"And, as usual, I was right. You *have* been a good husband to her. For the most part I've been proud to have you as my son-in-law. That's why I didn't hesitate to help you get started in your own business. You've done a fine job with The Page and you should be proud."

Why do I get the feeling this is all leading up to my execution? Michael wondered.

"Of course, we both know The Sports Page would never have existed if I hadn't backed you financially from the beginning and opened all the right doors for you. Granted, you've exceeded my highest expectations and that's to your credit, Michael. That's what makes this whole unfortunate situation doubly hard for me. Because it won't involve just you and Amelia. The company is at stake as well."

"Now just a minute!"

"Hear me out." Elliot raised his hands to halt Michael's outburst. "There's no sense whatsoever in trying to fight me on this. You've been very foolish, Michael. And I must say, you've surprised me. Oh, not that I'm surprised at your infidelities so much. Only disappointed to think you really thought you could get away with it. Son, surely you know me well enough by now—you can run but you can't hide from Elliot Thomas. Don't ever forget that."

Elliot's steely gray eyes pierced through Michael. He felt like a caged animal. The implication of losing his company made his blood run cold. Although he had carefully protected his business through the proper legal channels, it suddenly occurred to him that Elliot Thomas wouldn't necessarily attack through those same channels. Just as Elliot had used certain connections to pave the way for the company, he would no doubt use similar connections to yank it out from under Michael.

His mind raced, searching for answers. He exhaled slowly, attempting to calm himself. "Elliot, you're absolutely right. There's no reason we can't discuss this like two civilized men. Marriages fall apart everyday. That's just part of life."

Elliot slammed his fist on the table. "Not when it's *my* daughter's marriage!"

Michael jumped to his feet, holding up his hands in defense. "I would simply ask that you give me a chance to explain my side of the matter." He began pacing. "No reason we can't handle this as gentlemen. You said so yourself."

The cold, stony stare of Elliot Thomas dared him.

Think, Michael, think!

He walked back and forth behind his chair, his footsteps hushed on the deep carpet beneath him. He was thoughtful and pensive, much more in control. Or so he hoped it would appear. He strolled casually over to the open bar and poured himself a drink.

"Elliot, you must surely know that this marriage has been in trouble a long time now. It's obvious that Amelia is anything but happy. Her moods change constantly. I never know what I'll find at home—a raving lunatic or a sleeping beauty that can't get out of bed. I mean, she's on so many antidepressants I hardly know her anymore! She blames everything on me because she can't get pregnant, but she refuses to see any more doctors. All we ever do is fight, and I've just had enough of it. I'm through."

Elliot remained silent. Michael continued, heading back to his seat. "I have no intention of making this any harder on Amelia than it has to be. I plan to make a clean break. Make this as amicable as possible. There's no sense in dragging all this through the mud. It would only hurt her."

"Perhaps you should have considered Amelia's feelings *before* all your sordid affairs, Michael. I find it a little difficult to buy into this compassionate husband act of yours."

"You make it sound like I've bedded half the women in Houston! I admit I've seen a couple of women over the last few months. But I told you—things haven't been good between Amelia and me for a long time. In fact, it's been miserable."

Elliot stood up and walked confidently toward the bar. He opened a bottle of Perrier and poured it into a glass. "And somehow you thought that spending time with other women would help you work out your problems with Amelia. Interesting logic."

"Don't be ridiculous. I didn't go out looking for someone. It just happened, that's all. You have to believe that! You know how it is—you start talking to someone, you have a couple of laughs. You start to remember what it's like to have a good time again. And the next thing you know you're looking for excuses to make a phone call or stop by—"

"Now let's see, which one are we talking about here," Elliot interrupted, dropping a wedge of lemon into his glass. "Would this be a Ms. Anderson or—"

"How *dare* you!"

"—or would it be a Ms. Lindsey?" Elliot was back in his seat once again searching through a file he had withdrawn from his briefcase. "Let's see, I believe that's her name. Ah yes, *Mrs.* Lindsay. She would be the married lady whose husband travels internationally. Rather convenient, I suppose."

Michael forced himself to bridle his temper before responding. "Look, Elliot. I'm not proud of any of this. But I'm not gonna sit here while you parade through a list of women you suspect me of having affairs with! It has nothing to do with the fact that I'm going to divorce Amelia. It's just over between us! And that's all there is to it. It's time to move on. But I'm warning you—stay away from Cathy and Rachel. I mean it, Elliot. Back off."

"Well, we'll just see about that," Elliot responded dryly. "I don't see how you're in any position to be asking favors of me, son. No, I believe I'll be the one calling the shots on this one."

Michael sat down opposite his father-in-law at the long conference table. He threw back the shot of bourbon and felt it burn down his throat. He had to remain calm—that much he knew. And with each accusation, he felt his stomach knot tighter. The heat of the alcohol was coursing through his veins now, relaxing the grip of fear that had strangled him for the duration of Elliot's interrogation. Just as he was about to speak, Elliot turned his chair to face Michael and leaned back heavily.

"Michael, I think it's about time we got to the nuts and bolts of all this. You want to divorce my daughter. I will not have it. That puts us in quite a quandary. Now, the way I see it, you can either comply with my wishes or we'll have to discuss other considerably unpleasant alternatives."

Michael rubbed his face then suddenly stood up and headed back to the bar. He quickly downed another shot of bourbon then slammed down the glass. His head was beginning to relax, easing his mind into position for battle.

He slowly turned to face Elliot. "I'm getting *real* tired of all this," he said in a forced whisper, his words measured. "I will *never* again 'comply' with any of your wishes, congressman, so deal with it. If you're going to threaten me, then do it. I'm sick to death of your stupid little games."

"Have it your way," Elliot answered. "But never forget I gave you the choice to handle this with diplomacy. If you insist on taking this path, I assure you—you will most certainly regret it. I'm a very powerful man, and I have no problem whatsoever doing whatever it takes to get my way. And that certainly includes removing you from *The Sports Page*. Unfortunately, you don't seem to comprehend the fire you're playing with here, boy. It's clear to see you don't take me very seriously. That's a real shame, as I'm sure you'll soon discover."

"Spare me the speeches, Elliot. Just spit it out!"

Elliot inhaled deeply. "Fine. You will either drop these divorce proceedings first thing tomorrow morning, or I will take full ownership of *The Sports Page* immediately. And never mind the protests. I can do it in a heartbeat. You may hold forty percent of the stock, but what you failed to recognize was the fact that I control all of your remaining stockholders."

Elliot stretched his neck again, emerging with a mischievous grin. "Son, how stupid can you get? You were so all-fire sure that this little business was all yours by making sure I never got too big a chunk of the pie. Thought you had me, didn't you? But if you'd ever done your homework instead of chasing golf balls and fast women, you might have noted a couple of very important facts.

"Oh, you are absolutely right. I only hold fifteen percent of your precious little company. But I hand-picked the remaining members of your stockholders myself and they all answer to *me!*" Elliot burst into laughter.

Michael froze. "That's impossible!"

"Not hardly. Why, eighty percent of Texas resides in my back pocket, in case you haven't noticed. I can buy anyone and anything I choose. I have so many folks beholdin' to me—they practically stand in line to do favors for Elliot Thomas." He chortled once again. "Oh, me . . . this time it's been a real pleasure calling in those markers. As soon as I got wind of this divorce nonsense of yours, I made a few quick phone calls. Made sure all my ducks were still in a row." He rubbed his hands together, clearly enjoying the bomb he was dropping.

"Listen, you little punk, you've played your last card." Then, as if the clever thought just popped into his mind, he continued, "This is your last inning and the game's over!" He croaked his self-absorbed laughter. "And guess what? You're out!"

Michael's mind spun out of control. As Elliot laughed himself into a fit of wheezing coughs, Michael desperately groped for *anything* to stop this nightmare. He could see *The Sports Page*—his whole life—vaporizing before his eyes.

And then he remembered.

Suddenly the fog cleared and the answer broke through. *How could I have forgotten?*

While Elliot finally caught his breath and took another sip of his drink, Michael nonchalantly wandered back to his seat. He sat down slowly, giving his mind ample time to devise a plan of action. It had been a long, long time since his thoughts had traveled down this secret passageway, but he was relieved by its mere existence.

Not to worry.

A resurgent smile stretched across Michael's face. His confidence restored, he spoke slowly, his words calculated. "Elliot, you're an egotistical fool. Think you have all the answers, don't you? Think you can control everybody you meet by just snapping your pudgy little fingers. Well, I'm afraid you've pathetically miscalculated this time.

"You see, I still have one card left to play."

Chapter 4

Weber Creek, Colorado

The carefully lettered wooden sign over the door read *Williamson's*. The long front porch adorned with several old wooden rockers welcomed customers who stopped by. Stepping inside the old country store was like stepping back in time. The Ingalls family should be browsing these aisles. At the back of the spacious store, a stone fireplace boasted a bright, crackling fire from a fireplace tucked beneath an extended mantle sporting every imaginable gadget for the winter home. Four more rustic rockers sat ready and waiting for weary customers, a worn and colorfully braided rug resting beneath them. The long wooden store counter stretched along the entire length of the wall to the left, overshadowed by shelves reaching all the way to the ceiling. Each was packed with everything from Band-Aids to Borax to bubble gum.

The hardwood floors creaked melodically under the tread of all who entered. Four short aisles offered an array of necessities and a few luxuries here and there. Along the opposite wall to the right, a refrigerated case installed back in the seventies held dairy products and assorted chilled beverages. Overhead, an umbrella of baskets and dried flowers cascaded from broad beams of sturdy oak.

But it was the unique blend of aromas which first welcomed customers to Williamson's. Freshly ground coffees and homemade pastries beckoned the clientele into the heart of the store. A pot of complimentary coffee enticed regulars to pause for a moment of small town gossip; the comforting fragrance of the logs burning in the fireplace, at times intoxicating. Even an occasional whiff of moth balls or liniment only added to the homespun ambience of this country store.

Owners Bob and Mary Jean Williamson inherited their family store from Bob's dad, now deceased, who had passed it along before retiring. None of the locals could remember Weber Creek without Williamson's. The colorful products stocked on the shelves may have changed through the years, but the hospitality and courtesy remained the same.

Mary Jean sliced a fresh pan of Scottish shortbread into long perfect pieces. "Bob, I want you to run that kettle of soup over to Emma before it gets cold. That way she can have a bowl of it with her cornbread for supper."

"Supper?" Bob snapped. "It's only three o'clock in the afternoon. Nobody eats supper at three in the afternoon."

"Stop being so ornery and just do as I ask. That's when she likes it and who are you to tell her any different?" Mary Jean placed the sandy rectangles of shortbread on an antique platter.

"Whoever heard of supper at three o'clock," Bob grumbled. "Why, I'd have to have a whole 'nother meal by seven or eight or listen to a growling stomach half the night."

The front door opened with its familiar squeak as the verbal sparing continued. "Bob, just gather up the basket and get on over to Emma's. Stop all your jabbering! The good Lord knows I've endured enough of your mindless arguments over the last fifty years, and I don't want to hear another word of it today. I'm just plum sick of it."

"Who's sick? Is somebody sick? Should we call a doctor?" a voice piped in from the front of the store. The kindly face of Dr. George Wilkins lit up with a subtle twinkle in his eyes. "Are you two pretending to fight again or is someone really sick?"

"You bet I'm sick, George," Bob answered. "I'm sick of this cantankerous old woman snapping orders at me as if I were some kind of hired help. Would you remind her that the name over the door was mine long before she ever had the good sense to marry me?" Bob tried his best to sound mad, but he was as always, totally unsuccessful.

Mary Jean tipped her head back and forth, humming a familiar tune. She walked the basket over to Bob, pecked him on his cheek, and started back to her task. Bob gave her a swat on her ample back side then quickly made his getaway.

The doctor tracked his usual path over to the coffee pot, filled the mug with "Doc" on the side, then shuffled toward one of the rockers.

"MJ, come sit a spell and take a rest. Doctor's orders. Let's enjoy this nice fire for a few minutes, shall we?"

And with those words began Doc's daily visit as he did each and every day of the year, weather permitting. It was one of Mary Jean's favorite times of the day. She and Doc Wilkins had grown up together not far away in Remington. Though not related they had remained as close as a brother and sister. Since the death of George's wife some eight years ago, she and Bob had become Doc's family. The good doctor treasured their friendship deeply. Mary Jean wiped her hands on her red bib apron, poured herself a cup of coffee, and sighed heavily as she sat down in the rocker.

"Mercy, George, I just can't seem to help myself when I start in on Bob. Anybody else would think we hated each other by the way we carry on." She paused, sipping the hot coffee, then continued. "Funny how over the years you just grow into a pattern of playfully picking on each other 'til before you know it, it becomes a silly way of showing affection. I suppose that doesn't make much sense, does it?"

"Makes sense to me," Doc said, rocking quietly. "Ina and I had our own special ways of doing the same thing. Nobody else would understand at all. Like how we'd always bicker over the last biscuit at breakfast. I'd offer it to her, she'd refuse it. She'd say 'Gotta watch my weight, George,' just as serious as all get out. Then we'd fuss back and forth three or four more times—use those same identical words every single morning of our married life together. Then, of course, I'd say 'Well, Ina, if it'll help you stay as beautiful as you are today, I'll eat it. But only because you insist.' Then she'd flip a dish towel and pop me on the shoulder with it and say 'George Wilkins, you just beat all!' We'd go through that little ritual every morning just like clockwork. Pretty silly, I suppose." Doc sipped his coffee. "But it just goes to show we all have our quirky little ways of saying I love you. Doesn't make a lick of sense to anyone else, but then I guess it doesn't have to." He smiled, gazing into the fire.

ʔ

Annie stomped her snow-covered boots on the welcome mat then opened the door to the quaint country store. The slow squeak of the door announced her arrival.

"Afternoon, we're back here," a voice called out from the rear of the store. A jovial woman stepped behind the long counter. She smiled warmly. "C'mon in here, honey, and warm yourself by the fire. You look like one big shiver with an exclamation point thrown in for good measure!"

"It's freezing out there," Annie answered, pushing back the hood of her coat.

"Freezing? Heavens, this is practically a balmy day for Weber Creek. But stick around a few days if you want to see freezing," the woman continued. "Big storm rolling in that'll curl your toes. Can I get you some coffee? I just made a fresh pot."

"Oh, that sounds wonderful. Thank you, I'd love some." Annie moved toward the oversized hearth, pulling off her brightly colored mittens to warm her hands by the fire. She nodded at an older gentleman with a thick head of white hair who was gently rocking his chair.

"How do."

"Hello." She returned his smile. "This is just what I needed. It's lovely."

"Well here, young lady," he said, standing. "Let me give these old logs a nudge and see if we can't give you a real fire." He grabbed the poker and stoked the giant logs. "Name's George Wilkins, but most folks 'round here just call me Doc."

She took his outstretched hand firmly, relishing its warmth. "Nice to meet you. I'm Annie."

Mary Jean handed her the steaming mug of coffee. "Hi, Annie. I'm Mary Jean Williamson. What brings you to our little neck of the woods?"

Annie warmed both her hands around the large mug and sat down. "I'm on my way up to a cabin just a little further up the road. It belongs to an old friend of mine, Christine Benson—I mean Christine Benson-Hamilton. I haven't seen her since college, and I'm still not used to her married name. Although she's not married anymore so I'm not sure what name she goes by?"

Annie yawned. "Oh, I'm so sorry. I've been on the road for several hours and I'm afraid it's just about worn me out."

Mary Jean sat down on one of the remaining rockers as

Doc continued to stand with his back to the fire. "Don't often see a young lady traveling alone around here, what with the roads so tough this time of year."

Annie looked into her mug for a moment, then carefully sipped the brew. Her eyes misted over. Clearing her throat, she filled the uneasy silence. "Actually, I'm on a long overdue vacation. Christine has begged me for years to come up here and stay at her cabin." She paused a moment then added, "I finally decided to take her up on it."

She got up to avoid their stares, moving closer to the crackling fire.

"You'll love it up there at Eagle's Nest," Doc said. "Christine inherited that cabin. It's been in the family for years. Of course, it looks completely different than when her parents vacationed there. Through the years, she's renovated it considerably. Made a few additions along the way. In fact, a few years back it was featured in some fancy magazine. What was the name of that, MJ?"

"*Southern Living.* Four page color spread. They did a beautiful job."

"It has a breathtaking view of the valley," Doc continued. "Quite a place."

"It sure is, and I'd say you're in for a real treat if you're aiming to rest," Mary Jean offered. "It's pretty remote up there, so you won't have any traffic or neighbors bothering you. The only folks nearby are the Swensons and they're out of town. Had a death in the family up in Minnesota."

Doc interrupted, "Well now, MJ, I reckon Annie will get

along just fine. Knowing Christine, she left a well-stocked pantry and freezer. But with this storm coming in, we might want to get a few extras for Annie here in case the power goes or she can't make it back down the road for a few days. Power's liable to be off for several days if it goes. But she's got a good back-up generator, far as I know. You'll be fine, I reckon."

"Happens a lot this time of year," Mary Jean added. "But never you worry. We'll get you all fixed up."

The seconds ticked by. Other than an occasional hiss or pop from the fire and creaking of the floor under the rockers, they sat in silence. Finally, Annie took a deep breath then blew it out. She didn't miss the expression of concern that wafted across Mary Jean's wrinkled face. Thankfully, the moment was interrupted by the door creaking open.

"Bob, how was Emma?" Mary Jean asked as an elderly gentleman pulled off his knit hat and muffler. What was left of his white hair fanned out in every direction.

"Well now, that depends. If you ask her, she's on her death bed. If you ask me, she's just enjoying all the fuss folks are making over her. Though she was mighty interested in your chicken and rice soup, MJ."

Doc shook his head, "Ah, Miss Emma. Weber Creek's resident hypochondriac. Hard to complain, though. She keeps me busy when everyone else is well."

Bob turned to Annie. "And who do we have here?"

Mary Jean patted down the wayward hairs on her husband's balding head. "Bob, this is Annie. She's on her way up to Christine's place. We need to get her all fixed up in case this storm decides to stick around when it hits. Oh, and Annie, if we forget anything or if you find you need more, just give us a call and Bob here will run it up to you. Gets him out of my hair, if you know what I mean, so don't hesitate to call. As often as you can." Mary Jean snorted at her own joke.

"Thanks, but I'm sure I'll be fine."

Bob grabbed a shopping basket then asked, "So, where is Christine these days? Italy? Australia? Never seen anyone hop around the globe like that girl."

Annie finished her coffee and took the empty mug to the counter. "She's in Israel for several months. I'm not exactly sure what she's doing there. Some sort of photo shoot, I suppose. The only way I connected with her was over the phone. She called me out of the blue awhile back, and . . . well, turns out it was a good time for me to get away. We've been in touch ever since working out details."

Mary Jean looked at their newest customer. "Don't you worry about a thing. We're a lot closer than Israel and glad to help. Here's a card with our number on it. Just a phone call away, though you're welcome to stop by anytime. Anytime at all. How long will you be here?"

Annie looked down at her hands as she put on her mittens again. "I don't really know. I haven't actually decided, to be honest." She quickly looked up at Mary Jean then back at her hands.

"Well, you just relax and enjoy that incredible view up there," Mary Jean said, patting her arm. "You'll going to have a wonderful time."

Doc Wilkins cleared his throat. "Some R&R, a little peace and quiet, well sir, that'll do wonders for just about anyone."

"Okay, Annie, let's you and I make a list of what you'll need," Bob added, reaching for a pen and paper.

Annie felt a warm smile spread across face. "Thank you so much. You all are so kind. I'm really very grateful."

Chapter 5

Seminole, Florida

After reading Annie's letter over and over, David finally pulled himself together enough to pray. He couldn't begin to find the words. Instead, he felt his soul cry out to God, asking for direction, for answers. He was too stunned to cry, though he felt a desperate need to do just that.

Later, when his mother gently tapped on the door, he lifted his head, got up off his knees and sat heavily on the bed.

"David? Are you about ready to—" She stopped, staring at the expression on her son's face. "David! What's the matter? What's wrong?"

She shut the door behind her and moved quickly across the room to sit beside him. He leaned over, resting his elbows on his knees, burying his head in his hands.

"Mom, where are the kids?" he whispered.

"Jessie and Jeremy are downstairs watching cartoons, and Max is studying in his room. Why?"

"Annie's gone."

"What? Of course she's gone. I told you she had some things to do. Meetings, I suppose. I told you she'd be late, dear. What's the problem?"

David kept shaking his head. "No, Mom. I mean she's *gone*. She took a flight out of town. Only she didn't say where."

"What? But I don't understand."

"I mean just what I said. She's *gone*."

Caroline uttered a baffled sigh. "Are you sure? That doesn't sound like Annie at all. She wouldn't just up and leave without telling you!"

"Here—read this," he said as he gathered up the pages and handed them to his mother. She looked at him, her face contorted with the urgency of her desire to understand.

"But I—"

"Read it, Mom."

Cartoon sound effects drifted up the stairs and under the door. David walked over to Annie's side of their king-size bed. He noticed the framed family portrait was missing from the bedside table. So was Annie's Bible. He wondered what else was missing from their room.

"Oh no," Caroline groaned, her voice cracking with emotion. "That poor child . . . she's been hurting so badly and all the while hiding it—from all of us."

"Mom, where could she have gone? Why wouldn't she at least tell me? I've got to find her. I have to." He began pacing the floor. "I'll call the airlines. Surely one of them will be able to tell us something. Or maybe I should call Pete Nardozzi at the Sheriff's office. He could probably—"

"No, David."

"Pete could help us find her. The airlines would talk to him if they knew it was a missing person situation and—"

"Son? Don't."

"What do you mean 'don't'?"

"She doesn't want to be found. She obviously needs some time alone. She's made that very clear. Annie's an intelligent girl. She wouldn't do anything foolish or unwise. It sounds to me as if she's planned all this out very carefully for a reason. Sometimes we have to be able to love someone enough to let them go—even for just a little while."

David stopped pacing and leaned against the closet door. He shook his head, still refusing to believe it.

His mother continued, her voice soft. "Honey, when did all this start? What happened?"

"Not now, Mom. I don't want to talk about that right now. All I want to do is find her." David felt his mother's eyes on him but refused to raise his head. Moments passed.

"Isn't it just like Annie to be thinking about all the rest of us even at a time when she's suffering so much?" Caroline added quietly. "To think she's hidden all this from us. And for her to be thinking about *me* right now. About the anniversary of Wade's death . . . she's quite a girl, David." Caroline took a deep breath. "Quite a girl."

He shuffled back over to the bed and sat back down.

They sat together in silence for several moments. Finally, David spoke. "I don't know what to do. I'm at a total loss here. But I do know we can't tell the kids. At least not now. They can't possibly understand this. Who am I kidding? *I* don't even understand this! But with so many of their friends going through family break-ups right now—no, we'll just have to tell them she's had to leave town for awhile. To visit a sick relative or something."

"I'll back you in whatever you decide to do. I prefer not to tell the kids a half-truth, but God willing, maybe Annie will be back home in three or four days. I can stay over in the guest room and help out however you need me. But what will you tell the church? You know how badly the rumors fly around there."

David stood up. "I don't know. Let's get through tonight and take it one day at a time."

"Hey Dad? Gran? You up there?" Jeremy yelled from the bottom of the stairs. "I'm starving! When are we gonna eat?"

Caroline walked over and hugged her son, her head barely reaching his shoulder. "I'll take care of the kids. You come down when you're ready."

David nodded, his thoughts still searching for meaning. "Oh Annie. Where are you?"

Chapter 6

Tulsa, Oklahoma

Grady Brewster tossed the stack of papers from his desk into his briefcase and snapped it shut. He would most likely never get around to working on them, but it never hurt to go through the motions. It had been an endless day of meetings, and he was exhausted. He walked over to the glass wall and stood, silently gazing at the panoramic view before him. The skyline of Tulsa was etched against the amber and violet streaks of the sunset.

He stretched his arms and arched his back, then thrust his hands deep into the pockets of his Dockers. From his office on the sixty-first floor of the Williams Center, he watched the massive exodus of cars and buses heading out to the suburbs, too tired to join them just yet. The quiet ringing of his phone interrupted his thoughts. He stepped over to his desk and picked up the slim receiver. "This is Grady."

"Grady the Brewmeister? The one and only Brewster Rooster of the College World Series Champions of 1983? One and the same?"

"Well, if it isn't Mr. Baseball himself!" Grady grinned as he sat back down. "To what do I owe this high privilege, big guy? I haven't heard from you since you made Fortune 500."

Grady relaxed in the familiar teasing from his old college buddy. It was true. He hadn't heard from Michael for at least a couple of years. Hard to believe they had once been as close as brothers. In fact, since parting their ways after graduation, their friendship had suffered dismally from lack of attention due to the miles and years between them. Only these intermittent calls had survived through the years.

He knew Michael suspected jealousy of invading their friendship. After all, they had both played baseball at Oklahoma State. And while Grady was extremely competitive, the same doors had not opened for him as the myriad of offers Michael enjoyed after college. While Michael rode off on the crest of a wave headed for athletic prestige and national stardom, Grady had stayed behind struggling in the precarious world of finance.

I wonder what he wants after all this time?

"Forget Fortune 500, man," Michael teased, interrupted Grady's thoughts. "It's been *way* too long! You still up there hobnobbing with the rich and famous? Ever get the itch to move on up to Wall Street and find some real action?"

"Nah, I'm happy right here where I am, Michael. I'll

leave Wall Street to the demented crazies who crave that sort of life. I couldn't be happier anywhere else. Built a new home out south of town, got a beautiful wife who still thinks I'm hot, and two incredible kids who adore their father. What else could I ask for, right?"

Silence.

"Michael? You still there?"

"Yeah, sorry. I was just thinking—how ironic life can be sometimes."

"What do you mean?"

Another pause. "When you mentioned your family just now, and how happy you are, I realized I was feeling a little jealous. That's all. Kinda funny, isn't it?"

Grady let that sink in for a moment. "So why don't you come up sometime and see us? Let me rub your nose in it while I can."

"How does tonight sound?"

Grady leaned forward in his chair. "Are you in town? Where are you?" The sounds of laughter and clinking glasses drifted through the phone line.

"I'm calling from a hangout here in Houston. But if you've got some time available, I can be up there in a few hours. I,uh . . . Grady, I really need to talk to you."

"What's up, Michael? You okay?"

"Nothing I can get into over the phone. I can catch a flight out of here in about an hour and a half and be there about eight o'clock. Can you pick me up at the airport?"

"No problem. What airline?"

"American. Just meet me curbside, okay? Maybe we can go grab a bite to eat."

"Sounds great. You sure you're all right?"

Another hesitation on the other end. "Just give me a few hours of your time," Michael answered, his voice hushed. "That's all I need. Thanks, buddy."

"No problem. See you at eight."

Grady hung up the phone and leaned back in his leather chair. He swung around to face the credenza behind him. Among the cluster of framed photographs was a five by seven autographed picture of Michael in uniform at the World Series. He stared blankly at the picture for some time, his memories drifting to another place and time. Then, releasing a heavy sigh, he stood up, reached for his briefcase, and left his office.

✐

Michael returned the receiver to the wall phone near the restroom. His eyes darted around the crowded bar as his heart beat against his chest. He had sought out a public place to make this call from a pay phone. He knew any of his personal lines or even his cell phone would surely be bugged. He couldn't risk Elliot knowing about this sudden side trip.

The concern in Grady's voice had caught him off guard. Michael visualized the wide grin of his old buddy and was strangely comforted by the warm feelings of camaraderie that swept over him. He wanted to believe it was like old times. And tonight he urgently needed a friend he could trust.

In the urgency of this hour, Grady Brewster was the only person Michael had even considered calling. There was no one else.

CR

American Airlines Flight 1021

The flight from Houston to Tulsa would take only two hours. As soon as Michael took his seat in First Class, he got to work with a keen sense of urgency. He knew it was imperative to record the information that had remained locked in his memory for so many years, and this was his only chance. He still didn't know how he would approach Grady with this volatile story once they met face to face. Or if he even could.

But as long as I have it in writing, at least I know the truth will come out. Especially if something should happen to me . . . He buried the thought, despite the chill running down his spine.

Lowering the tray table in front of him, he slid his laptop onto it. Taking a quick look around, he was grateful for his privacy. While the coach section was bustling with passengers, there were only five others riding with him in First Class, and no one in the seat directly beside him.

Where do I start?

He stared out the window at the sparkling city lights

now tilting into view as the plane arced its path across the night sky, leaving Houston in its wake. With a shrug of his shoulders, his fingers began pecking the keyboard, telling the strange story.

Grady,

I'm writing this letter to you in the event that something unfortunate happens to me. I realize I am in a great deal of danger. I also realize it is crucial that the truth be finally exposed. I ask that you personally forward this information to the United States Attorney General immediately. I'm not kidding, Grady. This is serious.

I guess I need to begin at the beginning, with my marriage to Amelia Thomas, the daughter of U.S. Congressman Elliot Thomas of Texas, in 1991. As you know, a few years later, after a successful career in major league baseball, I retired and pursued my present career as CEO of The Sports Page. A couple of years ago my company made the Fortune 500. While my father-in-law initially helped me get the company started with his financial backing, The Sports Page belongs to me and my shareholders.

Or so I thought. I've recently learned that Elliot has, in fact, manipulated my shareholders from the start. They are his cronies and they answer to him directly. Every single one of them. This deception apparently began from the inception of my company. It is with a deep sense of betrayal that I now know my entire staff,

71

which I have always believed to be totally loyal to me, has instead been loyal to Elliot from the outset.

I suppose this information would have remained a secret indefinitely had Elliot's direct "spies" not reported to him of my plans to divorce Amelia. He confronted me with this report and made it clear that he would not allow a divorce. I wasn't actually surprised by his reaction. Anything that could remotely cause an unfavorable reflection on Elliot Thomas or his family is never tolerated—even something as simple as a divorce. People get divorced. It happens. But to blue-bloods like the Thomases, divorce is apparently not acceptable. It's not an option. You have to know Elliot Thomas to understand that. Everything, but everything revolves around his political career. And if he deems it bad for his political standing, he won't stand for it. He'll do whatever it takes to avoid a controversy, no matter how big or how small. No matter how ridiculous it may seem to anyone else.

But it was the threat that caused my alarm. It was more than a threat—it was blackmail. Elliot said he would pull The Sports Page out from under me if I divorced Amelia, and he proceeded to tell me just how he could do it.

At first, I thought it was hopeless. I would certainly lose my company. Then I remembered an incident that happened several years ago. An incident that implicates Congressman Elliot Thomas of conspiracy to commit first degree murder.

It happened in 1992, about a year after Amelia and I got married. Elliot invited me to join him and his chief of staff, a guy named Duke, on a weekend hunting trip. We went to a place near Natchitoches, Texas, where Elliot always goes on his hunting trips. We stayed at a big cabin out in the woods. He thought it would give us a chance to get to know each other better. It was my off-season so I figured, why not?

The last night we were there, we built a big fire in the fireplace and pulled up some chairs and a sofa in front of it. We were all drinking and telling stories. The usual kind of stuff. They wanted to hear stories about some of the ball players I knew, and they were telling all kinds of stories about people in Washington. Some unbelievably private stuff about presidents, first ladies, Supreme Court justices. The two of them talked and laughed long into the night.

Duke and Elliot kept drinking like a couple of sailors on leave. I stopped earlier in the evening because I wasn't feeling well. I felt awful—my head hurt, I was nauseated, I had chills—the whole flu thing. I finally stretched out on the sofa, right in front of the fireplace and tried to go to sleep. By then they were both drunk. Completely smashed. They were giving me a hard time for not keeping up, but I felt so rotten I didn't care. I just ignored them, rolled over with my back to them, and finally drifted off to sleep.

I must have slept a couple of hours or so. Evidently I had a pretty bad fever because even with that fire going, I was freezing. I guess that's why I began to wake up. I didn't move or anything, just started to become aware that I wasn't sleeping anymore. Elliot and Duke were sitting over at the kitchen table by then, still carrying on, talking and laughing. They had no idea I was awake. I'm sure they thought I was out for the night.

All of a sudden I heard them mention Christopher Jordan, the senator who was killed in a boating explosion several years ago.

I knew from Amelia that Elliot had hated Christopher Jordan. Actually, 'hate' doesn't even begin to describe it. They despised each other. At the time, Jordan was the Chairman of the House Ways and Means Committee. Elliot had worked on a project to build a huge new addition to the space center in Houston. NASA had planned to build it at the Cape in Florida, but Elliot wasn't about to let that happen. He'd promised some major pork to his buddies back home. He had a whole slew of land developers falling all over themselves to get this one. All Elliot had to do was deliver the deal to Texas.

Obviously, Jordan and Elliot butted heads. Actually, this NASA project was just the last of a long line of bones Elliot had to pick with Jordan. These two had bad blood between them that goes way back. Seems Jordan has been Elliot's nemesis since the two of them were back in law school at Harvard. I don't know exactly what started their feud. Probably just a natural contempt for each other that continued to fester over the years. Problem was, Jordan was always at least one or two steps ahead of Elliot. Every committee, every key appointment, every prestigious chairmanship—Jordan seemed to float right in and sail off with the prize. Elliot despised him for that.

Anyone who knows Elliot knows the kind of ego that drives him. Guys like him won't put up with playing second fiddle forever. When Jordan was appointed Chairman of the House Ways & Means Committee, Elliot was furious. That, coupled with the humiliation he experienced when Jordan made him grovel over that NASA deal. I think it was more than Elliot could take.

I realize how ridiculous this may sound. To imply that a United States congressman would try to pull off cold-blooded murder out of pure jealousy must sound crazy. But please hear me out.

Let me get back to that night at the cabin. As I said, Elliot and Duke were absolutely smashed. I'd never seen either one of them even slightly inebriated, let alone drunk. Elliot kept giggling like a little kid. That's probably what woke me up in the first place. He isn't exactly the sort of man who "giggles" if you know what I mean. But Duke had him going with something about the "risks of nautical life." They were coming up with every possible pun you could imagine. Elliot was actually singing and making up all sorts of dumb songs.

They were laughing so hard, Duke even fell out of his chair onto the floor. Elliot was practically gasping for air, he was laughing so hard. Then once they started to calm down, Elliot began to mumble a lot. I could still understand him just the same. I remember his exact words. He said, "Ol' Jordan thought he could threaten me, didn't he? Said to me, 'Thomas, you'll take that pork to Texas over my dead body!' Well sir, he didn't have to ask but once now, did he!" And off they went again, howling and laughing as if it was the funniest thing ever said.

By then, I was wide awake but I didn't move an inch. I didn't miss a word, but they had no idea I was listening. They kept talking about some guy named "Bo." I didn't have a clue who that was at first. I had never heard Elliot mention anyone by that name. But Duke said, "I told you I never liked that name! I wanted to give him a code name like Popeye—it was the perfect name for him and you knew it! But nooo! You had to go and pick some sissy name like Beauregard. What kind of a stupid name is that?" Then Elliot said, "We name this guy something like Popeye and we might as well take out a full page ad in the Washington Post. Just print a full confession in black and white! Anybody with half a brain would link us to that bombing. Thank God, one of us has a brain, you moron."

They started singing again. They even harmonized on one song over and over—"My Jordan lies over the ocean, my Jordan lies over the sea, my Jordan lies ALL over the ocean, can't bring back ol' Jordan to me!"

They started singing more stupid songs, and the drunken laughter went on all night. With each one I began to piece together what must have happened. If only I'd had a tape recorder.

Eventually they passed out. Fell sound asleep right there sprawled all over the kitchen table. My mind was racing in a thousand directions. And then I remembered something. The television coverage of Christopher Jordan's death. The remnants of his yacht. Even though it had been years ago, long before I knew Elliot, I could still see those images in my mind. Scenes filmed at his funeral. His wife and children consumed by their grief. The twenty-one gun salute. Taps.

And then I remembered seeing the new Chairman of the House Ways and Means Committee—none other than Elliot Thomas—the bereaving Congressman, at times too choked up to continue as he eulogized the "beloved statesman and American hero." And it all started to make sense to me.

So why didn't I go to the authorities? Why didn't I turn them in? After all, this was the murder of a prominent congressman of the United States. Why didn't I tell someone?

For several reasons, and all of them selfish, I'm

sorry to say. I had only been married to Amelia for a year, but I already knew how much power Elliot Thomas carried. To be perfectly honest, he scared me to death. Still does. And I was primarily concerned with how it would affect me. I wasn't about to risk having my reputation tainted with this story if Elliot was brought down. I wanted to be known as a Major League baseball player—not forever remembered as the man who blew the whistle on a dirty politician. It's no secret that athletic accomplishments are quickly forgotten when scandal enters the picture.

I knew I had to keep my mouth shut. And in a perverted way of thinking, I realized I could always use the information if Elliot ever crossed me. That may sound rather calloused, but at that point in my life, it was the way my mind worked.

However, I did a little investigation on my own over those next few months. An odd guy named Bo would show up at the country club from time to time when Elliot and Duke were around. Eventually, I began to put two and two together, so I hired a private investigator to check him out. I have in my possession a complete background document on him—along with some rather incriminating evidence—phone records, flight logs, receipts, photographs. This information clearly links Mitch Creason—aka "Beauregard" aka "Bo"—to Elliot Thomas, implicating the congressman in the murder of Christopher Jordan.

Now, the tables have all been turned. It's time to use my secret files. Elliot isn't the only one who knows how to use blackmail. I have no other choice. This guy plays in a ballpark that's way out of my league. He knows no limits whatsoever. I am fully aware of that and always have been since that weekend in the backwoods of Texas.

My whole life is my company now. Elliot may have helped me with the start up, but it was my blood, sweat and tears that made The Sports Page *what it is today. I refuse to stand by and watch him steal it from me.*

Michael Dean

Michael hit the return key several times, leaving a short break in the text before adding a final personal note.

Grady,

Elliot gave me twenty-four hours to give him an answer. The clock is ticking. This is literally a matter of life and death for me. Once I have confronted Elliot with this information, I can only imagine what his reaction will be. I believe it could be deadly.

As I instructed you before, please make sure this document goes to the Attorney General's office ASAP. Before you make that contact, I need you to go to Houston and pick up the file of evidence. You can find it in Locker 486 in the men's locker room at The Page. The combination is 21-6-15. Please turn this evidence over to the Attorney General along with this document.

I apologize for having to involve you in this mess, Grady. But with the stakes so high, I knew you were the only one I could trust. You're the best, Brewster.

—M

Checking once more to make sure the letter was saved, he entered the appropriate commands then saved it to a flash drive which he removed and placed in a small envelope. He scrawled Grady's name on the front.

Michael sat back in his seat and closed his eyes. He released a long, exhausted sigh. The well-kept secret had taken its toll on him, much to his surprise. Having the sordid details finally off his chest—even if only in writing—proved a remarkable relief.

He leaned his seat back hoping to take a short nap just as the flight attendant announced the plane would be landing in ten minutes. Michael pushed the button, returning his seat to its upright position, but his eyes remained closed.

"Excuse me, sir, but you'll need to disembark. This is our final destination tonight." Michael looked up into the kind eyes of the flight attendant before realizing he was the last passenger left on board.

❧

You're gonna love this place, Dean. Best Mexican food

anywhere. And that includes any of those dives down in Texas."

Grady eased his spotless black Lexus into the parking space he selected far away from the other cars parked outside of Ricardo's. Since picking his friend up curbside at the airport, Michael had kept the conversation light and superficial. The usual kidding and reminiscing shared by old friends was apparently all Michael was willing to handle for the time being. Grady knew when his buddy was ready to talk, he would do so and not before.

"Hey, Mr. Brewster. How are you? You want your usual table?" The attractive young waitress grabbed two menus and started down the aisle.

"That would be great, Maria." Grady and Michael followed her lead through two levels of the crowded restaurant. She seated them in a tall booth of polished dark wood. An upside down copper kettle served as the lampshade hanging over the table between them. It was a comfortable atmosphere brimming with colorful decor from south of the border, cheerful waiters, and happy customers—all against a background of festive Mexican music. A waiter brought two glasses of iced water, a basket of crisp, fresh tortilla chips, and a small bowl of salsa.

"You need some time to look over the menus, Mr. Brewster?" the waiter asked, setting the chips on the table.

"I'll have the usual. Michael, do you like chili rellenos?"

"Sure—whatever."

"We'll have two chili rellenos dinners and two drafts," Grady ordered, already reaching for a chip and dipping into the bowl of chunky red sauce.

Michael followed Grady's lead and dug into the chips. "Whoa—I didn't realize how hungry I was. This was a great idea," he mumbled over a mouthful of chips.

"Yeah, this place is amazing. We come here all the time. I carry the portfolio for Rick, the guy who owns this place."

"Grady, I didn't even think to ask on the phone. How's Shari? And how are the kids?"

That's a switch. In their usual encounters, Michael dominated the conversation with his endless list of achievements and name-dropping. For a change, Michael seemed genuinely interested in what he had to say.

"Shari's great. Up to her eyeballs in PTA meetings, team mom for Jason's soccer team," Grady answered, ticking off the list on his fingers. "She's always carting Molly somewhere—back and forth to piano lessons, gymnastics, Girl Scouts—you name it. I don't know how she does it, but she seems to keep up with all of us and seems to love doing it. We went through some rocky times when we first got married, y'know. I had some tough challenges with the business and almost didn't make it—financially, that is. But Shari stuck by me through all of it. She was incredible. Still is."

Michael smiled. "Who would ever think you and Shari would be the all-American family? Geez, Grady, you guys sound like June and Ward Cleaver."

Grady laughed. "So squeaky clean, it makes you sick, right? But I can't complain. How about you? How's Amelia?"

The waiter returned with their beer then slipped away.

Michael took a thirsty swallow, then set the glass back down. Seconds passed in silence.

"Michael, what's going on? I mean, it's great to see you, but flying up to see me at a moment's notice? After all these years? I seriously doubt you came all this way just to hear about my family."

Michael looked down his glass as he pulled another long, slow swallow. Grady noticed a palpable hesitance floating across the table. His friend started to reach into his jacket pocket, then stopped, as he tucked something back into the pocket.

"Michael?"

It was obvious he was stalling, thinking. Some kind of debate going on inside his head. Suddenly, he blew out a heavy sigh. "Grady, I—" He paused. He threw back the rest of his beer and set the empty glass gently back on the table. "I need your help," he began quietly. "I didn't know who else to turn to."

"What is it? What's wrong?"

"I'm in some trouble. Nothing I can't handle, but I— well, I just need a little security to fall back on."

"*You?* Michael Dean needs a loan? Get outta here!"

"Not money. It isn't anything like that. I . . . I just need to know if I get into a bind, if I find myself in danger, that I can count on you. That's all." He sighed again, apparently relieved to get it off his chest. Whatever *it* was.

A silent alarm sounded somewhere in Grady's mind. He blinked rapidly, hoping to downplay his concern. "What kind of danger? Don't you think you ought to tell me a little more about this? Whatever this 'trouble' is you've gotten into, don't you think you should tell me what's going on?"

Michael sat back, tapping his fork on the table. "It's Elliot."

The conversation stopped as the waiter set two platters of steaming food before them. "The plates are hot, so be careful. Can I get you a refill on your drafts?"

Grady spoke up, "Tell you what, just bring us a pitcher then you won't have to make so many trips."

Michael held up his hand. "Mind if we make it a pitcher of Coke? I've got to keep my head straight tonight."

"Sure—no problem." Grady nodded to the waiter.

The waiter returned shortly setting a bubbly pitcher between them. As he turned to leave, Michael and Grady hungrily attacked the plates loaded with rice, beans, and deep-fried chili rellenos smothered with a white cheese sauce.

Grady grew increasingly uncomfortable with the silence. "Now you've *really* got me worried. I've never known Michael Dean to pass up a pitcher of beer. So out with it. The suspense is killing me. What's Elliot done this time?"

Michael cleared his mouth and wiped it slowly with the red cloth napkin. He leaned forward over the table and spoke as softly as he could. "Grady, surely you've run into Elliot somewhere along the line in your business?"

"Yeah, I hear a lot about him. He's got a reputation for being obnoxious. He's a jerk—so what? Aren't most politicians?" He concentrated on the food before him, stabbing another bite.

"He's making my life miserable right now. In ways you

could never *imagine.*" Michael's eyes locked on Grady's. "Bottom line is I can't talk about this. I just need to know you'll be there for me if things take a turn for the worse."

"What's in your pocket? What were you reaching for?"

Michael blinked, patting his hand over his jacket. "It's nothing. Really."

Grady stared into his friend's eyes, uneasy with the ominous pleading he saw there. "So that's it? You're in some kind of trouble with Elliot but you don't trust me enough to tell me about it? C'mon, Michael!" he snapped. "Who do you think I'm going to tell? You think I'm going to call up the *New York Times* and give them some kind of scoop on a—a domestic problem a friend of mine is having with his father-in-law? Give me a little credit here!" He dropped his fork on his plate and pushed it away.

Michael leaned forward, his voice strained. "Grady, will you stop and just hear me out? It isn't a matter of whether or not I trust you! Geez, if I didn't trust you, do you honestly think I'd hop on a plane and come all the way up here to see you about this? I trust you completely." He paused then quietly continued. "But it finally dawned on me that I might be putting *your* life in jeopardy and I can't do that. I *won't* do that. You've got a family to think about. No, I've got to do this thing my way. You'll have to accept it on my terms or we drop this. Right here, right now. That's the best I can do."

Michael slowly shoved his half-eaten plate aside and dropped his napkin on top of it. "Take it or leave it." He looked up, his eyes determined.

Grady fought his temper. He broke eye contact, staring instead at nothing in particular. Then finally, with a heavy sigh, "I'm sorry, Michael. I had no right to demand anything from you. It's obvious you have your reasons for keeping this to yourself. I suppose I can respect that."

He rolled his neck. "You need a friend—you've got one." He extended his hand across the table. Michael responded with a firm handshake. Their eyes met only briefly.

"So what do you need me to do?" Grady asked, trying to mask his irritation with nonchalance.

"Just be available. That's all. In the next twenty-four hours or so, I may need to call you. I'll be okay as long as I know I can reach you."

"No problem." Grady removed his wallet from his coat pocket and pulled out his business card. He scribbled a number on it and slid it across to Michael. "This is my private cell phone number. It's with me wherever I go."

Michael cleared his throat. "Thanks. I appreciate it."

"Thanks for what?" Grady laughed. "I haven't done anything. Just do me a favor and take care of yourself, okay? I don't like the sound of this thing at all. What little you've told me, anyway. Although, I don't know why I'm not surprised. You always were the one in the middle of every barroom brawl in town while I was back at the dorm with my nose in the books."

"Some things never change, do they, Brewster?" Michael smiled weakly.

"Evidently not, Dean. Evidently not."

Chapter 7

Eagle's Nest, near Weber Creek, Colorado

The inside windshield of her Jeep Cherokee rental kept fogging up, no matter how many times Annie wiped it with her mittened hand. The snow was falling much heavier now. She scolded herself for continuing up the treacherous road in such bad weather.

David, what am I doing? You would never have let me drive in this kind of weather.

The wipers beat back a nervous rhythm, adding to her tension. She knew she must be getting close to Christine's cabin. It had been over half an hour since she left the Williamson's store.

I wonder if I took a wrong turn? She tried to squelch the knot of fear in her stomach. The Jeep was creeping so slowly, she was afraid she might slip backwards at any moment. *Thank goodness for the gravel road. I'd be slipping all over the place if it were regular pavement. Oh God, help me. I'm lost and I don't know what to do! I feel so all alone— please show me what to do!*

At that moment Annie felt a strange grinding of the tires against the gravel road. She anxiously tapped the brakes, attempting to stop the vehicle. The window had steamed up again, blurring her vision and filling her with panic. As she wiped it again, she gasped as a huge evergreen appeared suddenly out of nowhere. Jerking the steering wheel to the left, she felt the wheels skid then lose traction. The Jeep sailed, airborne off the side of the snow-covered mountain, suspended in mid-air—

Ring . . .

Ring . . .

Annie bolted straight up off the sofa as the phone rattled her back to reality.

Ring . . .

Her heart raced as she gulped for air. Slowly gathering her bearings, she realized she wasn't falling off a cliff. She found herself standing in front of the oversized sofa. Putting a hand to her head, she felt drenched in perspiration despite the chill that gripped her.

Ring . . .

Annie tried to pace her breathing as she reached for the relentless phone on the table. She stammered, trying to speak. "Uh . . . hello?"

"Annie, is that you?"

She paused, still trying to regulate her heart rate. "Yes . . . uh . . . yes, who's this?"

"This is Mary Jean Williamson down at the store. Are you all right? Bob and I were concerned about you, what with this storm hitting so hard."

Annie began to look around. The light from the lamp shone softly in spite of a bright glow from the windows, illuminating the entire room. *I must have fallen asleep last night on the sofa.*

"Yes, Mary Jean, I . . . I'm fine. I must have dozed off."

"Oh goodness, I apologize. I didn't think about waking you up. Bob and I just wanted to make sure you still had electricity and your phone lines were still working."

"Everything seems to be working. I'll take a look around and call you back if there's a problem." She paused to take a deep breath, finally relaxing. "I really appreciate knowing you're there in case of an emergency."

Mary Jean laughed. "Oh don't you worry. We want you to have a nice visit, but we don't want to interfere with your peace and quiet. Just let us know if you need anything, okay?"

Annie rubbed her foot on the inside of her other leg. The heavy socks felt good, but they weren't enough in this kind of cold. "Thanks, Mary Jean. I'll be in touch."

She wrapped the colorful quilt around her and tip-toed to the bedroom to find her slippers. Upon her arrival last night, she had slung her suitcase on the pine love chest at the foot of the queen-sized brass bed. She'd intended to unpack, but fatigue had quickly overcome her. She dug through her bag and found the fleece-lined slippers, then quickly put them on.

She was drawn to the huge window cut into the rustic logs of the cabin wall. The brightness made her squint before wiping the condensation off the glass panes. She used a corner of the hand-stitched quilt to rub the pane in a circular motion, then stopped. Her hand still poised on the glass before her, she shuddered, remembering the deadly dream. It seemed so real! She could still feel the car soaring through the frigid air. Another shudder swept over her.

Now that she thought of it, there had been many nights over the last few months when she was awakened by dreams. Usually, they made no sense at all, but the nightmares like the one she had just experienced were happening more often. She remembered reading once that dreams often dealt with unresolved conflicts. If that was the case, what was the significance of falling off the side of a mountain?

But, of course. Her life was out of control, and just like the Jeep Cherokee in her dream, she felt powerless to do anything to stop it.

Annie stomped her feet to get the blood circulating and pulled the quilt more tightly around her. Cautiously, she reached toward the window again, this time clearing it enough to see the panoramic view before her. She sighed, taking in the majesty of the mountains surrounding her. The snow blew hard, but she was able to make out the breathtaking landscape. Doc had been right. It was an incredible view.

She shuffled back out to the great room to revive the embers in the massive stone fireplace. In no time at all, a blaze was crackling behind the hearth, finally warming her. She tossed the quilt back on the sofa and padded over to the kitchen. Unwrapping one of Mary Jean's oatmeal muffins, she popped it into the microwave for a few seconds and started brewing a pot of hazelnut coffee. She poured a small glass of icy cold milk, wrapped the muffin in a napkin and headed back for the sofa.

She sighed with contentment. *This is heaven.*

She dismissed the tug in her soul, warding off the inevitable thoughts and truths she must face. Looking around, she marveled at the cozy and comforting ambiance around her. It was truly a beautiful retreat. Everywhere she looked were memorabilia from Christine's life—bits and pieces of her hobbies, treasures from travels to distant lands, and an amazing array of her award-winning photographs from around the world. Antiques here and there mingled with more modern accessories, tastefully blended in a way only Christine could pull off. Candles in every size and shape graced every surface of the room. *Signature Christine.*

Annie finished off the glass of milk and headed back to the kitchen for a mug of coffee. Finally settling down on the cream-colored sofa, she plopped her feet up on the coffee table, covered her legs once more with the quilt, and sunk down in the cushions to relax. She stared into the fire, realizing this was exactly how she had fallen asleep the night before.

It felt so incredibly good to be here. And yet, she felt plagued by the emotions still harboring inside. She wasn't ready to let go. Not yet. For now she needed only the soothing knowledge that there were no schedules to keep, no calls to make, no meetings or lunches required, no laundry to fold, no crisis to resolve—and no absent husband to be mad at. If she chose to sit in this very spot all day and all night, it was perfectly all right.

And for now, it was enough.

❧

Seminole, Florida

David's head throbbed. He felt awful. He hadn't slept more than fifteen minutes at a stretch all night, and the day was creeping by equally as bad. He had no idea how long he'd been sitting in his easy chair. His worn, leather Bible was spread across his lap, but he couldn't remember what it was he last read. He rubbed his eyes wearily and scratched the day's growth on his chin. The quiet ticking of the grandfather clock irritated him.

He shut his burning eyes, leaning back on the headrest. Just then he heard the sound of a vehicle pulling around to the garage.

Mom's back.

Caroline had left the house several hours earlier to run some errands, or so she said. He knew she needed to pack a bag for her indefinite stay with them, but he wasn't fooled by her supposed need to run errands. She wanted to give him some solitude before the kids came home from school.

Time to think. To pray.

He wanted to believe that last night was nothing more than a bizarre nightmare. It wasn't real, was it? Over and over, his mind replayed the previous evening. With the night mercifully behind him now, David shook his head hoping to get rid of the sense of helplessness that engulfed him. He ran his hand through his hair then stood up, stretching his arms over his head.

"David, are you up?"

"In here, Mom," he answered. He could hear the crinkling of the grocery bags settling on the kitchen counter.

"David, I've been thinking." She stopped in the doorway, placing a hand on her hip.

"Good. I'm glad one of us still has the ability."

"Now, don't start. Listen to me. You and I must be very careful how we handle this whole thing with the kids."

"I know. I've been thinking the same thing."

Caroline turned back around. "Come in here while I put the groceries away. I'll make you a cup of tea. We need to talk."

What would I ever do without her? He lumbered over to the counter, hopping up to sit on it.

Caroline unpacked a variety of packages and produce from the paper bags. "Part of me wishes we could lie through our teeth about this whole thing. Tell them Annie went to visit her sister in Vermont who just had a baby."

David crinkled his face in confusion. "Annie doesn't have a sister in Vermont. She doesn't have a sister anywhere, so I know there certainly can't be a new baby."

"I know that, son, but it sure would've made it a lot

easier if she did." Her smile was vaguely mischievous.

"Great. I'll be sure to bring that up when she calls. Or I guess I should say *if* she calls."

"You know, you aren't making this any easier with comments like that," she answered, leveling her gaze at him over her glasses.

"Okay, okay. Go on."

"The thing is, I despise people who lie and I know that God isn't too keen on it either. Which, as far as I'm concerned, rules out that option."

"So what do you suggest?"

"I suggest being totally up front with them. Tell them she needed a little getaway vacation. Remind them that everyone needs a break now and then, and she's getting one right now. Be as honest as you can possibly be with them, David. But I don't think it's necessary for them to know anything more."

David stared out the window at a bright cardinal feasting on the miniature log-cabin bird feeder. "I suppose you're right," he said, absently picking at the worn knee of his jeans. "Jessie doesn't miss much for a kid her age. What do I say if she digs for more answers?" he said, jumping down from the counter and pacing the floor. "And you know Max will drill us. And what do I say when the questions start flooding in from church members? They're going to wonder where she is. Mom, these people know me! They know I don't lie. How will I ever be able to do this? I can't face a hundred questions. I can't do this." He stopped, plopping down into a ladder-back chair at the kitchen table.

He rustled his hair again then rubbed his face.

Caroline walked over to her son, grabbing his arm and turning him to face her. "David, did you hear yourself just now? 'I can't do this.' Of course you can't! But you know you are not alone. Aren't you the guy who's always preaching to us how God is most able to work in our lives when we come to the realization we cannot do it ourselves? That we are totally dependent on Him? So how about letting Him take over and intervene for this shepherd?" She poked his chest with her forefingers.

David dropped his head again. Caroline wrapped her arms around him, hugging him with all her strength. "Besides, you have your old, white-haired mother here for you, remember? And I'll be here for as long as you need me. So don't even think about carrying this thing alone, okay? Between you, me and the Lord, we'll make it through this."

David finally responded, hugging his mother. "You're pretty feisty for an old, white-haired mother, did you know that?"

"Hey, I earned every single one of these white hairs and I'm mighty proud of each and every one. Now, what do you say we hit our knees and spend some time with the Lord since He's the one with all the answers?"

❧

Caroline? Is that you, dear? Did I dial your number by mistake?"

Caroline took a deep breath before responding, "Why, hello Darlene. What a nice surprise."

Even as the words slipped out of her mouth, Caroline winced at what she knew was an untruth. She offered up a silent apology to the Lord. "No, you didn't dial wrong. I just happened to be here and was by the phone in the kitchen when it rang. How are you, Darlene?"

To call it a "strained" relationship would be a generous description at best. Annie's mother was the kind of in-law every parent dreads. More like a blight joining the family tree. Fortunately, Annie was nothing at all like her mother, favoring instead her father who had died when she was only ten. Thank goodness she had been a "daddy's girl" from the day she was born. Caroline often wondered how such a dear child could ever descend from such an insufferable matriarch.

Darlene no doubt meant well. She simply had the uncanny knack of stirring up a hornet's nest where there weren't any hornets within miles. David called it the "spiritual gift of aggravation."

Caroline quickly tried to think how best to divert Darlene without compounding her previous half-truth. One thing she knew: Darlene must not find out that Annie had left. At least not yet.

This would have to be *creative.*

Darlene jumped right in, "Oh Caroline, I'm fine! Just fine! Randolph and I just got back from our trip to Australia. Annie did tell you we were going, didn't she?"

"Yes, she—"

"Well, we had the most WONDERFUL time! It's such an AMAZING country, Caroline. You just HAVE to go one of these days. Oh! I know! You could go on one of those Merry Widow cruises. Wouldn't that be terrific? And who knows, Caroline, maybe you'll meet some handsome, debonair, RICH widower! You know, like on those *Love Boat* reruns. Wouldn't that be just wonderful?"

Caroline sat on one of the kitchen stools. She uttered another quick prayer for patience. Wisdom alone wouldn't cut it.

"Darlene, I'd never thought of that. Who knows—maybe I'll look into it one of these days."

"Say! Caroline, I'll be going by our travel agent's office tomorrow. I'll just check on that for you. See when the next widow's cruise goes to Australia!"

"Oh thank you, Darlene, but—"

"Oh, nonsense, Caroline. No need to thank me. Glad to help in any way I can. Say, is Annie there? I haven't had a chance to chat with my baby girl since I got back. Thought I might stop by in a little while if she's going to be there and tell her all about our trip. We'll have everyone over sometime soon to see the videos we took, but for now I just MUST see Annie. Oh, say, Caroline, you come on over too when we show the videos. You'll get the bug for Australia if you do! Such a BEAUTIFUL country, and you'd just love their adorable accents! We recorded lots of them saying things in that cute little accent. They all sound just like that Crocodile Hunter on TV, God rest his soul. Oh, it was SO funny—I'd stop one of them on the street, ask for directions and Randolph would start taping our conversation, and—"

Does she ever breathe?

"—then I'd get to chatting with them. You know me—I'll talk to a chair if no one's around!" Darlene burst into laughter. Caroline arched her eyebrows as she rolled her eyes, the phone cradled on her shoulder.

"Oh goodness me! I just keep Randolph in stitches! Caroline? Are you still there, dear?"

"I'm here, Darlene," Caroline answered, biting off the sarcastic response bouncing around her head.

Darlene continued. "Oh dear, I've just been carrying on so and you haven't had a chance to get a word in edgewise, as Mama used to say. But then you know me—yak, yak, yak! Hardly have time to breathe!"

Oh really?

"Caroline, honey, are you all right?"

"Oh, I'm just fine, Darlene. Just a little weary, that's all."

"Yes, I know, dear," Darlene said, sliding into her syrupy sympathetic tone. "You must be just devastated since Wade had that awful heart attack and left you."

"Well, now, Darlene, I'm really getting along just fine. After all, it's been almost a year since—"

Darlene sucked in a shrill burst of air. "NOT REALLY! Has it really been a YEAR? You poor dear! Well, all I can say is, we've just got to do something about that. I'll tell you what we're going to do. I'm going to finish unpacking today and then tomorrow I'm going to spend the whole day with you! Why, we'll just go shopping and go eat a fabulous lunch at The Club, maybe even indulge ourselves and to go The Dessert Tray for some kind of sinfully good dessert! Oh—unless you're still dieting? Are you still watching your weight, dear?"

Caroline slammed the receiver down. For a moment she just stared at the phone, not believing the audacity of the woman behind that voice. *Lord! I just can't handle her today! Give me strength.*

Ring.

"I'm so sorry, Darlene, we got cut off. Listen, I've got to run anyway. Annie's not here right now but I'll leave a note that you called. Bye!"

Chapter 8

Eagle's Nest

Annie reached for the blue and white checked dish towel hanging inside the cabinet door below her. She wiped her eyes, now blurred with tears. She laughed out loud. With everything else on her mind, the last thing she expected to bring tears to her eyes was onions.

She finished dabbing her eyes then scraped the chopped onions off the cutting board and into the deep pot of sizzling ground beef. For some reason, she had craved homemade chili since she first set foot in this winter paradise. She couldn't wait to smell the mixture of spices, beef, and tomatoes.

Drying her hands on the towel, she ambled over to the entertainment center to find some suitable music. Christine's taste in music knew no boundaries so the selection was limitless—Billy Joel, Madonna, Pavarotti, Garth Brooks, Michael Jackson, Springsteen, Big Band, the London Symphony Orchestra . . . it was all there and more.

And suddenly, Annie was transported back to another day and time. Oklahoma State University—the year, 1981. In the huge university arena which normally housed raucous basketball games, she was surrounded by all her friends and thousands of students from her campus. The driving beat and killer tunes of The Police entertained them long into the autumn night.

Annie realized she was smiling. The memories of that night rolled tenderly through her mind like the gentle tide on the beach back home.

That night, they had laughed and sung and danced in the aisles. The blaring guitars and pounding drums pressed them upward like a thousand hands reaching up to lift the roof off the arena. She could see Christine, decked out in an oversized sweatshirt and her favorite jeans, her thick blond hair a splash of curls in constant motion. Always the carefree spirit, she was dancing up and down the aisle with any willing partner. At one point a "gorgeous hunk of a man," as Christine would later describe him, grabbed her hand and pulled her to the front of the auditorium near the stage. For a few minutes Annie couldn't see her through the throng of wild fans surrounding them. Suddenly, there was Christine—on stage with her new-found friend, dancing in perfect choreography to the driving beat of the music. That was Christine—right at home in front of a massive sea of strangers and side by side with Sting.

Only Christine.

Those years were jam-packed with good times and great friends. Life was one big party with an occasional exam thrown in the mix. No worries about tomorrow, no regrets about yesterday. Just happy in the here and now.

Annie scanned through the enormous CD rack to find Sting's Greatest Hits and gently placed it into the system. As the smooth melody of *Fields of Gold* filled the room, she made her way back to the kitchen. She quickly tossed the remaining ingredients into the chili and turned the heat down to let it simmer for an hour. After cleaning her mess, she made a cup of tea then headed for a look out the window. The snow continued to blow, but it appeared to be slowing at the moment. She would take a walk in a little while if it got no worse. The frigid air would be refreshing. Besides, she was dying to build a snowman, though even thinking of it made her feel a little guilty.

She pressed her forehead against the cold pane of glass and inwardly scolded herself. *Coming up here was a pretty selfish thing to do. Think how much David and the kids would love it here. The kids have never even seen snow except on TV.*

And at that moment, a voice spoke quietly inside her head.

Annie, it's all right for you to build a snowman. And it's all right for you to be here, to have some time to yourself. Quit beating yourself up and just relax. You needed Me—and this is how you felt you must find Me. I am here for you.

With only the slightest shiver down her back, she felt strangely calm. This was nice. Yes, this was good. Yet, something stubborn was tugging at her heart. She had avoided the thoughts and feelings dammed up inside her long enough.

It was time to face the volcano inside.

The scripture came to her mind at once. *Come to Me, all you who are weary and burdened, and I will give you rest . . . for I am gentle and humble in heart, and you will find rest for your souls.* She clung to the words as though lost at sea, clinging to a life raft. She had to believe those words even though doubts assailed her. She *needed* to believe those words.

Annie turned off the music and returned to her spot on the sofa. The sense of dread about confronting this moment had diminished. Now, taking God at His word, she allowed the door to her heart to gently open.

I don't even know where to begin, Lord. I've tried so desperately to bury these thoughts for so long, and now when I need to uncover them, I don't seem to know where to start. God, you alone know the pain that has burned inside me all these months. You alone know all the feelings I have experienced. Show me, God. Open my eyes to examine all of it. Don't let me hold anything back anymore. God, I'm begging You to help me. Give me strength to do this.

Once again, in the depths of her soul, the familiar words of the Psalmist spoke to her heart. *I lift up my eyes unto the hills—from whence does my help come? My help comes from the Lord, the Maker of heaven and earth.*

She took a deep breath and tried to clear her head. This was not going to be easy. When did it first begin? She closed her eyes, mentally watching a parade of faces and situations. It was like walking down a long, dark corridor lined with doors on either side. Doors she had barricaded. But she knew healing would only come as she unlocked each and every one of them. Skimming through her journal on the plane, she had cracked open a few of those doors. Now it was time to face the memories and individuals behind every single one of them.

The apprehension crawled back into her heart. Any one of these doors would stir up a myriad thoughts and feelings she had kept safely entombed. Annie shook her head, as if she could toss aside the months—no, years—of unacknowledged bitterness that had given root to these painful thorns in her soul. She sprang up to stoke the fire, poking the logs with unusual force, causing a fierce blaze to roar against the hearth. She stood transfixed, staring into the flames, surprised by her racing heart rate.

She tossed the poker back into its place and began to pace. Back and forth, back and forth. "Look at me! I'm like a wild animal here." She stopped in her tracks at the sound of her voice. "But who cares? I'm all alone here. Who cares if I sound like a raving lunatic? I can pace if I want to!"

It felt odd to talk out loud like this. Then again, it felt good. *Real* good.

"Hey! I can shout out loud if I want to! I can talk to myself, I can stomp all over the room, I can even scream if I have to!" She nodded in satisfaction with her new-found freedom and continued her pacing. "This is good. This is good.

"Okay, Lord, I'm ready. You asked for it. Well, here it

is." Rubbing her hands together, she took several deep breaths, bolstering her courage. "I am *sick to death* of being a pastor's wife.

"There. I said it!" She blew out a lungful of air. "In fact, I might as well be totally honest. I absolutely *despise* being a pastor's wife. I love David—at least the David I *used* to know—but I abhor the role I've been forced to accept just because I married him. I know, I know. I didn't object when he answered your call into the ministry. We both accepted that call. We were so sure it was what you wanted us to do. To devote our lives to serving you by leading a church family. Ministering to their needs. Using our talents and gifts to care for your people.

"But I'm not so sure any more.

"Maybe we were just young and idealistic. Maybe we were caught up in the emotional whirlwind of it all and somehow misunderstood what you wanted us to do. Maybe you only meant for us to be active members of a church. Use those same gifts but not necessarily as pastor and wife. I don't know, but all I *do* know is for the last year or so I've grown to hate it. I *hate* it."

Her words tumbled out in rapid succession to her unseen Audience. "I hate it because everything that's good and right about church is constantly overshadowed by the negatives. For every sweet child or dear widow who comes to give their heart to Jesus, there are ten others who find some kind of sick pleasure in tearing each other's eyeball's out. They'd rather burn up the phone lines spreading all kinds of ridiculous lies about each other. They call it 'sharing prayer concerns.' Oh God, how I've come to *hate* that stupid phrase! It's nothing more than pure gossip and they all know it!

"Of course, it's basically open season on anyone at all, but the target usually finds its way back to David in one way or another. Why is that? Just because he's the pastor? Because he's kind and considerate and approachable? Everybody *loves* David. So why do they pick on him all the time?"

The cabin grew quiet as the verbal outburst gave way to pounding thoughts. *It wouldn't be so difficult to handle if they were just open and honest with us. Tell us what they dislike or why they're upset. But why is it Christians seem to prefer the back door when it comes to criticism? They call me under some false pretense to take a back-handed slap at my husband. They pick on our kids unmercifully instead of coming directly to us if they have a problem or complaint. I mean, who in their right mind would harass an* eight year old child *just because they don't like the color of carpet his father approved for the new sanctuary? Or who would bother complaining to the pastor's* teenage son *just because they don't like the turn of a phrase in the Sunday sermon? Or just because they have some bone to pick with David, why would someone accost me in the parking lot at the grocery store—*

Annie stopped, the memory burning in her mind. Her chest heaved with the anger. She wiped her brow, surprised to find it damp with perspiration.

"Oh God, forgive me," she whispered. "I sound like such a whining child. Here I am, wailing and grumbling about each and every little burr that has pricked me at one time or another. I'm no better than any of them, am I? Oh God, how tired you must be of hearing me whine."

She took another lap, slowly passing the fireplace, deciding to give the blaze another jab or two. The words continued pouring out, like a dam unleashing its fury. "For *so long* I've put on my little mask and marched off to church every time the doors opened. Ever the happy little pastor's wife. Always careful to hide behind a plastered smile, even at times when my heart was breaking into a thousand tiny pieces. When I was missing David so much I could hardly function. Playing the part, going through the motions, and hating myself for the lie I was living. I constructed this huge wall around myself to try and keep the hurt out. To protect myself from the arrows aimed at my David and the kids and myself.

"And I'm so tired of having to stay on constant guard against potential friendships that might prove traitorous, when all I wanted was someone to be my friend. I need a *true friend.* Is that so much to ask? Yes, I know I have friends—people I have lunch with, go to Bible study with. But sometimes I need someone to talk to. Someone I can open my heart to. Someone who won't use our friendship for some hidden personal agenda."

She plopped down on the sofa, tired of her treks around the room. She grabbed a throw pillow, wrapping her arms around it. "It's even worse to sit by and watch when someone befriends David for all the wrong reasons. David, with a heart the size of Texas, who never met a stranger and tries to believe the best of everyone. How many times has he been betrayed? Only men play the game a lot tougher. They use a whole different strategy.

David, take the afternoon off and let me take you out to the club for some golf.

David, I want you and Annie to come over to my dealership and pick out any new car on my lot! It's my gift to you—a way to say thank-you for all your hard work!

David, you and Annie come by sometime and pick out some house plans to best suit your needs. I'll build it for you at cost. After all, you deserve it!

Pastor! We want you and your family to join us for a week of skiing up at Vail! Our treat!

"It all sounds so nice and generous and innocent. But it always backfires. It's nothing more than a bribe. A power play." Annie pounded her fist into the pillow, harder and harder. Faster and faster.

"What makes it even more disgusting is this, this 'residue' of suspicion it leaves on your heart. There are so many wonderful people—folks who have hearts filled with nothing but genuine love, whose only ambition is to honestly serve. No strings attached. No hidden agendas. They're just human extensions of Your love in everything they do. Yet I find myself immediately skeptical of *everyone* who comes along. They're completely unaware of the fact they must prove themselves to me before earning my trust. And I utterly hate myself for even having to doubt their sincerity.

"Oh Lord! Why do You put up with it? If it makes *me*

this crazy, it's got to be exasperating to You!"

She threw the pillow aside, jumping up to reach for the poker again, nervously tapping it against the stone hearth. "I just don't get it. How did Christians get so screwed up? When did we all stop living in your love and start being so cruel to each other? Surely you despise all this skepticism and criticism and suspicion a lot more than I do. You never meant for it to be like this, did You? Why don't you just—I don't know, send another flood or something. Or blast us out of here. Just be done with us, once and for all."

She stopped beating the hearth when she noticed tiny chips of stone flying with each strike. She carefully put the poker back into the stand with the other fireplace tools. She stared into the dancing flames, losing herself in the silence. Minutes slipped by.

Suddenly, she noticed her thoughts drifting away from all the disappointments of church life and hitting much closer to home.

David.

The ache in her chest was real. *When did we cross the line, David? Did we even know it? When did you sell your soul to the church? Do you remember when it happened? When the line between serving God and serving the institution became so completely blurred? When did it enslave you? When did it bind you in chains so strong, you stopped trying to fight it?*

When did it blind you from seeing the family you left behind? Blind you to what we once had? Do you even realize you're never home? Never available? I know your work is important. Your ministry is important. I get that. But don't we even register on the radar screen anymore? Can you remember the last time you worked us into your schedule? Made even the slightest effort to get home on time or have dinner with us?

And what about us? You and me. Can you tell me the last time we went out, just the two of us? Can you tell me the last time you even thought of me more than just in passing? For more than a quick kiss on the cheek on your way out the door? Or to hand me a list of social appearances we have to make dictated by the church calendar?

A sob caught in her throat. The tears burned trails down her cheeks. *David, do you have any idea how long it's been since you held me in your arms? Since you made love to me?*

Annie buried her head in her arms and cried. The sobs racked her body until she thought she would be sick. Her head throbbed, but the tears kept coming.

Finally, completely drained, she raised her head. She wiped her tears with the quilt, still trying to catch her breath. Mentally, she steeled herself against the pain. She closed that door, unable to face another second of so much sorrow.

Forcing her mind to change tracks, she faced one last frontier. This time, her words stammered out in a hushed whisper. "But worse than all of that, God—what bothers me most . . . is that I've lost *You*." The lump in her throat caught her words. "I've lost you because of all this." The flames hissed against her silence. "And I can't seem to find my way back."

She tried to take a deep breath, but couldn't. "God, I need You *so* much. Please let me find You."

Annie finally collapsed. The process had begun. The suffocating burdens in her heart were now laid out on the altar of her soul. She fell back into the open arms of the easy chair, thoroughly spent and exhausted. Surprisingly, she found it difficult to regain control of her breathing. It seemed as if her heart itself would surely tear away, unanchored from her soul.

When at last the storm inside her began to subside, she sat in silence, absorbed by the truths she had finally forced herself to confront. She waited. Patiently at first, then not so patiently.

Where was the peace? Shouldn't there be some kind of relief flooding over her now? Some afterglow of satisfaction for her unveiled confession? A feeling of accomplishment for facing this monster she had avoided for so long?

God, where are you?

Nothing. Only a chilled numbness. Even the quiet voice of the Lord had vanished in a deafening hush. Annie pleaded, screaming through stunned anger, "GOD, WHERE ARE YOU!"

Only the soft ticking of the clock echoed her pleas. The silence filled her with frightening doubt. This was not how it was supposed to happen. She was not even close to feeling any sense of resolution. Instead, she was even more confused than ever before.

And deeply, deeply disappointed.

Chapter 9

Seminole, Florida

Dad? What're you doing home? Are you sick or something?" Max yelled from the kitchen. After bursting through the back door after school, he had peeked around the corner at his father stretched out on the sofa in the family room.

"I guess you could say that, Max. But I'll be all right," David answered, trying to sound much more positive than he felt. He sat up and rubbed his eyes. "How was school today?"

"All right, I guess. But I could kill Mr. Harrison. He kept needling me in class today. The whole hour! He kept asking me all these outrageous questions. I didn't finish reading the chapter last night because I had to study for my Advanced Latin exam. So I couldn't answer all his stupid questions to his satisfaction. What a jerk!"

"Max—"

"But Dad, he really is a jerk! He's like, 'Mr. McGregor, one would think that a pastor's son could see the importance of understanding economics.' Max donned the imaginary and quite sarcastic posture of his teacher, complete with proper voice intonation. 'After all, good stewardship is one of the fundamentals of being a good Christian. Perhaps you should spend some time discussing this subject in depth with your father. I'm sure he has an acute perception when it comes to fiscal responsibility.' Then he peers over his half-glasses sitting on that schnauze of his and says 'If not, perhaps you can enlighten him on the basics, Mr. McGregor.' I wanted to smack those glasses right off his big fat face!"

"Whoa there, buddy. That's a little harsh, don't you think? Granted, I don't appreciate his comments, but I don't want to hear any more of this 'jerk' business or regrets because you didn't punch him out. Got it?"

"Yeah, but Dad—"

"No buts, Max. I mean it. Whether you like the man or not is beside the point. You may not enjoy being picked on like that—and I don't blame you. But I want you to show respect to him if for no other reason than the fact he's your teacher." David stood up and squeezed the shoulder of his oldest son. "You can't stoop to that level. Just don't let him get to you. It isn't worth it, believe me."

"But Dad, listen to me. He's *always* taking shots at you. It makes me sick. And it's not fair. If he doesn't get along with you, he shouldn't hassle me because of it."

114

David stood face to face with Max who stretched only an inch shorter. He grasped both of his shoulders. "Trust me, Max. It just isn't worth it to get that upset. Old Chet has been giving me fits since my first day on the job here. For some reason, which God only knows, he apparently feels called to be our resident devil's advocate. Every church has at least one, and Chet Harrison is ours.

"When Dr. Billings died, a year before we came here, Chet moved himself into a position of leadership while the church was without a pastor. He pretty much called all the shots. He hired the interim pastors, he oversaw the day-to-day details in the office, took care of the payroll, you name it. And I'm sure he enjoyed having a free run of power in the process. Naturally, a lot of folks admired him for such a 'sacrifice' of his time and effort. They looked up to him and rallied behind him.

"He was also chairman of the search committee for a new pastor, of course. And initially, Chet and I hit it off pretty well. I think he really liked me. Must have, or I'm sure it wouldn't have been a unanimous vote. But not long after I came, we began to butt heads. Chet realized I wouldn't be the puppet he hoped I'd be, and he began to fight me on every issue that came up.

"Then the final straw was when I steered the building committee away from choosing his son's company to build the new sanctuary. I had done my research and learned that Junior's company had a bad reputation in Pinellas County. You wouldn't believe some of the stories I heard about him. I wasn't about to lead this church into that kind of fiasco. And old Chet has never gotten over it. He's not used to having someone stand up to him, and he can't handle it.

"I tell you all that to say this—just try to ignore his little digs and do your best in his class. However, I *don't* expect you to have to fight my battles for me in his classroom. If you think his attitude bleeds over into unfair grading on your papers or tests, you let me know about it. I'll have a talk with him and settle that before it gets out of hand. Sound fair enough?"

"Yeah, whatever. I'll be so glad to get out of that class once this semester is over." Max's voice became noticeably more quiet. "Hey, Dad, what's going on with Mom? Gran tried to make some kind of explanation to us at dinner last night, but I didn't exactly buy it."

David walked over and sat down on the large brick hearth. Max followed, sitting beside him. He pressed on. "I mean, Jess and Jeremy might not put two and two together, but I can see something's up. Mom would never just up and take off without saying good-bye to us. And it's obvious you're really upset about something too. I mean, look at you—you're *never* home, let alone the middle of the day! I just wish you'd give me a little credit and stop treating me like I'm five years old. If something's wrong, I want to know, Dad."

David patted his son on the knee and rested his hand there. He smiled, stealing a sideways glance at the young man beside him. "I wish you could understand how hard it is to sit back and watch your son becoming a grown man right before your eyes. It can be a little overwhelming at times. Doesn't seem like that long ago that you were splashing around the pool with those bright orange floaties on your little arms."

Max rolled his eyes and laughed. "Dad, give me a break. I'm almost seventeen. I'm not a little kid anymore."

"You can say that again." He squeezed his son's upper arm. "Get a load of these now, will ya'? Move over, Schwarzenegger." His weary smile did little to answer Max's questions. "No, seriously, Max—I know you're old enough to have a better explanation than what you heard last night. I suppose I should have spoken to all three of you. The problem is, I don't even really understand it."

David was up again, adjusting books here, a slightly crooked picture frame there. He took a swipe of dust off the armoire that housed the television, then wiped his hands together. "Max, you mother is going through a rough time right now. From everything she's said, it sounds to me like she thinks she's about to have some kind of emotional breakdown."

"Mom? No way. You've got to be kidding! She seems fine to me. Maybe a little more tired than usual, but that's no shock. We keep a pretty hectic schedule around here. Not to mention all the stuff at church. But she's never let on that anything was wrong. Are you sure, Dad?"

"Unfortunately, yes. She left me a note. She—"

"A note? You mean, you didn't *know* she was leaving?"

"No, I didn't know. She left without telling me. I didn't know until last night when I found the note she'd left me."

"So where'd she go? Have you called her?"

"That's just it. She doesn't want to tell me where she is because she knows I'd try to find her, and she's right. It's killing me to sit around here when I know she needs me. I can't stand this! But she made it very clear that she needed some time away all to herself. Like it was something she had to do. And as much as I want to go to her, I don't seem to have much choice."

Max jumped up. "I don't believe this! You mean to tell me she just took off? Why was she so upset? I mean, c'mon—maybe it gets a little nuts around here at times, but hey, we survive!" He stopped, looking directly at his father. He paused a moment. "Dad, are you and Mom having problems? I mean, has something happened between you guys? You don't think she—"

"No Max, don't even think like that. We're fine." He stopped, locking eyes with his son. "Well, at least I thought we were fine. I had no idea. That is, I didn't know she was—"

"Dad?" Max stiffened. "What are you trying to say?"

David began pacing, rubbing his hands together again. "I'm never home. I know that. Of *course* I know that! It's just the way it is. There's always too much to do, and never enough time and never enough help and—" He stopped, searching for Max's eyes again. He dropped his shoulders. "Who am I trying to fool? She's absolutely right. I'm never home. I'm *never* here for my family. I've been so blind . . . such a blind fool." He fell onto the sofa.

"So she left because of you? Is that what you're telling

me?" Max asked quietly. The expression on his face daggered David's soul.

"Max, what I'm telling you is that she needed a break. She needed time to herself. She's upset with me, she's tired of the rat race, tired of all the stuff that goes on at church . . . But mostly, tired of having to do it all herself." He stared at the floor. "I've blown it. I pushed her away and now she's gone."

"But she's coming back, right? She didn't just pack up and leave for good, did she?"

David heard the panic in his son's voice. "No. No, it's only for awhile. She'll be back. I don't know when, but she'll be back. As mad at she may be at me, or whatever else is bugging her, I know Annie. She would never walk away from us like that. Trust me, son." He tried to smile. "I promise she'll be back."

Max sat still, frozen in thought, his eyes searching those of his father. David could tell from the seriousness registered in his eyes that his son's thoughts were running in a thousand directions. "Everything is going to work out okay, Max. We just need to give her some space right now. You know, like a chance to emotionally catch her breath, I guess you could say. She's probably very, very tired and needs a vacation, that's all. What we *all* need to do is pray for her. Ask God to help her get some rest, clear her mind. Restore her energy."

He paused. "And try to find it in her heart to forgive me." David swallowed hard. "Then before you know it, she'll be back home and back to her same old self."

"You really think so?"

"Yeah, I really think so." He knew he had to reassure his son that the situation wasn't as bad as it seemed. He was also suddenly very restless. "Hey, have you got a lot of homework or do you have time for a little one-on-one hoop?"

"Are you kidding? The homework can wait. Let's do it. I'll clean your clock, old man!"

❧

Eagle's Nest

As if emerging from a time capsule, Annie suddenly noticed her surroundings. It was dark outside. The hands on the grandfather clock clicked into place and the chimes rang their announcement. Six-thirty.

I can't believe it. Where did the day go? She shook off the doom surrounding her and made her way into the kitchen. At some point in her emotional rounds she had evidently turned off the burner beneath the pot of chili. Realizing her hunger, she dished up a bowl and put it in the microwave.

And then she remembered. She needed to call David. Despite everything else, she would not make him worry.

Annie pressed each number on the phone then hesitated. She hung up the receiver. *You can't call home like this. Get a hold of yourself. It will only make matters worse and upset David even more if he hears you in this state of mind.*

She took a deep breath and forced herself to calm

down. She put another log on the fire before sitting back down. A few moments later, she gently touched the numbers on the phone.

Annie was surprised to hear her own voice responding on the other end of the line.

". . . and if you will leave your name and number at the sound of the tone, we'll be more than happy to call you back. Thank you and God bless you today." Beep.

"David? It's Annie. I . . ." She paused, unsure what sort of message to leave. "Well, I just wanted to check in. I'm fine. Really. I'm okay. Give my love to Max and Jeremy and Jessica. And please thank Caroline again for me."

She rolled her eyes to keep them from tearing. "I guess that's all. I'll call you tomorrow. Good night."

It was just as well. David would have picked up on her frustration in a heartbeat.

&

Seminole, Florida

Oh no," Caroline sighed. She had stepped outside only for a moment to deposit the empty milk carton into the recycle bin and look at the evening sky. As she walked back into the kitchen she noticed the flashing red light on the answering machine.

Jeremy slid across the kitchen floor in his gym socks toward the refrigerator at full speed. "Hey, Gran. Who called?"

"What do you mean who called? Why didn't you answer it?"

"Me and Jessie are watching TV and I figured you'd probably get it," he answered casually, pouring himself a tumbler full of orange juice.

"Jessie and I. And why aren't you two in bed yet?" Caroline asked.

"'Cause *Jessie and I* are watching a movie. Can I have some popcorn?"

"No, Jeremy, you can't have any popcorn. I want you to march out there, turn off that television, and you and your sister go to bed. Right this minute!"

As her grandson flew out of the room just as he'd entered it, Caroline replayed the message on the machine. After another post-dinner game of basketball, David and Max emerged through the back door just as Annie's message was ending. The expression on David's face said it all.

"I'm so sorry, honey," Caroline apologized. "I stepped outside for just a moment and the kids assumed one of us answered it."

"That's okay, Mom." He gave her a passing hug and made his way upstairs.

"Is he okay?" she asked Max.

"About as okay as the rest of us, I guess. I gotta get back to my homework. G'night, Gran." Max kissed her cheek and followed his father up the stairs.

"Why isn't that at all comforting?" she mumbled.

Chapter 10

Houston, Texas

No, Amelia, I haven't heard from him either," Michael's executive secretary responded. "He called in after his golf game at the club yesterday and said he wouldn't be in the office until today, but that's all I know. If he checks in, shall I have him call you?"

Amelia Dean tapped perfectly manicured nails on her desk. "Oh, Jane, I don't mean to be a pest. I just need a quick answer from him on this fundraiser and I haven't had any luck tracking him down on his cell phone. But sure, go ahead and have him call me if you hear from him. I'd appreciate that."

"No problem, Amelia. Happy to help."

"Thanks, Jane."

How embarrassing. Amelia couldn't decide if she was

more embarrassed, worried, or just plain angry with her elusive husband. In the wee hours of the morning, she had glanced at the clock when Michael finally came home. It was 4:00 a.m. Before her thoughts could accelerate down the usual irritating path, she had rolled over, retreating into the familiar escape of slumber.

When the alarm sounded at seven, she had awakened to find Michael's side of the bed undisturbed. There was the usual evidence that he had indeed been home—a towel on the floor in the bathroom, his dirty clothes lying on the floor of his closet. Downstairs she had found the remnants of an early breakfast. He had left out the tub of margarine and peach preserves and an empty carton of creamer. Shaking her head, she had switched off the coffee maker. Fortunately there had been enough coffee left so it didn't burn to the bottom of the carafe.

Where are you, Michael?

She had blinked away the tears that stung her eyes and busied herself picking up the dishes. Even though Eva would be there any moment to begin her housecleaning duties, Amelia knew she had to stay occupied if she was to fight another bout of depression.

Now, several hours later, she absorbed herself in the plans for the upcoming *Evening of Stars,* the fundraiser for the Democratic Party of Houston. Michael had been a tremendous help in years past as he used his influence in the sports world to draw many of the biggest names to appear. But this year he had been impossible. He continually made promises to contact the various athletic stars he knew so well only to forget and promise again. The deadline for print advertising was approaching. Amelia had to produce a list of names to the committee.

But as was always the case, any frustration or anger she felt toward Michael would eventually dissipate into the familiar pangs of her breaking heart. She had never stopped adoring him, her charming and intelligent husband. She had loved him from the moment they first met. He had brought such joy and laughter into her life.

Oh Michael, what's happened to us?

☙

Congressman, Michael Dean on line one."

"Thank you, Helen." Elliot Thomas punched the flashing button on his phone, then leaned back in his chair. "Well, Michael, I was about to give up on you. Thought you'd decided to throw in the towel."

"Hardly, Elliot. We need to talk."

Elliot chewed on his unlit pipe. "I'm all ears, son. Give it your best shot."

"Not on the phone. And this time it's just you and me. We don't need your little entourage of muscle. After all, this is a family matter. At least out of respect for Amelia, we should be able to handle this one on one."

Elliot sat up to his desk. "Now that's pretty funny coming from you, Michael," he laughed. "'Respect'," he chuckled. "Yessir, that's a good one."

"Elliot, I'm on my way to your office. I'll be there in ten minutes. I suggest you be ready to go. Meet me downstairs in the garage."

He was answered with a sarcastic guffaw. "You really are a comedian, Michael. You think you can just ring me up and snap out orders when you—"

"That's exactly what I think," Michael interrupted. "You played hard ball with me yesterday—today it's my turn. I'll be there in ten minutes." *Click.*

∼

Precisely ten minutes later Michael pulled out of the parking garage with the congressman riding in his passenger seat. He joined the flow of traffic and adjusted his rear view mirror.

"So how do you like playing the big shot, Michael? I'll bet it makes you feel pretty good barking out orders at me, doesn't it? And I'll bet you didn't really expect me to oblige you on this one, did you?" Elliot shifted his ample body to better face his son-in-law.

Michael's eyes stayed glued to the traffic surrounding him. "You're right. I didn't expect you to come along without a fight."

Elliot laughed again, that wheezy, good ol' boy laugh Michael despised.

"Well sir, I don't take much to being ordered around, of course. But in your case I made an exception. Your little teaser yesterday has got me right curious. So tell me. What is this surprise you have up your sleeve?"

"Ah, looks like you're gonna have to wait a few more minutes for that one," Michael answered, his glare intent on the review mirror. "I do believe we have a little tail to get rid of first."

Elliot jerked his head around to look behind them. Michael stole a quick glance sideways just in time to see a fleeting grimace that swept across his father-in-law's face.

"Michael, I think you must be seeing things. There's no one following us."

"Uh-huh . . ." Michael sped up, taking a sharp turn to the right. He raced through the crowded streets, making a series of breakneck turns, throwing Elliot from side to side against the strain of his seatbelt.

"Are you trying to get us killed? Stop this car! Stop it this minute!"

But Michael was too close to losing Elliot's brute squad to stop now. He flew through a corner parking lot and into a narrow alley. The alley emptied onto the approach ramp to the interstate. Within minutes, his sleek black Escalade was racing along the expressway toward the wide open plains, away from the sprawling metropolitan heart of Houston. Elliot turned completely around, no doubt hoping to find his backup.

"All right, all right. So you can outmaneuver my boys. Big deal. Now just pull this car over and stop all these theatrics. I've had enough of your games. Pull over!"

"What's the matter, Elliot? Afraid of having a little fun? Don't tell me you're gonna go chicken on me just because you don't have your body guards protecting you?" Now it was Michael's turn to laugh. "Oh, I wish you could see yourself. Where's that rock solid self-confidence? Where's the cockiness? Hmm?"

Later, as Michael exited the interstate, Elliot pulled out his monogrammed handkerchief and wiped his brow. "I suggest you get to the point. My boys will have the police out here in a matter of minutes, so whatever you have to say, spit it out."

"You know, you are absolutely pitiful." Michael pulled into a secluded area surrounded by a thick stand of trees and bushes. "When it's just you, just plain ol' Elliot Thomas, without your goons or assistants or mindless constituents, you are flat-out pathetic. All you can do is threaten to call your boys, threaten to have the entire Houston police force out looking for poor, helpless you. I sure hope Amelia has never seen you like this. It would ruin her perfect image of dear Daddy."

"Just shut up and get on with it."

"Fine." Michael stomped the brake, forcing a short skid in the dry Texas dirt and gravel. He put the car in park and turned off the ignition. "There's no way you're going to steal my company from me," he stated without emotion. "I've made sure of that. We just need to work out the details so there's no misunderstanding between us."

Once again Eliot's sarcasm prevailed. "Oh yes. And I'm sure you have all the answers. So, just how do you propose to keep your little company?"

Michael raised his head, looking Elliot straight in the

eye. "Easy. I have a file of some valuable information that I'm pretty sure you'll want to keep confidential. Phone records, photographs . . . Yesterday you tried to blackmail me. Today it's my turn."

"Well now, I believe you're confused. I believe *I'm* the one with a rather large file on *you*. Concerning certain of your 'indiscretions?' Must we go over all this again?"

Michael hoped his laugh didn't betray his anxiety. "Oh, I'm not confused at all. Fact is, I have a file of my own. I've tucked it away in a very secure place. And I have no intention of making it public unless you force me to do so. It's strictly up to you. However, in the event anything should 'accidentally' happen to me, I have given explicit instructions for that file to be released to the proper authorities." *Poker face. Don't let him see you're bluffing.*

"What in tar nation are you talking about?"

Michael took a deep breath. Though the late afternoon breeze drifting through his open window was cool, he felt the perspiration under his shirt. *Here we go, Dean. Better make this good.*

"Christopher Jordan."

With eyes locked, the silence beat between them. For a split second, the tiny muscles around Elliot's eyes flinched. Then just as abruptly, the wall of steel returned to his glare. The game continued.

"Is that supposed to mean something to me?"

Michael threw his head back against the headrest. "C'mon, Elliot. You know exactly what it means. It means a hunting trip back in 1992." He paused for effect. "It means you and Duke should be more careful when you get drunk."

"And I suppose this is where I'm supposed to act shocked and appalled and fall all over myself. But the problem is—I have absolutely no idea what you're talking about."

Michael pressed on. "Oh, you remember the news reports. Christopher Jordan, out in the gulf relaxing on his boat. Suddenly, a deadly explosion blow him to bits. Is this sounding at all familiar? There was hardly anything left by the time the Coast Guard happened onto the scene. It was dismissed as a freak accident. A 'faulty gas tank.' But it was no accident, was it? That night in the cabin near Natchitoches, you and Duke were pretty careless in your conversation. And maybe, just maybe, I wasn't as soundly asleep as you thought."

The stare down continued. "So you figure to try to hang me somehow with Jordan's unfortunate demise. Think you can peg me with that one, do you? That should be mighty interesting, Michael. If it wasn't so ludicrous, it would be downright comical. But you and I both know you haven't got a leg to stand on."

"No?" Michael questioned, his eyebrows arched in mock dismay. He paused, gathering his courage despite the growing knot in his stomach. He also hoped to give Elliot time to squirm. "Does this ring any bells? *'My Jordan lies over the ocean,"* he sang quietly. *"'My Jordan lies over the sea.'"*

Elliot stared straight ahead into the dusk enveloping the SUV. His teeth were clenched, his jaw throbbing rhythmically. He spoke not a word.

Good. A crack in the ice, thought Michael. He continued the concert. *"'My Jordan lies ALL over the o—'"*

"That's enough," Elliot growled in an eerie hush. He moved cautiously, slowly turning to face Michael. "Now you listen to me, boy. I don't care what kind of so-called evidence you think you have on me. You'll *never* prove I had anything to do with that explosion. And just in case you're tempted to parade your little pack of lies out in public, you best remember who you're dealing with. Do I make myself clear?"

Michael felt his heart racing. "I'm not afraid of you, Elliot," he lied. "I've nailed your hide on this one and you know it. Your only choice here is to hand over your shares in my company or see your dirty little secret spread all over the front page of tomorrow's *Chronicle.*"

"So you overheard some talk. You can't prove a thing."

"Oh, but I can. I have all the evidence I could possibly need. I hired a private investigator to follow Duke and your little friend Beauregard. I have a whole file of pictures, receipts, phone records . . . and they all lead back to you. Well, that is—you and your good friend Duke. I've gotta tell you, Elliot. For being such a shrewd politician, you sure blew it placing your trust in someone like Duke. Not exactly the sharpest knife in the drawer."

By now Michael felt much more sure of himself. Flaunting his evidence pumped up his confidence. But it was short lived. Even before he'd finished speaking, he noticed Elliot stealing glances here and there. Michael tensed, sensing danger.

Then all of a sudden, Elliot seemed to relax. He sat back in his seat and released a long breath. "I guess you're right, Michael. You've outfoxed me this time. It's a little hard to digest, but I'm afraid you've got me over a barrel on this one."

Well, what do you know? Michael gave himself a mental pat on the back. He relaxed somewhat cautiously, stretching his arms out against the steering wheel. "I'm glad to hear you say that, Elliot. I've kept my mouth shut this long. No reason to open it now as long as you're willing to relinquish The Page to me once and for all."

As he turned to face his father-in-law, he heard the indisputable pop of a gunshot.

"Noooo!" he shrieked, instantly fighting back as reality rushed in. A white hot burn in his bicep screamed in pain as he struggled to seize the pistol out of Elliot's hand.

Elliot's face contorted with rage. Age was no issue with stakes so high. Michael's hands locked around Elliot's grip on the pistol. Elliot fired off another shot which whizzed past Michael's ear and out his open window.

Elliot cursed. As the struggle intensified, he groped for the door handle with his right hand. Then, with a sudden burst of force, he jabbed his fist into the bleeding wound on Michael's shoulder. Michael's grip broke free as he recoiled, grabbing his shoulder and screaming in agony. Elliot threw open the door behind him.

Michael knew it was now or never. He turned the key in the ignition, shifted into reverse, and slammed his foot on the accelerator. Elliot catapulted backwards out the door, but not before firing off another shot.

The Escalade spun backward in a wild cloudburst of dust. Michael threw the car into drive, keeping the pedal on the floor. Careening off into the darkness, he felt a second pinpoint of searing heat on his right side just below his ribs. He forced himself to ignore the wounds, trying to make sense of what was happening. He flipped on his headlights and peered into the rearview window. A bright red glow shrouded the trail of dust in his wake, his rear lights mercifully swallowing the scene behind him.

The will to survive consumed him. Instinctively, he approached the interstate and headed north, the engine roaring against the accelerated speed.

This can't be happening . . .

I have to drop out of sight . . .

Gotta go somewhere I can think . . .

Have to get some help . . .

He reached down to the festering pain below his ribs. His hand was soaked immediately with bright scarlet blood. The sight shocked him, sending an involuntary shudder over him. Wiping his hand on his pant leg, he continued speeding toward an unknown destination.

The desperate prayer escaped his lips. *God if you're out there, help me . . . please help me!*

❧

The clock on the wall of Elliot's dark office read eight o'clock. He slammed his door shut and rushed to pick up the telephone on his desk. With a trembling hand, he punched each number, then collapsed into his chair.

At the second ring, he cursed. *Answer, Duke!*

"Hello?"

"Get your butt to my office immediately. We've got trouble." Elliot slammed the phone down and cursed again.

By 8:20, Elliot was on his second shot of bourbon. He heard the outer doors of his office open and close, then a rapid knock on his door as it opened.

"What's up?" Duke Willis asked, obviously trying to remain calm as he hurried into the inner sanctuary of Elliot's office. "Good grief! You look like you've seen a ghost!"

"Maybe that's because I have," he spat. "Maybe that's because I've been hitchhiking for the last hour. Maybe that's because I had to catch a ride with a bunch of brain-dead illegal aliens in a pickup loaded with filthy, stinkin' snot-nosed kids," he shouted, wiping his hands on his shirt.

Duke dropped into the leather chair behind him. "What in the world were you doing out there hitchhiking? Don't you realize how dangerous that is in this town?"

Elliot's face heated with anger. "Of course I know how dangerous it is, you imbecile!" he bellowed. "That idiot son-in-law of mine dumped me out in the middle of nowhere! Tried to blackmail me! Thought he could stop me from squeezin' him out of his stupid company!"

Duke scrunched up his face. *"Blackmail* you?" he

laughed. "With what?"

Elliot leaned forward, clutching the edge of his desk. "With Christopher Jordan," he growled, his eyes narrowing.

Duke went pale. His mouth fell open. "Wha—what does he know about Jordan?"

"*Everything.*"

For half a minute the two men locked eyes. No words were necessary. Unspoken scenarios rifled through Elliot's mind. And by the look on his assistant's face, he was confident the same scenarios pummeled Duke's mind as well. Finally, Elliot got up and walked over to his bar. He replenished his drink and poured one for Duke. He sauntered slowly over to the sofa and handed the glass to the silent, frail man whose face was now buried in his delicate hands.

"Now, listen to me very carefully, Duke." Elliot sat down in the wing chair adjacent to him. "I've already called Gus and Marcus. I called them from my cell phone right after Michael took off before the useless thing went dead on me. I sent them up I-45 north toward Dallas to track him down. He's in his Escalade—they shouldn't have any trouble spotting him. I gave them explicit directions to call me the minute they find him. And I told them to stay out of sight. Told them not to go near Michael, just tail him."

"But—"

"I told them this is stealth surveillance. Of course I had to explain that since the morons didn't a clue what it meant. But I made it absolutely clear—under no circumstances were they to stop him or in any way warn him of their presence."

"Why can't they bring him in? Or dispose of him?"

"Because I want to know just exactly where it is our Mr. Dean is going. He claims to have all the evidence he needs to link us to Jordan's murder. If he's got it stashed somewhere, I want him to lead us to it. There's too much at stake. If we play this smart we can eliminate him *and* his little packet of goodies."

Duke shifted under Elliot's stare.

"Here's what I want you to do. I want you to find Bo. I don't care where he is, you find him. Then you put him on a plane out of the country. Send him where no one will find him. And you make sure we can reach him at all times wherever it is you stash him. You got that?"

"I haven't talked to him in years! I have no idea where—"

"FIND HIM!" Elliot roared. He paused, exhaled, then continued. "Now Michael probably hasn't gotten very far. I got a couple of shots into him so—"

"You *what?*" Duke jumped up. "Are you out of your mind? Elliot! He's threatening to implicate us with Jordan's murder! You can't go blasting away at him like some Keystone cop! Do you realize what you've done?"

Elliot felt his face heat once again. He slammed down his drink and stood nose to nose with Duke. "You shut up and listen to me! If you hadn't been so careless, Michael would never have come up with any proof in the first place. It's *your* fault this has blown up in our faces and I'll see you hang before I'll let them pin this on me!"

Duke stared silently at him. Elliot could almost read his

thoughts. Duke knew perfectly well he would be six feet under before he blinked if he didn't do just as he was told.

His assistant quietly sipped from the glass in his trembling hand and sat back down in resignation. "I'll do whatever you ask of me, Elliot. You know that. We'll find Michael. Don't worry."

"That's more like it." Elliot made his way back to his desk.

"How bad is he hurt?"

"I don't know. For all I know he may be dead on the side of the road even as we speak. But I doubt we can count on it. Oh, and get rid of this, will you?" He handed Duke the small handgun out of his pocket. "Wipe it clean and make sure it doesn't mysteriously appear again. Bury it in concrete if you have to."

Chapter 11

Huntsville, Texas

An hour after his exit from his explosive encounter with Elliot, Michael pulled off the interstate on the outskirts of Huntsville. His gas tank was low, but more urgently, he needed to care for his wounds. His arm and side were bleeding too much. Already the towel he'd pulled from his gym bag was soaked with blood.

He spotted a Shell Super Station and pulled in, pleased to find the restrooms tucked back behind the station. He pulled up next to the men's room and slowly slipped inside carrying his bag with him. Once inside, he locked the door and assessed the damage. The mere sight of so much blood sent the room spinning. Holding onto the sink to brace himself, he waited for the dizziness to subside, then splashed his face with cold water. He carefully peeled off his

shirt and threw it in the sink under the running tap.

Just don't even think about it. Just clean it up and get out of here. No time to think. No time to think . . .

Michael held a wad of wet paper towels over the dark wound on his side hoping to slow the flow of blood. Apparently the bullet must have grazed him, tearing in then back out his side. At least that's how it looked. He pulled his Astros sweatshirt out of his bag and carefully crawled into it. He ran his fingers through his wet hair and took another assessment through the mirror. It would have to do, at least until he could get some medical supplies. He cleaned up his mess, throwing the blood-soaked shirt into his bag.

Holding his arm tight against his body, Michael walked as casually as he could across the pavement to the store. Avoiding eye contact with other customers, he gathered his supplies into the small shopping basket—a traveler's first aid kit, some antiseptic, extra gauze and medical tape, and a large bottle of pain reliever. He grabbed a handful of snacks and a six-pack of bottled water, then headed for the counter. He realized he was the only customer left in the store. For the first time, the young clerk, dressed in a yellow Shell Super Store shirt and tight blue jeans, looked up to greet him.

"Hey-how-ya-doin?" she drawled. Nineteen, maybe twenty, Michael figured. She chomped on a wad of purple bubblegum.

Michael opened his mouth to answer, but nothing came out. He coughed and cleared his throat then tried again. "Whoa, sorry. Guess I must be thirstier than I thought. But I'm fine."

Ringing up his purchases, she looked back at him with

a questioning glance. "Say what?"

"Oh, sorry. You asked how I was and I said I'm fine." He tried to smile.

"Oh. Yeah, right." A purple bubble exploded out the frosted pink lips. She stopped smacking for a second. "Are you okay, mister? You don't look so good."

"I don't?"

"No, you sure don't." She handed him his change. "Maybe you oughta' sit down for a minute. Go git ya one of them iced down bottles of water in the cooler back there. You said you was thirsty. Maybe you just got dehydrated or somethin'."

Michael stuck the change in his pocket then wiped his brow. "Yeah, maybe I will. Thanks." He slowly walked back to the refrigerated section and picked out a tall bottle of natural spring water.

"Oh hey, mister. That one's on the house. You just take it easy now, okay?"

"Yeah, thanks. I appreciate it," Michael answered, awkwardly grabbing his bag of supplies and heading out the door. He looked back to see her craning her neck to watch him.

Great, Dean. Draw attention to yourself.

Finally out of sight, he quickened his pace back to the men's room. He undressed again, this time using the first aid supplies to treat his wounds. After the thorough and painful cleansing with the antiseptic, he bandaged and wrapped both wounds with gauze. Finally, he taped the last piece firmly in place and cleaned up the bloody paper towels around him.

He backed the car around to the gas pump and got out.

Okay, now be cool. Act natural. Just gas up the car, pay Miss Maybelline, and get out of here.

He filled his tank, his clumsy moves making him realize how handicapped he was without the full use of his right arm. The pain was becoming unbearable. He shuffled over to the window, handing a fifty dollar bill to the same young clerk.

"Wow. That was quick! You back again already? And you changed your clothes, huh?" It was a statement, not a question. Michael cracked a lame smile and looked away. She was still checking him out when he noticed the name monogrammed on her Shell uniform blouse.

Christine.

She looked puzzled. She followed his gaze down to her blouse and looked back at him, her eyes widened. "Wh— what's the matter? Mister, you want me to call a doctor or somethin'? You're actin' kinda weird, know-what-I-mean?"

Michael came back to his senses. "Oh, no—no! I'm sorry. No, I'm okay. But thanks. You've been great." He began walking away. "Really. I'm fine. No problem."

Moments later he pulled into the drive-thru of a McDonald's. "A large coffee. Black. That's all."

"That'll be a buck twenty-five. Drive up to the next window, please."

Michael knew he had to get some serious caffeine in his system if he was to make the long drive. He knew he was taking a risk by making another stop, but the Golden Arches offered a speedy solution to his caffeine dilemma. As he waited, his eyes made a quick check for tails or cops. Even as the thought crossed his mind, a police cruiser slowed to make a left-hand turn into the McDonald's parking lot.

Come on, come on . . .

"Do you want sugar with—?"

Michael grabbed the cup and pressed the accelerator. The cruiser turned into the entrance as Michael pulled out. He was careful to keep his face out of view. As fast as he dared to go, he headed toward the interstate entrance ramp and freedom.

Careful, careful . . .

He slowly began accelerating, hoping to put plenty of distance between himself and Huntsville's finest. He was just starting to relax when he noticed the cruiser catching up with him. The officer was keeping his distance but obviously in pursuit.

Come on, man, if you want me, flip on your stupid siren on and come after me!

The cruiser followed Michael for almost ten minutes before dropping back then taking the next exit.

That's odd. He had plenty of time to call in my plate.

He checked the digital clock on his dash. *Maybe Elliot hasn't had time to catch a ride back to town. Or maybe he's afraid to call the police in on this.*

Fat chance.

Juggling a hot cup of coffee and a steering wheel with only one functional limb proved a challenge. The combination of pain relievers and caffeine was easing the discomfort. At least a little, anyway. He pressed the automatic window button to let in the cool night air. It was a habit he learned back in college after partying 'til the early morning hours. To stay awake and try to keep the lines on the pavement from multiplying, he'd roll down the windows for a good stiff breeze. Worked every time.

College . . . it seemed like a lifetime ago. So many memories. So many faces.

And tonight, an embroidered name on a yellow shirt flashed a forgotten face through his mind. In that instant, he knew exactly where to go.

The perfect hideaway.

❧

Yes, sir. We know. He's a few cars in front of us."

The voice on the speaker phone echoed through Elliot's home office. He took a puff of the cigar and watched the smoke circle around him as he listened to the report.

"We haven't lost him for a moment. He stopped at a convenience store. Got some gas and medical supplies. Looks like he may have cleaned up in the bathroom."

Gus Rainey's report did little to relieve Elliot's worries. Gus and Marcus were loyal enough, just not too bright. He had to stay on them, calling them every hour.

"We thought one of the local boys was tailing him for awhile, but he took an exit and we haven't seen him again."

"Keep your eyes open. You let me know if anything or anyone looks the least bit suspicious. And whatever you do, don't lose Michael!"

❧

Houston, Texas

Daddy, it's after midnight. Are you all right?"

"Oh sure, honey," Elliot laughed as if he hadn't a care in the world. "Your daddy's just fine. I'm awful sorry to be bothering you so late, but I had a concern about something and I just couldn't go to sleep until I talked to Michael. Some business matters. Could you put him on the line for me, darlin'?"

"He's not home, Daddy. I don't know where he is. I tried to contact him several times today but I never got through." Elliot could hear the rustle of sheets when she paused. He could hear her snap on the bedside light.

"I'm sorry I woke you, darlin'. I assumed Michael would still be up and would answer."

"He's been so distant with me lately." Her voice caught. "Things are awful between us. He's completely avoiding me."

Elliot clenched his jaw. "Oh now, Amelia, I'm sure it's not as bad as all that. You know how busy Michael is with the company right now." He heard her soft sniffles through the line.

"No, Daddy, you *don't* know what it's really like. He's hardly ever home anymore and he never talks to me. It's like he totally ignores my existence. I don't know what to do anymore." She cried into the receiver.

His hand knotted into a fist. "Well, you just don't worry your sweet little head, honey. Daddy's gonna work it out for you. Just give it some time and I'm sure Michael will come back around. Maybe I can take some of the pressure off of him in his work. Daddy's gonna take care of you. You'll see, sweetheart."

She paused. "I love you, Daddy."

"Good night, honey. I'll talk to you in the morning."

Elliot sat back in his recliner. Encircled by the pleasing aroma of his cigar, he sat alone in the darkness of his study at home. The house was quiet. Only the urgent voices of panic deep in his soul kept him company. He stared at the telephone, willing it to ring with news of Michael Dean.

Yes, honey, Daddy's going to take care of your husband. Don't you worry.

&

Plainview, Texas

The music on the radio blared as the brisk wind blew through Michael's car. But even cold air and loud music could not compete with the fatigue overtaking him with each passing mile. He had been driving all night and knew he had to stop and get some sleep. It was a risk, but without a couple hours of uninterrupted sleep, he would never make his destination.

Neon lights and billboards began multiplying as Michael neared the outskirts of Plainview, Texas. He searched for a small motel knowing the larger chain motels would require identification. He couldn't take that chance. He had to find a small mom-and-pop place. He could live with a few bugs and a lumpy mattress. Then he spotted the sign:

KINCAID'S KOTTAGES

VACANCY

He parked to the side of the main entrance, relieved to feel the absence of motion replaced by the stillness of the breaking dawn. He looked down at his wounds, disappointed to find the crimson stain still spreading on his shirt beneath his arm. The shot embedded in his upper arm ached horribly but at least the bleeding had slowed. Painfully, he reached to the passenger seat for his leather jacket. He tugged it on through some awkward maneuvering and opened the door, slowly attempting to stand up. For a moment, he was sure he would pass out. He grasped the open door with his left hand and braced himself as the car and pavement swirled around him.

Oh God, please don't let me pass out. Just get to a room.

The spinning slowed though he was still light-headed. He closed the car door then steered himself toward the office door. A bell above the door announced his arrival, beckoning a plump woman to her station behind the desk.

"Good morning. How can I help you?" A strong whiff of cheap cologne wafted across the counter. Nausea roiled in his stomach, shooting a metallic taste to his mouth.

"I just need to get some rest for a few hours. Been driving all night and I can't seem to keep my eyes open any longer. Have you got a room?"

"Oh sure. Will that be a single?"

"Uh, yes. It's just me."

The woman made an entry in a large ledger then asked him to sign the registry. His John Smith looked like the work of a kindergartner. When he finished, he leaned forward for a better look at his barely legible signature then gently slid the book back to her. He noticed the long braid of white hair piled up on her head like a cinnamon roll. The thought made him hungry.

"Where can I get something to eat around here?'"

She eyed the scribbled name on her registry. Thick, penciled eyebrows rose to meet his gaze. "Why yes, Mr. . . Smith. 'Course the diner won't open for another hour but you could pick up some packaged food over at the Shop 'N Go just down the street. They keep a fresh pot of coffee going if you're so inclined."

"Thanks."

"That'll be thirty-five dollars cash or I can take a credit card, if you'd prefer."

He handed her a pair of twenties and turned to check out the store down the street. He could hear her panty hose swishing as she made her way to the cash register behind her. "Here's your change and your key. Cottage 12 is located around back. You can just pull your car around and park right by the door."

"Thanks," he answered, then added, "Oh, could you give me a wake-up call around ten?"

"Be happy to, Mr. Smith."

"Oh, one more thing. Is there a bus station around here?"

"On Broadway just off Tenth. Take Sixteenth here on up about two miles then take a right on Columbia, left on Twelfth then another right on Broadway. You'll see it."

He hoped he'd remember. He made a brief visit to the convenience store to pick up a couple of packaged muffins. Back at Cottage 12, he was pleased to find the room out of sight from the road. He gathered his things and went inside. The cozy room was spotless despite its early sixties decor. His legs felt like concrete as he made his way over to the sink. He peeled off his jacket with what energy he had left and let it drop to the floor. The bright red stains on his shirt alarmed him. He made his way over to the bed despite the dizziness.

I've got to change these bandages before I—

The fatigue overpowered him as he looked at the large, comfortable bed. His medical needs would have to wait. Even as his head rested gently on the pillow, a desperate slumber devoured him.

Chapter 12

Eagle's Nest

After a long and restless night, Annie knew she had to get some fresh air. She had to shake off the nagging despair that was creeping into her heart. If she could just go outside and breathe in the crisp, clear mountain air, maybe she would feel some sense of release. One thing was for sure: she couldn't wallow in this outburst of disappointment or anger. That was not why she came to this paradise.

Bundled up in layers of winter clothing, Annie sensed a deep longing for something—*anything* to take her mind off her problems. She pulled on the heavy waterproof boots and clomped her way to the door. Unlocking the heavy oak door, she threw it open and felt like she was breathing for the first time in her life. The frigid air stung as she inhaled deeply, but the slight discomfort was worth it. It felt clean and fresh and wonderful. She was grateful for the momentary break in the storm, though the snow continued to fall. Maybe the worst was over. Then again, maybe not. In the distance she could see more ominous clouds rolling in. She wouldn't go far.

Annie felt the smile on her face as she basked in the awesome display before her. Yesterday's frustration and heartache seemed miles away. Now, as she inhaled the cold, perfect air, its bite was already invigorating her, reaffirming her need to be right here, right now. This was where she was supposed to be.

She welcomed the crunching beneath her boots as she blazed a new trail in the untouched blanket of glistening snow. Staying as close to the road as possible, she was careful, not wishing to lose her way in such unfamiliar surroundings. Bob and Mary Jean were right; there wasn't any traffic up this way. At other times, such solitude would have made her uneasy, but she welcomed it today.

If only God would speak to her heart again.

She forced herself to block out all the negative feelings still unspent. For now, they would have to wait. In this moment she wanted to ponder only the blessings in her life. Any residue of angst in her spirit must give way to the good. At least for now.

She thought about her children. Three of the most delightful gifts on the face of the earth. Max, their precious first child. Now they could see only rare traces of the dark-haired little boy as he was blossoming into manhood. So tall and handsome. There was something so intriguing about those dark brown eyes. His wide grin, deep dimples, and contagious laughter made him popular in any crowd. His good looks attracted plenty of attention from the girls at church and school, but his strength of character set him apart. She and David had loved him from the moment they laid eyes on him. He was only eight months old when they adopted him into their arms and into their hearts forever. He had been a joy every single day of his life. Oh, but where did all the years go? Was it really possible he was almost as tall as David now?

And Jeremy, her little fireball always bursting with energy and imagination. Caroline had shown her pictures of David as a boy. The resemblance was incredible. Jeremy, so much like his father in both looks and personality. That McGregor nose already struggling to claim its rightful place on Jeremy's handsome young face. How he could make her laugh! Even when he got into mischief, which happened almost everyday, he could reduce her to gales of laughter. The way he arched his right eyebrow when he wanted to appear more mature. The way he mimicked famous characters. She loved his Elvis impersonation of Noah greeting the animals into the ark . . . *Mr. Giraffe, nice to see you. You and the little lady step right on up. Thank you—thank you very much.* She laughed out loud at the memory.

Oh Jeremy, you make our lives so much fun.

And sweet little Jessica, with her innocent smile, twinkling sapphire eyes and head full of bouncing blond curls. *You're Daddy's little heart-stopper, and my angel bunny. God sent you as a reminder to us of all the wonders of life. The simple joys around us. I love that picture we have of you—the one where your eyes are all lit up in awe of the baby bunny you found in your Easter basket. And how I love the hugs you give me for no special reason. "Just because" hugs, you call them. The sweet sound of your voice singing Christmas carols while you bake cookies with me . . . oh sweetie, how I love you.*

They're all my pride and joy, each in their own special way. I cannot imagine life without them.

Caroline, far more like a mother to her than Annie's own, was the real mentor in her life. David had loved and respected his father, but his mother had always been the foundation of the family. Her solid faith in God and her intimate walk with Him made her an irresistible strength to every life she encountered.

But before there was Max or Jeremy or Jessie or Caroline, there was David. Annie closed her eyes to see his face. She forced up a wall to block out all the recent hurts and resentments. She wanted to remember the David she fell in love with. She needed to focus on those memories right now.

Her life forever changed from the moment they'd met. After the bitter break-up from her college sweetheart, she had vowed to never again trust any man. She would never allow herself to be that vulnerable again. Determined to live her life as an independent single, she'd landed a teaching job in Tulsa immediately after graduation. She planned to take night classes to first earn a masters degree, then a doctorate in education. Her goal was to one day teach on the college level.

With a heavy background in American history, she planned to travel extensively throughout the United States in her quest to learn everything she could about the birth and beginning years of America. She passionately believed the recent cultural trends had transported America far away from the goals and dreams of its forefathers. She wanted to make a difference. She wanted to teach the truth.

Such plans made no provision for marriage. Annie didn't need a man in her life. They were nothing but heartache and trouble. Her own father, whom she adored with a childlike wonder, had died suddenly and without warning. On a family vacation, he dropped dead, the victim of a cerebral hemorrhage. Just ten years old, she mourned his unexpected absence for years before finally accepting it. While all around her, her friends' parents were ripped apart by nasty divorces, Annie soon realized that men weren't around for the long haul, regardless of the circumstances.

Men could not be counted on. Period. A life without the complication of a romantic relationship was much more suitable to the overall vision for her life.

Then one rainy October evening, on the way home from a late faculty meeting at school, a UPS truck flew through a red light, hitting her broadside. Her compact car spun out of control before slamming into a street light. When it finally stopped, she was dazed; not so much worried about the sticky pain on her forehead as the chaos of her students' test papers now strewn across the front seat of her car. Staring at the huge raindrops splattering the papers, she found herself unable to think what to do about it.

The next thing she remembered was waking up in the emergency room, bright lights and loud voices drifting around her like some surrealistic dream. A nagging female voice repeatedly asked for a name or number to notify a family member or friend. She couldn't think of a soul. Then a cloud of total blackness swallowed her into a merciful sleep.

A mild concussion accompanied the more serious internal injuries she sustained, including a ruptured spleen, several broken ribs and a broken arm. She lost track of how many times people said she was lucky to be alive. She certainly didn't feel very lucky. Recovery from the physical injuries was slow and painful, parking her in the hospital for over a month.

The emotional recovery was something altogether different.

For hours, she would stare out the window of her hospital room. Too angry to cry, she pondered the ramifications of her setback. Between insurance from the UPS people and her own salary, the financial aspects of the ordeal didn't concern her.

It was the lost time in the scope of her precise and well-ordered plans which frustrated her most. It would be weeks, maybe months, before she would be able to return to the classroom. The disruption in her lesson plans would throw them far behind schedule, her agenda shot to oblivion. During visiting hours, a steady stream of students and their parents always lifted her spirits on the one hand, but caused additional anxiety as she listened to their complaints about their "boring and crabby" substitute. Catching up from this despised leave of absence would be gruesome.

Then there was her graduate work. The university was sympathetic to her misfortune, but such a long absence from her classes necessitated dropping them for the remainder of the semester. The work on her research project also came to a screeching halt. Another postponement in her grandiose plans.

All in all, it wasn't fair.

Annie had always thrived on the hectic pace of her established lifestyle. So much idle time in her hospital room depressed her. It sucked her into a downward spiral which consumed her more each day. Too much time to think. Too many unsolicited thoughts and memories.

A couple weeks into her hospitalization, in the midst of this despondency, came a quiet knock on her door one afternoon.

"Chaplain," announced a man's voice from outside her partially opened door. "Mind if I come in?" Annie rolled her eyes and kept silent. *Maybe he'll go away.*

Another gentle knock as the door silently opened. "Oh, I'm sorry—I assumed since you didn't answer you were either asleep or out of the room. Is it okay if I come in for a minute?"

Annie visualized a retired, bald preacher, no doubt obese, with gravy stains on his too-short tie and nose hairs grossly in need of a trim. She was not prepared for the tall, well-built handsome man strolling into her room. He was young, probably not much older than she was. And his eyes immediately captivated her. She'd never seen such a deep shade of blue. His whole demeanor seemed to warm the room even as he entered.

This guy's a chaplain? "Um, okay."

He walked toward her, extending his right hand. "I'm David McGregor, one of the chaplains assigned to this floor." He grasped her hand in a confident, firm handshake then looked down at a clipboard in his other hand. He wore a long-sleeved freshly starched shirt, forest green with some sort of tan insignia on the pocket. The rich color seemed to enhance his thick, black hair and those mesmerizing blue eyes. It wasn't the striking face of a male model, but his broad smile and sheepish expression could surely melt an ice cube from ten paces.

"And you are . . . Annie Franklin. Nice to meet you, Annie Franklin." His smile seemed genuine and sincere. Annie was astonished to feel herself blushing. She busied herself arranging her covers. Attempting to pull herself up by grabbing the overhead bar, she grimaced.

"Here, let me help you." He fluffed the pillows behind her for support. "So I understand you were in a pretty serious accident." He pulled up a chair beside the bed and sat down, tossing the clipboard toward the foot of her bed. He stretched out his long legs, folding his arms across his chest, obviously quite comfortable and ready to talk. "Tell me about it."

Annie glanced out the window to avoid the expectant

expression on his face. "Actually, Mr. McGregor, I'd—"

"David. Just call me David." That smile again.

"Okay . . . David, I was just going to say I'd rather not talk about the accident right now. So maybe there are some other folks on this floor you might want to—"

He twisted his mouth to one side as if puzzled. "That's okay. We don't have to talk about your accident, but you look like you could use some company."

He paused for a moment then bounced out of the chair and headed toward the wall across from Annie's bed. "Whoa! Will you look at all these cards!" He examined the cluster of get-well cards and numerous hand-made posters taped to the wall then tossed a knowing smile over his shoulder at her. "Looks like you have quite a fan club. Who are all these kids?" he asked, pointing to an assortment of snapshots.

"I teach second grade. Those are my students."

"You like it?"

"Like what?"

"Teaching school."

"Yes, I love it. I really hate being laid up here. I can't stand watching the calendar tick off day after day."

He wandered over to the windowsill filled with flower arrangements. "Oh, I'll bet you don't miss them half as much as they miss you." He drifted over to her beside table, leaning over to smell a bouquet of red roses. Standing right beside her, he turned his head to face her, obviously waiting for a response.

That smile. Like some irresistible magnetic field that's pulling me in. She scolded herself for such a ridiculous thought. She tried focusing on her folded hands. "I'm not so sure. They're great kids."

"Tell me more about Annie Franklin." He dug his hands deep into the pockets of his khaki slacks and strolled casually back to his chair and sat down. "You from around here? From Tulsa?"

"No, I was born and raised in Tennessee. I've only lived here a couple of months. Graduated from OSU last spring. Got a teaching job, found an apartment, and here I am."

"So, that explains it."

"Explains what?"

"Why you sound so normal. I'd expect a girl born and raised in Tennessee to have quite a drawl, but you sound normal to me. Guess all those years at OSU will straighten out just about anybody with a hillbilly accent."

She didn't laugh, but felt a smile slowly spread across her face. She leaned her head to one side.

He grinned. "What? Did I say something wrong?"

She studied him a moment longer. "No, not at all. I was just thinking you don't exactly fit the mold when it comes to being a chaplain."

"I don't?" He laughed, as if shocked. "What—should I act real somber? Maybe I need to practice looking more . . . *reverent* or something. Or maybe I should use 'thee' and 'thou' when I speak? Would that help?"

Now it was her turn to laugh. "No, I mean, aren't chaplains supposed to pray with their patients?"

He smiled. "You want me to pray?"

Annie hesitated. "Maybe another time."

"I'll take that as an invitation to stop by again sometime." He stood to leave, making his way to the door. Just before he slipped out, he stopped and winked over his shoulder, "See you tomorrow, Annie Franklin."

In the following weeks, David McGregor stopped by every day. Sometimes twice a day. Without pressure or any form of intimidation, he slowly broke through the barriers of her sadness. Eventually she opened up and shared her disappointments and frustrations of this untimely accident. She talked about her students, her dreams, her goals.

Yet, there were definite limits to the subjects she was willing to discuss with this "preacher boy." And David McGregor would later tell her he was eminently aware of her carefully constructed wall of mistrust.

Whenever she turned the conversation to him, David talked openly about his background, his calling into the ministry, and his plans to one day pastor a church. The chaplaincy was part of his training for ministry. She evaded the subject of faith whenever possible, but he always seemed to sneak in a reference or two to God. Nothing heavy.

Gradually, she realized it was not so much the "religion" she observed in him. It was the apparent and obviously intimate relationship he had with the Lord. It was simply a natural part of who he was. He seemed so *real.*

Growing up, Annie's mother had always taken her to church, but she was not impressed by the people she met there.

They weren't at all real. They *played* church. But the church and God had no impact whatsoever on their everyday lives. And Annie recognized that inconsistency in her own mother as much as anyone. She hated the hypocrisy.

Ironically, Annie believed in God with all her heart. She had learned enough in Sunday school to know the difference between right and wrong. And she believed that God gave his son Jesus to save the world. She just never quite knew what to do about it.

Yet, here was a guy who really lived what he believed in a way that was appealing, spiritually speaking. It baffled her.

On the day of her release from the hospital, David stopped by early. "So you're finally going to blow this joint and get on with your life!" he announced as he waltzed in her door.

She was dressed, packed, seated in the chair beside her bed and waiting for an orderly to bring a wheelchair. "Yes, I am. And I'm not going to miss this place at all. But I have to admit, I'll miss our visits. You've been wonderful, David. I can't thank you enough for all your help. I think you'll make a great pastor one of these days."

He hopped up to sit on her empty bed. There was a different expression on his face. He looked at her briefly then concentrated on his legs which were swinging nervously off the edge of the bed.

Annie cocked her head and laughed. "What's up with *you?*"

"I need to ask you something," he said, still not looking up.

"So—ask."

He tucked his hands under his legs. "Well, the thing

is . . . what I wanted to say was . . . "

"Y'know, you're acting very peculiar, David," she teased.

Just then, a young orderly wheeled a chair into the room. "Limo at your service, ma'am. Is this all you've got?" He pointed to the small tapestry bag sitting by her feet.

"I had a friend take all my flowers home for me yesterday. So this is it."

"You sure know how to travel light! Oughta' make you show some of these other birds how to pack. You should see 'em. They come rollin' in here—got a whole fleet of moving vans lined up outside!"

David and Annie looked at each other and laughed. David stood and offered to escort Annie downstairs for the orderly. The young man checked out the photo ID clipped to David's shirt. "Well, sure enough, Reverend. I'm sure that would be just fine. You can leave the chair down there by the entrance for me."

"No problem," David answered. He turned to Annie. "Now, let's see if I can get you into this wheelchair without putting you back in traction." He carefully assisted her into the chair and hung her bag on the handle. "Okay, let's get you out of here."

Annie reached her good hand up to stop him. "David, wait. Sit down. You had a question for me."

"Oh . . . that! Well, see, I just thought . . . I was wondering—"

"Will you just spit it out?"

"Okay. The problem here . . . well, see—*officially* I'm not allowed to ask for your phone number."

Annie felt the heat rising up her neck. "Uh, well, I don't—"

"Wait. Here—" he said, snapping off his ID badge. "I'm not even supposed to be on the clock yet, so you can consider this on my personal time. So it's not 'Chaplain McGregor' or anything. It's just me. David." He flashed a nervous smile and rubbed his hands together.

"No, it isn't that," she said. "I'm just not sure you really want to do that. To call me. There's a lot you don't know about me, David. And I wouldn't want to hurt you."

He blew out a gust of air. "Oh, *that's* all! I thought you were going to tell me you were married or something." And with an air of relief, he jumped up, twirled her chair around and headed out the door. "See, the way I figure it, you're going to be a gimp for quite awhile—"

"A gimp?" She laughed as he rolled her down the hall.

"Oh yeah. Big time gimp. And you're going to need somebody to take you to the store, carry your groceries in for you, take you to your doctor's appointments. That kind of thing."

He paused. She missed his next comment as he mumbled behind her. "What was that?" she asked.

"I said someone needs to get you out of the house occasionally. Like to a movie or something." He wheeled her onto an elevator full of passengers. He left her facing all of them with her back to the doors as he joined the rest of them staring at her or the lighted numbers above her. *Awkward.*

"They'll all tell you it would be a big, big mistake to turn down such an incredible offer," he continued casually, nodding his head at the fellow passengers, his eyes still focused above her. All ten strangers simultaneously turned their confused attention toward her.

Annie couldn't help but laugh. He lowered his gaze to look into her face, his deep blue eyes alive with mischief, that irresistible smile melting her heart.

In that moment, she knew her resistance was history. That carefully constructed, protective wall came crumbling down.

In the days that followed, she received lots of flowers and a strange variety of thoughtful gifts. A bakery delivered a huge chocolate chip cookie the size of an extra large pizza. The message written in squiggly lines of vanilla frosting read, "How I Spent My Fall Vacation." A brown icing UPS truck with a frowning face zoomed below the words.

One afternoon he showed up with a small fishbowl, complete with blue gravel, green plastic seaweed, and a plastic scuba diver. In the sloshing water, a bright orange goldfish with wide, frightened eyes swam frantically in circles. When Annie's questioning eyes searched his, David responded. "Company to keep an eye on you when I can't be around. His name is Spike. Think of him like a dangerous watchdog if any of your other boyfriends show up. He's been trained to attack."

They were inseparable. Little by little, day by day, Annie Franklin fell in love with David McGregor.

Then one evening a couple months later, much to her disappointment, he called to cancel the quiet evening they had planned together. An hour later, as she sat reading in her living room, she began to hear music outside. She peeked out the window of her second floor apartment. Still unable to see anything, she stepped out onto her balcony. There on the courtyard below her, dressed in a black tuxedo and holding a huge bouquet of red roses, stood David McGregor. With the assistance of a professional stringed quartet, he sang of his love to her in the clear night air, completely at ease in front of the growing crowd of curious neighbors.

Since the beginning of time
Since words first rhymed
No one ever loved you more.
Since birds took flight,
Since day shared with night,
Your heart I have longed for.

I'm here before you now,
Down upon my knees,
I'm making you a vow
Asking will you please?
Be mine
Be mine
Forever will you be my mine?
My wife
My life,
Forever will you be mine?
Together for the rest of time,
Be mine.

When the realization finally registered that this was a concert for her alone, Annie covered her face with her hands. For a brief moment, she began to laugh at the spectacle below. Then as she looked up once again, the tenderness of it swept over her and the tears of joy began to fall. David's smooth voice continued the sweet serenade. And even as her neighbors began to gather in the moonlight surrounding his entourage, his eyes remained on her alone.

> *Forever will you be mine?*
> *Together for the rest of time,*
> *Be mine.*

As the stringed instruments continued softly in the background, David cleared his throat and knelt down on one knee. "Annie Franklin, with these fine musicians and kind, albeit *nosy* neighbors as my witnesses, and more important, before Almighty God, I, David Jeremy McGregor, do humbly ask for your hand in marriage." His face beamed as he cleared his throat once again. "Annie, will you marry me?"

Cheers erupted as she mouthed her reply through her happy tears, unable to speak. Once convinced that such pure a love could never exist, Annie knew she had found her knight in shining armor.

They were married a few weeks later on New Year's Eve.

But in Annie's case, she got two for the price of one. For David gave her not only his love, he gave her a Savior as well. What started as a mere curiosity of the unique, personal relationship he shared with Christ, quickly grew to an eager yearning for a personal relationship all her own. She surrendered her life to the Lord, astonished at the difference he made in her life.

All because a UPS truck ran a red light.

Blinking as her mind returned to the present, Annie realized the storm clouds had rolled in. She shivered and knew it was time to head back to the cabin. Still fresh from the long, personal glimpse into her most precious memories, Annie could not even imagine her life without David. All he had meant to her, from that first moment they met at the hospital.

Oh God, please help us. There has to be a way for us to take our lives back again. Someway to restore the love we once shared. Forgive me for ignoring the blessings you've given me, for an ungrateful heart when we travel through the tough times. I cannot imagine my life without David. Oh, God please show us what to do! Tug at his heart as you've tugged at mine. Help him see what we've lost, and oh God, please help him want to find it again. Save the relationship you designed for us, Lord. Oh, Father, please hear my—

Suddenly, Annie's foot skidded off a steep embankment, dragging her helplessly downward. Her hands, buried deep in the warm pockets of her coat, were of little help as she struggled to pull them free. She screamed, her voice echoing across the snow-covered landscape. Woolen mittens grasped uselessly at the fleeting drifts of snow until her foot caught on something below the surface of the snow. Her ankle snapped as she came to a stop.

She fell back onto the covered ground behind her, grimacing in pain. *I don't believe this!* She tried to lift her leg with both hands to free it. With a heavy sigh, she fought the urge to cry out again. She knew she had to get back up to the road and back to the cabin. She felt along the ground, pushing away the snow in search of a branch to grab on to. She found a large pile of boulders completely hidden in the huge snowdrift. Clearing off the snow, she grabbed the biggest stone and pulled herself up, balancing on her good foot. She found herself right beside an aspen tree its branches in reach. She hobbled over to the trunk for safety, then reached for the lowest branch.

Climbing back up the embankment proved to be a daunting challenge. With a throbbing, useless ankle, it might as well have been Mt. Everest. Annie paced herself, making progress in unbearably slow intervals. The snow fell harder. It took almost fifteen minutes to ascend the distance up to the road. Once she reached the summit, she paused to catch her breath. This wasn't going to be easy. It was still a long way home.

A full hour passed before she reached the base of the steps of the cabin leading up to the wrap-around porch. Annie was exhausted, but she resisted the urge to sit down and rest on the bottom step. She had to get inside before she froze to death. Dark gray clouds now covered the sky behind the thick swirls of snowflakes falling around her.

Using the rustic banister, she pulled herself up the

steps one at a time then crept inside. She hobbled into the great room before shedding her garments and lowering herself onto the soft, inviting sofa. The exhaustion overwhelmed her immediately.

Fearing she would give in to her fatigue, Annie picked up the phone and dialed the number for information. After a moment, she hung up and dialed the number for Doc Wilkins.

"Dr. Wilkins? This is Annie McGregor up at Christine's cabin. Do you remember me?"

"Why, of course I remember you. What can I do for you?"

"I think I may have broken my ankle."

"What happened?"

She started to cry. "It was such a silly accident. I decided to go out for a walk and somehow I must have lost my footing and slid down an embankment off the side of the road and—I feel so stupid but it hurts *so* much!"

"Well, you just try to make yourself comfortable and I'll be right up. Elevate your foot and stay off it, okay?"

She whimpered, trying to get the words out but realized he had already hung up.

Annie gingerly lifted her foot and propped it on the coffee table. She grabbed a throw pillow and stuffed it beneath the throbbing foot, then rested her head on the back of the sofa and shut her eyes. She didn't even have the strength to pull off her boots before drifting off into a fitful sleep.

❧

A gentle knock preceded the sound of an opening door as Annie's mind struggled to break through the seal of her restless slumber. "Dr. Wilkins, is that you?"

"Yes, Annie. You stay put. Let me get out of my overcoat and I'll be right there." He stomped the snow off his boots on the welcome mat. Discarding his muffler, coat, and gloves, he reached for his worn leather medical bag and made his way over to Annie. "Well, well, well, what have we here? Took a little spill, did you?"

Annie looked up into his kind eyes and relaxed in the surprising comfort of his mere presence. "I'm so glad you're here. I can't believe I did this! I've hardly been here twenty-four hours and already I've injured myself. What a klutz." She laughed then moaned as she tried to lift her foot from the coffee table.

"Now hold on, you let me do the doctoring, young lady. Let's pile a couple of these pillows behind you then I'll take a look at that ankle."

As he made a thorough examination of her foot, she found the country doctor to be a welcomed guest as well as a gifted physician. His amiable bedside manner was exceeded only by his wise comprehension of physical matters. Relieved to have such kind-hearted attention, she remained irritated with her clumsiness.

"For heaven's sake, we all take a tumble now and then. Why should you be any different?" He continued his work.

His question found a vulnerable mark and struck hard. She stared at the wrinkled countenance of this man she barely knew. It was an innocent question offered in compassion. Still, his question echoed through her soul.

Why should you be any different?

That's just it. She was no different from any other person on this planet. So why couldn't she handle her life? Why couldn't she just suck up her aggravations like everybody else and get on with her life? And why on earth did she leave behind her home and all the people she loved to come up on this stupid mountain?

"Annie?"

The doctor's voice broke her train of thought and she blinked, causing a single tear to escape from her eye.

"Are you all right? Aside from your ankle, I mean." Doc Wilkins paused in his work to search her face. Embarrassed by her emotional display, Annie wiped her cheek with the back of her hand. She sniffled before attempting to answer.

"Yes, I'm fine. Well, except . . ." She paused, uncertain what to say. "No, really—I'll be fine. I suppose the long walk back up here must have knocked the wind out of me." She faked a smile, knowing her words didn't fool either of them.

"I think you've got a pretty bad sprain, but it doesn't look like you've broken any bones. Which means a speedier recovery. But you'll need to stay off it as much as possible. Try to keep an ice pack on it as much as you can stand it. If there's not one in the freezer, just use a bag of frozen peas or corn. That'll do just as well. I'm sure Mary Jean will be more than happy to come up and bring you a meal or two if you'd be open to that."

"Oh no, I'm sure I'll be fine, Dr. Wilkins."

"Please—just call me Doc. Everyone does."

She smiled. "Okay, Doc. Thanks for the offer. If I run into trouble, I'll give you a call. I just need—" Her voice disappeared.

Doc leveled his gaze at her over the top of his glasses. "Young lady, I know I'm practically a stranger to you, and you have no reason whatsoever to feel compelled to talk to an old codger like me. Just the same, I'd be mighty blind not to notice you're hurting pretty badly in here." He tapped his finger on his heart. He smiled at her with knowing eyes. "A sprain like this may be a nuisance, but it's not too serious. But if you keep whatever it is that's bothering you all stuffed down inside you like some turkey all dressed for Thanksgiving, you'll bring on all kinds of illnesses. Physical *and* emotional. The good Lord didn't design these old bodies to cart around so much stress."

"You're a believer?" she asked softly.

"Good heavens, yes. Mercy, you don't think I could understand the human body without knowing the One who made it in the first place? Yes, I've been a believer longer than you've been alive, I reckon'. Don't know how people live without the Lord. Can't imagine."

Annie took a ragged breath before trusting her voice again. "I am too," she responded, then added, "I'm also a pastor's wife, but . . . I guess you'd say I'm . . ." She struggled to find the words. Nothing.

They sat in silence. The wind howled through the trees outside. Finally, the doctor finished taping her ankle and stood up. He reached down to pat her hand. "You just let me know if you need anything—and that *includes* an experienced listener," he added, once again peering over his glasses. "You can ask anyone in this county and they'll tell you that Doc Wilkins knows how to keep his mouth shut. It's a rare quality, of course. But it comes in mighty handy sometimes.

"Now, I'm going to fix you a hot cup of tea before I go. I'll build your fire back up, then look around for the crutches Christine keeps around here somewhere. Up here in ski country, everyone has a pair of crutches around the house. You just try and take it easy, okay? Doctor's orders," he added over his shoulder.

Annie relaxed. In a strange way, she knew her fall had been no accident. It was a "divine appointment," as Caroline liked to call it. An unexpected mishap requiring an unlikely visitor. An angel disguised as a sweet, country doctor with plenty of time on his hands.

Chapter 13

Plainview, Texas

Michael groped for the phone. He started to lift the receiver until a pain shot through his arm, startling him out of his sleep. "Aaahhh!" He dropped the phone.

"Mr. Smith? Mr. Smith! Are you all right?"

A far away, muffled voice beckoned from beneath the bed. "Just a minute . . . I dropped the phone. Hold on." With his good arm, he pulled the cord until the receiver followed it up the side of the bed. "Uh, yes, I'm here."

"Mr. Smith, this is Peg at the front desk. You asked for a wake-up call at ten o'clock. It's just a shade after ten now. Are you all right?"

"Sure . . . I'm fine, just knocked the phone off . . . no problem. Thanks. I, uh . . . appreciate it." He hung up before another wave of pain rolled over him. He cried out, cradling his side, shocked at the continuing intensity of his pain. For a moment, he remained totally still. *What am I going to do? I've got to get out of here.*

He checked his watch. Five after ten. There was no time to baby himself, not another minute to rest. If he had any chance at all, he must keep moving. With bold determination, he inched himself up to a sitting position and waited for the dizziness to pass before opening his eyes.

A voice in his head badgered him. *You're never gonna make it. Give it up. Just crawl back in bed and forget about Elliot. Forget about your company. Who cares? Nobody gives a rip about you anyway.*

Michael snapped his head from side to side. "No. No! I won't give up," he whispered. He crawled out of bed and began to make his way to the bathroom. The sight in the mirror was even worse than before. His skin looked pale and pasty. Dark puffy half-circles hung below his eyes. When he peeled the bandages away from his wounds, the sight took his breath away. His work was cut out for him.

An hour later, he emerged from his room carefully scoping out his surroundings. The hot shower had given him renewed hope, soothing his tired body and washing away the dirt and grime and dried blood from the nightmare he was living. Even with only a couple hours of sleep, he felt at least partially refreshed and eager to get on the road. He recognized the elevated adrenaline in his system and knew he had to ride it out for as long as it would last. It was his only hope.

Michael pulled through the motel parking lot and back onto the road. He spotted another fast food restaurant with a drive-thru and pulled in. As he approached the window, a freckle-faced teenage boy gave a long, admiring whistle to Michael's SUV. "Nice wheels, dude!"

Michael smiled and placed his order. After evading the barrage of questions and comments about his car, he reached out for the bag containing his breakfast and pulled out onto the highway. He popped the lid off the tall Styrofoam cup of coffee and carefully took a sip. The fresh, hot flavor of the coffee instantly revitalized him.

He tried to remember Peg's directions to the local bus station. Fifteen minutes later, he walked out of the noisy complex, coughing from the diesel fumes of idling buses. He folded a piece of paper with a locker number scribbled on it and wrapped it around a key. Tucking both into his pocket, he felt a noticeable weight off his shoulders and hurried to his car. The flash drive with evidence of Elliot's involvement in the murder of Christopher Jordan was safely out of his hands now. He would call Grady the first chance he got and give him the number off that paper. Now he had backup.

Life insurance.

Setting his coffee in the console holder, he turned on the radio and began to search for a news station as he pulled out of the parking lot. He skipped through an array of country love songs, indistinguishable rap music, a radio preacher's blistering sermon, and a station playing an old Captain and Tennille song before he found what he wanted.

"And now a look at today's weather. Expect increasing snowstorms for much of the panhandle today as this second front, which looks to be much stronger, continues to bear down from Canada. By this evening we expect a traveler's advisory to be issued as this storm moves into our area from the northwest. Stay tuned to KCOL for your weather report every hour on the tens."

Michael unwrapped his sausage and cheese biscuit and took a bite. "Once again, here are the stories we're following for you here on 990 KCOL . . ."

As the reporter rambled on with the news of the hour, Michael's mind raced back to the questions that still plagued him. *Where were Elliot's hounds? Elliot wouldn't give up this easily. Where was he right now? And what about Amelia? Surely she's called Daddy by now complaining about my absence. I wonder how Elliot covered that one?*

Michael took another sip of coffee and looked at his cell phone. He had kept it turned off, avoiding anyone's efforts to trace him. But he had to call Grady. He would find a pay phone in the next town. His eyes were drawn to the green sign along the side of the road.

Edmonson—13 miles
Amarillo—89 miles
Pueblo, Colorado—409 miles

While calculating how much longer his drive would take, his pain reminded him of the immediate need for more medication. Suddenly, it dawned on him.

Why didn't I think of it before?

He had always kept a supply of prescription muscle relaxers in his gym bag, his desk at the office, his brief case, and the bedside drawer at home. For years he had used the pain medication for relief from a knee injury he suffered back in his last days with the Astros. It didn't bother him all the time, but when it did the pain could be intense. He scolded himself for not remembering the meds earlier.

With a bum arm, he knew he couldn't dig through the bag while he drove. He pulled off on the side of the road, grateful for the cover of an old, abandoned stretch of wooden fencing. Awkwardly, he reached across his body with his good arm to pull the black vinyl bag up to the front seat beside him. His clumsy movements frustrated him until he finally jerked the bag around the seat. In a split second, the bag tipped the edge of his coffee cup sitting on the console. Automatically his other hand reached to stop it from spilling. Pain shot through the arm as the reaction tore through his bullet wound. He screamed in agony only to be answered with a steaming splash of coffee still hot enough to burn his right hand.

He cursed until his anger gave way to the urgency of relief. He tore open the bag, digging out the first aid kit he'd bought the night before, then tended to his wound. After treating his injuries, he finally found the bottle of muscle relaxers. It wasn't until he opened the bottle of pills that he allowed himself a glimmer of hope. He washed the capsule down with a gulp from his water bottle and turned the key once again in the ignition.

❧

He's where?"

"I told you, Mr. Thomas—he's just now leaving Plainview. Going north toward Amarillo. Could be he's headed for Colorado. He got any friends up there? Family? You all got one of them chalets up there anywhere?"

"No, of course not," Elliot snapped, changing the receiver to his other ear. "Our chalet is in Switzerland. If he has friends up there, it's nobody I know about. Just keep your eyes open and whatever you do, don't lose him."

"No sir. We won't let him out of our sight."

"Make sure you don't."

"Only thing is, sir, you sure we can't just grab him and haul him back to Houston? What's with this cat and mouse game anyway?"

"That's not your concern. Just stay on his tail but don't let him see you, got it? And Gus—don't you and Marcus screw this one up, understand? I'll make it well worth your while as long as you follow my strict instructions. Are we clear on that?"

"No problem, sir. And don't you worry none. We won't blow it. You can count on us, sir."

Elliot slammed down the phone. "Why does that give me no comfort?"

Chapter 14

Seminole, Florida

Don't even say that! How could you!" Jessie cried, shoving her chair back as she jumped up. She threw down the rest of her sandwich and bolted from the school cafeteria, shouting, "You're not my friend anymore!"

She was halfway down the hall when she heard a stern, commanding voice behind her. "Stop right there, young lady!"

She turned around, quickly wiping her tears. Jessie kept her head down, afraid to face whoever belonged to that mean voice. As the footsteps approached her, the voice softened.

"Why, Miss McGregor! What's wrong?"

Jessie looked up into a familiar face, recognizing the man from church. She sniffed a couple of times and wiped her eyes on her sleeve.

He dropped to one knee and put a hand on Jessica's

shoulder. "Now what could be so bad to send you running out of the cafeteria?" His tone was gentle and compassionate. "You can tell me, honey. My name is Mr. Harrison. Your daddy and I are good friends."

"You are?" She looked up at him, studying his face.

"Why, of course we are! And I know that if my little girl was upset and your daddy was there, I'd want him to help her. Sure I would! Here now—here's my nice clean handkerchief for you. You go ahead and use it to dry those pretty big blue eyes of yours. And then you can tell me what's happened."

Jessie wiped her nose and her eyes and began telling her daddy's friend how she was missing her mommy.

"Where did Mommy go, sweetheart?"

"I don't know. Gran just told us she had to go away for awhile and she doesn't know when she's coming back."

"Oh. Is that so?"

"Yes, and then Samantha said maybe my Mommy and Daddy are getting the Big D."

"The Big D?"

"A di-divorce!" The tears erupted all over again. Jessica hid her face in the handkerchief with the fancy monogrammed initials. When she finally peered over the cloth at her daddy's friend, he had a strange look on his face.

"Well, now, Miss McGregor, there's no need for you to get so upset. I'm *sure* if your mom and dad were getting a divorce, then I'd know all about it. 'Course, I suppose your mama could have left for awhile. She might have needed to get away for a little vacation or something. See, sometimes kids, and especially little kids, can just wear a mama out. You know how it is—a mama gets so busy with cooking and cleaning up and doing laundry and driving her kids all over the place. And then kids are always fighting and arguing and making even more messes for her to clean up—"

Jessica tried to keep her lower lip from trembling.

"—and I'm sure your daddy's probably never at home hardly at all, is he?" Her head slowly nodded in agreement. "And of course, that just makes it *extra* hard for a mama. She feels all alone. Has to do everything herself.

"So it's not so hard to see why your mommy probably just felt like she was all tuckered out. We grown-ups call it 'burn-out.' Happens all the time to busy people. Especially someone like your mother. So maybe she just needed to get away from everything for awhile. That's all! Certainly nothing for a pretty little girl like you to worry about."

Her daddy's friend stood up and moved in alongside of Jessica, his arm draped protectively on her shoulders. She blew her nose as they began walking down the hall. Daddy's friend sounded like a nice man. He seemed to know a lot more about her mommy and daddy than she did. That didn't seem right somehow.

I don't care. I just want Mommy to come home. I want my mommy and I want her now!

She didn't want to hear Daddy's friend talk anymore. Jessie pulled free from him and took off down the hall, whimpering as she ran.

❧

Max was torn between taking notes and stealing glances at the clock on the wall. Missing the closing words of a lecture by Mr. Harrison could prove deadly on an exam. Still, the countdown was irresistible. Only three more minutes until freedom. The second hand crept along its circular path unbearably slow today, as if hesitating to pass each and every numeral. *C'mon . . . c'mon . . .*

"Mr. McGregor, how would you explain their dilemma?"

"Excuse me, sir?"

Mr. Harrison clasped his hands behind his back as he turned to stroll toward Max's desk. "Just as I expected. Too enthralled with the clock on the wall to have even the remotest idea what I just asked you, correct?"

"No, sir. I just got behind taking my notes and missed your last couple of statements. That's all."

Harrison stood directly above him now, his fingers tapping impatiently on his desk. "What is it with you McGregors? Do you have some sort of attention deficit disorder, or are you just simple? Our subject matter today isn't so complex. But since you can't seem to grasp it, perhaps you should stay after class so I can spell it out for you—reeeaaal slooooow."

Max shifted in his desk as his classmates laughed. "That's okay. I think I've got it."

"No, I don't believe you do. You'll remain after class, Mr. McGregor." The bell rang, mocking Max as he remained seated. He caught several of his friends rolling their eyes in knowing sympathy as they left the room. He stole a glance at Megan as she passed his desk. *I'll wait for you outside*, she mouthed. Her expression of consolation provided the only encouragement he was willing to accept.

He set his pen down, folded his arms against his chest and leaned back in his seat. His long legs crossed at the ankles reached far under the vacant seat in front of him.

Once the room cleared, Harrison paced himself slowly, putting away his lecture notes and various texts. He straightened everything on his desk then turned his back and began erasing names and dates on the blackboard. Max watched his every move, confident it was all orchestrated for his benefit.

He's trying to eat you up. Don't let him get to you. Remember what Dad said.

Whap!

Max jumped. Harrison smiled sardonically, quite pleased with his little trick. The map behind him still flapped from his sudden release. Max refolded his arms, silently counting down his impatience. *One, two, three, four . . .*

Harrison sat down behind his desk at the front of the room and folded his hands atop his desk. "Well, well, well. It's about time you and I had a nice little personal chat like this, Mr. McGregor."

"Look, Mr. Harrison, I've got basketball practice starting right now. I've got to get suited up. Is there any chance this could wait until another time?"

"Not a chance. Your sports will just have to wait. We

need to clear the air a bit between us. I've sensed a real problem with your attitude for some time now. And quite frankly, I find that it's interfering with your participation in this class. Now I would think that being a preacher's kid—"

"Hold it, Mr. Harrison. Let's leave that out of this. I'm just an ordinary kid like every other kid in your classroom."

"Quite the contrary. You are Max McGregor, son of the good pastor David McGregor. And that makes you stand completely apart from every other student in this class or any other. The other students look up to you. They even set their standards by you if for no other reason than the fact that you're their preacher's kid. They expect you to be their leader. Just as we all expect your father to be the leader of our church, whether we like it or not."

Max shifted in his seat. "With all due respect, Mr. Harrison, that's where you step over the line. I'm just a student in your class. You have no right to keep bringing up my father's name or the fact that he's my dad. You think you can keep picking on me just because you have a problem with him, don't you?"

Harrison stood up and slowly walked over to the bank of windows. "Oh now, just calm down, McGregor. No use getting yourself all in a huff. I'd just like to *see* a little of that respect from you. That's all. You sit there staring up at me with a real chip on your shoulder. I suppose I do expect more from you than I should." Harrison leaned against the counter under the windows. "If I were a betting man, I'd wager there have been quite a few sessions about me at your home. Am I right?"

Max scoffed. "What kind of question is that?"

"Don't play games with me. It's no secret that your father and I don't get along. Anybody associated with the church or this school knows that."

"So?"

"So I'm betting my name has been batted around your home quite a bit. And most likely, not in the kindest of terms."

"Look, I still don't know what you're asking. You want me to tell you things that are said in the privacy of our home? I don't think so!"

"I'm sure your mother has probably had plenty to say—"

"What about my mother?" Max stood up, hiking his backpack up on his shoulder. "Y'know, you've got some nerve. It's none of your business what my mom or my dad say about you! But I'll tell you this much—neither one of them come close to the kind of crap I have to put up with from you. And you know what? I just made a decision. I'm not putting up with your crap anymore! You got that?"

Max shoved open the door in a burst of anger, slamming it back against the wall as hard as he could. Its glass window shattered in a thousand pieces then dropped like a waterfall, crashing to the floor. Max stood frozen in his tracks, his back still turned on the disaster behind him. He closed his eyes, knowing his fate was now surely sealed.

From inside the classroom came the quiet, unprovoked voice of his history teacher. "My, my, what a temper, Mr. McGregor. No wonder your mother ran away from home."

In that split millisecond, Max felt his blood boil over. He clenched his fists, trying to steel himself. With bold, deliberate steps, he forced himself to walk away from actions that most certainly would get him expelled.

Or land him behind bars.

৵

Max, wait up! What happened?"

Max fumbled in his pocket for his keys. He unlocked the passenger door of his car and held it open for Megan. He refused to look at her. "I lost my temper. I broke the glass in his stupid door, okay?"

He slammed the door after she got in then slammed his own before turning the key in the ignition, immediately throwing it into reverse. His wheels squealed in protest as he backed out, leaving a patch of rubber as a black tribute to his anger. Megan quickly buckled her seat belt and braced her hands against the dash and the door handle.

After roaring out of the school parking lot and onto the road that sliced in front of the church and school property, Max rolled his head back against the headrest and slowly let out a long sigh. His foot moved to the brake as he sought to bring the car back under control. They drove for several minutes without speaking. Finally, Max pulled off the road into the Sonic Drive-In. He placed their usual order over the intercom, then turned to face Megan, leaning against his door.

"Hey, I'm sorry. I shouldn't have peeled out like that.

Are you okay?"

Megan unfastened her seatbelt and turned to face him. "Yeah, I'm fine now. A little worried about you, though. I've never seen you like this. You really scared me back there." She sandwiched his hand between hers. "This is more than the usual stuff from Mr. Harrison, isn't it?"

Max tightened his grip on her hands. "Yeah, a lot more. He just kept pushing me! It's like he knows if he pushes me hard enough then gives me one more solid punch, I'll go over the edge. And this time he actually pulled it off. And I lost it, Megan. I was already heading out the door, for cryin' out loud!"

He pulled his hand free and ran his fingers through his hair.

"What in the world could he possibly have said to put you over the edge? To make you that mad?"

He stopped agitating his hair. "He brought up Mom."

"That's it? He mentioned your mom and you went ballistic?"

"Megan, there's something I haven't told you. I was hoping I wouldn't have to, but it's killing me not to be able to talk to you about it."

"What is it?"

He reached over for her hand again. "It's about Mom. She's been gone for a couple of days and we don't know where."

Megan cocked her head sideways. "I don't understand."

"Dad wasn't going to tell us, I think because he knew how much we'd worry. But I knew something was up. Yesterday he finally told me 'she had to get away.' Whatever that means. Like maybe an emotional breakdown or something . . ." His voiced grew husky and he looked away.

"Oh Max, I'm so sorry. Why didn't you tell me? You know I'd never say anything to anyone." She held his hand up to her cheek then gently kissed it. "No wonder you've been so upset. I can't imagine what your dad must be going through. He doesn't know where she is?"

"No. She left a note but didn't say where she was going. Only that she was having a tough time and had to have some time to herself. I keep wondering if it was something I might have done."

"You can't blame yourself for this. It probably has nothing to do with you."

"Easy for you to say."

"What's that supposed to mean?"

"Nothing. Forget it." Max dropped her hand and stretched his arms against the steering wheel.

Megan paused for a moment, looking out her window. "No, I don't want to forget it. What did you mean?"

"Stop trying to read something into it. I hate it when you do that."

"Wait a minute. How did this get back to me? I haven't done anything. I was just trying to help."

"Right, Megan. Always the innocent. You're never to blame for anything. You never do anything wrong. You're always perfect, every hair in place. No, it's always me. *I'm* the one who's always in trouble. Like I *asked* Mr. Harrison to pick on me! Yeah, right."

Megan's chin began to tremble. "I never said that! And I don't pretend to be perfect. How could you say that?"

The waitress approached his window with two frosty mugs of root beer on a tray. "Just forget it!" he shouted, throwing the car into reverse again, screeching backward.

Moments later, his tires squealed to a stop at the curb in front of her house. Megan wiped her nose and gathered her backpack and purse then opened the door. "Max, I don't know why you're so upset with me. And I'm really sorry about your mom," her words warbling with emotion. "But if you don't get control of your temper, you're going to chase away everyone who loves you. And that includes me." She slammed the door and ran up her driveway.

And for the third time in less than an hour, he left a trail of black rubber smoking behind him.

❧

It's about time! Where've you been?" Jeremy blasted as Max opened the door to the kitchen. "You were supposed to take me to buy a new pair of Nikes this afternoon. You promised you'd take me after your basketball practice!"

"Jeremy, you're not the only one in this family with a life, okay? So I forgot. Big deal. I'll take you this weekend, so get over it." Max kept moving, heading for the solitude and privacy of his room. He hoped this little skirmish had gone undetected by his dad and grandmother. No such luck.

"Whoa, hold up there, buddy," his dad called out from his study. "I think you owe your brother an apology. He's been counting on you to help him pick out those shoes for a long time. You promised him."

Max made the turn and started up the stairs, calling over his shoulder, "Fine. Jeremy, I apologize. Now, is everyone satisfied?" He flew up the steps three at a time.

"Max, stop. Right there." His father stood at the foot of the staircase. "What's going on? Jeremy didn't deserve that kind of reaction. And I'd like to know where you've been. It's almost six-thirty."

Max stood with his back to his father then sighed and turned around. His eyes stayed focused on the backpack hanging from his shoulder. "I had to stay at school a little late, that's all. Then I took Megan home and we had a fight. Okay? I've got homework to do."

He could feel his father's eyes on him. Silence.

Finally, "We'll talk later."

He didn't wait for a response, nor did he get one.

Upstairs, Max threw his backpack on his bed and touched the ON button on his CD remote. Guitars and drums blasted, filling the room. It hammered his soul, matching rhythm with his anxiety. He started to pull the books from his bag, then decided against it for the moment. In one swift motion he shoved all of it off on the floor and flopped onto his bed.

Max shut his eyes and tried to put the events of the last few hours out of his head, but it was too fresh. Images assaulted his mind. The smirk on Mr. Harrison's face. The crash of the glass on the floor. The warmth of Megan's hands wrapped in his, then the hurt in her eyes as she began to cry. He remembered the urge he'd had to bite somebody's head off as he drove home. And he remembered the battle inside his heart as he flew up the stairs with his back to his father.

Dad has enough to worry about right now. The last thing he needs is more fires to put out like this crap from Mr. Harrison. He'll find out soon enough when the school calls.

But something his teacher had said was echoing through the back of his mind. *"My, my, what a temper, Mr. McGregor. No wonder your mother ran away."*

Max felt a sudden wave of nausea. *How in the world could Mr. Harrison possibly know about Mom? And even if he did know, why would he have any reason to think she ran away?* Max rolled over on his side, cradling his queasiness. Harrison was to blame for everything—the busted window, his fight with Megan, his trouble with Jeremy and his dad's disappointment in him. But none of that bothered him half as much as the gnawing fact that Harrison knew about his mother.

Chapter 15

The Texas Panhandle

A knot of fear tightened in Michael's stomach. A state trooper's cruiser was two cars back. He casually put on his blinker and changed lanes. The cruiser did the same. Michael changed back to the right lane and eased back on the accelerator. The cruiser passed him then exited a mile later.

Michael took a deep breath and blew out a long sigh. Relieved, he still couldn't relax. Surely Elliot had put some kind of APB out on him by now. It didn't make sense. You don't escape someone as powerful as Elliot Thomas. Yet he was already 600 miles out of Houston. It didn't add up. And *because* it didn't add up, Michael felt even more insecure. He decided to get off the highway and find some back roads just to be safe.

The two-lane road wasn't shown on Michael's U.S. map.

He needed state maps so he could plot his way to Weber Creek. Three miles down the road he spotted a run-down gas station that must have been around since the invention of the automobile. But the gas was cheap and more important, the old man sitting behind the dusty counter could supply him with maps of Texas and Colorado. The proprietor never took his eyes off the tiny black and white television screen. He was deeply immersed in a *Wheel of Fortune* rerun.

Good. If anyone stops in to ask if he's seen me, he won't know a thing. Thank you, Vanna White.

Michael had driven a couple of hours when he realized the muscle relaxer had obviously given him the boost he needed to continue his long drive north. Outside, the temperature was dropping as the daunting sky continued to release its payload. For a Texan from Houston, he was unaccustomed to driving in frigid conditions like these. He hoped this country road would remain drivable if the storm got worse. His Escalade might own the road in Texas, but it was an alien to the rough back roads he now traveled.

A twinge of sadness descended on him as he looked at the wintry scenes around him. It was far too beautiful. The flat barren panhandle of Texas had delivered him into a mystical landscape with majestic mountain ranges looming in the distance. These were visions designed for families on their way to the slopes. Couples heading for a romantic honeymoon in a secluded chalet. Carloads of college kids traveling to ski lodges for the weekend.

Much too beautiful for someone running for his life.

As he followed the narrow road through the rising mountains, he spotted a roadside store approaching. He pulled off and steered his car toward the phone booth on the far right side of the old brick building. The car door flew open once he turned the handle, whipped by a strong gust of wind. Shivering, he hurried to the booth, grateful it still had a door. He inched his bandaged hand into the pocket of his sweat pants and pulled out a handful of change.

"Operator. How may I help you?"

The wind rattled the booth as he backed against the door to hold it shut. The operator placed the call. In a few moments Michael heard the familiar voice on the other end of the line.

"Michael!"

"Yeah, Grady, it's me."

"Where are you, man? I've been worried sick about you! Why haven't you called me?"

"Hold on, Brewster. I'm in trouble, man. I'm on the road—"

"What? Where are you? What's—"

"Let me finish!" Michael yelled into the receiver. "Grady, you have no idea what's been going down in the last twenty-four hours. I told you there's been some trouble. After I met with you the other night, there was a confrontation between me and Elliot. He's trying to shut me up. It was bad, Grady. *Really* bad."

"What happened? Are you all right?"

"It got really ugly. He pulled a gun on me—"

"He *what?* Michael, are you okay?"

"Yeah, I'm fine. Well, not exactly. He pulled a gun and unloaded a couple of bullets into me—"

"He *shot* you?! You must be kidding! He's a United States congressman! Guys like that don't go around shooting people!"

"What, you think I'm making this up?" he yelled. "He was IN THE CAR with me, Brewster!" He paused, surprised at Grady's silence. "Grady . . . look, I'm sorry," he apologized quietly. "I didn't mean to yell at you like that."

"No, Michael, I'm the one who's sorry. I just can't believe it, that's all. I'm not saying it didn't happen. It's just so outrageous. What was he thinking? What could be so bad that he—"

"There's not time for that now. I'll tell you all about it later. I just wanted to call you." Michael slid down onto the floor. He was dizzy again and chilled to the bone.

"Geez, buddy, are you okay? Where are the bullet wounds?"

Michael took a deep breath and closed his eyes. The booth was swaying around him. "One in my shoulder, the other under my ribs on my right side. I've lost a lot of blood."

"Now you listen to me. You get yourself to a hospital and I mean now! You can't fool around with this kind of—"

"I can't go to a hospital. I have to disappear for awhile. Elliot wants me dead. He *needs* me dead, man, and next time he won't miss. I'm not about to give him another chance. I had to get away as far and as fast as I could. I've stopped a few times to clean up these wounds but I'm not much of a doctor."

"Then find yourself one! It doesn't have to be a hospital. Pull off somewhere and find some small town clinic or—"

"But Grady, I can't leave a trail behind me. I can't stop, can't take any chances. I'll get help as soon as I reach my destination."

"Where are you headed? I'll hop on a plane and—"

"No, Grady. Don't. Stay right where you are. I need you where I can reach you once I get there."

"So where are you going?" An audible edge filtered Grady's voice.

"I don't want to say. They can't beat it out of you if you don't know."

"Are you crazy? Nobody's gonna come asking *me* about all this! You're not thinking rationally. You're being completely paranoid, Dean. Just tell me where—"

"No! I can't take that chance!" He shivered, trying to stay focused. "I'll call you in a few hours. I need time to think, time to figure out what I'm going to do. In the meantime, I need you to write this number down for me and keep it somewhere safe—89. It's the number of a locker at the bus station in Plainview, Texas. If anything happens to me, you give that number to the authorities and tell them where it's located. There's a lot of evidence in a packet there. Documentation, that sort of thing. But swear to me, you won't breathe a word of that to anybody unless something happens to me. Swear to me, Grady."

"Okay, okay! I swear. Do I need to go get it now? Are you there in Plainview now?"

"No, I'm not in Plainview. And don't even think of going after that yourself. Leave it to the authorities. And only if something goes down. I have the only key, so the police would have to order the postal employees to open it. Just promise me you'll pursue it, but only if something happens to me. Promise me!" Michael heard another frustrated sigh over the phone line.

"Fine. Whatever you say."

"Grady, my whole life is slipping out from under me . . . I don't know what to do. I just need to get somewhere safe so I can think. I need to think. That's all. I need to think . . ."

"Okay, Michael. Have it your way. I'm here for you. Just don't take so long to call me back. I want to hear from you again in a couple of hours, you got that?"

"I'll do my best. Hey, I'm sorry. I'm—" His voice cracked.

"Hey, don't go soft on me, man. You hang in there, okay? You can do it. I'm going to help you get through this. We'll handle Elliot. But you've got to *let* me help you. Okay?"

Michael swallowed hard. "Yeah, I will. I promise. Thanks, man."

He climbed his way up the wall of the phone booth and replaced the receiver. He fell against the door again, frightened by his weakened condition. *Gotta keep driving. Gotta get to Christine's. I gotta make it . . .*

He straightened himself as best he could, still cradling his throbbing right side. He slowly made his way back into his car then fell into the driver's seat. *Take more muscle relaxers. You're never gonna make it like this.* He grabbed the bottle of pills and poured several into the palm of his hand then swallowed them with a gulp of cold coffee.

Backing out the car, he rolled down the front windows with the press of a button. The arctic blast of air hit him like a brick of ice, awaking every sense in his body. He drove only a few miles before his shivering fingers reached for the automatic window button to close them.

The winding road beckoned him closer and closer to his refuge. Only a couple more hours and he could relax. Christine could find a doctor for him. She'd put him up for awhile, at least until he could come up with a plan.

Christine. Crazy Christine . . .

His delirious mind took a detour back to college. It was early summer following his senior year at Oklahoma State. With the College World Series only days behind him, he waited impatiently for the upcoming November baseball draft, hoping to land a major league contract. To stay in shape, he played on a local semi-pro team for the summer. His girlfriend had joined a group of friends on an extended graduation trip to Hawaii. Christine, her best friend, had planned to go but had to back out at the last minute when her father had a sudden heart attack.

Christine. Always the life of the party. She had one of those husky voices from too many years of cheerleading. He could still hear the contagious sound of her raucous laughter. But aside from her enormous popularity, everyone knew how close she was to her father. With Christine's mother deceased, her dad bought an apartment in Stillwater where he lived part of the year so he could be close to Christine while she was in college. Occasionally he would visit the family vacation home in Colorado, but when he wasn't traveling on business—which was most of the time—

he stayed in Stillwater. Christine loved having him close by.

So when Harold Benson had a massive heart attack, Christine was devastated. Michael became the shoulder she needed to cry on, the friend she needed to lean on. They had been good friends for years. After all, she was Annie's best friend. And with Annie and all their friends off in Hawaii, it was only natural for him to take care of her at a time like this.

Take care of her . . . at least that's how it began. Christine was falling apart, watching her father's life slip away. In a matter of days he was gone. And as she went through the motions of the funeral and all its demands, Michael was there for her.

The night after the funeral, Christine asked him to take her for a long drive out into the country. They iced down a few six-packs in a cooler and took off as the sun began to set. They had no destination. They drove until they were well into their second six-pack. With the subsequent need for a bathroom, they pulled off the road near Lake Keystone and like any respectable college drunk, headed into the woods to Mother Nature's "restroom" under the stars. Michael went back for the cooler and an old quilt he kept in the trunk of his Camaro. They walked down a moonlit path to a deserted beach.

They laughed and they drank. They sang old Beatles' songs and they drank some more. When the cooler was empty and the laughter died, Christine began to sob. Michael held her in his arms and let her cry.

And in a moment of quite unexpected intimacy, they

were swept away by their passion.

Even now, all these years later, it still made him feel uneasy. It wasn't like they'd intended for it to happen. It just happened. And in the days that followed, it happened again and again and again. Did he love her? Maybe. In a different kind of way.

And Christine? For her it was perhaps nothing more than a peculiar part of her grieving process. Michael had always known that. He was sure she loved him in her own special way. But she was a free spirit. The day before their friends were due back from Hawaii, she told him good-bye and took off. She offered some lame excuse of a possible job offer in New York, but Michael knew she was just making it easier for everyone concerned. Maybe she was right.

Everyone knew he had planned to marry Annie. After the draft, they would make plans and set a date for their wedding. Everyone, but *everyone* expected Michael and Annie to get married. For four years, they had been inseparable.

Until that summer. In four short weeks, everything had changed. Before, his entire world had been consumed with two things: baseball and Annie Franklin. Baseball was his life, and Annie was the love of his life. She was beautiful and funny and smart and amazing. And he had never even imagined his life without her.

But all that had changed. Maybe it was guilt. Who knows? Maybe he knew he could never face Annie—those four weeks with Christine hidden in his heart, buried forever like a burning secret. Or maybe he'd realized he wasn't ready to be tied down. He didn't want to wake up one morning and feel suffocated by the confines of marriage. After all, the scouts all predicted he'd go in the top five rounds of the draft. He had a career to think of. He'd be traveling constantly. This was no time to settle down. He had to be free to pursue his life-long dream to play major league baseball. Right?

It would be hard, but he could do it. He'd make a clean break with Annie as soon as possible. He'd try not to hurt her too much. Maybe they could still be friends once she got over the blow. *Yeah, Dean. In your dreams. You broke her heart and you know it.*

Suddenly, the blaring air-horn of a tractor trailer slapped Michael back to reality. He had crossed the middle line. He jerked the steering wheel, throwing his car into a radical spin. The semi flew past him with its deafening horn. By the time his brakes grabbed the snow-covered road and stopped the car, he was facing the blinding lights of the oncoming cars which had been following him a split-second before. He slammed his foot on the accelerator and jerked the steering wheel again. His Escalade flew off the road and into a deep snow drift.

One. Two. Three. Four. Five cars careened past him before they vanished into the darkness. Michael laid his head against the steering wheel. *When did it get dark? How long have I been driving in this stupor?* He looked at the digital clock on the dash. He couldn't even remember driving for the last couple of hours. *You idiot! How could you be so stupid!*

And then it dawned on him. The muscle relaxers.

He didn't remember how many he'd taken. He had no clue where he was.

Without warning, his body was wracked with pain. The initial shock of his blunder had worn off. Now his injuries reminded him how seriously hurt he was. The abrupt maneuvering to escape what surely would have been the death of him now pierced his shoulder and side. He was overcome with dizziness and fatigue. In his mind, he relived the sight of those headlights coming straight at him. That horn blaring down on him.

And again without warning, a severe nausea erupted in his stomach. He pushed the car door open just in time to splatter the pure white snow with the remnants of whatever was left in his stomach. He heaved until nothing more was left. He wiped his mouth against the sleeve of his good arm and tried to catch his breath. He climbed out of the SUV, careful to avoid where he'd puked.

The physical regurgitation was nothing compared to the rage that spewed from his soul. He cussed and cursed and screamed, his fury echoing off the silent darkness around him. For a moment, he stopped. He surveyed the position of his car in the bank of snow, the headlights casting two eerie tunnels of light through the white mound. Then he burst back into his uncontrollable frenzy of wrath, even more fiery than before. He damned everyone and everything he could think of, then repeated his tirade all over again.

With his anger finally emptied, he sat down in the snow

and fell back against the soft, icy cold blanket beneath him. He panted hard from his outburst, his breath forming huge puffs of fog that swirled away into the night. He was wiped out, the bullet wound in his side feeling like the white hot irons used to brand the cattle back in Texas.

"Oh God, please don't let me die."

Michael shook with raw fear as a brilliant light suddenly engulfed him. He opened his eyes only to shut them again against the glare of a bright wall of light. *Oh no . . .* "Oh God, no! Please! I don't want to die!"

"Hey! Are you okay, mister?"

Michael shielded his eyes against the lights. He could make out the silhouette of someone against the headlights of a vehicle. Relief swept over him as he tried to get up.

"Yeah, I'm fine. I lost control of my car and ended up in this snow bank." He was standing, wiping the snow off his wet clothes.

"Son, it looks to me like you're bleeding pretty bad there. Do you want me to go call an ambulance?" The stranger's face was still hidden in the blinding light, but Michael felt comforted by the kind tone of concern in his voice.

"Uh, no. No, that's okay. It's nothing serious. But I'd appreciate it if you could help me pull my car back out of this ditch."

"No problem. I've got a chain in the back of my truck. Just take it easy and I'll try to get it hooked up to your bumper."

The stranger went about the task as if he'd done it a thousand times. In no time at all, the Escalade was sitting back on the side of the road apparently undamaged.

"Are you sure I can't take you into town to see the doctor? You're bleeding an awful lot there, son."

Michael tried in vain to conceal his blood-soaked clothes. His sweats and jacket were soaked all the way through. He rubbed his hands together to warm them. "No, I'll be okay. I really appreciate your help. Except—do you happen to know where Weber Creek is? I'm not even sure I'm on the right road. Am I in Colorado?"

"You're only about five miles east of Weber Creek. I'll lead you to the turn-off if you'd like?"

Michael hesitated. "Well—sure. Thanks. At this point, that would be a big help. I really appreciate this. Can I pay you for—"

"No need. I wouldn't think of it, son. Just pass the favor on. That's all I ask."

Chapter 16

Seminole, Florida

Jessica appeared at the door of his study holding the phone against her chest. "Nana's on the phone, Daddy. She wants to talk to you. She's kinda upset," she whispered.

David took the phone from her, pressing the mute button on the receiver. His eyes silently communicated with those of his mother across the hall. She raised her eyebrows then turned her attention to her granddaughter. "Jessie, honey, why don't you come help me finish setting the table. We're just about ready to eat and I could use your help." She took Jessica's eager hand and steered her toward the kitchen.

David closed the door to his study while uttering a silent prayer to find the right words. He'd dreaded this call from his mother-in-law. "Hello Darlene, how are you?"

"DAVID! What's going on! Where's Annie? Why didn't

anyone TELL me she was leaving? Jessie just told me she's gone on a trip. WHAT trip? She didn't tell ME she was going on a trip! That's not like—"

"Whoa Darlene—hold on! Just calm down and let me explain. Don't get yourself all worked up, okay?"

"But David, why didn't—"

"It's all right. Really. Annie just needed some time away. A little vacation. Some time to herself. I think she—"

"What do you MEAN she needed some time to herself? Annie would never—"

David was fighting a losing battle with his temper. "Darlene, you've got to stop talking so I can tell you! Okay? Can you do that? Because there's no way I can begin to explain as long as you keep interrupting me."

David heard a frustrated sigh through the phone line. His mother-in-law detested any manner of correction directed toward her. She dished out plenty of it, but clearly couldn't take it in return. "Very well. I'm listening," she patronized.

"Apparently Annie has felt a tremendous burden lately, and I think the continuous stress we've been living under just caught up with her. The best thing for her now is to have a stress-free period of time when she can work through some of this and—well, I suppose, get her bearings back. The kids are fine. I'm fine. My mother is staying with us while she's away, so there's no need to worry. I'm sure this is going to do Annie a world of good. She's never had an extended time away just for herself since we've been married. I think you'd agree that sometimes we all need a chance to step away, take a good deep breath, and regroup."

David paused, searching for anything else he ought to say. He hated this.

"May I speak now?" Darlene snapped.

"Of course."

"Let's get one thing straight. Annie is MY child. I believe I know her better than anyone since I was the one who gave her LIFE." She addressed him as if he were five. "And if something was bothering MY Annie, I can ASSURE you, I'd be the first to know."

Oh Darlene, you have no idea. You are the last *person Annie would ever go to with her problems. You live in a fantasy land, believing you have the perfect mother/daughter relationship. Oh Lord, give me the right words here. Help me be kind but truthful.*

"Darlene," he responded as graciously as he could. "I'm sure you didn't know about any of this only because you've been away on your cruise. I'm sure Annie would have called you if you'd been in town."

Pause. "Oh."

David could almost hear the wheels churning in her mind as the realization slowly sunk in. Annie couldn't possibly have reached her.

"Yes, well, I suppose you're right. I forgot about my cruise. But David, when do you expect her back? Where did she go? I want her number. She isn't answering her cell."

"Darlene, she's asked us to give her the freedom she needs right now. She calls in, but we're trying to give her all the space we can. I promise when she calls tonight I'll tell her you called."

"David! WHERE IS SHE?!"

Her tone startled him. He wasn't used to being yelled at, even by his crazy mother-in-law. But he wasn't about to be drawn into a fight. Not tonight. He paused, then answered softly, "She didn't say. Good-night, Darlene." He placed the receiver gently back down on its console.

God, You are going to have to handle her for me. I don't know what else to do.

The door bell rang just as he stood up. "I'll get it!" Jeremy yelled. David hoped it was only one of the neighborhood children asking Jeremy or Jessie to play. He started to sit back again in his chair when someone knocked on the door to his study.

"Come on in," David answered. Jeremy opened the door. His eyes were wide as saucers.

"Jeremy? What's wrong?"

Jeremy closed the door behind him and sprinted over to his father. "Dad!" he whispered. "There're two cops at the door and they want to talk to Max! What should I do?"

David stood up. "Well, I supposed you ought to go upstairs and get your brother. I'll let them in."

Jeremy bolted up the stairs as David walked to the front door. "Hello, I'm Max's father, David McGregor. Come on in. Max will be down in just a minute. Please, have a seat." He ushered them into the living room wondering what this was all about. "Is there some kind of problem, officers?"

A tall uniformed policeman offered his hand as he

introduced himself, "Mr. McGregor, I'm Officer Todd Kelly and this is my partner, Phil Brantley. It seems there was a little trouble up at your son's school today and we need to ask him a couple of questions."

At that moment, Max came around the corner of the room, his hands buried deep in his pockets. David could tell by the sheepish look on his face that something was definitely wrong.

"Max, this is Officers Kelly and Brantley. They want to ask you some questions."

Max walked over to sit down on the arm of his father's chair. "Okay."

Office Kelly began, "We had a call from the Tall Pines Christian School today at approximately 4:00 p.m. concerning some alleged vandalism."

Max looked down at the knee of his jeans and began to run his finger roughly along the seam.

"A complaint was filed by one of the school's teachers, a Mr. Chet Harrison. Now this Mr. Harrison claims that a student by the name of Max McGregor destroyed the door to his classroom this afternoon following a heated discussion."

"It didn't happen anything like that!" Max cut in. He shot a look at his father. "Dad, I promise. It was an accident."

Officer Brantley interrupted, "Max, why don't you start at the beginning and tell us just exactly what transpired this afternoon."

Max described the entire scenario, beginning with the harassment from Mr. Harrison while class was still in session and ending with the shattering glass. He discreetly left out the

209

parting comment Harrison made concerning his mother. "And that's exactly how it came down. It wasn't 'vandalism' and I didn't 'destroy' the door, it was just an accident." He looked to his father, his eyes pleading for understanding.

"I think I can explain at least part of this," David began. "You see, I'm the pastor at Tall Pines Community Church. The school is a part of our ministry there on the church grounds. Mr. Harrison is a member of our church in addition to his teaching position at the school. Unfortunately, Chet has some bones to pick with me, and he's apparently allowed his personal grudges against me to carry over into the classroom. Max has told me about some of the problems he's had with Mr. Harrison in the past, and it's obvious now I should have done something about this before."

He put his arm around his son's shoulder. "I'm sorry, Max. I should've talked to Chet before it came to this."

Max looked up into his eyes. "It's okay, Dad. I shouldn't have lost my temper and slammed that door so hard." He looked at the policemen sitting across from him. "I'll pay for the broken window."

Officer Kelly responded. "It sounds as if this whole episode was just an unfortunate accident. Max, we appreciate your honesty. However, I think we may still have a bit of a problem. Mr. Harrison wants to press charges. That means unless you discuss this with him and he agrees to drop the whole thing, we will have to make an official arrest. But Pastor McGregor, under the circumstances, I believe we can give you some time to talk to Mr. Harrison and see if you can't work this out."

❧

Eagle's Nest

Hello-this-is-the-McGregor's-home-Jessica-speaking."

"Jessie? Jess, it's Mommy. How are you, sweetheart?"

"Mommy! Oh, Mommy, I miss you so much! When can you come home?"

"Oh, sweetheart, it's going to be awhile yet," Annie said, hoping to change the subject to evade any more questions. "How is everything with you, honey? How's school?"

"School is fine, Mom, but guess what? There's two policemen here and they're talking to Max and Daddy. I think Max must'a got in real big trouble!"

Annie sat up. "Jessie, what do you mean? What's happened? Did Max get a speeding ticket?" *Jessie must be confused. Max never gets in any kind of trouble.*

"I don't know, Mommy. They made me leave and come in here to the kitchen."

"Sweetie, I think I better speak to Daddy. Can you go get him for me?" Annie tried to sound as casual as possible.

"Sure, Mom. I'll go get him. Just a minute, okay?"

Annie felt another deep stab of guilt. *What am I doing out here in the middle of nowhere when—*

"Annie? I'm so sorry we missed your call last night. The kids were—"

"David, what's going on? Jessie said the police were there and Max was in some kind of trouble?"

"Honey, it's nothing to worry about. Max had a little

run-in with Chet Harrison at school today. That's all. And evidently Chet wanted to spook Max so he called the police. The whole thing is ridiculous. We've told the police exactly what happened and it's no big deal. I would tell you if it were otherwise."

"But what about Max? Did he get hurt? Is he all right?"

"Honey, I'm telling you—he's just fine. A little ticked off at his teacher, but no more than I am."

"Chet Harrison . . ."

"Yeah, that's what I said. It was Chet."

Silence.

"Annie, what is it? What's the matter?"

"Oh—I'm sorry. You know how I feel about Chet."

David softly chuckled. "I know how *lots* of folks feel about Chet. He's a challenge even on his best days." He paused. "Annie, how are you?"

She looked at her carefully wrapped foot propped upon on a couple of pillows. She truthfully felt no pain at the moment so answered, "I'm okay, I guess. I've had a lot of time for some serious soul-searching and that's why I'm here. But it's even more obvious to me now than when I came just how much I have yet to work through."

"I'm glad you're making some headway. But I miss you *so* much. I can't even begin to tell you how sorry I am, sweetheart. I've been such a—"

"No, David, please. That's not why I called. I really don't want to get into that now. We can talk about all of it when I get back."

"But I *have* to tell you. You need to know. I will do

whatever it takes."

"Honey, please. Not now."

"I'll walk away from this church if that's what it takes. We'll move if we need to. We'll find something—"

"I'm going to hang up if you keep this up. I'm not ready to talk about it!" She didn't mean to snap at him.

His weary sigh washed over the line. "Okay, okay. But if you hear nothing else, hear this. I love you, Annie McGregor. I *love* you." Hearing his voice quiver sent a bruising ache to her heart.

"I know. I love you too. But I know this is where I'm supposed to be right now. I have to do this."

"I just wish you'd let me come to you. I wouldn't interfere, Annie. I promise you that. I'd just be there with you. Help you in any way I can. I'd stay out of your way—hey, I can be your butler. How about it? You know, cook your meals, clean up for you—anything you need. What do you say?"

Annie couldn't help laughing. He sounded just like Jeremy when he was younger, begging for quarters to buy something from the ice cream truck. "David, I've got to do this alone. Please don't make it any harder than it already is."

"Then at least give me a phone number where I can reach you."

"No. Please stop this. Don't you see? I came here to get away from the pressures. *All* the pressures. If you keep this up, I'll have to stop calling." She hated the edge in her voice. "It's just important to me that you understand my need for this time alone."

"I know and I'm the one who's sorry. I won't pressure you anymore. At least I'll try not to. Just don't stop calling me. That would make *me* crazy. Promise?"

Annie sighed. "I promise, David." She wiped her nose on a Kleenex. "Let's change the subject. Is everyone else all right?"

"Everyone else is fine. We're getting by, I guess. Mom's been great. Oh—speaking of moms—"

"Oh no."

"I'm afraid so. Darlene called again. And poor Jessie—she didn't know any better. She told Darlene you'd gone away and—well, you can probably figure out your mother's response."

"Don't tell me. I don't even want to know." She could imagine her mother's reaction practically word for word. "That bad, huh?"

"Yeah, that bad. But we've stalled her as best as we could. I'm sure she'll come exploding in here any time now. But we'll handle her. I've had years of practice when it comes to dodging Darlene."

Annie smiled but didn't comment.

"Annie, I'm—" He paused.

She knew he was struggling. "David, I've got to go. I'll call you tomorrow. Give my love to Jeremy and Max and Jessie. Oh, and Caroline too. Thank her for me, okay? For everything. And tell Max I'll be praying for him." She felt her throat tighten. "I love you, David McGregor."

"I love you too. Take care, sweetheart."

Annie slowly hung up the receiver. Her eyes tracked toward the crackling fire. Out of the dancing flames rose the sneering face of Chet Harrison. He threw his head back in an evil, mocking guffaw. Her mind replayed the exchange she had tried so hard to forget. It was, after all, the final straw. The scene rolled through her mind like a forbidden video.

"Mrs. McGregor!"

An invisible shiver crawled down her back at the sound of the familiar voice. She continued pushing the cart of groceries to her van, hoping and praying that voice and that man wouldn't follow her.

No such luck.

"Why, Mrs. McGregor—you wouldn't be ignoring one of your fellow church members now, would you?"

"Oh hello, Chet." She opened the rear door of her van and began to load her groceries.

He had purposefully wedged himself between her and her cart, hindering her task. She could hear him jangling the change in his pockets as he seemed to inch even closer. It was an annoying habit, his trademark. To maintain her "safety zone" she backed up until she felt the bumper press against the back of her legs.

She put her hands on her hips. "Chet, do you mind? I'm a little busy here, okay?"

"Why, am I bothering you? Have I done something to upset you?" His feigned innocence pushed her blood pressure through the roof. "You know I would never do anything to upset my pastor's lovely wife, now would I?"

"Chet, it was nice seeing you. A real pleasure, as always. But if you'll excuse me, I'd like to get these groceries home before the ice cream melts."

He moved in even closer. "Oh, I can assure you the treat

was all mine, Annie. Everyone is always telling me what a fine, friendly Christian woman you are and I thought this coincidental little meeting of ours would be just the opportunity for me to find out how friendly you really are. See if you really are as nice as they all say. Especially to someone like me who's not one of your husband's favorite deacons. In fact, I've even heard it said he considers me his 'thorn in the flesh.' Now, why do you suppose he would say something like that? Or maybe I should ask you. Am I a thorn in your flesh?"

She tried to estimate the distance between their noses. Four? Maybe five inches? Definitely too close. "I have no idea what you're talking about Chet," she said casually, shoving him out of her way and forcing the cart between them. "I think you'd better go." She turned her back to deposit two more bags into the van.

"Oh, come now, Annie. You don't mind me calling you Annie, do you? A pretty lady like you probably has lots of men around town calling you all sorts of things."

Another chill raced up her back. She turned to face him, forcing an indifferent expression on her countenance. "Do you have something to say, Chet, or are you just trying to harass me?"

"Well now! Aren't you just the sassy little wench?" His suggestive chuckle arced between them as he drew even closer. "Spirited—ooooooh, I like that in a woman. Oh, I bet you and our fine pastor have some pretty naughty times together behind closed doors, don't you? Why, I'd wager a feisty little thing like you knows just how to—"

She slapped him across the face. Stunned, Harrison reeled backward, his hand protectively guarding his cheek.

Annie teetered dangerously close to the edge of control. "You pathetic excuse for a human being! You may have fooled everyone else, but you don't fool me. You parade around like some pious, holier-than-thou saint, but you're nothing but a fraud, Chet Harrison. You're a despicable hypocrite—I know it, you know it, David knows it—and God sure as hell knows it!"

His face crimsoned, his eyes narrowed. His hand curled into a fist as he lowered it from his face, his entire body shaking. She'd never seen him so angry. Her heart raced as she grabbed the rest of her groceries. Suddenly, Harrison grabbed the cart and hurled it as hard has he could, sailing it across the parking lot. It crashed into a shiny red sports car setting off the security alarm in a piercing shriek.

"Have a nice day, Mrs. McGregor," he hissed, casually walking away as if he hadn't a care in the world.

Too angry to cry, Annie's chest heaved as she fought to slow her breath. She walked toward her cart as it slowly rolled backwards. Fortunately, no visible damage was done to the convertible. Her hands trembled as she searched for a scrap of paper in her purse and wrote down her name and number to leave for the owner in case he wished to contact her. The alarm wailed on as she headed back to her car towing the cart behind her.

David never heard about the incident. When he had returned home that evening, it was after midnight. The two-year-old child of a young couple at church had tragically *drowned in the family pool that afternoon. The teenage baby-sitter, having a fight on her cell with her boyfriend, did not realize the child had wandered outside. David had remained at the hospital with the devastated parents until they made the decision to pull the life-support plug on their brain-dead child.*

He arrived home emotionally and physically drained. Any lingering anger Annie may have harbored toward Chet Harrison was immediately buried deep inside. That bitterness would have to be resolved some other time. It seemed so trivial at a time like this. She felt only the purest heartache for these grieving parents.

Still, as selfish or childish as it may seem, she couldn't release the fact that David, as always, was available to minister to everyone else in need, but had no time or emotional strength left for the needs of his own family—trivial or otherwise. He had no clue of the pain in his own home.

It had happened only days ago. Annie had tried to pray about it, hoping to find some forgiveness in her heart with God's help. Instead, the smoldering anger from that encounter had burned incessantly, along with the sting of unintentional neglect from David. In the days following, she couldn't bring herself to tell him. As always, he was too overwhelmed with everything else that was going on. It was as if the heartaches and illnesses and tragedies within the church family and within her own heart were snowballing faster and faster.

But Annie had sensed for quite some time that there was more to it than that. Up until the last few months, she had never given serious thought to the possibility of spiritual warfare. The whole subject had always been rather obscure to her. A little frightened by it, she avoided any study on the concept. Yet, deep inside, she knew there were factors involved beyond the superficial. Too many attacks from too many different angles to be mere coincidence.

Yet, every time Annie's thoughts drifted into that spiritual arena, she felt uneasy, like she was tiptoeing into dangerous waters. She resisted the urge to think about it further. Not now. Not like this.

God, your silence is filling me with fear. I don't understand it. I want so much to work through all of these things with You. But everything is wrong. At home, here— everything! I need you to answer me!

Chapter 17

Weber Creek, Colorado

After trailing along behind the stranger's truck, Michael made his exit on the side road, waving to the kind man who had helped him. The heater in his car was turned on high, but Michael couldn't stop shivering. His clothes were soaked. He was freezing. He refused to take any more medication after his near-accident, though the pain was excruciating. Mostly, he feared the weakness sweeping over his body. He could hardly keep his eyes open.

Michael had been to Christine's cabin once before a few years ago. In the area while on a ski trip with several of his former Astros teammates, he had slipped away in a rental car to make a surprise visit. After getting directions in town, he made his way to her cabin only to find it locked up tight and no sign of Christine. He left a note wedged in the door but never heard from her.

Now, as if driving in a slow-motion dream, he remembered the way up to her mountain. He drove up the twisting snow-packed road grateful for the powerful strength of his four-wheel drive. His breath came in shallow, anxious pants, quickly steaming up the windshield. Normally pristine about his automobiles, Michael made messy, careless swipes on the glass leaving broad, wet smears that only blurred his vision worse.

Unspoken prayers drifted through his mind in fragments. *Oh God, please help me.*

He came to another fork in the road and instinctively knew which way to turn. Heavy eyelids impaired his vision, but he sensed the cabin was near. Michael slowed to a stop, the windshield wipers beating a frantic rhythm against the quiet hum of his engine. He backed up the car to aim his headlights at the entrance of a driveway. A large stone mailbox boasted shiny brass numerals but no name. Then he spotted a slate sign hanging from a log post. It flew wildly in the blustering wind making it impossible for Michael to read. Then, in the briefest of moments, the wind died just long enough for the sign to right itself.

Eagle's Nest

Private Property

Overcome with emotion, tears rolled down Michael's cheeks. His breathing puffed faster now as he willed himself to go on. The Escalade crunched carefully over the long, snow-packed drive that climbed gently higher. At last he made a final turn, the cabin appearing like a mirage before him. A sob caught in his throat as he stopped the car and turned off the ignition. And yes, there were lights glowing through the windows and a trail of smoke rising from the great stone chimney.

She's home! Christine will help me now. I'm safe!

Every movement made his head swim. His left hand shook wildly as he reached for the door handle of his car. It took every ounce of his strength and determination to turn his body toward the door. He shoved the door open with his left foot, ducking down against the gust of snow that blew in.

"Christine . . ." His shout was little more than a whisper.

He curled his body around his bleeding right side and took careful, agonizing steps around the car.

Please God, just a few more steps . . . help me!

He peered up just enough to see the cabin sway from side to side. *The house is dancing. Why is Christine's house dancing? I don't hear any music . . .*

And with that strange, whimsical thought puzzling his fevered mind, he collapsed in a heap of snow.

శ

What was that?

Annie jolted out of a dead sleep, her eyes darting around the room. A moment later, a pair of lights traveled across the room followed by the sound of a car's engine.

Who would it be at this time of night? Doc?

She noticed the fireplace, a low flame skirting along a smaller pile of logs. Annie checked her wristwatch. Eleven forty-five. *Doc Wilkins wouldn't come back to check on me this late at night.*

The sound of an idling engine, much closer now, interrupted her thoughts. She started to stand up then remembered her foot. Straining to reach for the crutches beside the sofa, she fumbled them awkwardly in her attempt to stand up. Once she got her balance, she slowly hobbled toward the window.

She held back the curtain enough to peek outside. The wind swirled the heavy snowfall in a wild dance in front of the cabin. Parked a few yards out in the driveway was a large dark automobile, its headlights still beaming. She cupped her hand against the window pane. The onslaught of snow made it all but impossible to detect any movement.

A shiver fingered Annie's back. Torn between a sense of danger and an unsettling curiosity, she debated what to do. What if someone was in trouble and had stopped by for help? Then again, what if it were a prowler or some other kind of criminal? Here she was—all alone out in the middle of nowhere.

She limped on her crutches to the front door, stealing another look through the curtains. She reached for the light switch and turned on the porch light. Still nothing. No movement outside. Only an idling car.

Wait—the driver's car door stood wide open. The hairs on the back of her neck lifted. Annie ducked out of sight, clinging to the rustic log wall beside the door frame. Her heart rate accelerated to match her fear. *What should I do!*

God, please don't be silent any longer. I'm all alone and I'm scared!

Before she uttered the last words of her hushed prayer, she sensed the warm familiar presence surrounding her again. Her heartbeat slowed. She felt strangely calm, knowing without question God was with her.

Something drew her outside. Someone out there needed help. She knew it, felt it in her soul. She unlocked the deadbolt and the regular lock before opening the large wooden door. The brisk snap of cold air caught her breath, but she continued, slowly pushing open the screen door with the end of her crutch, and feeling somehow propelled to move out into the darkness.

The chill of the wind blew right through her as she made small, careful steps with her crutches. Nearing the edge of the porch at the top of the steps, she stopped cold.

Someone was lying in a heap at the foot of the stairs.

Annie dropped her crutches and reached for the banister. Clumsily hopping down the steps as quickly as she dared, she finally reached the body crumpled in a mound of snow. The car lights offered little help, shining off into the dark wintry woods like two misguided eyes. Annie dropped down to sit on the last step. She reached out her hand then pulled it back, uncertain. Gathering her courage, she stretched it out once more to see if this body was still alive.

He was sprawled face down in the snow. Annie tapped

his back. "Hello?" There was a slight movement, a shifting, then a hand attempting to respond. She reached for the hand, trying to gently grasp the wrist. The pulse was barely detectable but it was there. Even in the darkness she could tell it was a large hand, ice cold and lifeless.

"Mister? Can you hear me?" She leaned closer, firmly tapping his right shoulder. He screamed, recoiling from her touch. He curled into a ball, his head tucked deep into his shoulder so that she couldn't see his face. His whole body jerked and trembled as he groaned in obvious, horrible pain.

"I'm sorry! I didn't mean to hurt you! Please, can you hear me? I need to get help for you—"

The left arm shot out, searching for her. "Christine—don't!" his whisper, hoarse. "No help . . ." The stranger shivered in spasms, curling tighter.

"I'm not—" Annie began, then paused. *This must be a friend of Christine's. Obviously not a criminal, just a friend who's come looking for help from Christine.* "Look, I just want to help you. We've got to get you inside. Can you help me get you up the steps?"

She got up, moving closer to him, hoping for a better angle to help lift him. "C'mon, now—try to crawl your knees up under you so we can stand you up. Take it slow and easy—that's good. Try to get your feet underneath you."

Their progress was slow but sure. Annie put his left arm around her shoulder as she balanced on her good foot. "Okay now, just lean as much of your weight on me as you need to. I'll try to pull you up. That's good. Here we go . . . take it slow.

"Whoa!" His weight overwhelmed her as he gradually stretched to stand beside her. Even doubled over with pain, she could tell he was a big man, tall and muscular. The trip up the steps would not be easy. Her foot protested with every step.

"That's it—we're almost to the first step. We'll take it slow. Just don't give up on me, okay?" She grimaced from the sharp pain in her ankle feeling woozy each time she had to put the slightest weight on it. She forced as much of their shared weight onto her other foot as possible.

The stranger lifted his head, resting it in the crook of Annie's neck. She still couldn't see his face. He was struggling to say something.

"Christine, don't . . . call . . ." His breath was warm against her ear. "No police, Christine. Promise . . . they're trying . . . he shot me."

Annie's eyes flew wide. A shot of adrenaline coursed through her veins, moving both of them up the remaining steps at a much faster pace.

She tried to keep her voice calm. "Just don't talk. We're almost inside. Just a few more steps now, here we are. " Her mind raced. *Should I call the police? Should I even be taking this man inside? Are there people out there even now coming to kill this stranger?* They crossed the threshold and Annie reached back to slam the door and bolt it.

He tried to speak again, his words escaping in short, breathy gasps now. "Please, Christine . . . don't . . . tell anyone I'm . . . he'll kill me . . ." And with that he passed out, collapsing onto the floor and throwing Annie off balance. She landed awkwardly, sprawled across him, the wind knocked out of her.

Carefully lifting herself off him, she realized his clothes were soaked all the way through. She could only see the back of his head, but his hair was drenched as well. Tiny drops of water dripped off the ends of the dark brown tendrils covering his head.

Annie sat back, panting hard but relieved to be off her injured foot. She peeled the wet sock off her other foot and rubbed her ankle, closing her eyes. *I need to wake up. This has to be another bad dream. Has to be.* She massaged her neck and shoulders and tried to make some sense of it all.

She opened her eyes and looked at this lump of a predicament before her. She felt something sticky on her hands and was startled to find his blood on her palms. The sight of it put her back in motion. There was no time to lose. Crawling across the floor to the kitchen, she pulled open a drawer full of wash rags and hand towels. She pulled herself up on the cabinets and threw the linens into the sink under running water. After quickly squeezing out the excess water, she hopped across the floor, grabbing a pillow and quilt off the sofa. She worked quickly trying to pull off his saturated jacket. She gasped, seeing the large patch of blood clinging to his sleeve.

No wonder he screamed when I tapped his shoulder! Oh God, tell me what to do here!

She had to get him onto his back. He obviously had another wound that was seeping all over the floor. "Okay, mister—I'm going to roll you over on your back now. Just take it easy."

Annie stood beside him, carefully turning him over while lodging the pillow beneath his head. Her eyes locked on the grotesque blood stain covering his entire right side.

"Oh God! What do I do?" Instinctively, she began peeling the sweat shirt away from his skin to find the wound. She discovered a massive bandage soaked with blood. Easing her fingers gently along its edge, she began to take it off. A hideous black wound festered with infection.

She scrambled backwards at the sight of it, gagging against the bile filling her mouth.

Burying her face in her hands, she leaned back against the wall.

God, what am I going to do? This man needs a doctor or he's going to die!

The thought slammed into her mind. Maybe he was already dead.

Annie sobbed, her hands knotted against her mouth. She squeezed her eyes shut as tears cascaded down her face.

Please, Lord, help me!

Slowly, she sucked in enough breath to quell the involuntary sobs. Still trembling, she leaned over to take a good look at this stranger. His head was turned away from her. *Who are you?* Gently pushing the wet hair from the side of his face, she felt a burning fever on his skin. Shaking her head with the helplessness of it all, she reached for a clean rag to wipe his face. Turning his head slightly toward her, she finally got a better look at his face.

Annie froze.

It can't be . . .

She felt a vacuum suck the air from her lungs. She threw herself back up against the wall, ignoring the pain in her foot, her eyes glued to this face of a thousand memories. And even as she stared at features once so familiar, he uttered an unconscious groan, his head slowly falling in her direction.

Her heart stood still. She slid down the wall behind her. A single tear escaped her eyes as his name fell silently from her lips.

Michael . . .

Chapter 18

Eagle's Nest

Dr. Wilkins?"

"Yes? Who's calling?"

"This is Annie McGregor," she answered, her voice catching.

"What's the matter, Annie? What's wrong?"

Annie paused, cupping the end of the receiver in her other hand. She couldn't control the trembling of her hands, much less her voice. "I . . . he—"

"Who? What are you talking about?"

She couldn't speak.

"Annie, are you all right? Has someone come up there? Who's 'he'?"

"It's . . . he's hurt. Hurt really bad. I think . . . I think he's been shot."

"Shot!? Who's been shot?"

Annie turned around, afraid to look at the still form splayed on the hard wood floor of the entry way. "It's . . . please, Dr. Wilkins! You have to come quickly! I don't know if he'll make it if you don't."

"Annie, are *you* all right? Are you in any danger, dear? Should I call Sheriff—"

"No! No, don't call anyone! I'm okay. It's someone I know. Just please *hurry,* Dr. Wilkins!"

"I'll be right there, Annie. Now, just calm down. I'll be right there."

Annie limped carefully on one of her crutches, backing up to the wall again. She could hardly breathe, her eyes riveted to the body stretched out before her. Were it not for the uneven rising and falling of his chest, she would have thought he was surely dead.

"Michael, what happened to you?" she whispered.

As if in response, he jerked, screaming out in pain. "Don't tell them! Please!" he cried, coiling once again to cradle his injured side. "He's trying to kill me . . ."

Annie was at his side, reaching out to touch his forehead. Finally, she laid her palm against his brow, frightened by the ravaging heat she felt there. "Michael, you're burning up with fever. Oh God, help me—I don't know what to do!"

He wagged his head in delirium, haunted by whatever nightmare he was living. The moaning wore on, staggered only by his effort to breathe. "You've got to hide me. Don't let them . . . "

But he was again incoherent, his lips moving silently.

His torment broke her heart. Overwhelmed with helplessness, she forced herself to gather the blood-soaked towels and hobble over to the kitchen. She rinsed out the cloths, sickened by the crimson trails of water swirling in the sink. After filling the dishpan with cold water, she headed back to her patient. She wrung out a wash rag and began gently patting his troubled face. She continued, hoping the cool cloth would relieve at least part of his suffering. With her other hand, she carefully pushed his hair back out of his face, her fingers combing through his thick dark hair.

A strange mix of sadness and fear etched Michael's face. She paused, pulling back her hand, uneasy with the odd feelings accosting her. *This can't be happening. After all these years* . She tried to dismiss the thoughts, rinsing the washcloth again. Folding it lengthwise, she laid it gently across his forehead, then sat back, her eyes wide in disbelief.

Moments passed until she heard a car pull up outside. She pulled herself up, making her way to the door. Rushed footsteps clomped up the steps followed by a rapid knocking. "Annie! Where are you?"

She threw open the door. "Oh, Dr. Wilkins, thank God you're here!"

He stepped inside then stopped abruptly. "Good heavens, what happened?" He dropped down beside the still figure.

Annie shook as she cried. "You have to save him, Dr. Wilkins! Please don't let him die. You can't let him die— "

"Now, listen to me." He grabbed her arms. "I don't know

who this is, but it's obvious he's lost a lot of blood. His color is bad. I need your help. You've got to pull yourself together and help me if we're going to save him. Can you do that?"

She pulled in a ragged breath and wiped her tears with the back of her hand. "Yes, yes I'll help you. I will—just tell me what to do."

"Good girl. Now, we must work very quickly. Our first job is to get him up on that kitchen table."

❧

What's the matter?" Annie asked, disturbed by the troubled sigh of the doctor. He stood over Michael after making a thorough examination. It had been no easy job for them to move him from the floor to the long, pine table in the kitchen. The jostling aroused some weakened moans from Michael, but nothing more.

"The bullet I can remove. But my concern at this point is his loss of blood. We've got to get some fresh blood into him. You wouldn't happen to know his blood type, would you?" he mused out loud.

Annie looked up, her eyes widening. "Yes, I do. He's O-negative. The same as me—O-negative."

"Are you absolutely sure? How could you possibly know that?"

"Michael is—he's an old friend from college. And I remember once going together to one of those blood drives on campus. We thought it was odd that we were both O-negative. Everyone teased us about being sister and brother instead of—" She paused. "The thing is, Michael and I were engaged. A long time ago."

"You don't have to tell me anything more. If you're absolutely sure he's the same blood type as you are, we can get this started right now. We don't have much time."

"I'm positive. I mean, negative. Oh, you know what I mean."

Doc Wilkins smiled briefly at her unintentional humor. "All right, I want you to have a seat. When was the last time you had anything to eat?"

"I don't even remember, to tell you the truth, but I'm really not hungry—"

"Maybe not, but I can't have you passing out on me. So I want you to drink some orange juice and—" he continued, looking quickly around the kitchen. "Here, eat one of these muffins. Go on now. Don't argue with me. We don't have time." He pointed to her hands. "But give those a good scrub first."

She lathered her hands at the sink then rinsed then in hot water. Taking a seat at the table, Annie took an oversized bite of the muffin, trying to eat as fast as she could. She was surprised, watching the swift moves of the elderly doctor as he put together a makeshift system to transfer Annie's blood directly into Michael. She finished her hasty snack and washed it down with orange juice, just as Doc reached for her arm, thumping it for a vein. Satisfied he found one suitable, he tied a rubber strap above her elbow.

"Here we go." He inserted a needle into her vein. "You can relax your fist now." He monitored the process with extreme efficiency. Annie was relieved at his competency.

"You may be a small town doctor, but you work like someone who's spent his entire career in a big city hospital," she said quietly. "I'm impressed."

"It may be a small town, but trust me, I've seen it all. When you're the only physician around, you see a little bit of everything. Births, automobile accidents, cancer, you name it. Not to mention lots of skiing mishaps. You just never know what a day will bring along."

Annie was starting to feel light-headed. "But not too many shooting victims."

"No. Not many. Though I remember a freak hunting accident a few years back. Ol' Jeb Townsend and his son Cooper were out turkey shooting. Along the way they got separated and ended up on opposite sides of a clearing. Ol' Jeb spotted a great big tom out in the middle of that clearing and fired off a shot, never realizing Cooper was directly in his range. Filled Cooper up with 180 pieces of buckshot."

Dr. Wilkins leaned over Michael, checking for a response. He seemed satisfied for the moment.

"Did he die?"

"Who?"

"Hi son, Cooper. Did he die from the buckshot wounds?"

"No, he pulled through. Quite a miracle. That many pellets and not a single one hit any vital organs or arteries. We took out as many of those pellets as we could. Left in what we had to. Fortunately, Cooper's stayed around here. Otherwise, he'd probably set off airport security systems from here to eternity."

"His father must have felt awful."

"Oh my, yes. Ol' Jeb was a basket case 'til he knew for sure Cooper would be all right. I'll tell you one thing for sure—that's one father and son who are mighty, mighty close now. Never saw anything like it. Incredible."

"That's a nice ending to the story."

"Annie? Are you getting queasy on me?"

"A little. I think I'll rest my head for a moment if that's okay with you."

"No problem," he answered, looking over his glasses at her. She put her head down on her other arm. After a couple of moments, he asked quietly, "Annie?"

"Yes?"

"How did Michael get shot? Any idea?"

She turned her head sidewise, still resting it on her forearm. Her eyes traveled slowly from Doc to Michael. Even as her gaze took him in, she felt her heart skip a beat. So many memories, so many feelings, and far too many emotions. It all came flooding back into her mind and her heart. She shook off her thoughts to answer Doc.

"I don't know. We haven't talked in years. I can't even imagine." She felt a drowsy smile pull at her mouth. "Michael always lived life right on the edge. He could be quite the daredevil at times. But the thing is, he got more breaks than any one human being should be allowed to have. Maybe his luck just finally ran out."

"Did he say anything to you?"

"He kept mumbling about someone trying to kill him.

He thought I was Christine. I guess he came here looking for a place to hide . . . though I didn't know that Michael and Christine were . . ." Her thoughts drifted.

"Were what?"

She hesitated, ignoring his question. "Obviously, he's in some kind of trouble. It's been such a long time since I've seen Michael. After we—well, we haven't spoken to each other since college. Occasionally I've seen him on TV, of course. He used to play baseball. First base for the Houston Astros."

"Ah. That's why he looks so familiar. I'm a Cubs fan myself, but Michael Dean was quite a celebrity a few years back. He could crack a bat like the best of them. I lost count of all those years he was MVP for the National League. Great ball player."

"Incredible ball player," she added, her thoughts traveling the gracious distance of time. "I used to love watching him play back when we were together. Never missed a game."

A few moments passed. "Annie?"

She snapped out of her thoughts. "Yes?"

"I'm still concerned about your safety. Whoever shot your friend here could still be out there, you know."

"I know."

"Do you know anything else about him? Does he have a family? Where's he been living? That sort of thing."

"No, only bits and pieces. I heard he was married to the daughter of someone famous. Some actor or—I just can't remember. And to be honest, I've tried very hard *not* to keep track of him."

"I see." Doc finished the procedure. "All right, that's about all you can spare right now. You okay?" He looked up at her while pressing a cotton ball to the tiny hole in her arm.

"Oh, I'm fine. Not even dizzy any more."

"Well, keep your seat there for a few minutes. You'll be light-headed when you stand up again."

He moved back to the kitchen sink to run more hot water. "Once we get Mr. Dean all fixed up, I think we need to move his car into the garage. Might be best to keep it out of sight."

"I'll take care of it," she offered.

"You'll do no such thing. I can do it myself. You just keep an eye on your baseball player for me. He's going to be with us for awhile," he continued. "If the weather wasn't so bad, I'd try to pack him up and drive him over to the hospital in Pueblo, but it's too far and we can't take that chance. We could lose him if we ran into even the slightest problem along the road. So we'll just have to do the best we can."

He dried his hands then began setting out the instruments he would need from his bag. "Let's get started."

Three hours later, Doc helped Annie to her room, insisting she get some rest. They had moved Michael to the guest room where he seemed to be resting comfortably. Doc was able to remove the bullet that had lodged in Michael's shoulder fairly easy. But the abdominal wound was another story. He found no bullet there and surmised that it had evidently grazed Michael's side, just passing through, but doing a substantial amount of damage in the process. Fortunately no internal organs were damaged, but the infection had spread. He estimated the wounds to be at least a day old.

"Are you sure he's okay?" Annie asked, climbing into bed.

"His pulse has steadied and his blood pressure has stabilized. Right now we need to let the antibiotics do their work and help his body begin to heal." He tucked her in, turning off the bedside lamp.

"If Michael wakes up—"

"If Michael wakes up, he'll see the face of an old doctor who's sitting by his side watching his every move. Now, you get some rest."

"Doc?"

"Yes?"

"Do you think there's someone out there?"

Annie heard him exhale before answering. "I don't know. I'm going to pull Michael's car into the garage and take a look around. Then I'll be in his room if you need me. Once the sun comes up, I'll have to make a quick run down to my clinic. I don't have enough medication to keep him adequately sedated for the duration of his recovery. I'll pick up some supplies and come right back."

He walked over to the window. "Storm's getting worse."

"Do you think you should go now? What if you can't get out in the morning?"

"I need to stay with Michael for the next couple of hours or so. You go on and get some sleep."

Annie yawned. "I don't know how to thank you."

"No need. That's what I'm here for." With that, he closed the door quietly behind him leaving her alone. For the first time since this nightmare began, she heard the howling of the wind outside. Though the cabin was warm and secure, she felt a chill pass from her head to her toes.

Who would want to you kill you, Michael?

As tiny pellets of ice and snow tapped against the window pane, she fell into a restless slumber.

Chapter 19

Eagle's Nest

Annie?"

"Huh?"

"Are you awake?" A soft knock on the door followed Doc's question.

"Sure, come on in," she answered, still half asleep. The room was still dark. "What time is it?"

He walked over to the bedside chair and sat down. "It's coming up on six o'clock. Sun won't come up for another hour. Still snowing mighty hard out there."

All at once she sat up, her mind suddenly clear. "Is Michael okay?"

"Yes, he's fine. He's resting. Thrashed around a bit, mumbled a lot, then dozed back off. Best thing he can do is sleep right now."

Annie leaned back against her pillows. "Do you think he's going to be okay? Can he make it if we don't get him to a hospital?"

Doc stretched his arms over his head. "Oh, I think he'll pull through, if that's what you mean. He'd recover a lot faster in a hospital, but I'll do my best to see he gets the care he needs. I need to make that trip down to my office. Think I better bring a back-up generator up here in case the power goes out. I know for a fact Christine never got one. Never saw the need since she's gone so much during the winter months.

"I'll stock up on pain medication and supplies for our patient in there. Not a lot we can do for him but we can at least keep him comfortable. I put what medication I have left on the top of the dresser in his room. There's plenty for the time being. If for any reason I don't get back before he wakes, you can certainly administer it to him. I wrote out some instructions in case that happens. Will you be all right?"

"I'm fine. I'll go sit with him while you're gone."

Doc made his way for the door. "I shouldn't be gone long." He pointed toward the window. "The wind just started kicking up again and it's snowing pretty hard, so I'll try to get back as quickly as I can. You sure you'll be okay?"

"Go. I'm fine."

He stopped at the door, his back turned to her. "Listen, Annie," he paused looking over his shoulder. "I'm going to pay a visit to Sheriff Patterson while I'm in town."

"No! Dr. Wilkins, please don't do that!" Annie sat up,

clutching the comforter around her.

He turned back around to face her, his hand held up to stop her protests. "Now just listen to me. You or I neither one know what Mr. Dean has gotten himself into. We don't know if those are criminals who shot him or if he's running from the law."

"But Doc—"

"It's my responsibility as a physician to report this kind of injury. I need to at least let Patterson know I've got a patient with gunshot wounds up here."

"Please don't say anything! At least not until Michael wakes up and can tell us what happened. He's not going anywhere. If we find out he's done something wrong, we'll do the right thing. I promise you. But please don't tell anyone else he's here. I'm begging you."

He stared at her long and hard. Finally, he rubbed his hand over his face. "I suppose it won't hurt to wait awhile before going to the sheriff. If those gunmen had followed him, they would have barged in here by now. I don't know how Michael made it up these roads, let alone anyone else. Besides, if they're some kind of law enforcement officers, they'll go to Sheriff Patterson themselves."

Annie relaxed, sighing again. "Thank you."

"Just promise me you'll keep the door locked and won't open it for anyone but me. Understood? I'm still concerned that whatever trouble Mr. Dean has gotten himself into may eventually follow him up this mountain."

"Don't worry. I'll be careful."

"You better be. Good nurses are hard to find around these parts, especially when they're as pretty as you." With a wink of his eye, he was gone.

&

"NO! Don't shoot! Oh God, don't let him shoot me!"

Annie jumped from her chair. "Michael! It's okay! No one's trying to shoot you." She took hold of his left hand and held it firmly in her own. His breathing was rapid, his mind surely reliving a scene Annie didn't want to think about.

"Shhhh, you're safe here now. No one's going to hurt you. Just take it easy." His eyes were open but focused somewhere far away. He slowly relaxed, his breathing gradually easing back to normal.

His face glistened with perspiration. She found the ceramic bowl of water Doc had set on the bedside table and reached for the wash rag floating in it. Wringing out the cold water, she began carefully patting the damp cloth against his face.

"Oh, Michael, what have you done?" she whispered. She brushed aside his hair surprised to find it peppered with strands of gray. *How odd. In my mind, you never aged at all.*

She continued wiping his face with the cool cloth, finding herself drawn to study his ruggedly handsome face. *The years have been kind to you, Michael Dean.* The lines and creases of age had only helped to define his good looks. Despite the trace of fear still locked in his brow, she noticed a collection of tiny laugh lines around his eyes. *Sculpted from that perpetual smile of yours, no doubt.* She caught herself smiling, remembering his wonderful sense of humor.

A wistful chasm of time pulled her back to a day long ago.

Michael had just led his college team to win the conference title by hitting a grand slam home run at the bottom of the ninth. Through the wild celebration on the field that followed, he kept searching the stands to find her—waving, bouncing into the air, dancing in wild circles, laughing like a crazy man. She made her way down to the field along with their horde of friends. When Michael finally spotted her, he flew across the infield, catching her as she jumped into his arms.

"Annie! We did it! We won! We're going to Omaha! We're going to the College World Series!" He spun her around and around until she begged him to put her down.

"You won it! Your grand slam won the game! You were AMAZING! Michael, you won it!"

"Annie, we've got to celebrate! Oh, baby, I love you!" He took hold of her face with both of his hands and kissed her hard. He pulled back, grabbing her hand as he headed for the celebration out on the pitcher's mound, whooping and hollering at the top of his lungs.

Before she knew what was happening, Michael leaned over, lifting her up onto his shoulders then parading all through the crowd of his teammates, coaches and friends. A reporter pulled Michael aside for an on-air interview. Michael conducted himself with complete attentiveness, as if doing so with a girl on his shoulders was the most natural thing in the world. Annie couldn't stop laughing. She could only imagine what they must look like—a double-decker scoop of ice cream on a cone in constant motion.

After the usual questions, the reporter asked, "Michael, what are your plans for the future? Can we look for you in the majors next year?"

"You better believe it. I hope to go first or second round in the draft, I'm gonna marry this beautiful woman, and play major league ball!"

It was a moment in time forever captured in her heart, like some favorite movie that would be played over and over again.

An eternity ago.

Suddenly, the room darkened, awaking Annie out of her thoughts. A weak glow from the snow-covered landscape outside began to filter through the curtains offering the only source of light. Annie's heart pounded in her ears. Had the storm knocked out the power? Or was someone out there? An eerie silence filled the cabin.

"Doc, please hurry," she whispered.

She tiptoed across the bedroom floor with the aid of her crutches putting as little weight on her swollen ankle as possible, then peeked out into the great room. Steeling her courage, she made her way into the kitchen and looked out across the room. Everything still in place, she hobbled toward the front door to check the locks. Both were secure. *Thank God.* Then she realized what was missing. No hum of the refrigerator. No digital clock glowing the time on the microwave. *The power's gone.*

Unaware she had been holding her breath, Annie felt her eyes sting. Limping back to the front window, she peered outside, careful not to rustle the curtains.

The storm unleashed its fury. Annie had never seen anything like it. It was dark as night with thousands of angry white flakes swirling in a mad frenzy. Then, as if in sudden orchestration, a wall of powder shifted to pound against the cabin. She wrapped her arms around herself and prayed. *Oh God, why now? Why couldn't this blizzard hold off until Dr. Wilkins got back?*

Startled by the unexpected ringing of the phone, Annie jumped, the air exploding out of her lungs. She reached over to pick up the receiver, not at all surprised when her voice wouldn't budge.

"Annie? Are you there?"

"Yes," she croaked. "Yes, I'm here. The phone just startled me, that's all. Dr. Wilkins, where are you? The power's gone out!"

"I know. That's why I'm calling. Apparently this whole side of the mountain is down. I've got a back-up generator here, but I'm sorry to say I didn't get one up to you in time. How's Michael doing?"

"He's still sleeping, but I think his fever is still awfully high. How long until you can be back?" Annie felt her heart sink at the pause on the line.

"Well, now don't worry—"

"Doc, Michael *needs* you," she urged, fearing what he was about to say.

"I'm afraid it's going to be awhile. The road is out. Some

fool trucker tried to beat out the storm. Came flying through town and missed the curve in the road. It was a logging truck—he was hauling a full load, too. You've never seen such a mess. It knocked out our transformer that sits a good twenty yards from the road. That's why we've all lost power. The road is completely shut down. We'll have to wait until the power company can send some trucks over from Canon City, and in this weather, who knows when that will be. I'm sorry, Annie. There's just no way for me to drive up there."

"But surely there's some other—"

"No, I'm afraid not. You've got to remember, you're sitting up on top of a mountain. There's nothing but a steep wilderness all around you. I've hunted up in that area my whole life, and I can assure you, it's not a place to be in this kind of weather. This is quite a storm, even for this neck of the woods. Wind this strong, snow this heavy—it can be a deadly combination. And it won't do you or Michael any good if I'm off in a ditch or down a ravine."

"But what are we going to do?" Annie pleaded. "I don't know how to take care of someone in Michael's condition! He needs *you*."

"Now, don't sell yourself short. What Michael needs most right now is lots of rest. All you have to do is try to keep him comfortable. And if you run into any trouble, all you have to do is call me. I don't expect these phone lines to go down so there's no reason we can't stay in touch. Besides, I don't have to remind you that you aren't alone. The Lord is fully aware of your situation—and Michael's too for that matter. He'll keep you safe.

"Annie, are you still there?"

"Yes. I just wish the Lord would give me a break. This is the last thing I need." She felt a rush of impatience. "I came here to get away. I needed time to think. And now look at this—this whole ridiculous situation. After all these years, at the worst possible time in my life, God dumps Michael on my doorstep. And if that wasn't enough, He has to go and dump a blizzard on us, too! Now I'm the one stuck having to help Michael. Michael Dean! Of all the people on the face of the earth, why did it have to be him?"

She suddenly realized she was shouting at the phone. Shouting at Doc Wilkins, no less. She buried her face, frustrated and embarrassed. She tried to stifle her sobs as she heard the quiet voice coming through the telephone line.

"Annie? It's okay, dear. I think maybe there's a whole lot more here than just a bizarre series of coincidences."

She sniffled, wiping her nose with the back of her hand. "What do you mean?"

"Well now, I don't have a clue about what it is you ran away from—"

"I didn't run away!" Annie snapped, immediately sorry. She knew she should apologize. He was absolutely right.

Doc continued. "I knew the minute I met you over at Williamson's that something was burdening you. Doesn't take a psychologist to know when someone is in that much pain. And you've alluded to it just about every time we've crossed each other's path. I haven't wanted to pry. Thought you needed your privacy.

"But under the circumstances, with what's happened in the last twenty-four hours, I would have to assume the Lord may be trying to tell you something. Sometimes He allows the strangest events to befall us just so He can get our attention—"

"Yeah, well He already *had* my attention," she interrupted. "I laid all my cards on the table. I poured it all out and left it as His feet. And I was waiting on Him for some—some kind of guidance. Some answers. Anything! But He just disappeared on me! I begged for answers and He totally turned His back on me."

"But that's exactly what I'm trying to say," Doc answered patiently. "You may think He deserted you when in fact all these circumstances may hold the very answers you've been searching for all along."

Silence drifted across the line. She knew he was waiting for a response.

"Annie, what I want you to do is go sit down by Michael's bedside and just relax. Make sure he's okay and take some time to get a hold of yourself, all right? Then try to get your thoughts organized. You'll need to make some preparations because it could get mighty cold up there if this power is down for as long as I think it will be. Put some more logs on the fire. I left a good supply of them on the hearth for you, and there's a whole rack of them out in the garage as well. You'll also find a Coleman stove out there. Better bring that in so you can heat up some soup or stew or something. Make some tea. Michael is going to need some good food once he wakes up. Then I want you to find some lanterns, some candles, dig out some more blankets and quilts—that sort of thing. That's a lot to do with that ankle of yours but you've got to do it anyway.

"I'm going to see what I can find out on this end and I'll call you back in a little while. Don't worry—I'm not going to leave you stranded up there a minute longer than I have to."

Annie resigned herself to the situation. "I know. I'll be fine." Her voice sounded husky. "And I'll make sure Michael stays comfortable."

"That's more like it. If you have any questions, just give me a call. If I'm not here, leave a message on my machine. I'll talk to you soon."

❧

Houston, Texas

Eliot approached the open door of his office, hearing a familiar voice inside.

"Helen, any word from Daddy?"

"Who's that wanting to know where her daddy is?" He strode through the door to his office, noticing his daughter sitting behind his desk, his secretary handing her a cup of coffee, and Duke sitting in an armchair.

Amelia stood. "There you are."

He dropped his brief case on the floor and made his way to her, taking her into his arms. She hung on a second longer than usual. He pulled back enough to look into her face. The facade didn't fool him.

251

"Would you like some coffee, Congressman?" Helen asked. "I just brewed a fresh pot."

"No, thank you. Duke, Helen, would you give us a few moments together?"

"No problem," Helen responded, heading for the door.

Duke stood up. "But Elliot, we have some very important details to discuss, if you'll recall."

"It'll have to wait."

"But I've *been* waiting. We had an appointment and you're late as it is."

Elliot turned to face him. "I believe I asked for some privacy with my daughter, and I would appreciate it if you would follow my very intelligent secretary and leave us alone."

Duke huffed as he turned to go. "Can I expect to hear from you when she's gone?"

"Of course," answered Elliot, slamming the door behind his departed associate. "Now, sweetheart, what's the matter? Come, have a seat. You look upset." He escorted her to the couch. She sat down, warming her hands around the cup of coffee.

"Daddy, he's still gone. No phone call, no note, nothing. He's just gone. Jane hasn't heard from him either and I'm—"

"Now, just hold on," he interrupted, sitting beside her. "You know Michael. He gets a little restless now and then. He probably took a trip out to California to see some of his buddies or. . . who knows, maybe he's trying to do some business behind my back." He laughed easily. "Michael is always trying to outfox me. Trying to prove himself, I suppose. He's probably on some 'secret' mission. He'll show up in a day or two. Don't worry."

Amelia stared at her father. "Daddy, I'm his *wife*! Don't you think he would tell me if he left on a business trip? Or even . . . even if he was going to see some of his old friends, don't you think he'd at least tell me he was going?"

"I don't know, would he?"

"Daddy!" she scolded.

"Well, you said it yourself—you're his wife. Don't you two ever talk? You're still living in the same house, aren't you?"

Tears filled her eyes as she stood. "Are you mocking me? I came here to talk to you because I'm scared and angry and—how can you talk to me this way?"

He stood up to comfort his daughter, but she pulled away from him, crossing the room to look out the huge bank of windows. He followed her. Massaging her shoulders, he spoke quietly. "Amelia, I didn't mean to upset you. I just think it's time we began to take a long, hard look at your marriage and make some sort of assessment. Michael has changed. You know it and I know it. He's not the hungry, eager-to-please son-in-law or husband anymore. Somewhere along the line, I suppose he decided he's done all this on his own, made this company a success all by himself. Made himself an awful lot of money. And maybe, just maybe, he doesn't think he needs us anymore."

Amelia dropped her head, giving in to the comforting hands of her father. "But Daddy, I still love him. And the more he seems to pull away, the more I need him. The more I want him."

Elliot walked back to his desk. "I should have known from the first time we met Michael Dean that he'd eventually hurt you. A celebrity athlete like him? They're all alike. They feed on all that attention, then they can't live without it. I thought he'd be content owning a successful business. Apparently I was wrong."

Amelia remained where she was, her back to her father.

"And we have to be very frank here, sweetheart. There's always the possibility he's seeing other women—"

"No!" she bellowed, spinning around. "He wouldn't do that. He loves me! I know he does. He's just distracted right now. That's all. And you've got to help him, Daddy." She paced the floor. "You have to hire more people to take the pressure off of him. Get someone else to take all these business trips. Get Duke to do it—he obviously has nothing better to do. Make Duke run all over the country and give Michael time to be at home with me. Time to come back—"

She broke. In the anguish of her tears, she sank down onto the couch, burying her face in her hands. "Oh, Daddy, what am I going to do? I can't go on without him."

He returned to her side and wrapped his arms around her. "Nonsense. I won't listen to that kind of talk. Do you hear me?"

"No, I'm serious. I can't make it without him," she whispered. She looked up at her father, the tears streaming down her face. "I can't live without him, Daddy."

Torn between the deep love he felt for his brokenhearted daughter and the growing fury burning inside him toward the one who caused her this pain, Elliot groped for the right words. Blinded by his own masquerade, he wanted nothing more than to end her sorrow. For a brief moment, he fantasized . . . there he was, consoling Amelia, much as he was now. Standing above an expensive casket covered with a blanket of flowers as it was lowered into the ground. He held her, the grieving young widow dressed in black, as she watched her deceased husband laid to rest.

"Daddy, why are you smiling? How can you be happy at a time like this?" Her irritation hung between them.

Elliot caught himself, quickly reverting to his guise as the concerned father. "I'm not happy, sweetheart. Just thinking of brighter days ahead for you. And I'm sure you'll get through this just fine." He found his place behind his desk and continued. "Here's what I'll do. I'll find out where Michael is."

"Do you really think you can find him?"

"Of course, I can, honey. Are you forgetting who your daddy is? Just give me some time and I'll track him down. For the meantime, you stay busy. Get back to work on that benefit and don't be running in here every five minutes wearing me down about it. Understood?"

She flew into his arms. "Oh thank you, Daddy!"

"Enough!" Handing her the designer purse, he guided her to the door. "Don't be thanking me until I find him, all right? And stop worrying about him. I told you before—I'll take care of Michael. You just wait and see."

With a new assurance, she smiled and kissed his cheek before leaving.

As the door closed, Elliot cursed. He walked back to his desk and sat down, slamming his fist on the dark cherry desktop.

"So how many lies did you tell her this time?" The door slammed behind Duke as he barged into the office.

"Shut up, Duke."

"Elliot, we can't let this thing drag on. Sooner or later Amelia's going to find out and she's going to hate you—"

"I said shut up!" Elliot dug his hands deep into his pockets and slowly walked over to the window. Standing precisely where Amelia had stood moments before, he swore again under his breath. "If we eliminate him now," he began quietly, "we risk the chance that his mysterious 'evidence' will surface later. We'd be naturally linked to his disappearance or murder and we'd both hang."

Duke shifted in his chair, coughing.

"But if we wait much longer," he continued, "we risk him beating us and taking his so-called evidence to the authorities. And still, we hang."

"We find him now and force him to hand over the evidence. We don't take *any* risks," Duke responded.

Elliot remained silent.

The ringing of Elliot's phone broke the tension in the room. He hesitated then moved to answer it. Noticing the flashing red light on his private line, he stole an inquisitive look at Duke.

He picked up the receiver. "Yes? Yes, this is Elliot Thomas. Who's calling?"

Elliot sat down in his chair, turning it around to leave Duke's wondering expression behind him. He said little, only an occasional "yes" or "no" or "I see." After what seemed like an eternity, he turned his chair back around.

And laughed out loud.

Placing the receiver back on its cradle, Elliot released a long sigh of relief. "Duke, my boy, we have nothing to worry about. No sir, nothing at all."

~

Eagle's Nest

Confident that Michael was resting as well as could be expected, Annie ventured into Christine's kitchen, attempting to collect the provisions she would need. Shaking off her fear and aggravation, she hobbled around the kitchen, opening the door to the oversized pantry. She gathered whatever she could find that didn't require cooking, collecting her choices into a laundry basket which she placed on the kitchen counter. Realizing she hadn't eaten in hours, she opened a box of cinnamon toaster pastries. She took a bite and headed to the great room to add more logs to the fire.

Thankfully, Doc had restocked the pile of chopped logs on the far side of the hearth. She awkwardly crafted another stack of logs and girdled it with kindling to produce a comforting, blazing fire.

Snatching the box of pastries, she tottered back to Michael's room. She reached for a couple of blankets stacked on the pine love chest at the foot of his bed and spread them gently over Michael's still form, careful not to disturb him.

Annie stopped, steeling another peek at her unexpected guest. Resting her palm on his forehead, she was disappointed to feel the relentless heat there. Repeating the ritual with the cool wash cloth, she let the prayer drift from her lips. *Don't let him die, God.*

As if on cue, Michael began moaning, his head jerking from side to side. "No . . . please . . . NO!"

She sat beside him on the bed. She watched in silence as he thrashed about against some unseen enemy. Somewhere locked in that nightmare was a threat that haunted her as well. She reached for his hand, taking it between both of hers.

"Shhh, Michael, you're all right," she murmured. "Take it easy. I'm right here beside you. No one's going to hurt you now." She prayed he couldn't hear the tremble in her voice. Gradually, he stopped the unconscious struggle, appearing to respond to her soothing words. His expression relaxed.

"I promise not to leave you," she whispered. "I promise."

Chapter 20

Seminole, Florida

I don't care what you say, Caroline! I have as much right to be here as you do, so just stay out of my way! Annie is MY DAUGHTER in case you've forgotten. And I won't be treated like an outsider! Now where is David?"

Darlene stormed past Caroline, who stood flabbergasted beside the kitchen table. She had barely finished putting away the dishes when the blond tornado blew through the back door.

Darlene spun around and took off for the staircase. "David! Come down here at once. I want to talk to you and I mean to do it right now!" she yelled, planting her hand on the banister. "Oh, for heaven's sake, Caroline. Where is he?"

"Darlene, if you'll just give him a minute, I'm sure he'll be right down."

"Then what's taking him so long?"

"He was trying to get some rest. Just calm down."

Her jaw dropped. "Well, isn't that just precious. His wife is missing and he's taking a NAP? Well, he's not anymore, if I have anything to say about it! DAVID McGREGOR, you get yourself down here this instant or I'm coming up! Do you hear me?"

"I heard you the first time, Darlene." David rubbed his eyes and started down the stairs.

"How in God's name can you sleep at a time like this? David, YOUR WIFE IS MISSING! My sweet Annie is MISSING! She could've been kidnapped for all we know! She could be in terrible danger! And you just lie around the house and SLEEP? What's the matter with—"

"Darlene, calm down!" he shouted, removing her knotted fists from his face. Both mothers stopped cold at the tone of his voice.

Darlene jerked her wrists free of his hold. "How DARE you talk to me that way!"

David stared at her. He ran his hand through his hair, then reached out to embrace her in apology only to be rebuked.

"Don't come crawling to me for forgiveness! I don't want your righteous little acts of pity. You hung up on me and don't think I have forgotten it! I want to know where my daughter is and I want to know RIGHT NOW!"

"Darlene, we don't *know* where she is or we would tell you!" Caroline pleaded.

Darlene scowled at her. "You stay out of this, Caroline! You lied to me when I called you yesterday. Evidently it runs in the family." Her eyes shot back at David. "Either you give me some answers right this minute, or I'm calling the police. And don't think I won't! I have friends on the force, you know!"

Suddenly, all three of them realized a presence in their midst. Simultaneously, their heads turned upward to the top of the stairs where Jessica was sitting on the top step. Tears pooled in her wide, frightened eyes, her lower lip trembling.

"Jessie—" David bound up the stairs two at a time. In one fluid motion, he scooped her into his arms. She wailed in her father's embrace. "Daddy! Where is Mommyyyyy? Who took my mommy? I want my mommyyyyy!"

He hushed her cries, gently rocking her in his arms as he took her seat on the top step. "Jess, it's all right. Mommy's just fine, honey. I talked to her on the phone last night. She's not in any danger at all, okay? She's away on a little vacation, remember? No one has harmed her," he reassured, peering over her head at Darlene. His eyes dared her to keep silent.

"Well, you can all pretend that everything is rosy and ignore the situation until you rot and die for all I care! My daughter needs me and I'm going to find her if it's the last thing I do." Darlene held her head high, turning her attention to her granddaughter. "Jessie, your mommy is NOT all right. Your Daddy has no idea where she is. And if HE doesn't care enough to try and find her, then you can certainly count on ME!"

Suddenly, she was propelled around and found herself escorted toward the front door. "Caroline! What are you doing?!"

"Darlene, get out of this house and *stay* out! You are no

longer welcome in this home. Is that clear?" She threw open the door. Then, in a whisper coated with contempt, "Get. Out."

Darlene stood motionless for a split second before grabbing the door handle out of Caroline's hand. In a storm of defiance, she slammed the door behind her.

"Oh my goodness!" Caroline gasped, her hands flying to her face. She turned, searching for her son. When their eyes met, she could only stare at him in disbelief. "I've never spoken to anyone like that before in my entire life!"

A hint of a smile pulled at one side of his mouth as he winked at her. The smile disappeared as he kissed his daughter on the top of her head, holding her tight.

❧

Hey, Seth. Is Megan home?"

"Yeah. Come on in. Boy, has she been in a rotten mood. You guys have a fight or what?"

Max followed the thirteen-year-old into the kitchen, the scent of fried chicken wafting through the door. Megan ignored him, focusing on the contents of the cast iron skillet. He dug his hands deep into the pockets of his jeans and walked over to her.

"Megan, I'm sorry."

She turned a chicken leg over. It sizzled in protest.

"Please give me a chance to apologize. I was horrible yesterday. I'm really sorry."

She wiped her hands on a dishcloth and turned

around. "Max—" she started only to stop again. "I don't even know how to respond to you. You said you're sorry and I believe you really mean it. But what happens next time? You hold your temper with everyone else, but when we're alone, you make no effort to restrain it. I just don't understand that at all. And it scares me. It scares me a lot."

She moved away from him, clearing dishes off the counter. He knew she was right. Every word she said was true. Problem was, he didn't know what to do about it.

He leaned against the kitchen table. "It's like—I feel like I always have to do my best. In *everything*. I have to behave all the time, make the best grades, be the best athlete—all of it. I'm so afraid I'm going to embarrass my parents or my family, y'know? It's like I have to be so careful all the time.

"But when I'm with you, I feel like I can just be myself. I feel safe. Like I don't have to worry because I know you'll still love me regardless of my grades or my athletics—or even who my dad is. Any of that stuff."

Megan put some dishes into the dishwasher. "So what are you saying? You feel comfortable with me? Like I'm an old pair of tennis shoes or something?"

He detected a slight smile on her face. "No, I was thinking more like a faithful puppy. Y'know, kinda cute and cuddly."

Seth opened the refrigerator. "I'm puking here. Do you mind?"

"Seth, get lost. I'm talking to your sister."

"'I love you like a puppy, Megan!'" Seth mimicked as he left the room. "Gag me."

"Have you ever thought of selling him? I'm sure there's

somebody out there who needs a munchkin with a big mouth."

"Not a bad idea. Look, I'm done with this," she said, lifting the last piece of chicken out of the skillet. "Why don't you go out in the back yard. I'll be right there."

A few minutes later, she joined him in the tree swing, handing him a glass of Coke. "Sorry about Seth. I think he's happiest when he's torturing me."

"It comes with his age. He can't help himself." He sipped his drink then smiled.

Megan leaned back in the swing. He rested his arm along the top of it gently squeezing her shoulder.

"So have you forgiven me or what?"

She looked across the yard, avoiding his gaze. "This isn't a joke, Max. It's serious. We have to work through this. We have to learn how to handle our relationship when you get upset about something. I don't want to be your punching bag any more."

"I never punched you! I would never do that!"

"No, but you know what I mean. I'm talking about using me as a *verbal* punching bag. Taking your temper out on me. It's not right. I want to always be here for you, but I don't want to be on the receiving end of your fury every time Mr. Harrison or anybody else gives you a hard time. It's got to stop."

"I know, I know. You're right."

She turned to face him. "Max, I love you with all my heart. And I want to be your best friend. But please— promise me the next time you get angry, you won't make me your target. I'll be here for you. And you can share anything with me. You surely know that by now. Just don't push me away. Let me help you work through it." She reached for his hand. "All right?"

Max felt a lump the size of a baseball in his throat. He wasn't sure he could speak. Looking into her eyes, his heart pounded against his chest. He set his Coke on the ground beside them, then took her into his arms. "I'm so sorry I hurt you. Don't give up on me. I don't know what I'd do without you."

"I'll never give up on you," she whispered. She sat back in the swing resting her head against his shoulder. "Talk to me about your mom. What's going on?"

He pushed his foot against the ground, setting the swing in motion, then looked directly at her. "I don't know how we're going to do it, but we're going to find her. We've *got* to find her."

❧

I think I've got it!"

"Got what?" Max cradled his phone while checking his digital clock. It was after eleven. "And Megan, why are you whispering?" He stretched out across his bed, his cell phone lodged against his shoulder.

"A way to find your mom. I think I know a way to access the files at the phone company! We can trace her calls!"

"You can't just call up—"

"Max, just be quiet and listen to me," she scolded gently.

"She's not using her cell phone so you can't just—"

"Listen to me!"

"Okay, okay! I'm listening!"

"Good. Remember Denton, that guy my mom dated last year? The one with the Harley? "

"Yeah, the one who was always taking her on trips. Nice guy. Why'd she ever ditch him?"

"She didn't ditch him. Anyway, he still calls now and then because they're still friends. So guess who called after you left?"

"Um, give me a second here, I'm thinking."

"Max, this is really important! I remembered that Denton works for the phone company. So I asked him if he could help us and he said he could check your records and easily trace the number your mom's been calling from!"

He sat up. "He can really do that?"

"Yes! I gave him your home number so he could look up the records. He said he'll call me back as soon as he knows anything. And he promised not to mention it to my mom or anybody. He said he could get in a *lot* of trouble so we have to keep our mouths shut. I think he really wants to help. And just between you and me, I think he's hoping I'll put in a good word about him to Mom. The guy's hopelessly in love with her."

"This is awesome! Call me when you hear something, okay?"

"I will, Max. But be sure not to say anything to your dad or your grandmother."

"I won't. And Megan?"

"Yeah?"

"You're incredible."

Megan laughed. "I know. You' just now figuring that out?"

Chapter 21

Eagle's Nest

For Michael Dean, an urgency laced with raw fear would no longer allow him to sleep. Fighting to drag himself from the depths of the vast black abyss, he called on every ounce of will he possessed. Slowly, slowly . . . not unlike a swimmer stroking his way toward the surface of the water, he found his way. With a final surge of strength and determination, he broke through the barrier, his eyes flashing open.

Gasping, he lifted his head from the pillow only for a millisecond before the pain in his side knifed a reminder of his injuries. His head fell back on the pillows. He cursed his weakness. Michael looked around, taking in his surroundings. He had no clue where he was, but he felt oddly at ease. There was something nagging at him inside his soul . . . something wrong, yet a quiet calmness in not remembering what it was.

A mound of quilts kept his body warm, though his arms were exposed above the covers. A shiver raced across him. *Why is the room so cold?* Abruptly, he sensed he was not alone. His eyes darted far to his left. Out of his periphery he could see someone's feet covered with blankets and propped up on an ottoman. He swallowed, letting his eyes trail up the body until—

Annie?

Seeing her, the realization hit him. *Of course. I'm still asleep. Or unconscious.* Amused at himself, he let a lazy smile crawl up the side of his mouth as he mumbled. "Dreamin' . . . still dreamin' . . . "

"Michael?"

His eyes flew open.

"Michael! You're awake!"

He blinked at her.

"Michael, you're awake!" she cried out again.

He stared at her, disbelieving. "Annie?" he croaked.

She threw off her covers and moved to his side, grasping his hand in hers. "Oh Michael! I wasn't sure if you'd—" Her eyes pooled with tears as she reached to touch his face. "Oh thank God! Your fever finally broke. You're okay!"

I'm obviously hallucinating. Can't be right. Can't be—

He felt a wet kiss on his cheek.

"I'm so glad you're all right. I prayed so hard! And look at you—you're really alive!" She laughed, gulping back a sob in the process.

"Annie?" He whispered her name again. "Where am I? Why are you here? I don't understand—" He tried to sit up, the pain shooting through his side again. "Ahhhh! What the—"

"Careful, take it easy. You've got some nasty wounds. Don't try to sit up."

Panic washed over him. "What kind of wounds? What are you talking about?"

Her eyes met his. "Gunshot wounds."

The words lingered mid-air. He searched her face while his mind raced through the obstacles of his memory.

"Michael, you've been through a lot. Don't try to make sense of everything just yet. There will be plenty of time—"

"But where am I? Is this your home?"

Her face broke into a nervous smile. "No, I don't live here. This is Christine's cabin. Up in the mountains of Colorado, remember?"

His eyes remained locked on hers, searching for meaning. "Christine?"

And then the veil lifted. Thoughts pounced his mind all at once. It all came rushing back. Elliot. The gunshots. The muscle relaxers. The long, exhausting drive from Texas.

Fear instantly replaced confusion; he gripped a wad of quilts. "Annie, you've got to help me." He threw the covers back. "I've got to get out of here. Help me get up and get my clothes on. Hurry!"

She grabbed both his wrists, pinning them to his sides. "Stop it, Michael. Listen to me! You're in no shape to go anywhere. Now just calm down and sit still, will you?"

"Annie, I—"

"No! You have two gunshot wounds. The one in your

side was seriously infected by the time you got here. If Dr. Wilkins hadn't made it up here in time—"

"You called a doctor? No! That's the *worst* thing you could have done!"

"He saved your life, you big ox!" she yelled back, planting her hands on her hips. "You'd be dead by now if he hadn't operated on you! He's just a country doctor. He's hardly going to place a call to *America's Most Wanted*." For heaven's sake, Michael. What did you do anyway? Rob a bank?"

His eyes narrowed at her question. The fight with Elliot replayed vividly in his mind. The flash of his gun . . . the echo of his own scream . . . the grinding wheel spinning in the dirt as he slammed his foot to the floorboard. He shivered and tried to refocus on Annie.

"Michael? What's the matter? What is it?"

Once the tremor passed, the fatigue began to swallow him again. Too many facts muddled his mind too soon. He looked toward the windows as he spoke. "It's a long story, Annie." He sighed. "A long story."

She paused a moment, moving in his line of vision to search his face. Her brow knit with concern as she busied herself smoothing his covers. "I'll let you in on a secret," she began. "There's a blizzard outside, the power has been off for several hours, and the roads are impassable. No one is within miles of this place. And since you and I are the only ones up on this mountain, I figure I'm a captive audience. So why don't I get you something to eat and you can tell me all about it. The way I see it, we've got all the time in the world."

A sense of reassurance emanated from what she said and the tenderness he saw in her face. For the first time in days, he felt safe. At least for the moment. He reached out for her hand and squeezed it, unable to express the deep gratitude he felt in his heart.

అ

The wind offered an eerie serenade as the snow continued to fall. The once warm and cozy cabin was now chilled to its very foundation. The glow of the oil lantern on the bedside table dimmed as nighttime once more stretched across the hidden horizon outside.

Michael spilled the bizarre details of his story to Annie. She listened intently, stunned by the frightening reality of his account. When at times he grew weary, she would make excuses to give him time to rest. She made frequent trips to heat water for tea using the old Coleman stove. When Michael expressed a hint of hunger, she warmed some chicken soup. Through it all she remained calm on the outside, caring for his needs while trying to mask the growing sense of terror as she listened to his tale. Her unspoken prayers for protection and wisdom flowed with every breath.

"I remember pulling into the drive here and seeing the lights on, but that's all," he finished, taking another sip of tea.

"That's because you passed out head-first in the snow at the foot of the porch. You scared me to death, Michael. I peeked out the window and all I could see was a car with its headlights on and the driver's door standing wide open."

"My Escalade! Where is it?"

"Doc pulled it into the garage once we had you stabilized. Don't worry, no one could have— "

The phone sliced through her reassurance. Annie reached for the receiver. "I'll bet that's him, even as we speak."

"Hello? Yes! Dr. Wilkins! He's awake!" She watched Michael's face cloud with concern with each piece of information she relayed to the doctor.

When she hung up the phone, he questioned her before she had a chance to speak. "Annie, how long have you known this man anyway?"

"Only two or three days, I guess, but—"

"But nothing! For all you know, he could be in touch with the local cops. He could be feeding them information—"

"No way. You've got him all wrong. He promised not to tell anyone and I trust him. He's a Marcus Welby, y'know? So relax about him, okay? He's the least of your worries."

"Why did he call just now?"

"Because he hadn't heard from me. I had promised to call him and when you woke up, I just forgot." Annie stopped, her hand covering her mouth. "Oh no—I forgot to call David. He'll be worried sick! I haven't called him since you got here."

"Who's David?"

"My husband," she answered as if he should know. "I promised to call him and it's been—I don't even know how many nights it's been since I've called him. He must be so upset."

She scrambled around the room in confusion before

landing back in her chair and reaching for the phone. "I can't believe I forgot to call him," she mumbled, dialing the phone. She stopped. Her eyes slowly tracked to Michael's. Then, with a heavy sigh, she put the phone down.

"Why are you looking at me like that?"

"I can't call David. What would I tell him? 'Oh hello dear, sorry you haven't heard from me but an old boyfriend showed up on my doorstep with a couple of gunshot wounds and now we're snowed in together?'" Her eyes grew wide as the implications ran through her mind. "No. No I can't tell him. No way. It just sounds so . . . so—"

"Unbelievable?"

"Unbelievable. That's right. Who would believe such a story?" She placed the phone back on the bedside table and bundled up again in her quilts. "I mean, this is crazy. Who would ever think, after all these years, that you and I would—I mean, it isn't like we *planned* this or anything. But then it would still look a little—"

"Annie, stop. Just take it easy. Besides, you're making me dizzy, and it's freezing in here. Can't you check and see if the power will come back on or something?"

She focused on him again. "You can forget about the power coming back on. Doc said an accident took out the transformer. It could be days before they get it all cleared and get the power restored. The road is completely blocked. That's why he can't get back up here to check on you. Most of the phone lines are down. I'm surprised he got through."

"Well, there you have it."

"Have what?"

"When this is all over just tell your husband the lines went down in the storm."

She looked away from him, remembering a time he could once read her mind.

"Annie, you still haven't told me what you're doing up here."

She felt her face heating. After a moment, she tossed off the quilts again and reached for her crutches. "We've got to get you out of that bed. The only way to keep you warm is to get you near the fireplace. So pull yourself together. This won't be easy."

≈

The move into the great room exhausted Michael—slow and painful, but worth the effort. Annie built a roaring fire which quickly warmed the oversized room. The soft glow of candles scattered around them cast a peaceful, quiet ambience and filled the room with scents of bayberry and vanilla.

But Michael never noticed. Once comfortably settled on the sofa, he fell into a deep sleep. His soft snores fell in rhythm with the crackling of the blaze on the hearth and the persistent howling of the wind outdoors.

Annie found it difficult to sleep despite her fatigue. Her chair and ottoman pulled alongside Michael's make-shift bed, she gazed at the man tucked safely under quilts and blankets, his head resting against a mound of pillows. She tried to understand the trepidation she felt from hearing his incomprehensible story. She tried to understand the agitation she experienced at remembering she had not called David . . . and now *couldn't* call him. She tried to understand it all.

And she tried to understand the strange beating of her heart caused by the man sleeping on that sofa.

❧

Michael awoke. He had no idea how long he had slept. Annie sat close by, her head turned as she stared into the fire. The golden glow outlined her features, dancing off the long, wispy curls of her shining brown hair. *She's hardly changed at all, even after all these years. She's even more beautiful than before. Amazing.*

A tiny glistening sparkle appeared on her cheek. He blinked, unsure he had seen it, until the sparkle began moving down her face. Her eyes clenched shut as she began to rock gently back and forth.

He reached out to touch her hand. Annie turned to look at him. She wiped her face with the quilt that enveloped her.

"Michael," she whispered, pulling her hand back. "How long have you been awake?"

"Long enough."

She stole a hesitant glance in his direction. She tried to smile through the remnant of her tears, then began twisting her hair up off her neck.

"Leave it down. I always liked it down."

She stopped, her hand in mid-air, then let the brown

trusses fall back down. She dropped her head, unable to look at him. "Michael, please. Don't."

"It's not like we're strangers," he spoke barely above a whisper. "Why won't you talk to me? Why won't you tell me what you're doing up here, all alone on this mountain?"

She sniffed, rubbing her face with her hand.

He reached again, grasping her hand firmly in his. "I've told you everything. *Everything.* It never crossed my mind to lie to you about what happened to me. After all these years, I never even questioned trusting you. I knew I could. I haven't seen you or talked to you in, what—fifteen, sixteen years or so? Yet I knew in a heartbeat I could still trust you. So what is it? You're obviously upset about something. Why can't you talk to me?"

Annie unwrapped herself from the quilts and stood up. She hobbled over to the fire, occupying herself by stoking it. "Look, it isn't that easy. You make it sound like it's perfectly all right for me to cry all over your shoulder when I don't even really *know* you any more. Sure, I used to see you play ball on television sometimes. And I read all about your big wedding—" She stopped suddenly and turned around. "I'm sorry. I didn't mean—"

"It's all right. Go on. What are you getting at?"

She put down the poker and sat down on the hearth. "Michael, it's just been too long. You've led your life and I've led mine. We live in two totally different worlds. You would have absolutely no idea about the kind of life I lead. Not a clue. It would be like speaking a foreign language, and I wouldn't begin to know how to translate it for you."

"You make it sound like you're living on Mars! C'mon,

Annie. So we've got a lot of catching up to do. Big deal. You're the one who told me we've got nothing but time here. And besides—" he paused, straining to sit up.

She rushed to his side. "Don't do that. You'll only make it worse. If you want to sit up, just ask for help." She propped the pillows behind him, lifting him to a more comfortable position.

He grabbed her arm and gently pushed her in the direction of her chair. "Sit."

She slowly obeyed. "Besides what?"

"Besides, there once was a time we shared everything, remember? And I do mean everything."

Her eyes met his and neither of them looked away. He watched her, knowing the same thoughts were trailing through her mind that were everywhere in his. The memories swirled through the air between them like the raging wind outside. They had shared so much. Theirs had been such a storybook romance. An unforgettable passion.

"Tell me what you're thinking, Annie."

જી

The gentle ticking of the grandfather clock marked the minutes that passed between them. When Michael closed his eyes at her long silence, Annie assumed he had drifted back to sleep. She stared into the fire, fighting the unspoken pull of her heart. That irresistible warmth invading her senses, filling her with an overpowering desire to crawl back into all those romantic memories.

It would be so easy. He was here. She was here. Far away from everything and everyone who had caused her so much frustration. It would be so nice. To be finally free of all the hurts and agonizing questions. Free from the heartache of God's continuous silence. To just let go.

She turned to find him watching her, the desire in his eyes so familiar.

"No, Michael."

"No what?"

"No."

She stood quietly and left the room.

Chapter 22

Seminole, Florida

Max walked into the kitchen just as the answering machine beeped and the red light began flashing. Ignoring it, he poured a glass of orange juice then opened the back door to let Snickers out. The cool morning air awoke his senses, reminding him how little he'd slept last night. His mind wouldn't unplug from the urgency of finding his mother. It consumed him, robbing the rest he craved. A thousand different ideas had flooded his mind.

He had finally given up any efforts to sleep and got up to take a shower. The rest of the house was still quiet. Noticing the flashing red light on the answering machine, he remembered Megan's promise to call with information from Denton. He pressed the button to replay the messages.

"David, Caroline—this is Sally. I know I'm calling

awfully early. Let's see, my clock says 6:08, but I just opened today's newspaper. If you haven't seen it yet, you'd better take a look. I think the dam just broke. Please call me. I want to help with flood control."

As he listened to the message from his father's secretary, the knot in his stomach cinched. He hurried to the front door, threw it open and searched for the paper on the lawn. Peeling off the wrapper, he walked back toward the house, stopping mid-step as he opened the paper.

The headline appeared in bold, black letters:

LOCAL PASTOR'S WIFE MISSING

Even before scanning the story, Max's eyes were drawn to the side-by-side photographs accompanying the article. He read the caption: *Annie Franklin McGregor, 39, has been missing from her Seminole home for four days. Her mother, Darlene Franklin Preston (right) fears foul play.* The photograph pictured his grandmother dabbing her eyes with a handkerchief, her expression woefully dramatic.

"Way to go, Nana. You've screwed up everything. As usual."

"You're up pretty early, aren't you?" his father asked, stepping out onto the front porch. Max folded the paper, hiding it behind him.

"Uh, yeah. Couldn't sleep."

"Max, why are you trying to hide the paper?"

He hesitated, then shrugged. "I was hoping you wouldn't have to see it. But I don't suppose there's much hope of that, is there?" He handed the folded copy to his father.

"What could be so bad you'd try to hide the newspaper? Don't tell me we missed the rapture?" He winked as he unfolded the paper. For a moment he stood perfectly still. "Oh no. Darlene, what have you done? No, no, no!" He crumpled the paper, then dropped his head.

"Mrs. Hampton called and left a message on the answering machine. She wanted to warn us. Dad, why would Nana do something like this?"

Something snapped. Max saw his father's wall of defense come crashing down. "Because she's nothing but a know-it-all busybody, Max! And there isn't *anything* on the face of this earth she wouldn't do to thrust her way into the center of attention—*even* at the expense of her own daughter!"

Max looked around then hurried to guide his father inside the house. "Take it easy, Dad! You'll wake the neighbors!"

"I don't care if I wake the neighbors! They need to get up anyway so they can READ THEIR PAPERS!"

Max pushed his father into the house. Once inside, he jerked out of his son's grasp. "Get your hands off me, Max!"

"What did *I* do?"

"Just leave me alone! I want you and everybody else in this stupid town to just leave me alone!" He turned and roared up the stairs. A moment later, Max heard him slam his bedroom door.

This time, it was Max who snapped. He flew up the stairs shouting. "Fine! Go ahead—have your own little pity party, Dad! You aren't the only one who's worried about Mom, y'know!"

Caroline appeared at the top of the stairs, wrapping her robe around her. "What on earth is going on?" Embarrassed in front of his grandmother, Max blew out an angry grunt then hurried back down the stairs. "Max? What happened?"

A few moments later, he heard his grandmother enter the room as he stormed around the kitchen. She caught hold of his arm and stopped him. "Hold it right there, young man. I asked you a question and I want an answer. What is going on?"

"Oh, it's no big deal," he answered, heavy on the sarcasm. "Dad just happened to get a good look at the front page of the paper this morning, that's all. Nana shot her mouth off to the press and now the whole world knows Mom is gone."

Caroline's jaw dropped. "Oh, Max, no—please tell me you're kidding." She drifted to a kitchen stool and took a seat. "She didn't—"

"Oh, yes she did. And she made sure she got not only Mom's picture plastered across it, but hers as well. No great surprise there, now is it?"

"Where's the paper? I want to see it."

"Then I guess you'll have to pry it out of Dad's hands. Look, Gran, it's not *my* fault Nana did this! But obviously Dad wants to blame me for it. You should've seen him! I didn't sleep one minute last night worrying about Mom! And *this* is what I get for being concerned?" Max grabbed his keys and opened the back door. "I'm outta here."

Just then, Snickers skipped inside. She barked playfully to remind him of her presence. "Get out of my way!" He shoved the pup out of the way with his foot. Snickers yelped as she skidded across the tiled floor. Max felt a fleeting moment of remorse. But as he turned to kneel beside the pitiful puppy, he was knocked off his feet with a head-butt from his younger brother.

"What's the matter with you?" Jeremy screamed, wrestling with his brother. "Why'd you kick her? Are you crazy? Why don't you just leave! Go away and don't ever come back!" He reached for the whimpering puppy, cradling her in his arms.

Heart racing, Max jumped up then flew out the door.

❧

The bells above the door at PJ's Donut Shop clanged like an emergency alarm as Max McGregor stormed in. Customers' heads turned in unison. Ignoring their stares, he stomped his way over to his usual stool at the end of the counter. He snatched a napkin out of the dispenser, wiping the perspiration off his forehead. Suddenly looking up, he noticed everyone frozen in place, their eyes fixed on him.

"What?!" he snapped.

PJ appeared from the back, wiping his hands on a dish towel. "Max! You gonna break my door if you keep that up!" he scolded, his thick Polish accent graveled with age. "What's the matter you?"

Max tried to relax. He tossed the crumbled napkin in the trash. "Sorry, PJ."

"Whatcha' mean 'sorry, PJ'? I never see you so upset. You have a fight with dat girlfriend of yours?"

"No." He avoided the old man's probing eyes.

PJ threw the towel on his work station and shuffled around the counter. He sat down beside Max and draped his arm over his shoulders.

He lowered his voice. "Now, you tell me, Max McGregor, what's got you so mad?"

Max could smell coffee on his breath. PJ leaned a little closer. "I seen dat newspaper this morning."

Max dropped his head in his hands. Had *everyone* seen it? His eyes stung. "PJ, what am I gonna do?"

"You come with me." He slapped Max on the back and led him back to the kitchen. "You sit," he ordered, pointing to a wooden stool. He poured Max a cold glass of milk from the refrigerator and with a tissue picked up a fresh cinnamon roll still warm from the oven. "Here. You eat. I be right back."

PJ hurried out to the front of the store through the swinging door. Max could hear him barking orders. "Tony, you take care of 'dose customers for me, yeah?"

"No problem, PJ. Gotcha covered."

Max had often heard the story his father told of discovering PJ's little shop shortly after moving to Seminole. On a whim, David had stopped by one morning to pick up some fresh donuts for his new office staff. Surprised by the rude demeanor of the shop's owner and sole employee, David ordered a cup of coffee so he could observe the old man gathering up his order. The other customers seemed to take PJ's abrupt manner in stride. David had wondered why so many people would patronize a business where they were treated so poorly.

In the months following, he made a point to visit the

odd little shop at least once a week. Gradually, over small talk and too many glazed donuts, he began to piece together the story behind the old man's ill-mannered behavior. It seemed the shop was originally named P&J's—short for Pearl and Jake's. But Jake had recently lost Pearl, his wife of sixty-three years, to a long and difficult battle with Alzheimer's. He'd grown bitter watching her waste away, no longer knowing him. Her sweet temperament vanished in the fog of dementia, leaving her mean as a snake and cussing him out with the vilest language he'd ever heard. Her eventual death nearly destroyed him. Only the daily task of running his tiny donut shop kept him going.

Little by little, David befriended the man who came to be known as PJ. Undaunted by the gruff responses, he persisted, drawing the Polish immigrant out of his shell until one day, with no other customers in the shop, PJ poured out his heartache to his new friend. David responded with compassion and understanding, comforting PJ with the love of Jesus.

It wasn't long before the McGregors adopted PJ into their family. He insisted on cooking the Thanksgiving turkey each year, his flamboyant carving of his masterpiece an annual tradition. He spoiled them with armloads of presents tucked under their Christmas tree, and never missed a single birthday party.

PJ was family.

Now, as Max sunk his teeth into the warm pastry, he relaxed under the old man's care. "Thanks, PJ. I didn't know I was so hungry."

"Sure you did." PJ poured himself a cup of coffee.

"Huh?"

"If you not hungry, why you come to PJ's? Unless, of course, you come here on account you need to talk?"

Max wiped his mouth with the back of his hand. "Okay, here's the deal. Dad lost it this morning. I've never seen him blow up like that. I didn't know he had it in him. You should have heard him."

PJ pulled up another stool. "Not good. Not good. Doesn't sound like your papa at all. Max, where your mama go? You got any idea?"

"Well, she wasn't kidnapped. That much we know for sure, regardless of what they wrote in the paper. Those idiots never even talked to us! They ran that whole story based on Nana's rants."

"Dat woman—she a pack of trouble. I never liked dat lady. But dat's just between you and me, okay?"

Max rolled his eyes, understanding all too well.

PJ took another sip of coffee. "You didn't answer my question. Where your mama?"

"We don't know. Dad said she was having some problems, like maybe she was about to have a breakdown or something," Max shrugged. He looked PJ straight in the eye. "She didn't leave *Dad,* she just left. There's a difference."

"Ah, you don't have to tell me that. 'Dem two never gonna split up. I seen 'em together—they like a couple of love-birds." PJ's smile widened across his weathered face. Bushy eyebrows danced over knowing eyes.

Max smiled. "Yeah, when I was a kid I used to get embarrassed because they were all the time holding hands and hugging and stuff. Dad was always pulling Mom over to sit in his lap and—"

Max didn't voice the realization dawning on him. He hadn't seen his mother and father's affectionate gestures in a long time. The thought twisted his stomach.

He hid his concern by taking another bite of his cinnamon roll. "Dad said Mom just needed to get away for a while. I mean, we're all worried and everything, but we just kept thinking any day she'll come home. Then her mom had to go and stick her big nose in it and blab it to the whole world.

"So Dad sees the paper this morning and it was like he came unglued or something. I've never seen him like that, PJ. *Never.* He just lost it. And naturally, *I* was the one in his line of fire. I know I shouldn't have let it get to me, but lately I just—I don't know what's gotten into me!"

He took a last gulp of milk and wiped his mouth. "Mom promised to call and check in so we wouldn't worry, but last night we never heard from her. Who knows what could have happened. She could be okay or she could be . . . I don't even want to *think* about all the stuff that might have happened. I just wish there was something I could do."

After moments of silence, PJ got in his face. "What? What you got cooking in dat head of yours?"

Max answered with resolve. "I know what I'm gonna do! I'm gonna find Mom, PJ! I know I can do it, but I'm going to need a little help."

PJ stood up and placed his hand on Max's shoulder. "You don't even got to ask. Whatever you need, you got it!"

"Just promise me you won't tell anybody what I'm going to do. I mean it. This has to be strictly confidential between us. Well, except for Megan, of course. She's already helping me track down Mom's whereabouts. But nobody else can know, okay? Especially Dad. Have I got your word?"

PJ stood as straight as his eighty-year-old body could muster. "You got it, buster," He put his hand out, "Partners?"

Max grasped PJ's hand firmly, finally beginning to feel a trace of optimism. "Partners." He slung his arm over the old man's shoulders. "Now here's what I need you to do."

❧

Max! I finally heard from Denton!" Megan blurted with excitement. "Your Mom is in Colorado!"

"Colorado? What the heck is she doing way out there?" He blew a long whistle. "Colorado is like a gazillion miles from here."

"Yeah. So?"

"So I've got an idea. But I need your help. Can you meet me at PJ's after school today?"

❧

As soon as Megan walked in, Max watched PJ pull the shades and flip the door sign to read CLOSED.

"PJ, what's going on?"

Though the donut shop was completely deserted, the proprietor looked around as if making sure the coast was clear. Without a word, he herded her back toward Max, standing at the kitchen door. Max led her into the warm kitchen, to a stainless steel table covered with maps.

She stopped cold. "Oh no . . . you're *not—*"

He held up his hand to stop her protest. "Now Megan, don't start with me until you've heard our plan."

"*'Our'* plan?" she asked, looking from Max to PJ and back again. "You have *got* to be kidding."

"Just hear me out. PJ here is going to help us find Mom. We've got it all figured out."

"Oh yeah, right. I suppose you two are taking off for Timbuktu?"

"Megan, will you just listen? PJ's not going anywhere. He's going to stay right here and man my control center for me. I'm the only one heading for Colorado. Do you have that phone number for Mom?"

Megan stared at him then slowly dug the notepaper out of her purse. "You aren't seriously thinking about driving alone all the way to Colorado, are you? You said yourself it's a gazillion miles!"

"Sit, Megan," PJ ordered as he pulled up two more stools for Megan and himself. "You listen to Max. Hear him out." He continued motioning with his head while peeking out the kitchen door to make sure no one was out front.

"What's with him?" Megan whispered close to Max's ear.

Max wrapped his arms around her waist and kissed her ear before answering. "Isn't he a trip?" he whispered. "Ever since he offered to help me out, he's been acting like James Bond."

"Hey, none of that kissy stuff, now. We got work to do!" PJ ranted, hustling back over to them. "You gotta call your mama, Max."

"Here's the number." Megan handed Max the slip of paper. "Denton said it originates out of Weber Creek, Colorado. He looked it up and said it's about forty miles west of Pueblo up in the mountains."

Max ignored the piece of paper and looked up Weber Creek on his map guide, then followed the coordinates to find its exact location.

"Max, look at this." Megan pointed at the note from Denton. "The number is listed under the name 'C. Benson.' Does that mean anything to you?"

He thought for a moment. "No, not off the top of my head. I assumed she was staying at a hotel or something. Is that a private residence?"

"Sounds like it. Best way to find out is to place a call." She looked at Max with eyes full of expectation.

"I guess you're right." He picked up the note and made his way over to the extension. "What am I supposed to do if she answers? What if she *doesn't* answer?"

"Well, you can't exactly say 'Hey, Mom—this is Max, what's happenin'?'" Megan mimicked. "If she thinks you know where she is, you're gonna freak her out."

"She's right," PJ added. "You can't say nothing. You

just listen and make sure dat's your mama's voice who answers dat phone."

"Well, here goes." Max took a deep breath then dialed the sticky cordless phone. "PJ, don't you ever wipe your hands before you pick up the phone? This is gross."

"You gonna call the health department or you gonna call your mama?"

"Yeah, yeah. Now you've made me forget what I've dialed." He pressed the button and started over. He listened impatiently as the connection worked its way across the miles. "Okay, Mom, answer the phone."

"Hello?"

Max motioned with his hand then froze.

"Hello? Is that you, Dr. Wilkins?"

His stomach doing a complete somersault, Max pressed the button to break the connection.

"It was her," he whispered.

"Max, that's wonderful! You found her!" Megan grabbed him, slapping him on the back.

"Did she sound okay, your mama?"

"Yeah . . ." He found the wooden stool and slowly sat back down. "But kind of anxious. She said 'Is that you, Dr. Wilkins?'" He paused again, his thoughts obviously running a thousand directions at once. "I wonder if—you don't suppose she left town because she was sick or something? What if she's got—"

"No, no," PJ interrupted. "Don't you start hopping to conclusions, Max."

Megan sat down again. "PJ's right. She wouldn't have left town if she was ill.

Dr. Wilkins could be anybody. Maybe he's the one who owns the place where she's staying."

Max blinked back to his present surroundings. "Yeah. Maybe. At least I know where she is. Now I've just got to figure out how to get there."

❧

Eagle's Nest
Hello?"

No response.

"Hello? Is that you, Dr. Wilkins?"

Click.

Doc's warning immediately echoed through Annie's mind. *I'm still concerned that whatever trouble Mr. Dean has gotten himself into may follow him up this mountain.*

Fear rushed through every fiber of her being. Grabbing her crutch, she hurried back out to the great room.

"Who called?"

She reached for her quilts. "I don't know. They hung up."

Her eyes met Michael's.

Nothing more was said.

Chapter 23

Seminole, Florida

Why don't you fly?" Megan suggested. "It would take you at least three days to drive there from here, and that's driving straight through without stopping. No way."

The unlikely trio continued their strategy. They all agreed Max had to find his mother. Getting there was the problem.

"We talked about that," Max said, looking at PJ. Their older partner stood up again, hiking his pants above his waist and sucking in his stomach. With a cocky shake of his head, he unfolded the plan.

"Max thought maybe he was gonna find him some money and just hop on some plane. Well, I told him that's not gonna work on account two reasons. One, the minute his daddy realizes he's gone, his daddy gonna call up the police and the next thing you know, they gonna be waiting for him at that airport in Colorado." He punctuated his concern with a nod of his head.

"Then, he gonna have to have himself a car and nooo-body gonna rent a car to a sixteen-year-old boy. Not gonna happen. Besides, the minute he pulls out that driver's license, they gonna know he's dat boy who's missin' from Florida. Am I right?" PJ thrust out his chest, hands on his hips.

Megan stifled her grin and turned to face Max. "You know, he's right. But what are you going to do?"

Before he could answer, PJ jumped in. "Well now, Megan, I'm glad you asked. Come and see for yourself!" He grabbed her elbow and led her to the back door. He threw it open then once outside, he rushed to strike a pose. "Ta-daaaaa!" Waving a broad sweep of his hands, PJ presented the getaway car: his very own 1968 Volkswagen bus.

Megan's mouth fell open. Her face registered a mix of disbelief and suppressed laughter. "Uh . . . PJ! This is really . . . *nice?*" She turned to her boyfriend. "So you're planning to drive to Colorado. In a *hippie bus?*"

Max laughed. "Isn't it great?" He walked over to slide open the side door. "And get a load of this—PJ fixed it up so I can sleep in it and everything. If I get tired, I can just pull off at some rest stop or truck stop and climb in back for a couple of hours. It's got everything—a small refrigerator, a mattress, pillow—"

Megan peeked into the van over Max's shoulder. "PJ, where on earth did you find this carpet?" Avocado shag lined the floor, walls and inside roof of the vintage vehicle.

He beamed. "Nice, huh?"

"Oh, very! And I suppose it has a tape deck so you can play some really groovy music?" She smiled at Max, trying desperate not to laugh.

"Eight-track in mint condition!" PJ's bushy eyebrows danced again.

"And PJ has offered to send his lifetime collection of polka music along for the ride. I mean, admit it, Megan. It just doesn't get any better than this."

PJ snapped his fingers. "Oh! I'll get that case of tapes right now!" He rushed back into the kitchen.

Max hung his arm across Megan's shoulder and looked at her, the mischief playing across his face. Before she could speak, they both burst into laughter.

"Max, are you really—"

"Yes, Megan, I'm really going to do it." He grinned with assurance. "And if it wouldn't shock everyone in the whole western hemisphere, not to mention the church *and* school, I'd take you along with me."

Megan rolled her eyes. "Sorry, no can do."

"'Cause I know how you like 'dos polkas, Miss Megan," Max teased in his horrible attempt at a Polish accent as he swept her into a silly dance.

Chapter 24

Seminole, Florida

Caroline sat quietly in the slip-covered chair, her legs stretched out comfortably on the matching ottoman. Peering out the windows of the quaint guest room, she could see the empty flowerbeds lining the back yard privacy fence. Faded winter mulch seemed to beg for the kaleidoscope of the impatiens, vinca, coneflowers, and zinnias Annie would plant with the arrival of spring. Morning's first light uncovered a thick blanket of grass the color of winter wheat. The weathered beams of the jungle gym stood guard like a silent fortress, its two lonesome swings tracing a lonely pattern in the early morning breeze.

A weary sigh escaped her wondering thoughts. Her hands rested on the Bible in her lap, palms pressed lightly against the worn pages as if willing the answers she sought to absorb through her fingertips. She'd exhausted her prayers. Now only the silent language deep in her soul could communicate the cries of her heart. She knew nothing else to do at this point. It was all in God's hands. Caroline rested her head back against the soft chair and closed her eyes. The long hours had eclipsed the night. It was time to face another day.

A quiet knock on her bedroom door interrupted her thoughts. "Come in."

A sleepy-eyed vision of pink flannel and soft curls padded across the room and into her lap. Jessie clutched the form of her stuffed kangaroo and burrowed into her grandmother's warm embrace. Caroline pulled the cream-colored afghan to cover them both. "Good morning, sweetheart."

"Uh-hum."

"What's my beautiful granddaughter doing up so early this morning?"

Jessie yawned. "I don't know. I just woke up. Didn't want to go in Mommy and Daddy's room so I came in here."

"Now, why wouldn't you want to go in your mommy and daddy's room?"

Jessie shrugged.

Caroline glanced down at the cherubic countenance. She hugged her granddaughter tighter and took a deep breath.

They sat in silence. Finally, Jessie squirmed a little then asked, "Where's Max?"

"What do you mean, honey?"

"I walked by his room and his door was open just a little bit and I peeked inside and he's not in there."

Caroline didn't like the sick feeling washing over her, but swallowed her angst. "Jessie, let's you and I go check it out and see what he's up to, okay?"

The first thing to catch Caroline's eye was the framed photograph of Megan and Max noticeably missing from his bedside table. She hurried over to his closet, throwing open the louvered doors. Her eyes flew to the top shelf above his rack of clothes—his Nike duffle bag noticeably missing. Max used it whenever he traveled.

"What's the matter, Gran?" Jessie grasped her Caroline's hand. "Why did you moan like that?"

Caroline faced her. "Oh sweetie, I'm afraid your brother has taken off. And I have a feeling I know where he's gone."

Jessie started to whimper as she clung to Caroline's waist.

"Shhh. Jessie, I'm right here and I'm not going to leave you." She grabbed her granddaughter's hand and held it tight. "Let's find out what this is all about." They peeked in Jeremy's room, relieved to find him snoring softly. They listened at David's door and could hear a much louder version of the same snore. A sad smile played across Caroline's lips.

They slowly descended the stairs together in silence. The house seemed unusually quiet, almost reverent somehow, as they made their way to the kitchen. Snickers waited eagerly at the back door until Jessie let her out. Caroline noticed the crocodile tears still brimming on her granddaughter's eyes as she looked back toward her.

Caroline's heart ached as she looked around the room hoping to find a note or some indication of Max's whereabouts.

Nothing was out of place, nor was there any sign of a note. Heaving another sigh, Caroline searched her heart for answers. *Now what? How am I going to tell David? Was it really just yesterday he lost it over that headline?*

Headline? Oh Lord, please don't let there be another headline this morning. Stealing a look out the kitchen window, Caroline grimaced at the vacant spot where Max always parked his car. "Jessie, why don't you pour us both a nice glass of orange juice? I'm going out to get the paper, then I'll come back and fix us some breakfast. How does that sound, honey?"

Damp eyes the size of saucers stared at her beneath a crinkled brow. Caroline headed for the front door. Opening it, she felt Jessie's presence behind her like a shadow.

"Don't leave me, Gran," Jessie warbled.

She dropped to her knees, scooping Jessie into her arms. They hugged for several moments, Caroline breathing in the sweet fragrance of her granddaughter's curls. She pulled back and with her index finger, lifted Jessie's chin so they could look into each other's eyes.

"Jessie, you can stick to me like super glue if that'll make you feel better. C'mon. Let's get the paper and hurry back in before the wind blows up our nightgowns!" At long last, she heard a tiny giggle escape as they dashed outside. Once back inside with the door safely shut, she grasped Jessie's hand and led her toward the kitchen. Heavy, slow steps descended the stairs behind them. She swallowed and uttered an unspoken prayer.

"Mom?"

The husky tone of her son's voice gripped her, but she fought the threatening wave of emotion. "Yes, dear? We're out here in the kitchen."

David looked awful. He had aged a hundred years in his mother's eyes. Appearing at the kitchen door, the dark circles under his eyes testified to another restless night.

"Jessie and I are going to have some breakfast. Would you like to join us?" she asked in a voice a little too cheerful.

"Sure. Thanks," he mumbled, sitting down at the table. "Did I miss Annie's call last night?"

Caroline busied herself gathering the ingredients for pancakes. "No, honey, I'm afraid she didn't call."

David looked at his mother. "Do you realize it's been *three days* now since she called?"

"Daddy, is Mommy all right?" Jessie interrupted, her voice hushed with apprehension. "You said she was just away on a little vacation." Her innocent eyes pleaded for truth.

Caroline watched them as she whisked the pancake batter. David took a long, deep breath and rubbed his eyes. His face still buried in his hands, he answered softly. "Pumpkin, she really is on a vacation like I told you. She's gone away to rest and think and pray, which is something we could all use about now." He looked up at his daughter's worried countenance. "The only thing is, she didn't tell us where she went."

They could see the words slowly drifting through Jessie's thoughts. Her eyebrows drew together in two miniature creases. "You mean she's lost and you can't find her?"

David paused for a moment. "Well, yes, I guess you could say it's something like that. Except that *Mommy's* not lost—*we're* the ones who don't know where she is." He looked to his mother for help.

"Oh, sweetie, we just need to pray for Mommy and at the same time ask God to bring her home to us. I'm sure she's somewhere safe and sound, and . . . and probably catching up on her sleep and just forgot to call," she finished with gaining speed. She turned around and poured the first six pancakes onto the griddle, avoiding further questions.

"But Daddy?"

Caroline peeked over her shoulder as David reached across the table to grasp his daughter's hand in reassurance. "Jessie, Gran's right. There's no reason for us to worry. She promised to take care of herself and we've all asked God to take care of her, so we just need to practice our trust a little more. Right? Don't you think God's big enough to watch over our Mommy for us even when we don't know where exactly she might be?" He nodded in affirmation to convince those questioning blue eyes.

"Well said, Pastor." *Practice what you preach,* she thought.

"Yeeeaaahhh." He yawned, stretching his arms high into the air. "So where are the boys? Still asleep?" he asked Jessica.

"Jeremy is but—"

"Would you like some coffee, David?" Caroline grabbed the carafe from the coffee maker.

"Sure, Mom. What were you saying, honey?" he asked his daughter.

"Cream and sugar?" Caroline held the carton of creamer directly in front of his face.

David turned to look at his mother. "You know I never put cream and sugar in my coffee, Mom." His eyes narrowed as he searched her face. "Mom?"

She set the carton on the table and handed David a steaming mug of coffee. "Why, of course you don't. I don't know what I was thinking."

He placed his hand on her extended wrist. "Mom."

"Yes, dear?"

"You've always been terrible at playing cards. You never learned how to bluff, remember?"

She smiled weakly. "Oh, well I—"

"Max is gone," Jessica blurted, disappearing behind her glass of juice.

"What?" he asked, turning to face her.

"I said Max is gone," the reply echoing from the glass.

He turned back toward his mother. She started to move, but his hand held her firmly in place. "Max is gone?"

"Now before you get upset again, let's just calm down and talk about this." Caroline quickly took a seat.

"Max is GONE?"

"David McGregor! Lower your voice this minute!" She jerked her hand free and subtly nodded in Jessica's direction. David's eyes grew wider as he started to say something, but Caroline jumped in. "Jessie, sweetheart, why don't you go see if Sesame Street is— "

"No!" she answered, pounding her fist on the table. "I don't *want* to watch Sesame Street. I'm not a little baby anymore! I'm just as much a part of this family as anybody else. And I'm tired of everybody trying to keep secrets from me." Lips pursed, she raised her chin and folded her arms across her chest.

"Okay, okay!" Caroline raised her hands in surrender. She drew an unsteady breath before continuing. "Now Jessica, David—both of you—just stop for a moment and calm down. Jessie, you're exactly right. You *are* as big a part of this family as the rest of us. So I suggest we all try to work through this together. Quietly. Calmly. But together."

She turned to face David. "Jessie discovered Max's absence just a little while ago when she came to my room. His room is neat, his bed is made." Pause. "And his duffel bag is missing."

David started to speak but his mother beat him to it again. "His car is also gone, so I think it's safe to assume he's taken off. And I believe with all my heart he's gone to find Annie."

"What?" David snapped. "Why would he—how does he think he can—"

"Because he feels as helpless as the rest of us! And unfortunately he was the closest bystander when you popped your cork yesterday." She leveled a knowing gaze at him.

"Popped your what?" Jessie asked.

David sighed. "Popped my cork. Lost my temper. Blew it."

"Honey, your father held in his feelings as long as he could, then—"

"Look, I'm sorry about exploding. I need to apologize to you about that, Jessica—to you too, Mom. I've never acted like that in my entire life. I don't know what got into me."

Jessie patted his hand. "You're forgiven."

"David, we know how hard this has been for you. Don't we, Jessie?" Caroline nodded toward her granddaughter, who nodded back. "But we're *all* struggling to get through this. And Max? Well, he's a lot like you, son. In his own way, he needed to explode too. And once he calmed down, I'm sure the wheels in his mind started spinning, no doubt searching for a solution to 'fix' this whole mess for all of us. Maybe it's not necessarily what we would have done, but I'm sure he thought it was something *he* had to do."

"So where could he have gone, Daddy?" Jessie tucked a curl behind her ear. "How could he know where Mommy might be?"

"I have no idea," David answered, mussing his daughter's hair. "Not a clue. But I promise you this. I'm going to find out."

Chapter 25

Eagle's Nest

Annie tucked Michael's blankets around him after dressing his wounds again. "Your coloring is better. That's a good sign. Here, take these." She handed him the medication with a glass of water. Her patient obliged, swallowing the pills.

"I'm starving. Do you mind fixing me something to eat?"

She rolled her eyes at him and limped back to the kitchen.

"How about a hot plate of cheese enchiladas, a couple tacos, and maybe some queso dip and chips? Can you rustle that up for me?"

"Dream on. I'm afraid you're hallucinating."

He watched her make two sandwiches and placed them on separate plates with a handful of chips.

"Can you heat up some tea while you're at it? I can't stop shaking."

"Neither can I. It feels like thirty below in here." She balanced the tray of food vicariously, hobbling on one crutch to carry it over to the coffee table. Setting it down within his reach, she headed back to the kitchen to fill the kettle with water. "This is getting really old."

"Oh, I don't know. It's really not so bad if you think of it." Michael chomped on the thick ham and Muenster sandwich as he studied the fire.

"I'm thinking of it and I'm thinking it's pretty bad." She put the kettle over the fire then sat back down.

"Then you're looking at it all wrong. The way I'm seeing it—it's like being marooned on a desert island, only colder."

Annie sighed then took a bite of her sandwich.

"Well, aside from the chill, it's really not so bad. Think about it. No one else can travel in this weather, which means no one can get up here, which means for now we're safe. That may not mean much to you, but you can't imagine how good it feels to me."

"That's great. I'm glad you're happy. If you're happy, then I'm happy. Just think how amused they'll be when they find the frozen smiles on our frozen faces on our frozen bodies."

"Whiner."

"I'm not whining."

"Cry baby."

"Stop it."

"Make me."

"Shut up, Michael."

"Okay."

"Okay what?"

"Okay, I'll shut up on one condition."

"What?"

"The fire needs stoking."

He heard her slam the bedroom door just as he realized she hadn't served him his tea.

"Annie?"

Silence.

He shook his head, amused and irritated at the same time. She wouldn't be in there long. The fire was out here.

But he wasn't amused for long. The constant, nagging sparks of fear gnawed at him. With every passing moment, Elliot and his legions were bound to be closing in on him. Despite the comforts of Christine's cabin and the strange companionship and assistance Annie provided, he still felt like a sitting duck. He resented the physical weakness that trapped him here on this sofa. He needed to *do* something.

His cell phone caught his eye. Earlier, he had asked Annie to get it out of his car, though he wasn't sure if he would use it or not. He just needed it near. Now with her out of the room, he felt an urgency to talk to Grady again. He pressed the on button, coughing to cover the sound of the beep. The instrument came to life, the panel glowing a florescent blue. He pulled the covers over his head to muffle the sound of his dialing.

"Hello?"

"Grady! It's Michael."

"Michael! Thank God! I thought you were dead by now."

"No such luck. I'm better—much better than the last

time we talked, that's for sure. I've had some medical attention, I'm in a secure location—"

"Where are you now?"

"I'm not sure it's a good idea to tell you."

"Michael, you promised me. The last time you called you promised to come clean and tell me where you are."

"I know, I know. I just don't want—hey, wait a minute. Maybe I can tell you without *telling* you."

"Meaning?"

"Meaning . . . what if I told you I was at *Tumbleweed's hideaway* and left it at that?"

A pause on the other end of the line. "You mean—"

"Don't say it! Don't say a word, okay? I still don't trust these cell phones. It's too easy for someone to intercept the lines. Are we on the same page here?"

Grady laughed. "We're good, Michael."

"Good. That's a big relief. So if anything should happen to me, you'll know exactly where to find me. And you still have the information I gave you about the—"

"Got it. Not to worry."

"There's one other thing I need to tell you. At the moment, I'm a bit *under the weather*, if you follow me—"

"I hear you."

"But once this all clears up—"

"I understand—"

"I'm going straight to the authorities myself. I just need to decide how to do that. Who I can trust."

"Michael, it will make it a lot easier if you'd just let me

go to the authorities now. Give them the location for the packet. Tell them to come rescue you. It makes sense!"

"No way."

"Don't be an idiot, Dean!"

"No! I've already endangered you by these phone calls. I don't want to involve you any more than I already have. I'll be careful who I contact. I'll cover my tracks. I'm only telling you now so that someone somewhere knows where I am and where there's information that pieces together the puzzle behind this nightmare."

"You sure you don't want me to handle it for you?'

"I value your friendship too much to do that to you."

No response.

"Grady, you still there?"

"I'm here. Look, you take care of yourself, okay? And call me back in the morning. Keep in touch. And for the love of Pete, try not to get yourself killed, okay?"

"I will, Grady. I will."

❧

Weber Creek, Colorado

Well, what do you think, Doc?" Bob Williamson asked his friend, leaning across the counter. "You think our guest up there can cope with this kind of storm?"

Doc Wilkins had trudged across the street through the piling snow to Williamson's Store. He was restless. Increasingly concerned about the troubles up at that cabin, his thoughts had little to do with the storm. He had a bad feeling about all of it. A feeling he couldn't shake. Someone had tried to kill Michael Dean. He could think of little else.

"Well?" Bob asked again, sliding Doc's coffee mug gently across the counter.

Doc wasn't used to keeping secrets, especially from his two best friends. But this time he had no choice. "Oh, I'm sure she'll be all right." He wrapped his hands around the warm mug. "She seems to be pretty resourceful. And that ankle should be improving right along. I expect she'll do what has to be done."

"Well, at least she can still use the phone," Bob added, following Doc to the fireplace.

"Who can still use the phone? Last I checked the phones were down," Mary Jean hollered as she made her way out of the storeroom. "Oh hi, George. Didn't hear you come in. Didn't you know the phones were down?"

"No, MJ. But I was afraid of that." Doc eased into one of the rocking chairs. "That changes everything."

Mary Jean sat down on the hearth, pulling her sweater tighter around her. "What do you mean by that? Are you talking about Annie?"

Doc nodded slowly, his eyes fixed on the blaze.

"But I thought you just said she could take care of herself," Bob countered.

"Well, of course she can take care of herself, Bob," Mary Jean argued. "But being cut off from the entire human race in this kind of a storm? And her, not being used to this kind of weather? Land sakes, I've been in these mountains all my life and I still say there's nothing lonelier than having the phones go down on you. Poor thing, she's probably scared to death up there. Surely there's something we can do?" She looked back and forth between the men.

Doc Wilkins stared at the steam coming from his coffee mug. *You're so right, Mary Jean,* he thought. *I'm quite certain Annie is scared to death by now, but her fears have little to do with the blizzard outside her window*

❧

Eagle's Nest
Hey!" He hated this. He was totally incapable of doing anything for himself. He despised the helplessness.

"Annie?"

The glow of the candle preceded her as she shuffled around the corner. "Michael, what is it? What's wrong?" She stood over him, alarm etched on her face. "Are you in pain?"

He huffed. "No, I'm not in pain. Nothing's wrong. Except that I need to, uh . . . I mean how I am supposed to—I need to go to the bathroom, okay?!"

"Oh!" A hint of a smile crossed her lips. "I wondered when that would hit you. You've been holding your liquids a long time. Course, you always did have a huge bladder. You could drink like a fish all night and never once have to go. I could never figure out how you did that."

"Strong will."

"Oh sure. But now you're embarrassed about this, are

you? Big guy like you? Humiliated because you need a little help to go potty?"

"Can we cut the jokes here? I wouldn't have asked if I didn't need help." He threw back the quilts.

"I don't know, Michael. I rather like having you helpless. Who's the crybaby now, huh? Besides, it keeps you humble," she continued, helping him to his feet. "Also keeps you completely at my mercy. Now there's a switch," she added dryly.

"Actually, come to think of it, you're right." The effort of walking strained his voice.

"Right about what?"

"About my being embarrassed. Why should I be embarrassed? After all, it's not like we didn't live together all those years or anything," he toyed, giving her the slightest hug his bad arm could muster.

Annie jerked to face him, their noses mere inches apart. Her eyes narrowed.

"What? What did I say?"

Just as quickly, she looked away. "That's all history and hardly relevant at this point in time."

They continued their slow journey to the bathroom. Michael enjoyed the ability to make her squirm. "History, maybe, but all history is relevant if you ask me."

"I didn't ask you."

"Fine. But the fact remains that you and I were once—"

"I know what we were, okay? Can we just skip this stroll down memory lane?" They reached the bathroom. "Why don't you just . . . just do what you need to do and let's get on with it."

311

Once he was situated, Annie pulled the door and gave him privacy. He could still see her through the crack in the door. She folded her arms across her chest, leaning against the door frame.

"Fact is, those were some of the happiest years of my life."

"Enough, Michael. I don't want to hear any more. I'm a married woman, thank you very much. I have three kids, and besides that, I'm a pastor's wife."

"A *pastor's* wife?" He laughed, rolling out several lengths of toilet paper. "Well now, that's quite a switch, isn't it? Actually, I think I'd heard about that somewhere along the line, but I didn't really believe it. Annie Franklin? A preacher's wife? *My* Annie? The girl who partied with me, danced with me—who *lived* with me?" He watched her shift uncomfortably from one foot to the other.

"I'm not 'your Annie' anymore, in case you've forgotten. That was a long time ago. I'm a different person now, though I'd hardly expect you to have a clue what it means to change your life for the better. If you'll recall, *you* were the one who walked out on me all those years ago. Without so much as a word of explanation, you just left." Her voice cracked.

Michael tried to think of something to say. For once in his life, he was speechless.

"Oh for heaven's sake! Why are we even talking about this," she mumbled, limping out of sight, though he could still hear her. "God, why him? Why now? Wasn't it all screwed up enough?"

He listened to her quiet pleas, certain she had no idea he could hear. He silently cursed himself for upsetting her.

"Uh, Annie?"

Silence.

"I could use a little help in here."

She groaned in protest. He could hear her unsteady clomping against the hard wood floor. He could also hear the words she muttered under her breath. "Nurse Nancy to the skeleton in my closet. Like I needed this?"

~

Houston, Texas

Those imbeciles! It's been three days!"

Elliot slammed down his phone and dropped back into his chair. His heart pounded in his chest, the anger rising to a boil.

He knew what they'd done. Gus and Marcus had lost Michael's trail. And rather than admit their failure, they'd turned off their cell phone or forgot to charge it. *I was a fool to trust them to do something this important. What was I thinking!*

He stood up and walked over to the bank of windows. Thirty stories below, pedestrians went about their business, rushing along the city sidewalks like ants on a mission. Elliot pressed his thumb against the glass as if he could squish them. All of them. People were such a nuisance.

Especially Gus and Marcus.

Especially Michael.

Wherever you are, Michael, I'll find you. And I'll squash you like the worthless ant you are. I'll squash you with my own bare hands.

Chapter 26

Near Little Rock, Arkansas

Max yanked the polka tape out of PJ's eight-track stereo and tossed it on the floor. "How do people stand that stuff? And they give us grief over rock & roll. Go figure."

The trip had been without incident so far, which Max attributed to his continuous prayers. The first three hundred miles had been exciting. He was on a rescue mission! He imagined the relief at home when they heard he had not only found his mom, but was on his way home with her. They would quickly forgive his impulsive decision to take off without permission. Their gratitude would far outweigh any anxiety they'd experienced.

Sure it would.

But as the miles stretched on, he had grown steadily more irritated at himself for making such a hasty departure.

I should have left a note. Maybe I should have spoken with Dad. At least a phone call—anything to keep from adding another burden on them right now. Way to go, Max. They're probably losing their minds with worry about now.

His thoughts spiraling downward, Max pulled over at a convenience store on the outskirts of Little Rock, Arkansas. He would have no peace until he placed the call. He was exhausted anyway, and knew he needed some serious sleep.

But first things first. He'd checked in with Megan a couple of times already, but he needed to hear her voice before placing his other call. He dialed the familiar number. The sound of Megan's voice pumped him up again. He told her about his decision to call home. After a brief discussion, she agreed it was the right thing to do.

"So how's PJ doing? He's not dressing up like 007 to serve donuts, is he?"

"He's such a riot, Max. But you know what? I think this whole escapade has made him feel really important somehow. Like he's a significant part of something very important. I'm not sure how long he'll be able to keep the secret, but so far he's been great. I think you should probably call him. Maybe after you get some rest. It would mean a lot to him."

"I'll do that. Well, I guess I better go. I miss you, Megan," he said softly. "I can't believe how good it is to hear your voice."

"I love you, Max McGregor."

"I love you, Megan Tanner."

"Keep in touch, okay?"

"I will. Talk to you later."

Max hung up the pay phone. He suddenly realized how hungry he was and decided to get some dinner before placing his next call.

He was stalling and he knew it.

అ

Max took a deep breath. *Oh God, please let him understand.*

"Hello?"

"Dad, it's me, Max."

"Max! Where are you? We've been worried to death!"

"I know, Dad. And I'm really sorry. I never should have left the way I did." The words tumbled over themselves. "I just . . . all I could think about was finding Mom and bringing her home. I thought maybe then you'd . . . maybe it would make you . . ."

"Make me what?" his father pressed.

Max struggled for the right words. "Dad, I feel like all I ever do is disappoint you. I'm always causing you grief, one way or another. And just about the time I think I'm finally making some progress, like staying out of your hair or not losing my temper, then I go and blow it big time."

"Max, you don't have to prove yourself to me!"

"But—"

"Look, son, I'm the one who needs to be making the apology here, so just hold on for a minute. The other morning when I—"

"Dad, you don't—"

"Yes, I do. I was way out of line. That headline sent me over the edge, but that's no excuse for taking it out on you. I'm asking you to forgive me, buddy."

Max absently fingered the lint in his pocket. "I do. Forget about it. But it goes both ways. I lost my temper, like I always seem to do. So I blew it too. And I'm sorry. Forgive me too?"

"Sure thing. But we need to talk about this trip you're on."

"Yeah, I know."

"Why didn't you talk to me first? If you've got information about your mother, why didn't you tell me? We could have made this trip together."

"Dad—" he hesitated. "Dad, I don't expect you to understand, but I have to do this alone. I'm being careful, I'm not taking any chances, but I've got to do this my way."

Max heard a heavy sigh on the other end of the line. He could imagine his father running his fingers through his hair like he always did when he was frustrated.

"You aren't going to believe this, but I think I *do* understand. As your father, I'm not sure *why* I understand, but I do. I know I've got to learn to let go enough to let you be the man God made you to be. But that's pretty scary for your old man. I'd be lying if I said otherwise."

"Yeah? Well, it's a little scary on this end too." Max laughed.

"Tell me this. How did you track down where your mother is?"

"Uh, actually I'd rather not say. Just think of it as . . . a miracle. I figure God must've *wanted* me to know, so let's just leave it at that."

"Max . . ." his father chided.

"Dad, really. You've just got to trust me. You have to accept that I know what I'm doing."

"If that's the way it has to be, then that's the way it has to be. But let's set some ground rules. I want you to call me twice a day if for no other reason than to give me peace of mind that you're safe. Three or four times would be even better. But at least twice. Is that acceptable?"

"No problem."

"And promise me if you get even remotely close to any kind of danger, you'll call immediately and tell me where you are. That's non-negotiable."

"All right, but don't worry about it. I'll be fine. Just pray this vehicle gets me there. It would cost more than it's worth just to tow it back home!"

"*What* vehicle? Aren't you in your Mustang?"

"I gotta get back on the road, Dad."

"Ma-ax?" he warned.

"I'm glad we talked. Thanks for being so cool about this. For an old man, you're okay."

"Keep in touch, son."

"Will do. Bye, Dad. I love you."

"Love you, too, Max."

Chapter 27

Houston, Texas

It's this phone you gave us, sir. We got off without the charger and it's about done."

Elliot nodded, congratulating himself for correctly guessing which excuse these idiots would use for not checking in. "And it didn't occur to you over the course of the last three days to stop and buy a charger for it?"

"Well, of course, sir, but we just haven't been able to track one down as yet."

"And you expect me to buy that excuse? Are you a complete idiot?"

"Well, nossir, but you have to—"

"SHUT UP!" Elliot screamed at the receiver. His breath came in rapid wheezes as he fought to control his temper.

"Now you listen and you listen good. I should have

known I couldn't trust you two with so simple a task as following a car. Fortunately I have other irons in the fire. And since you've obviously lost him again—"

"Oh, nossir!" Gus added. "Who said we lost him? Me 'n Marcus are—"

"Shut up and try to get it right this time."

"Yes, sir. Whatever you say, Mr. Thomas. We'll find him for you and—"

"Here's what I want you to do. Our Mr. Dean is more than likely planning to hide out near a town called Weber Creek."

"Hey! We saw a sign for Weber Creek!"

"Good. That means you must be close."

"Uh, well not exactly. I think it was yesterday. Or maybe the day before?"

Elliot took a deep breath, attempting to calm himself. "You will find Weber Creek. You will get there before I call again or you will kiss every dime of that reward goodbye."

"Yes, sir. We'll be there before you know it, sir. We won't goof up again, sir. I promise."

Elliot pinched the bridge of his nose. *Morons. Utter and complete morons.* But they were closer to Michael than he was at this point. He had to rely on them. He had to motivate them to get to Weber Creek as fast as possible. Against his better judgment, he continued. "And just for the record, the stakes just went up, gentlemen. You find Mr. Dean by this time tomorrow and I'll personally add $10,000. For each of you."

He could hear Gus's voice away from the receiver. "He's gonna give us $10,000 more each!"

"*Only* if you find him this time! Lose him again and I'll have *both* your heads. You find Michael Dean and you take him captive. We're going to end this thing."

⁕

Amelia rinsed off her dinner plate and put it in the dishwasher. Grabbing a bottle of wine, she uncorked it and poured the Chardonnay into a glass. She sat on a bar stool at the counter, the thoughts burning through her mind as she tried for the hundredth time to make sense of her husband's disappearance.

It didn't matter what her father said, or anyone else for that matter. Amelia knew Michael was not coming back. And she knew without a shadow of a doubt that wherever he was, he was with another woman.

It wasn't just the wine that warmed her. She could feel the anger surging through her veins. How many times had she endured this pain? How many times had he left without a word? For days at a time, sometimes weeks. How could he care so little for her feelings?

The tears coursed down her face spilling onto the counter. She poured another glass and cursed his name out loud. She drained the glass in mere moments and poured another. The alcohol seared through her body, numbing her mind to the harsh truths.

I'm too good for you, Michael. You're nothing without me. You're only a flea along for the ride. If it wasn't for Daddy,

322

you'd be nothing but a washed-up has-been jock.

"Did you hear that, Michael? You're worthless! You're garbage to me and I should have dumped you years ago!" she sobbed. "I HATE you! I HATE YOU!"

She hurled the bottle across the room, shattering it into a thousand pieces all over the kitchen cabinet and floors. Startled by the sound of it, she stopped. Amelia wiped her eyes with the back of her hand, her body still shaking. Smoothing her hair back away from her face, she took a deep ragged breath.

And then the hurt crashed over her again, this time a pain more intense than she'd ever known. She screamed his name again. She threw the near-full glass across the room. The sound of the exploding glass against tile goaded her on. She grabbed the vase of flowers off the counter, hurling them into the sink.

On and on it went, the damage extensive. When at last she found nothing else to throw, she snatched the only bottle that was left. Bourbon. Michael's precious bourbon.

She slid down onto the floor and opened the bottle, guzzling it. It burned but she didn't care. She didn't care about anything. Not anymore.

She didn't know how long she sat there on the floor. Her head throbbed. Her throat, raw. Her heart ached despite the effects of the alcohol. *Oh, how it ached . . .*

Broken glass and shards of crystal covered the tile floor. It was the elegant detail of the cut crystal, now shattered across the floor that first caught her eye.

She sighed, her resignation complete. Then, slowly, very slowly, she stretched out her hand, reaching for a jagged piece of glass.

Chapter 28

Seminole, Florida

The ring of the telephone and the chime of the doorbell had become increasingly annoying over the past few days at the McGregor home. They couldn't let the answering machine handle the calls, fearful they'd miss one of Max or Annie's calls. They couldn't take that chance. For now, they would simply have to live with the continuing barrage of calls and well-meaning visitors.

With a growing degree of aggravation, David headed to the entry hall to answer the doorbell once again. Pete Nardozzi stood on the porch, his uniform cap in his hands.

"Pete, you have no idea how glad I am to see you! In fact, I was just about to call you. Come on in," David said, patting the officer on the back.

"You were?" Pete replied, bewildered. "Now I really feel

like an idiot. I've been debating whether to talk to you for a couple of days now, but I didn't want to invade your privacy, under the circumstances."

David walked his friend into the study. "Don't be ridiculous. We're friends. You could never invade my privacy. Fact is, I should have called you days ago. I almost did—when I first found out Annie had left. I was going to make you find her for me. But at the time Mom seemed to think we needed to give Annie her 'space' and not chase after her. Now I'm not so sure."

He quietly closed the door. As both men sat down, Pete began, "Before we continue this conversation, you need to know the only reason I decided to come see you was after a lot of prayer. I couldn't get this whole situation out of my mind. And since I'm obviously in a position to be of some help, well—here I am." He smiled sheepishly then looked back down at his hands. "I'm here to offer my help in any way I can."

"Thanks, Pete. I appreciate that."

"So you've been in contact with her?"

"At first, yes. She left me a note and she's called a couple of times. But she doesn't want me to know where she is because she knows I'd be on the next plane. And she's right. I hate this! The person who means more to me than my own life is out of my reach and I can't call her, I can't find her . . ."

David bounced out of his chair, moving nowhere in particular, circling the room. "This one hit me broadside, Pete. Everyday, I help people work through their problems. I pray with them, I visit them in the hospital, I offer counseling . . . all kinds of advice. I'm there for them at the worst moments of their lives. I agonize with them over their heartaches, and I cry with them when they face hopeless situations.

"But now it's my own wife and I can't—I can't 'fix' this! Sure, I could send you off to track her down. But it's the last thing she wants right now. And I don't know what to do! I'm her husband and she wants me to stay away!"

He fell back into the chair behind his desk, embarrassed by his emotional display. The hot tears stinging his eyes surprised him.

Pete was quiet for several minutes. David felt comfortable in the silence, grateful that his friend would give him the ample time and space to blow off some steam. Finally Pete responded. "David, we've been friends a long time. You may be my pastor, but you're also my friend. And quite frankly, I don't think you've allowed yourself to just be a friend—*apart* from being a pastor or anything else. So please—don't be confined by some false need to be the perfect role model or the perfect pastor. Actually, I consider it quite an honor that you call me 'friend.' Not deacon, not church member, not any of that. Just friend."

David didn't look up, but was keenly aware Pete could see the imperceptible nod of his head. There was a decided difference in the air. A wall had come down and they both knew it.

Pete straightened his back. "Now, I want you to know a few things. When the story hit the papers—"

"Don't remind me," he moaned.

"—I took it upon myself to pay a visit to your mother-in-law."

David looked up. "You're kidding."

"No, I'm not. Maybe I was out of line, not talking to you first. But I knew the aftermath of that little stunt was going to be huge. I don't have to tell you, that's one *strange* woman."

They both laughed, the tension easing. "You don't know the half of it. God's been really merciful to give me a love for her over the years. But this—"

"Well, once we got passed the theatrics, I was very blunt with her. I pointed out the problems she had created for everyone concerned. Of course, she hadn't thought about any of that. I also warned her to stay away from the press. She didn't like that much until she agreed they hadn't been altogether accurate in their coverage. Said they 'highly exaggerated' her comments." Pete smiled. "And no, I didn't buy that for a moment."

"Sounds like you've got Darlene pretty well pegged. She is a piece of work, isn't she?"

"That she is." Pete's face turned more serious. "I've gotta tell you, I was rather stern with her. Folks can be intimidated by the uniform anyway, so I took advantage of that and let her have it. She went *way* over line with this, in my opinion."

"I'm sure you did fine. I wondered why we hadn't heard from her since all that hit the fan. It's not like her to be so silent. But trust me, it's a welcome silence. I'm not complaining."

Pete leaned forward, his elbows resting on his knees. "David, what can I do for you? How can I help you?"

"You tell me. Annie promised to keep in touch. I haven't heard from her in three days. And if that wasn't enough to drive me mad, now Max is gone."

Pete straightened again. "What?"

"He took off early this morning to find his mother. Not that I blame him. I should have done it as soon as I found her note. But Max is only sixteen!"

"So where is he?"

"He called in about an hour ago. I still don't know how he found out where Annie might be. Honestly, Pete, I think I'm about to lose my mind. I can't even think straight anymore. What should I do? What would *you* do?"

"For starters, I can put out an APB on him, if you'd like. That way we can locate him."

"I'm not so sure about that. If he gets pulled over, it's liable to spook him. Then again, I suppose it's not so unusual for a teenager to get pulled over, is it?"

Pete laughed. "No, it's not." He pulled his Blackberry out of his uniform pocket. "I'll need the year and make of his car as well as the license number."

"Then we have a problem. He's not in his car."

"Whose car does he have?"

"I don't know. He's trying to play this whole thing his way. I asked him about it, but he said he didn't want to involve anyone else or get anyone else in trouble. I guess we could ask a few of his friends."

"I can do that for you. If you can give me some names of his friends or school mates I can run them down. David, tell me something. Do you have any possible idea where Annie could have gone? Any place you've visited before? Maybe the

Diane Moody

home of a friend or a family member? Any idea at all?"

"I'm clueless. I've talked to everyone I can think of where she might have gone. Nothing. No one's seen her or heard from her. "

Pete returned the Blackberry to his pocket. He stood, prompting David to head for the door. "David, we'll work this out. We'll find them. Give me a little time to make some calls and I'll get back to you. You have my cell number if you need to reach me."

David patted him on the back. "Pete, I don't know how to thank you."

"Look, it's like I said—I consider it an honor for you to confide in me like this. And I take that level of confidentiality very seriously." He smiled as he turned to leave. "I mean, what are friends for, right?"

David fought the lump in his throat and grasped Pete's hand in a firm handshake. "Absolutely."

Chapter 29

Eagle's Nest

Annie settled Michael back onto the sofa then burrowed into her cocoon at the other end of the sofa. She covered both of them with piles of quilts and blankets. They couldn't stop shaking.

"One more favor."

"Michael, I'm not a slave here. Do you mind?"

"Hand me the guitar over there."

"No."

"Please?"

"Get it yourself."

"Very funny."

She dropped her head against her chest. Throwing back the covers, she hopped on her good foot across the room to the instrument resting in its stand by a wooden stool. "This is the last favor."

"Talk is cheap."

She handed him the guitar, growling at the cold. Once under her blankets again, she wrapped an afghan snugly around her head for warmth and glared at him.

"That's lovely. You look like one of Tevya's daughters in *Fiddler on the Roof.*" He smiled while tuning the acoustic guitar. She noticed a slight grimace, his efforts no doubt painful against the wound in his shoulder.

"Whatever."

His long fingers worked their magic, patiently finding the perfect pitch of each string. Finally satisfied, he strummed a few chords, humming no melody in particular.

"So help me, if you play—"

He interrupted, breaking into song with *Fiddler's* most famous tune.

"I knew it."

"What have you got against matchmaking?" he teased.

"Nothing. You're just so predictable."

"Okay, okay, I couldn't resist." He laughed, his fingers dancing across the strings as he played through the pain. She'd forgotten how well he played. She watched him, absorbed in his own little concert. Bits and pieces of old songs drifted through the air. Led Zeppelin's *Stairway to Heaven,* Emerson Lake & Palmer's *From the Beginning* . . . the haunting melodies, a part of every guitarist's repertoire.

When at last he settled into a quiet ballad, the first notes sent a spontaneous rush through her. The sweet familiar chords of a song once so intoxicating made her dizzy with memories. She closed her eyes, knowing the lyrics that would follow.

James Taylor. *Something in the Way She Moves.*

Their song.

Annie's heart fluttered at the caress of his voice, a sound so intimate she could feel the heat crawling across her face.

His serenade continued. James Taylor couldn't have done it better.

She couldn't help the smile that tugged her lips as she rocked gently to the rhythm of his concert.

He nudged her with his toe beneath the quilts as the melody continued. "I see that smile."

"Be quiet. I'm listening to the music."

"Are you now?" he teased, the bridge of the song filling the space between them.

"You know you wanna sing, Annie. "C'mon, sing with me."

Much to her own surprise, she did. Her voice, like so many times before, found its place alongside his in perfect harmony.

He finished with a flourish, the last guitar note hung in the air. She smiled shyly at him before turning her head and gazing back at the fire.

"That gave me goose bumps," he whispered. He laid the guitar across the coffee table. "But then you always did give me goose bumps."

The embers hissed as if on cue. Michael grew silent. She could feel his eyes following her. She prayed he couldn't read her thoughts as they drifted back in time, the images traipsing through her mind like an old home movie.

"We had it so good together, Annie," he said quietly.

She nodded ever so slightly, hearing his sustained deep sigh.

"I was such a fool to leave you. You were *everything* to me. We were soul-mates, you and I. Nothing was ever complete unless it included you."

Out of her periphery, she could see him turn to face her. "Remember that ancient little house we shared?"

She nodded again.

"Would you believe that little house was more of a home than any other place I've ever lived? I have a three million dollar estate outside of Houston. Most impersonal place I've ever lived. Why? Because there's not a trace of love in it. It's just brick and marble and paint and a lot of very expensive furniture. But our little house back in Stillwater—remember how tiny it was? We were *so* cramped living there. But we didn't care."

She smiled, lost in the memory. "I remember. The closet was so small I made you keep all your clothes in that makeshift dresser we picked up at the flea market. Ugliest piece of furniture ever made."

He laughed. "It was dog ugly, wasn't it? But I remember how you fixed up that whole house. Real cozy and comfortable. It was such a dump when we found it, but you transformed it into . . . a home. Remember how our friends loved to hang out there? There was always someone extra sleeping on the sofa or sharing a meal with us. They all loved being there with us."

She laughed, her elbow nudging his foot. "Michael, they hung around because they liked to sponge off us. Free food and a place to stay."

"Yeah, I guess you're right. No wonder we never had any money. We fed the entire baseball team most of the time as I recall. They *loved* your lasagna."

She smiled. "I never make it now that I don't think of those guys. But you know something?" she mused. "I didn't really mind. They were like family to us."

Michael leaned his head back. "Do you remember the time we had that big party after we won the conference playoffs? I think it was our junior year. All the guys and their girlfriends, all crammed into our house? Remember when we woke up the next morning and Lance Palmer was sprawled across the foot of our bed, sound asleep and snoring like a jackhammer—"

"—drooling all over our comforter! I was *so* mad at him!"

Michael laughed until the pain in his side protested. Which made Annie laugh, which made *him* laugh even harder until he winced with intense pain. She watched him until he finally caught his breath and turned to face her again. Their eyes met for a moment that seemed to stand still. Embarrassed by the intimacy of their shared memory, she looked away.

"Annie, I'm sorry. I didn't mean to make you uncomfortable." He paused, pulling up the quilts over his shoulders. He laid his head back once more and shut his eyes. "Maybe it's because I'm living such a nightmare now. I watched my perfect life just vaporize before my eyes. It's gone. All of it. Gone." He continued, his voice husky. "All of a sudden, I find myself fighting for my life."

He opened his eyes, turning to her with unmasked honesty. "And I'm scared. I have nothing left. Do you realize that? *Nothing.* My marriage—what there was of it—is over. My company is gone, my career is ruined. And unless a miracle comes along pretty soon, I'm a dead man."

Annie studied his face, captivated by the fear she found there. In all their years together, never had she ever seen Michael Dean afraid. Not once.

"Look, maybe I'm just asking for a little kindness," he pleaded. "A few moments to forget the nightmare and remember a better time. Is that so much to ask?"

Hearing the steady rhythm of his breathing, Annie felt suddenly tired, her mind weary from the swirl of thoughts and feelings and uncertainty. Still shivering, she dug down deeper into the blankets and rested her head against the back of the sofa. Despite her fatigue, an unwelcome struggle raged inside her. Somewhere, a fleeting wave of urgency beckoned. Was it caution?

Be careful. Be on your guard.

Another swarm of thoughts countered an attack. *He just needs a friend. He's right, you know. It's not so much to ask, is it? Just let go of all those problems you've been worried and obsessed about. He's just an old friend who needs you . . . he needs you . . .*

Slowly, she reached out her hand toward his. She felt him wrap his hand around hers, gently taking it back under the covers to stay warm against his leg. He squeezed her hand, the strength of his grasp so familiar, sending a soothing warmth through her. She let her head fall to the side so she could watch him, the ticking of the clock matching the beating of her heart.

He exhaled, his eyes closing again. "There has to be a reason, Annie," he whispered. "After all these years, we found each other. It can't be chance. Can't be." He sighed again before the restful pattern of his breathing resumed.

She gave in to the tugging lure of sleep as well, even as her thoughts battled on.

What am I doing . . . oh God, what am I doing?

Chapter 30

Seminole, Florida

From his study at home, David called his secretary's cell number. After a brief conversation, he changed the subject. "Listen, Sally, I'm heading into the office in few minutes. I've got to do some work or else lose my mind. And I'll be at the mid-week service tonight. I'm not sure what I'll preach on, but I'll manage somehow. I'll be in before anyone else this morning, but let's keep that between you and me at this point, all right? No appointments."

"Whatever you say."

"Thanks. Anything else I should know?"

Silence.

"Sally? What is it?"

"Something's up, David. The deacons have called a special business meeting, and I'm pretty sure Chet's behind it."

David groaned aloud. "I'm not surprised. But let's just take it one thing at a time, okay? See you in a little while, Sally."

ॐ

Pete Nardozzi eased his cruiser into a parking place marked PJ's CUSTOMERS ONLY. At eight in the morning, the popular donut shop was packed. As the jangling bell announced his arrival, he found his way to the far end of the counter near the archaic Frigidaire.

"Good-morning-how-you?" PJ's usual greeting drifted from behind the counter where the proprietor boxed up two dozen glazed donuts for a UPS driver.

"Morning, PJ," Nardozzi answered. "How's the day treating you, my friend?" He took a seat on one of the counter stools.

PJ snapped straight up at the sound of the officer's voice, shooting him a wrinkled, bewildered expression. His mouth fell open.

Startled, Pete set his hat on the counter then laughed. "PJ, you look like you've seen a ghost. What's gotten into you?"

"Uhhhhhh . . . Nothing wrong with me, Pete! No sir! No problem here!" he protested, busying himself with the truck driver's order. "Now I lose count. Let's see, that's sixteen, seventeen, eighteen—okay, now, I got it. That's twenty-four glazed for the UPS guys. Okay! See? I even give you guys a couple extra! See? Here—have a couple cinnamon rolls for the road, okay?"

The driver laughed and paid for the order then hustled out the door.

"Bye-bye-nice-day!" PJ's traditional farewell followed the man in brown out the door. He quickly began wiping down the counter opposite from Pete, then rushed around refilling coffee mugs. The bell on the front door rang again and the ritual repeated itself. "Good-morning-how-you?"

Pete waited. Normally, the donut maker scurried right over to serve Pete's usual cup of coffee and two buttermilk donuts. Not the case today. He rested his elbows on the counter, watching the curious owner dart around like a nervous mouse. He noticed the morning paper scattered on the counter and reached for the front page. In a box below the fold he noticed a short header: *Pastor's Wife Still Missing.*

"Don't they ever give up?" he mumbled to himself, scanning the brief story. As he continued to read the paper held in front of him, he sensed a presence. Slowly peeking over the newsprint, PJ's weathered face flashed from curiosity to feigned innocence.

Pete refolded the paper. "Okay, PJ. What's going on? For fourteen years I've come by here at least once a week and you always, *always* serve me my regular order without having to ask. You know exactly what I want. This morning I walk in and not only have you failed to bring me my food, you're ignoring me."

"What?" PJ protested. "I don't ignore you! I serve you like everybody else that comes in here!" He rushed to fill a cup of hot coffee and grab two buttermilk donuts. "See? I got your donuts. I got your coffee. I don't ignore you!"

Pete stared back at him. "Uh huh." The old man's eyes shifted mischievously. "PJ, could it be you know something you ought to be telling me?"

"Who me? Nobody ever tells me a thing. No sir. I just make the donuts, that's all I do. Always the last person on this earth to know anything! That's right, Officer Pete. Hey, you want a cinnamon roll?"

Pete laughed, raising his hands. "No, thank you, my friend. Sometimes I think this town would be downright boring without you, do you know that?" He continued to chuckle, making a mental note to keep an eye on the donut shop for the next couple of days. "It's like our buddy William Shakespeare used to say—'methinks thou dost protest too much.'"

PJ's brow knotted. Absently wiping the counter, he answered, "Well, okay. Yeah, oh sure, I know him. He's one of my regulars."

Pete donned his hat and put three bills on the counter. PJ shoved it back at him. "You know I don't let police pay for donuts! Put that away."

"Goodbye, PJ. Have a good day, and if you think of anything you might want to tell me, don't hesitate to call."

❧

The Texas Panhandle
The adrenaline of his mission was the only motivation keeping Max going. Miles melted into more miles. The hours flew as cities and small towns disappeared in his rear-view mirror.

State lines multiplied as he blazed toward his destination. With only an occasional stop for an hour's rest here and there, he inched ever closer to the Colorado state line.

Beyond exhaustion, his concern turned to weather. The reports on the radio sounded ominous. A Floridian driving on roads covered with ice and snow? Mounting concern gnawed at his empty stomach with each passing mile. Fortunately, the road crews had done their jobs well in clearing the main highways and roads. Much to his amazement, the old Volkswagen bus had performed fairly well for such a grueling trip.

He made his calls home right on schedule. His dad seemed more relieved with each call and his grandmother's oath of continuous prayers kept him going. He uttered his own prayer that neither of them tuned in to the Weather Channel.

He flipped on the wipers, attempting to clear the dirty windshield, uneasy with the sleet bouncing against the glass. "Come on, old hippie van, just get me there," he coaxed as he wiped down the foggy glass inside the windshield.

Then more quietly, he corrected himself. "Lord, just get me there. Please?"

❧

Seminole, Florida
David showered and headed for church. He slipped in through the private back entrance to his office. He needed to spend some time on his knees before talking to anyone.

Half an hour later, he heard a quiet knock on his door. Sally Hampton peeked around the corner. "Welcome back, boss. How's it going?"

David stretched his arms over his head. "Okay, I guess. It's good to be occupied with all this," his hand sweeping over the sea of papers. "Keeps my mind busy."

"Good. How about some coffee? I'll make us a fresh pot."

"Sounds great, Sally. You can catch me up on everything I've missed."

Returning minutes later with two steaming mugs, she began. "I'm sure you know, the church family is heartsick about everything that has happened to your family. I've fielded hundreds of calls for you. Most are very sympathetic, all promising to pray for you and the family."

David took a careful sip, then leaned back in his chair.

"And I've refused comment to the media as you requested."

"Thank you."

"Your mother-in-law made an appearance yesterday," she said with a hint of a smile.

"Darlene?"

"There's only one, thank goodness!"

"What was that all about?"

"She flew through here in all her glory. Ranting and raving and demanding to see you—the usual." Sally laughed, rolling her eyes.

"Any fall-out?"

"I don't think so. Fortunately, most of the office and staff were out for lunch at the time. Besides, everyone here knows all about Darlene. They recognize her for who she is."

"Attila the Hun?"

Sally laughed again. "Now, I didn't say that."

"She's unbelievable, isn't she? Aside from my mother-in-law, anything else I need to know about?"

Sally looked at the open door then back to David. "Only Chet," she whispered.

"Aha. Good ol' devil's advocate incarnate."

Sally kept her voice low. "Apparently he and Geneva hosted a 'prayer meeting' of sorts at their home the other night. The guest list was the usual who's-who among his adoring fan club. I have no idea what took place, but I have a bad feeling about all of it, David. He's up to something. I'm pretty sure he's behind the special business meeting called by the deacons."

"When has Chet *not* been up to something is the better question. I think it's time Chet and I went face to face on all this. Maybe I've been a fool to keep dodging him. He's given my kids a lot of grief, and I'm not going to put up with it any more.

"In fact, why don't you see if you can set up an appointment for Chet and me? And just so we do this the right way, let's have Justin and one of the other deacons sit in on this meeting. Safety in numbers, right?"

"Sure. I'll get right on it." She jotted herself a note, then stared at the pencil he was tapping against his coffee mug.

He stopped. "Sorry."

"Still no word from Annie?"

He drained the coffee and plunked down the mug on his

desk. "No, nothing. Hopefully Max will have some news for us shortly. Otherwise, all we can do is wait. God is teaching me whole new dimensions of the meaning of that word."

She stood to leave. "How about more coffee?"

"No thanks. I'm wired enough as it is."

Sally headed for the door. "I'll have the cleaners drop off your suit of armor."

"What?"

"Chet Harrison," she mouthed over her shoulder.

Chapter 31

Weber Creek, Colorado

We're back here by the fire," Mary Jean Williamson called out at the sound of the bell over the front door. She got up to greet her customers, surprised to see two unfamiliar faces. "Oh goodness, pardon me—I didn't expect any visitors in this kind of weather. Come on in, boys!"

The two men entered the quaint country store stomping snow off their shoes and rubbing their hands together.

"That's some kind of storm out there, ma'am!"

"Oh, we like to make a show of it this time of year, all right. You boys come back here by the fire and warm up. Can I get you a cup of coffee? I've kept it warm on the Coleman."

The two men headed for the back of the store. "Why, don't mind if we do at that. That's real kind of you, ma'am."

"Where you boys from?"

Her guests warmed their hands by the fire. She looked up just in time to see them make eye contact with each other before one of them answered. "Oh, we're pretty far from home. We're from down south."

She handed them each a mug of coffee. "South of here?"

The other one piped in this time. "Yeah, kinda far from here. We was just passing through when this storm stopped us."

His friend continued. "The roads are awful. Almost bought the farm a few miles back. Couple of near misses. Never seen anything like it before. So we figured we ought to find us some place to stop for awhile and wait it out."

Mary Jean gestured for the two men to have a seat in the rockers. "That's not a bad idea. I guess you heard the road just west of here is closed, so you wouldn't have gotten far anyway. Logging truck took the curve too fast and lost its whole load. Oh, it's a real pickle out there. Even knocked our power out. And now our phone lines are down. Glory be, what a mess."

For reasons she couldn't guess, the silence felt uncomfortable. "Yes, well, how can I help you gentlemen?"

"We was wondering if there was any place around here we could get a room for the night since it looks like we may be stuck here awhile."

The other man grimaced and cleared his throat. "What Gus here means is we need a place to ride out this storm. Any place you might be able to recommend?"

"Just down the street and around the corner is the Weber Creek Inn. Real nice place. I'm sure the Carters will be happy to help you out as best they can, all things considered."

Bob's voice drifted from the back room. "What'd you say, MJ?"

"Nothing, Bob. Just visiting with a couple of stranded travelers who stopped by." She turned back to them. "Is there anything else you all need? Any supplies? More coffee?"

Gus patted his pocket. "You got cell phone chargers?"

"We carry a few. Let's go see if we've got what you need."

Gus followed her, pleased when they located the exact brand his phone required. He smiled warmly at her. "Well, that's just great. Thank you, ma'am. I truly appreciate it."

"No problem. Anything else?" Mary Jean made her way toward the register.

"Actually, I was just wondering . . . "

"Yes?"

"Well, my buddy and I are trying to find a friend of ours. He was headed up into this area just a few days ago. So I was wondering if maybe you might have seen him. Tall, muscular, brown hair, real handsome like?"

"Hmmm, not so as I remember, but let me ask my other half. Bob? Honey, have you seen anybody new around here lately? A tall muscular guy with brown hair?"

"Nope. No one by that description, anyhow. But we'll keep our eyes open. If we hear anything, we'll get word over to you boys at the Inn. That okay?"

"That works just fine. Come on, Marcus, let's go."

Chapter 32

Seminole, Florida

Are you sure you're up to this?" Sally handed him the order of worship for the Wednesday evening service.

"Probably not, but it's what I've got to do." David pulled his sweater over his denim shirt, then attached the wireless microphone to his collar.

"By the way," she added, "I never got through to Chet. I left several messages at his home and also at the school office, but so far no response."

"Gee, why am I not surprised?" He stiffened, standing a little too tall as a smirk skirted his face. "He's scared of me, no doubt. Probably shaking in his boots somewhere as we speak. Keep trying." He winked then headed for the sanctuary.

Throwing open the side door to the auditorium, he bounced up the steps to the platform. Instantly, a hush fell over the sanctuary. His face warmed as he headed for his chair.

The keyboard player began quietly playing. Then slowly, applause broke out, spreading through the crowd until it drowned out the music.

David looked up, surprised to see his congregation on their feet, looking straight at him with smiles on their faces. A lump caught in his throat.

He held up his hand, acknowledging their spontaneous gesture of love. The applause grew louder until it thundered against the rafters.

Finally, he got up and approached the pulpit. He raised both his hands to quiet them. The roar subsided. He attempted to regain his composure as he looked around the auditorium. All around him, faces beamed with affection.

"You are . . . the *best*." His voice cracked but he didn't care. Clearing his throat, he started again. "If ever a man felt the love of God through human expression . . . I can't tell you how much I needed that."

He smiled at them through misty eyes. A familiar voice chimed from the front row. "We love you, Pastor."

"Thank you, Belinda—everyone." He paused a moment to gather his thoughts. "These last few days have been a nightmare for us, as you know. I've known disappointment and heartache before, but this has been—" He paused, swallowed. "So hard." He took a deep breath, determined to continue.

"But even when I've been weak, God has been there for me. Of course, that's something I preach to you all the time. He promises to always be there for us. *Always*. Even when I lost my patience or lost my temper and—"

"That's enough, Pastor McGregor," a voice boomed from the back of the auditorium.

David searched the crowd. Murmurs waved through the congregation. On the far right-hand side, last pew, he spotted him.

Chet Harrison stood up, straightening his coat jacket, adjusting his tie as if he had all the time in the world. He began to make his way down the aisle taking a deliberate, slow stride.

"I have something that needs to be said right here and right now." He stepped up onto the platform, approaching the pulpit without making eye contact.

David shrugged. "Chet, I don't think this is the time to—"

"It has come to my attention that the church family is not fully aware of all the facts in this unfortunate crisis in your family."

His hand covering the microphone on his collar, David quietly pleaded with him. "Chet, please. Can't we—"

Chet jerked his arm loose from David's touch and reached for the pulpit microphone.

"Ladies and gentlemen, as a long-time devoted member of this church family, I am compelled to speak to you."

"Sit down, Chet! You're out of order!" a voice yelled from the middle of the room.

He held up his hands, cocking his head to the side. "On the contrary. There are times when situations may circumvent the usual way of doing things, and this is one of those times."

David stepped aside, folding his arms across his chest. *Go ahead. Get it out of your system. Have your five minutes of fame.*

"No one is more sympathetic than I about the difficult week that has occurred in this man's family. All of us grieve for what must surely be a heart-wrenching experience for Pastor McGregor, his children, his mother—"

David looked across at the pew where his mother always sat. Their eyes met and he felt her prayers.

"And while we may not fully understand why his wife has suddenly disappeared—"

"Chet, I'm begging you," David tried one more time.

"—I am quite uncomfortable with some of the facts coming out of this situation. While I would not think to discuss these matters here in the house of our gracious Lord, I am nevertheless obliged to inform the church family of my opinion—and that of several others among us—that our Pastor is not fit to serve at this time and should be relieved of his position of leadership."

Boos and shouts erupted across the room, rolling through the crowd like a tsunami. A number of deacons stood, but they were too late. Chet nodded his head ever so slightly. His ready followers quickly filed across the front of the sanctuary. Standing shoulder to shoulder, they formed a human chain between the platform and the congregation.

A hush swept over the crowd. Several of the elderly ladies up front whispered among themselves. In the aisles now, the deacons slowed their pace as they watched the scene unfold.

Chet tapped the microphone forcing the room back into silence. "Ladies and gentlemen, I am not here to offend or upset you. But we cannot leave the leadership of this body of believers in the hands of a man who is emotionally unstable. Our just and righteous God would not have us do that."

David moved back to his chair, sat down and buried his face in his hands.

Chet continued. "I feel as much compassion as any one of you, as all of you. But duty dictates that we must do the right thing. As I have said, there are facts you do not know—"

"Such as what!" shouted one of the deacons on the side aisle. "You claim to know something, Chet. So spit it out!"

David looked up just as Chet took a handkerchief out of his pocket to wipe his brow. *Ever the drama king.*

"I didn't want it to come to this, I assure you. But word has come to me that our pastor's wife has disappeared all right. Right into the arms of another man."

A split second of silence. Before the shouts of protest could pass the lips of his congregation, David flew out of his seat, grabbing Chet Harrison by the back of his neck. Whirling the arrogant chump around to face him, he reared back and belted him right in the nose. Harrison fell back onto the floor as absolute silence paralyzed the brethren.

Oblivious to everything else, David reached out to pull up his adversary by his bloodied shirt only to feel himself being pulled away from his target. "Let me go!" he cried. "He can't get away with this! He has no right to—"

Chet crawled backward across the carpeted platform, yelling, "Help me! Somebody help me! He's crazy!"

David watched the surreal scene unfold around him.

Geneva Harrison ran to the front of the room howling for her poor husband.

Mary Bloom, the oldest member of the church at ninety-seven, fainted, sliding under the front pew like a piece of linguine. Sitting at the end of her aisle, PJ Ludwinski rushed to her side shouting in Polish. Her elderly friends wailed their dismay.

Men throughout the auditorium rushed forward, attempting to break through the barrier of Chet's men. Fist-fights broke out among them like a WWF brawl. Steve Anderson was shoved from behind by Dwight Eggers, one of Chet's men. In retaliation, Steve picked up his contender and threw him over his shoulder. The feisty little guy bonked him on the head, causing Steve to lose his balance. With the room spinning around him, Steve began to twirl around and around until he let go of his captive who catapulted against a stained glassed window, crashing on impact. The sight and sound of it sickened David.

He turned in time to see Mary Bloom's minion of friends come to her rescue. Leaving her to their care, PJ shuffled up to the platform. He checked to make sure David was safe under the protection of his friends, their eyes locking as the old man frowned in obvious concern for him. David's stomach churned as he saw PJ turn his attention to Chet. The troublemaker lay with his head in Geneva's lap, a handkerchief held to his nose to stop the bleeding.

"Shame on you!" PJ shouted, trying to push his way through the crowd of people. "You big blow hole! You see this?" he taunted, holding up a gnarled fist. "Let me at him!" He elbowed his way against the wall of men. "Nobody talks to David that way! Nobody!"

Then, amidst the mass confusion, David noticed the back doors of the church fly open. There, his own mother-in-law, her face flushed with excitement, escorted in a television crew.

"All right! This is great stuff!" A smiling camera man began to roll tape.

"He's a maniac! I told you the pastor was nuts! But no one listened to me!" Darlene ranted, hustling after the camera crew.

David groaned under his breath. He watched as the cameraman neared the platform. Moaning louder for the camera, Chet tried to sit up. "Help me, honey—I'm afraid the pastor may have given me a concussion."

❧

I've never witnessed anything so ridiculous in my entire life!" Caroline paced back and forth across the family room carpet. "I've a good mind to rush over there and give that man a piece of my mind!"

They had arrived home only moments earlier. Pete Nardozzi escorted them home after a parishioner called him to the scene at church. He joined them after placing a few phone calls from the privacy of David's study.

"They've already released Chet from the hospital. His buddy Dwight wasn't quite so lucky. They'll be plucking colored glass out of his, uh—*posterior* for another couple of days." Pete tried to hide his smile.

"Never in my life have I seen such an ungodly display of stupidity." Caroline continued. "To think that this church could have that many raving lunatics! Well, I can guarantee you one thing, David McGregor—that man will have a lot of explaining to do when he comes face to face with his Maker—*if* the good Lord lets him in those pearly gates." She stormed out of the room, ranting all the way into the kitchen.

"Daddy, did you really punch Mr. Harrison's lights out?" Jessica asked, her soulful eyes searching his.

He lifted her onto his lap. "I'm afraid so, princess. He said some unkind things, and unfortunately, I overreacted. It was a very *wrong* way for me to respond, and I'm sorry for what I did. Very sorry."

Her eyes grew even wider, her fingers gently caressing his face. "That's okay, Daddy. Somebody needed to teach him a lesson."

"No, sweetheart, it *isn't* okay. It's never okay to hit somebody—no matter who it is and no matter what the circumstances."

"David, don't be so hard on yourself," Pete interrupted. "Chet was out of control and had to be stopped."

"That may be, but not this way. I had no business decking him like that. And in front of the whole church? I don't know what came over me! What kind of a message does that send to my church family?" He hugged his daughter. "Sweetheart, why don't you go see if Gran could use some help?" She kissed his cheek and scampered out of the room.

Pete looked him straight in the eye. "You did the same thing I would have done, so enough of the guilt. Got it?"

The house phone rang. Pete grabbed it. "Officer Nardozzi." Pause. "Sure, Max. He's right here, just a minute." He handed the phone to David.

"Max!"

"Dad? Why did Mr. Nardozzi answer the phone?"

"It's a long story. One you'll probably enjoy, come to think of it. But I'll tell you all about it later when you and Mom get home. Where are you?"

"We had an agreement, Dad. Remember?"

"Oh sure, I know. I forgot. Are you all right?"

"I'm fine, but my transportation just died."

"What happened? You okay?"

"I think I just ran the life out of it. It was old to begin with and I've put a lot of miles on it."

"Can you get to a mechanic?"

"I'm at a truck stop right now and there's a mechanic here, but he's really busy. I'm hoping he can find out what's the matter with it. I don't know how long it's going to take. I'm really bummed."

"I know, Max. But take it easy, okay? It's probably good for you to stop and get some sleep. Is there a motel near by?"

"I think so. The thing is, Dad . . . I'm, uh, I'm a little nervous, I guess."

"Say the word and I'll come to you. Maybe that's the best thing anyway."

He didn't answer right away. "I don't know. Give me a

chance to think for a little while."

"Whatever you say, sport." David covered the receiver with his hand. "Pete—any way you can find out where this call is coming from?" he whispered.

"No problem."

David gave him the thumbs-up. "Are you still there, Max?"

"Yeah, sure, Dad. I'm pretty tired. Think I'll do like you said and get some sleep. I'll call you back in a couple of hours."

"Okay, just be careful."

"Love you, Dad."

"Same here, big guy."

He carefully hung up the phone and looked at Pete.

"Just press the star button and the numbers six and nine."

"Okay." David punched the keys. A long distance number appeared. "Wow, like magic! I didn't know you could do that. Okay, so what state has an area code with 719?

Pete worked his Blackberry, pulling up a directory. "It looks like area code 719 includes Pueblo and Colorado Springs."

"Max is in Colorado?" David asked in disbelief.

Pete whistled. "That kid of yours has covered a *lot* of territory. I'll get someone to track down that number. We can pinpoint his exact location. Shouldn't take but a minute." He activated the shoulder mic which squawked to life. A few moments later, he had his answer. "He's at Bailey's Truck Stop in Boone, Colorado. That's about twenty miles east of Pueblo off State Road 96."

David stood up. "Boone, Colorado. Pueblo . . . What's Annie doing in—" He slapped the heel of his hand against his forehead. "Christine! Why didn't I think of it before? That's got to be it! Pete, I know where she is!"

Chapter 33

Southeast Colorado

Max headed to the motel adjacent to the truck stop. A flashing neon sign caught his eye.

HOT HOMECOOKED MEALS

After living on pretzels, Little Debbie Oatmeal Cakes, and Big Macs, he was starving for something more substantial. He headed straight for the diner, his taste buds already gearing up for meatloaf, friend chicken, or maybe even a thick juicy steak.

The blast of warm air knocked the chill off his bones as he entered the spacious, austere diner. Max looked for an empty booth finding most of them occupied with truckers. He slipped into one on the end, sliding across the red vinyl seat.

A waitress brought him a glass of water and a menu, along with a quick rundown of the specials. He scanned the menu, deciding on the fried chicken dinner with mashed potatoes, gravy, macaroni and cheese, tossed salad with blue cheese dressing, and biscuits.

"Oh, and save me a slice of your cherry pie for dessert?"

"Sure thing. Anything to drink?"

"Coffee. Black. Thanks."

"No problem. Be right back with your salad."

He sat back in the booth, stretching his long legs beneath the table. He rubbed his face brusquely hoping to awaken his mind enough to enjoy the meal. Sipping the glass of water, he pulled the folded map of Colorado from the pocket in his jacket and spread it out across the table. Even if the mechanic could make time to look at the old van, he knew he couldn't afford a costly repair bill. Frustrated and weary, he breathed a silent prayer for direction.

With his eyes still closed, he couldn't help overhearing the animated conversation in the booth across the narrow aisle.

"Yes, I understand, ma'am. But I am not *in* Weber Creek. I'm the sheriff *from* Weber Creek, and I'm calling you from another location. I'm on my way *back* to Weber Creek. All I'm asking is how much longer you expect the phone lines to be down in that area."

Max peeked sideways to see who was talking. A uniformed sheriff sat alone in the booth talking on a cell phone.

"No, the phones here are fine. That's not the problem—

what? No, I'm not on a pay phone, I'm calling from my cell phone. What?"

An idea took shape even as Max continued to eavesdrop.

"Okay. No, forget it. Never mind!" The sheriff snapped off the phone and blew out an exasperated sigh.

"Excuse me?"

The sheriff jerked his head toward Max.

"I couldn't help overhearing. You're heading for Weber Creek, right?"

"Trying to, anyway. On my way back from a conference in Amarillo. I live in Weber Creek, but this storm hit pretty hard over there. Power's out, phones are down. Why do you ask?"

The waitress brought Max's meal, setting it out before him. He dodged around her attempting to carry on his conversation. "Actually, I'm headed there myself, but my van broke down. And I was wondering . . . I was thinking maybe, could I hitch a ride with you? Is it legal to hitchhike with a cop?"

The sheriff laughed. "Sure, no problem."

"Awesome! Thank you! Thank you so much, Officer!"

"I'm Brett Patterson." The sheriff stood, extending his hand to Max. "Mind if I join you?"

"No! Not at all. I'm Max Mc—" he hesitated, shaking the sheriff's hand. Relieved he hadn't said his whole name, he quickly changed the subject. "Can I buy you something to eat? Are you hungry? This chicken is outstanding. Want some?"

Patterson waved him off. "No, but thanks. I'll just have a refill on my coffee." He looked over Max's shoulder for the waitress. "And take your time. We're in no hurry."

Max bit into the crunchy chicken breast, savoring its flavor. "Oh man, this stuff is too good," he said around a mouthful. "I haven't had anything but McDonald's and Dunkin' Donuts for days. This—" he added, waving the chicken for emphasis, "is *great*."

"Where are you from? What brings you to Weber Creek?"

"Florida. My mom."

"You drove all the way from *Florida*?"

"Yes, sir. It's been a haul, let me tell you."

"I guess it has. Your mom lives in Weber Creek?"

"No, sir. Just visiting." Max took another mouthful wondering how much he should say.

The waitress slid his pie across the table toward him. "I'll scarf this down then we can hit the road. Oh, except I need to make a phone call if that's okay."

❧

Seminole, Florida

Pete Nardozzi looked up as the bell on the door of the donut shop rang again.

"Hey PJ. Any word from Ma—" Megan Tanner shot a look at Nardozzi, then the donut maker, then back at the officer.

Nardozzi looked back and forth between the two of them.

Megan smiled brightly at him then turned again to PJ. "Uh—oh hey, I just came by to, uh, to pick up those—"

"All right, you two. I think it's time the three of us had a nice little chat." Pete stood, waving Megan to the stool beside him. "Have a seat, Miss Tanner."

Her smile faded. She sat down then folded her hands on the counter in front of her.

Pete took his seat again and drummed his fingers on the counter. "You'll never guess what just happened. Pastor McGregor and I have discovered that Max is in Colorado. That's right. *Colorado.* Now I don't suppose you two would know anything about that, would you?"

"Colorado? Max in Colorado. Imagine dat," PJ mused.

Megan raised her brows in a sad attempt at surprise.

"Fact is, Max called his father just a little while ago. Seems his *mode of transportation* broke down on him." He studied PJ's evasive eyes. "So he's up there in Colorado, the roads are bad, he's thousands of miles from home, and he's sounding pretty scared." He didn't miss the fleeting trace of concern that flashed across Megan's face.

"And it strikes me as rather *coincidental* that your van has disappeared from out back, PJ. It's been gone since— wow, just about the time Max took off! So I'm wondering— could it be? Is it possible that Max borrowed that old VW bus to try to find his mother?"

"Okay, that's it." PJ threw his towel on the counter. "He got us, Megan. No use trying to hide the truth from this one, no sir!"

Megan dropped her head into her hands. "Okay, okay." She looked up again. "But we weren't trying to lie or anything. Honest! It's just that Max really wanted to do this all on his own. He thought if he could just find his mother, then everything else would be all right."

"I understand. I do," Pete said. "But the situation has moved beyond that. I've been in touch with the Highway Patrol up there. It's a near blizzard through that part of Colorado. The roads are a mess. We need to find Max and we need to find his mother. The McGregors haven't heard from her in several days.

"Game over. We need your help."

Chapter 34

Southeast Colorado

Thornton, this is Patterson. I've been trying to get through. How long have the regular phones been back up?"

Max woke up, his neck stiff from leaning against the cruiser's passenger window. He looked over to see the sheriff talking on his cell phone. Patterson continued his conversation then ended the call. "My deputy says the road should be cleared up from that accident in just a couple more hours. Power should be back on by daybreak."

Max stretched, trying to wake up. "Where are we?"

"Just a few miles out now."

He looked out the window at the mad flurry of snow. "Maybe so, but at this rate we'll be another six hours getting there. How slow are you going, anyway?"

Patterson dropped his gaze to check the speedometer.

"Looks like thirty-five miles per hour. Not bad with the roads in this condition. We're lucky to be moving at all."

The wipers whipped away the flakes beating a steady rhythm. Max watched them, back and forth, back and forth. "Would you believe I've never seen snow?"

"You're kidding."

"Nope. Never snows in Florida. This is pretty cool."

"You certainly timed it right this trip. Lived up here all my life and I still love the snow. It can cause a mess of things, but I never get tired of it. You should try to do some skiing while you're here."

Max rubbed his face and yawned, stalling. "We'll see."

℘

Houston, Texas

I don't want to hear any more of your ridiculous complaints!" Elliot growled into the receiver. "I want a visual confirmation that he's in that cabin and I want it now! Quit screwing around and get up that mountain!"

"Oh, nossir, I don't think you mean for us to get up there *tonight,* sir. You gotta understand—the roads here are *real* bad right now. It's too dangerous out there to drive."

"Then you'll walk up that mountain and you'll do it NOW!"

"You want us to *walk* up a mountain road that's nothing but a sheet of ice and snow at this—"

"That's exactly what I want! And the split second you mark him, you call me. Understood?"

"Yes, sir. Right now. Me and Marcus. We'll climb that mountain if it kills us."

❧

You boys back so soon?" Bob posted the CLOSED sign on the door.

"Afraid so. Me and my friend here need us some warmer clothes. We're about to freeze to death. You sell clothes?"

"A few. Come on in and follow me."

Mary Jean continued sweeping the floor, watching the two men. She worked her way over to the fireplace where Doc Wilkins sat on the hearth warming his back and reading a Tom Clancy novel. She tapped her broom against his leg.

"George," she whispered. "Look at those two."

Doc peered over his glasses, taking in the newcomers from head to toe. He looked back at Mary Jean, shrugging his shoulders as if to say "so?"

Mary Jean positioned herself between Doc and the others, her back to them. "They were in here earlier this afternoon. Said they were stuck here on account of the weather."

Doc tried to find his place in his book. "What's so strange about that and why are we whispering?"

"I don't know. Just a couple of weird ones, I suppose. Something strange about them. I can't quite put my finger on it. They were asking if we'd seen some other fellow. Said it was a friend of theirs they'd lost track of. But I'm thinking that's not it at all." She swept around Doc's feet, straining to see them.

He inserted the bookmark nonchalantly and closed the book. "How come?"

"I don't know, George. Something's just not right."

"Did they say who this person was they're looking for?"

"Didn't leave a name, come to think of it. And I didn't have sense enough to ask, I reckon. Described him as a tall fellow with dark hair. I think they said he was handsome or nice looking, or something like that." Mary Jean noticed a trace of alarm on Doc's face. She was glad he was finally starting to take her seriously.

"What else did they say?"

"Nothing."

Doc stole another glance at the two men now making their way to the counter with their arms full of long johns, flannel shirts, thick socks, and wool stocking caps.

Bob rang up their purchases on the old register. "That comes to a total of two-hundred and eighty-five dollars." Doc, Mary Jean and Bob all watched as the customer pull out a thick roll of crisp, new hundred dollar bills, peeling off three of them.

"Marcus, c'mon. We gotta get going," the other man beckoned from the front of the store.

The one called Marcus stuffed his money back in his jacket and lifted the oversized bags of their purchases. "Keep the change. Thanks for the help."

As soon as the door closed, Mary Jean dashed to Doc's side. "See what I mean, George? Something's fishy about those two. Mark my words."

"Any idea where they're staying? Are they over at the

Inn?" Doc asked.

"I think so. Least ways, that's where we recommended when they asked."

Doc put his book on a shelf behind the counter then reached for his coat. "Well, I wouldn't get all worked up, MJ. Just a couple of strange ducks passing through. Aren't the first. Won't be the last."

Bob helped him put his coat on. "Where are you off to? Why don't you stick around for dinner? MJ made her homemade chicken pot pie."

Doc was already heading for the door. "No thanks. I need to look in on some of the girls before it gets too late. Maybe I'll stop back by later this evening."

&

Doc was out the door before Bob or Mary Jean could protest, but his thoughts were definitely not on the widows in town.

He looked across the street just in time to see the two men turning the corner, no doubt heading for the inn. Pushing his hat down farther on his head, Doc followed them at a safe distance.

Once the two men entered the inn, he walked carefully over the ice-crusted road toward the inn's parking lot on the other side of the building. Grateful for the cover of darkness, he moved among the few cars parked there. Most were covered with several inches of snow, like caricatures of some weird Arctic creatures. In the far back corner near the hotel dumpster, he spotted a black sedan. The nondescript automobile was partially covered with snow. It was caked with dirty ice, the kind that hitches a ride along the bottom edge of a car's body when it travels on roads treated with salt and sand. Clearly a new arrival.

Glancing around, careful no one was watching him, Doc shuffled to the back of the car. With this gloved hand, he brushed the dirty snow off the license plate. It was too dark to make out the numbers and letters. He remembered the tiny flashlight on his keychain and dug it out of his pocket. Muffling the jangling keys with his gloves, he aimed the penlight at the plate as he knelt down, safely out of sight.

Texas tags. A Houston Ford dealership plate holder.

Bingo.

Chapter 35

Houston, Texas

Elliot heard the tremor of anger in his own voice. "I don't trust those clowns and I can't afford to have them let Michael get away. Not when we're this close." He wedged the phone against his shoulder as he continued packing his briefcase. "We've got to finish this and make sure it's done right. That's why I need you. You've helped me this far and I want you there at the finish line."

He sat back down as he listened to the response on the other end of the line. He checked his Rolex—it was just after three in the morning. "Good. I'll fly out of here in one hour. That should put me at your airport at five-thirty sharp. Meet me at Hangar 12. We'll get back in the air and be in Pueblo no later than seven."

He nodded, the cell phone still at his ear. "Don't worry

about it. I've got a Hummer waiting for us there with a driver who knows the roads. A little snow isn't about to stop me now. Just be at that hanger and don't be late."

Elliot disconnected the line. He looked around his study, inhaling the comforting scent of the leather books that lined his bookshelves. But in the darkness of this early morning, he found no comfort. His coffee mug shook in his hand, the sight of it setting his nerves on edge. He kneaded his throbbing temple. A sob escaped, startling him. He sat back in his chair, rubbing his hand roughly across his mouth then biting the knuckle of his fist.

Through blurred eyes, his gaze rested on the family photographs elegantly framed and lining his credenza. His eyes crinkled as they caressed the image of his beloved wife. He reached for the picture, cradling it in his hands. Taken the summer before she died, she smiled warmly beneath the brow of a large straw hat. She was sipping lemonade while stretched out on the porch swing of their lake house. Relaxed and happy and beautiful.

He took a deep and ragged breath. His eyes shifted to the ornate silver frame where Amelia and Michael smiled, proudly adorned in their wedding attire. *Amelia's eyes, so like her mother's . . .*

The last time he'd searched his daughter's eyes, they were dull and lifeless and bloodshot. Her hospital gown hung loosely around her, revealing pale and bony shoulders. She was curled in a fetal position, her wrists bound in stark white bandages as she rocked slowly back and forth.

He slammed the frame face-down on his desk and cried out. After a moment's thought, he grabbed the picture, holding it tightly in his hands as he stared at the images through broken glass. He felt the scorching heat of hatred swell through him again. Carefully, he replaced the photograph, snapped his briefcase shut, and left the room.

An hour later, seated aboard his Lear jet, he sipped a glass of orange juice as the plane sped through the ink black sky, leaving Houston's skyline behind. After a brief stop at five-thirty to board another passenger, the jet climbed once more the early morning sky and streamed westward toward Colorado.

Chapter 36

Eagle's Nest

Annie woke up, chilled to the bone and shivering. She got up, quietly leaving her spot on the sofa to put more logs on the fire. As her sleepiness gave way to reality, she shuddered against the uneasiness seeping through her. A few moments later, she welcomed the revived warmth billowing out of the fireplace, momentarily relieving her senses. She stood against the hearth, her hands outstretched. The heat thawing her icy fingers.

Wake up!

She jumped, startled to find Michael still sound asleep. She looked around, certain she had heard a voice.

Wake up! Listen to me!

Her eyes grew wide with recognition. There was no question in her mind. Turning back to face the fire, she fell to her knees before the hearth. "Oh God—I need You!" she whispered.

Shhhhh . . .

It wasn't an audible voice but one she knew without question. "Lord, I'm so confused. Please help me!"

Shhhhh . . .

"Lord, You've been so silent. Why did you desert me when I needed you most?"

I'm here. I've been here all along.

Then a rush of guilt flooded her heart. "Forgive me, Father. I should never have doubted you."

Words failed her. Yet, in a split second, every fear in her heart melted away. Every frustration that had rendered her spiritually powerless for these many months seemed instantly absolved. Every seed of bitterness and disappointment was plucked away in the blink of an eye. An overwhelming release sent tears spilling like the currents of a mighty river. Her body trembled as the incomprehensible warmth of his embrace surrounded her.

She rested her head on folded arms, warm against the stones of the hearth. "Thank You, Father. I don't understand. Why here, why now? After all of this . . . but oh God, thank you!"

Annie, here's what I want you to do. Hear what I say.

As her mission unfolded, Annie wept with tears of gratitude. Suddenly everything that had happened before and all that had happened here in this cabin became clear and focused. She laughed through her tears, wiping them against the fuzzy wool of her sweater.

"Show me how, Lord," she whispered, turning back to Michael's side.

"Michael. Michael, wake up!" She shook him, rubbing her hand against his cold cheek. "I have to talk to you. Wake up!"

"What? Who's there?" he jumped, startled. When his eyes focused on Annie, he relaxed. "Annie, don't do that to me! I thought someone was—what's the matter with you? You look—"

"I have to talk to you. I finally get it."

He tried to sit up, grimacing at the persistent pain in his side. "Get what?"

"This is really important. I need you to listen to me."

"I'm listening, I'm listening. What's this all about?"

She took a deep breath, kneeling beside the sofa. "I need to explain something to you. See, the reason I came up here to Christine's cabin was because I was dying inside. I realize that now. I was so frustrated with everything in my life. I couldn't go on anymore. I'd lost my way.

"It's not important for me to tell you everything right now, except this—the very reason I was here was because I'd become *so* distracted with all the wrong things in my life! I was blinded by the stupid stuff. I let all that insignificant junk weigh me down until I rendered myself absolutely worthless."

Michael stopped her, impatience written on his face. "Why are you telling me this? I don't think I need to hear—"

"Yes, you do. Just let me say what's on my heart. I know it sounds ridiculous but, the truth of the matter is, I ran away from home."

He yawned. "You ran away from home."

"Yes. I quite literally ran away from home! I'm a grown woman who left her husband, her kids, her whole life behind, to come up here.

"See, I thought I was losing my mind. I thought if I could just have some time to myself, time to think through everything, I would be all right. But I wasn't. I came up here to get a fresh sense of what my life was all about. But that didn't happen. All of that 'stuff' was still there, hovering over my head.

"Then I got angry. I kept asking why? Why was this happening to me? All I ever wanted was to be a good wife to David, and a good mother to my children. Why was all the rest of it such a stumbling block to my life? Why couldn't I handle it? Why was I giving up on David instead of fighting for him? Where was my backbone! I'd completely lost sight of everything that was right and good in my life.

"But now I see! It took coming here to this cabin—and you—and *all* of this for me to see the truth!"

"Annie, I have no clue what you're talking about. You've lost me."

She smiled, taking his hand in hers. "That's just it—you were lost! Don't you see? The same thing was happening in *your* life. Maybe the circumstances were different, but in your own way, you were stumbling all over your life just like I was. You said yourself that your life was ruined. Your marriage was ruined. Your career was ruined. Why? Because you tried to do it all your *own* way. You called all your own shots—" She stopped mid-sentence as a thought occurred to her . . . "—and got shot in the process!"

"Very funny. But what's that got to do—"

"It's got *everything* to do with it. Look, regardless of whose fault any of it was, the bottom line is that your life was a total disaster. Admit it! But you knew the answer, even though you didn't *know* you knew the answer."

He stared at her, blinking. "You're not making any sense."

She could tell his patience was wearing thin.

Say it, Annie. Tell him.

"You said it yourself. You said that unless a miracle came along, you were a dead man."

His eyes narrowed, daring her to continue.

"Michael," she whispered. "*This* is your miracle. And you were right about something else. None of this was by chance! It could never have happened by mere coincidence. You—me—here . . . together after all these years? What are the odds? It wasn't some obscure second chance at a long-lost relationship. We weren't brought here to rekindle a romance from way back when. We're here—now. You and me. Holed up in this cabin, snowed in, out of touch with the rest of the world. Why? For this very moment. *This* is your miracle."

He grabbed her shoulders. "ANNIE! Stop talking in circles! I. Don't. Understand!"

"But I do! That's just it! God had to yank me out of my pity party and out of my worn-out routine and drag me up this mountain in the middle of nowhere. He had to let me pour my heart out to Him and spill out all that venom and anger and hurt and frustration—because *he needed me*. It

Diane Moody

was his way to prepare me for something extraordinary."

"For WHAT?"

"He wants to use me. Like . . . like a life raft. For *you,*
Michael." She looked deeply into his eyes, searching for
some light of understanding. A tenderness so pure filled her
with a love that astounded her.

A very different kind of love.

"Michael Dean, you showed up here shot up like a piece
of Swiss cheese. Dumped on my doorstep half-dead. You are
completely at my mercy. And finally, *finally,* I have a chance
to tell you about Someone who totally turned my life
around. Someone who has all the answers, all the miracles,
all the hope you or I could ever need.

"Oh Michael, if only you knew. All those years ago, you
broke my heart. But instead of bitterness, I've carried a
secret heartache that had nothing to do with how you left
me. Because God changed my life. He gave me a new slate
to start all over. But deep inside, my heart has always ached
that I never had a chance to share Him with you. Over the
years, whenever you crossed my mind—if I heard our song
on the radio or saw you playing ball on TV—I prayed for
you, asking God somehow, some way, to get through to you.
To love you like He's loved me.

"Don't you see? All that emptiness you feel? It's because
God made each of us with a place in our hearts just for
Him. But He didn't force Himself on us. He designed it to be
'by invitation only.' We have to *want* Him to be a part of our
lives. And He wants desperately to be invited in. But even

when we ignore him or reject Him, He doesn't give up on us.

"And it's so simple. All we have to do is ask. Ask Him to forgive us for screwing up our lives, for leaving Him out of the picture, and for all the wrongs we've committed in the process. Then we only have to believe He's who He says He is. He's God! And He gave his Son to provide a way for us to come to Him. It's all about forgiveness, don't you see?"

"No, Annie. It isn't that simple. You don't understand. You have no idea what kind of person I've become. You don't know—"

"But that's just it. We've all made mistakes. We've all made messes of our lives in one way or another. And that's the whole point. We've tried to fill that void in our lives that was made just for Him. And we can't do that with anything else *but* Him. All the while He waits for us, and waits and waits, until we come to the end of the rope and realize we have no place else to turn but to Him.

"Yes, Michael. It really is that simple."

Tears filled his eyes despite the confusion she saw there. She knew a fierce and mighty battle raged behind those eyes.

She spoke urgently, barely above a whisper. "You've been in the driver's seat your whole life, and look where it got you. Just hand the keys over to Him. He wants so much for you to hand over those keys because He wants *you*. Let go, Michael. Give Him your life. He can make it whole and pure and good like it's never been before."

She searched his eyes for an answer. There was only one question left to ask. "What have you got to lose?"

He closed his eyes, his chin trembling. Now was his

moment of truth. She too closed her eyes, praying for God's peace and presence to overwhelm him and lead him out of the darkness forever.

She didn't know how long they remained that way. Finally, she heard him take a deep breath and felt him gently rub her hand. She looked up, his face familiar but now strangely different. Even the look in his eyes was different.

And for now, that was enough.

Chapter 37

Pueblo, Colorado

At the Pueblo Memorial Airport, the sleek white jet descended for landing. Nearly invisible in the heavy snowfall, the blinking lights on the aircraft flashed rapidly as though begging for assistance. The pilot of the jet had ignored the warnings from his radio. He wasn't daunted by a few flakes of snow. He had been instructed to land the plane regardless of the conditions on the tarmac. And land he would, paid generously for the effort.

The runway had been cleared sometime earlier, though a fresh layer of snow already covered it again. Fortunate for any renegade pilots, the salt trucks had prevented the pavement from icing. Still, the pilot cautiously touched down, careful to ease the brakes. It wasn't a pretty landing as the plane slipped to a stop before the end of the runway then taxied slowly to a hanger.

As the engines whined down, the side door lifted opened. Stair-steps lowered. Two figures quickly descended the steps and hurried into a waiting black Hummer. The large vehicle left immediately, disappearing into the storm before the jet's engines ever quieted.

❧

Weber Creek, Colorado

Doc Wilkins backed into Williamson's, kicking snow off his boots. "Bob? MJ? I want to try a run up to Christine's. Thought I might take Annie some—"

"You know Annie McGregor?"

He turned around and found himself face to face with a teenage boy he'd never seen before.

"Excuse me, I don't believe we've met." He held out his hand. "I'm Doc Wilkins, and you are?"

"Max McGregor. I'm trying to find my mother, Annie McGregor. You've met her? You know where she is?"

Sheriff Patterson joined them. "Doc? You know something about his mom?"

"Hold on. Just a minute. I only stopped by to pick up some groceries and—"

"But you said you were going to take something up to *Annie*." Max stepped closer. "That's gotta be my mom. I need to know where she is."

Doc looked over Max's shoulder at the sheriff.

Patterson scratched his chin. "The kid drove all the way from Florida. If you know where his mom is, help him out, Doc."

He hesitated, trying to think. He busied himself cleaning his glasses even though they were spotless. "I know exactly where she is, Max. But how about I go on up there and bring her back here to you?" He turned to leave.

The boy stepped around him, blocking his exit. "No, sir. I've come this far. I want you to take me to her. Besides, why wouldn't you want to take me up there to see my mom?"

Doc stared into the young man's anxious eyes. Finally, he pulled his gloves back on, and smiled in resignation.

"Then let's go see your mom, Max."

Chapter 38

Eagle's Nest

If the weight of the world had lifted off Michael Dean's shoulders, it paled in comparison to the thrill that washed over Annie McGregor. Never had she felt so overwhelmed with gratitude.

She remembered the words of Romans 8:28 as if the Apostle Paul had crafted them just for her. *And we know that in all things God works for the good of those who love him, who have been called according to his purpose.* To think that God had orchestrated all the infinite details that propelled her on this timely search for truth. All the stumbling blocks, lined up for a specific purpose. Every trace of exhaustion, every personal heartache, every emotional drain of her energy had contributed in part toward a divine appointment on this mountain. Even the sting of her humiliating confrontation with Chet Harrison had played a part . . . *for such a time as this.* If Chet hadn't crossed the line, she never would have experienced that final straw. That desperate, urgent need to get away from it all.

Annie could never have imagined that God would cross her path with Michael's again in such an extraordinary way to take care of "unfinished business." Now, her heart soaring from God's healing touch, she left Michael alone to his thoughts, busying herself by preparing something for them to eat. After toasting some stale bagels in a skillet on the Coleman stove, she heated water for tea.

"There's something else we need to talk about."

Carrying the tray to the coffee table, she set it down and handed him one of the warm mugs. "What's that?"

He blew on the steaming tea then cleared his voice. "It's just that . . . well, it seems like . . . uh—"

"Michael, what could possibly be so difficult for you to talk about? After what just happened here this morning?"

"Well, that's just it. There's something you need to know. And now, all of a sudden, I *know* I have to get this out. It has to do with what happened all those years ago."

She shrugged. "Maybe so, but that's all history. Just forget about it."

He shook his head. "I can't. I was such a fool to ever leave you, Annie. But I had a very valid reason for letting you go."

"Michael, I don't really think I want to—"

"Let me talk! And stop interrupting me. You need to hear this whether you want to or not."

She waited, quite certain she did not.

"It was Christine."

"What do you mean it was Christine?"

"When you and everyone else went to Hawaii after graduation, I stayed home to play in a semi-pro summer league, remember?"

"Okay. So?"

"Christine stayed home too, remember?"

"Yes, I remember. Her father was dying."

"And she was going through a tough time," he continued. "And all of her friends were out of the country. Except me."

She tilted her head.

"Christine needed a friend. She was alone. She was upset. Especially after her dad died. And . . . well, we became . . . close."

Silence.

"Close," he repeated. "As in, intimate."

She tented her eyebrows, tilting her head to the other side. A long-forgotten impish grin crossed his face. That crooked grin that used to melt her heart.

Not this time.

"Annie, it just happened. It wasn't planned, we didn't mean for it to happen—it just did."

"And you think I need to know this *now* because . . . ?"

"Because you need to know. Because I'm trying to make a fresh start of my life here. Because in order to do that, I need to start with a clean slate, and there are things you need to know. What else can I say?"

She dropped the bagel that had been dangling from her hand and blew out a lung full of air. "Well, let's see. For starters, how about 'I'm sorry'? We were together for *four years*, Michael. I left town for a few days and you bedded my best friend? How could you! Her father was dying, for heaven's sake! And you took advantage of her at a time like that? What kind of animal are you?"

She jumped up, the plate on her lap crashing to the floor. "Great. Just great." Ignoring the mess, she hopped over to the fireplace, angrily warming her hands. "I can't believe it. How could you be so heartless? How could you even think of being so heartless? And then, you turn around and dump me without so much as a single word of explanation?" She tossed the words over her shoulder like guided missiles. "You didn't even have the decency to at least be honest with me—after all those years together? It's unspeakable, Michael. How dare you. How *dare* you!"

"It would have been too much for you, Annie, and you know it! The last thing I wanted was to hurt you!"

"Well, it's a little late for that now because you most certainly *did* hurt me!" She wrapped her arms around herself, a sharp sob stealing her breath. "You broke my heart, Michael, and you know it."

Silence hung for seconds between them. But the spell was broken with the wild tapping of a heavy branch against the roof. Her shoulders slumped. She exhaled in defeat, a quiet moan in its wake.

"This is so typical," she finally whispered, realizing what had happened. She turned, peeking over her shoulder at him. A sad smile pulled across her lips. "*So* typical. One minute we're standing at the very throne of God as He's holding his arms open wide to greet you—and the next minute we're at each other's throats. It's so ridiculously predictable."

She collected the pieces of broken stoneware off the floor. "The enemy can't stand the fact that you've given your life to the Lord, Michael. He won't stand for it. So he does whatever he can to steal the joy of that decision. Even with a silly argument about ancient history like this."

"But I had to tell you."

"I suppose. I'm just amused by the timing of it and the way I over-reacted."

"Come here." He reached out his hand to her. She put the broken pieces on the tray and sat back down in the chair adjacent to him.

"I don't know much about that sort of stuff—about the 'enemy' or Satan or any of that. But I'm not finished. Let me say what I have to say so we can put this behind us and be done with it. Deal?"

"Deal."

"There's more to this and it's time you knew. When you all got back from Hawaii, if you'll remember, Christine was gone."

"I know. She went to New York to work on her master's degree while she interned for that big agency."

"Yes and no. The degree came later. She left because she was pregnant."

The air vanished from her lungs. He held her hand tight, refusing to let her pull it free.

He went on. "I was *so* . . . full of myself back then,

Annie. I told her I wanted no part of it. In fact, I tried to get her to have an abortion. Even as radical and free-spirited as she was back then, she wouldn't hear of it. That's why she left town. She made me promise not to tell a soul. But I knew I could never face you with it anyway. I may be a lot of things, but I'm an absolute coward when it comes to the emotional stuff. Which is probably no surprise to you.

"And that's why, when you came back, I had to break it off between us immediately. Only I didn't have the guts to tell you why."

She stared at him in disbelief, speechless.

He pressed on. "About a year later she called me. Said she'd had a baby boy. Said she had tried hard to take care of him, tried to be a good mother, but she just couldn't do it. She wanted something better for him. She was hoping I might volunteer to raise him, but naturally *that* didn't happen. My career was just taking off. No way I was gonna care for the kid.

"Christine said she figured as much. So she told me she was going to give him up for adoption. She wanted him to have a mother and a father and a real chance at a normal life. Of course I agreed.

"She kept the adoption very private, never gave me too many details, only that she was careful to make sure he was placed in a good home. She went through an attorney—it was all very anonymous. That was her requirement."

"You never saw him? You've never even met your own son?"

"No, I never did, at least not in person."

Annie studied him through narrowed eyes, trying to

understand. Trying to find some trace of sympathy about the whole bizarre situation. The analyses rolled awkwardly through her mind.

"What did you mean 'not in person'?" she asked.

"Christine sent me pictures of him from time to time. She had some kind of arrangement through her attorney to get pictures of him through the years. At least that's what she told me. I guess that sounds a little strange."

Annie nodded. "You could say that, considering neither of you wanted the kid." She rolled her eyes. She couldn't help it.

"In fact, I noticed an old picture of him in the other room. But Annie, you've got to understand, even though we went through this whole thing, we were still friends. It was never the same between us, but even so—we had a bond, obviously. I really cared about Christine. And I still do, believe it or not. I regret that I put her through all that. But then, you know as well as anyone what a jerk I've been."

"There's an understatement."

He smiled, squeezing her hand. "I had to tell you. Especially now. I know it isn't easy for you, but I feel like a ton of bricks has been lifted off me. I'm sorry if it's caused you pain. Again."

"What a strange twist to an already peculiar story. I never dreamed. It never even crossed my mind. Not once. And to think you're a father. Now *there's* a scary thought."

"No, I can't say I'm a father. I fathered a child, but there's a big difference. Someone else has been his father. Thank God."

"You said there's a picture of him in the other room. Where did you see it?"

"In that room where I was staying. It was his Little League picture from a long time ago. There's a bunch of framed photographs on the top of the dresser. I think there's even one of you, if I'm not mistaken."

She wrapped a quilt around her and stood up.

"Annie?"

"What?"

"Are you sure you're okay about all this now?"

"I'm okay about all this now, Michael. Shocked down to my socks maybe, but yeah, I'm okay. It'll take some getting used to, though. I'm just curious to see this mysterious little love-child," she trailed off heading into the bedroom.

Moments later, she returned. "There's a bunch of pictures in there, but the only one of a little boy is just this one of—"

"Of who?"

Nothing.

"But . . ."

"But what?" He twisted around to get a look at her. "Annie, what's the matter?"

Her lips were moving but nothing came out.

"Come over here. I can't hear a word you're saying. What's wrong with you?"

"But this is . . . Max." Her knees felt weak.

He took the framed photograph from her hands. "Yeah, that's him. But how did you know his name?"

She dropped into the chair like a rag doll.

"No. No, I'm sure you're mistaken."

"Annie, how could you possibly know his name if

Christine never told you about him?"

She shook her head. "No. There's got to be some mistake. Give me that!" She snatched the picture out of his hand. "This is NOT your son," she whispered angrily, jabbing her finger at the beaming young face in the picture. His image blurred, her voice gone. "Because this—this is *my* son."

He stared back at her. "That's impossible! That's the same kid she's been sending me pictures of for years! Why would she send me pictures of *your* kid? Don't be ridiculous."

Annie was lost in a web, her mind and heart tangled in tightening knots. She fought the rising volcano inside her as she searched for an explanation. *No. It's impossible.*

She spoke deliberately, slowly, as if to a child. "Michael, you said Christine gave your son up for adoption. When was that?"

"Well, let's see. She had the baby in March—"

"March?" she echoed, her heart sinking.

"Yeah, March. And then she called me sometime that fall. It was in the playoffs for the division . . . so I think it was in October. Sometime in October."

She forced herself to go on. "And did she tell you when they found a home for the baby?" she asked, her voice barely audible.

"What?"

Methodically this time. "Did she tell you when they found a home for the baby!"

"Well, I didn't hear about it until later. She knew I was busy with the playoffs—"

"I DON'T CARE ABOUT YOUR STUPID PLAYOFFS!"

"Geez, Annie! Calm down! I'm trying to remember!"

"Just tell me! When did Christine give up her baby?" A sob escaped.

He stared at her with eyes wide open. He began to nod as it came back to him. "It was at Christmas. I remember now because of the holidays. She was really sad about it. She said it was the hardest thing she ever had to do. But she was also glad because she was able to give someone a really amazing Christmas gift." He looked back at her. "Some Christmas gift, eh?" He chuckled.

Annie dropped her face into her hands and began to cry. "Oh God, please no."

Michael reached over to touch her shoulder. She pushed his hand away. "No! Just leave me alone."

"No, I won't leave you alone! I want some answers too. What makes you think Max could possibly be your son?"

"He *is* my son, you jerk! Don't you think I know my own son when I see him?" she cried, jabbing at the picture again. "He's my son!"

She rocked back and forth, tears streaming down her face. "God gave him to David and me when he was just eight months old. An attorney came to us at church. He said he couldn't reveal any information except that a young mother had requested that we consider adopting a little boy. He said she wanted a good and loving home for her child, and that she specifically asked for us. We assumed it was someone in the community who knew David was a pastor. Maybe even the estranged daughter of a church member. Something like that."

Her words slurred as the memories rushed by. "We were still newlyweds. We hadn't even thought about starting a family yet, but . . . after we prayed about it, we knew we were supposed to give this little guy a home." She caressed the picture, wishing she could feel the warmth of his skin through her fingers, smell the scent of his hair.

"On December 20th, they brought him to us. They placed Max in our arms and it was love at first sight." She wiped her nose and eyes, a sad smile not quite reaching her eyes. "I can't believe this."

"Why? Tell me! Why would Christine do this?" he yelled. "Why not just give the baby away to some stranger and be done with him? Was this some kind of bad joke? Some kind of sick revenge on the two of us? And I thought *I* was a jerk! This is unforgivable!" He tried to stand up but fell back in pain.

Annie didn't rush to his aid this time. "She did it out of love, Michael."

"But why? There are thousands of couples out there desperate to adopt a baby. Why did she have to pick *you?*"

"Because she knew me. She knew how much I loved kids. And she knew she would never have to worry about her son. She trusted us to take care of him and to love him."

The distinct sound of a car door thudded outside. They looked at each other.

"Michael, they must have cleared the roads! That means—"

He grabbed her arm. "Annie! Shhh!" he croaked. "Be quiet. We don't know who's out there. It could be Elliot's men!"

"What should we do?"

He was already tossing the quilts aside. "Get me off this sofa and over there, behind the kitchen counter. We have to stay out of sight!"

Chapter 39

Eagle's Nest

Michael sat on the cold kitchen floor, his back leaning against the cabinet doors, his chest heaving with anxiety.

"What should I do?" Annie whispered, fear etched on her face.

He cocked his head, listening for clues of who might be outside the cabin.

"Wait—" Annie stretched up to peek over the counter. "I think it's Doc."

Michael grabbed her elbow pulling her back down. "Get down! If it's Doc, we'll know soon enough. If it's not him, I don't want you getting your head blown off."

Hearing a muffled voice outside, she gasped. "Michael, did you hear that?"

He held up a finger, cautioning her to be silent.

"Mom! It's Max! Open up!"

The pounding on the door jolted her upright. Michael's stunned expression matched her own. "Max?" she mouthed.

Before Michael could stop her, she flew to the door. "Max! Oh Max! I'm here! Hold on!" she cried, her fingers recklessly unbolting the locks.

"Mom!"

She threw open the door and into his arms. "Oh Max! What are you—how did you—oh, sweetheart!" She hugged him, crying his name over and over.

"Mom! It's okay—I found you! We were so scared and I couldn't stand not knowing where you were and Dad was so upset and—"

Annie pulled back from their embrace and shot an anxious look over his shoulder. "Dad's here? He came with you?" She flinched at the tremor in her voice.

"Dad? No, he didn't come." He searched her eyes. "Mom? Why did you—"

She saw Doc Wilkins emerge from his Bronco at the foot of the porch steps. He stood with his hand on the open door, staring up at Annie. Seconds ticked by as they silently communicated. Finally, he shut the door. "Annie, I suppose we should have called before we came up, but Max here was in a big hurry to find you. I—well, I apologize."

She understood his meaning. "It's okay, Doc." Her eyes lingered only a moment more, then back at her son. She buried her head in his shoulder, hugging him again. "I'm just so surprised, Max! How did you know where to find me?"

"It's a long story. Can we come in? It's pretty cold out here."

"Oh, I'm sorry, of course! Come in."

Doc ascended the stairs, one hand grasping the handrail, his medical bag in the other. "Don't mind if I do," he mumbled.

They shuffled inside, drawn to the hearth where a fire was on its last embers. "Doc told me about your ankle. Here, let me help you." Max held her arm as she limped along. "He said it was a pretty bad sprain."

"It's much better," she assured him, reaching for a log as they neared the hearth. Let me get this fire going again. The power has been out so long and this has been our only source of heat but—"

"I'll check the breakers in just a minute," Doc offered. "The power came back on in town several hours ago."

"Our?" Max asked, his hand still on her arm.

"Our what, honey?"

"You said 'our' only source of heat."

She stopped, at a loss for words. "Did I say 'our'?" She turned to set the log on the embers. "Max, would you hand me a couple more logs?"

He walked to the end of the hearth and gathered several logs. He turned, his eyes grazing the furniture pulled close to the hearth. A pillow and lots of quilts spread out on the sofa. Another pillow, another pile of quilts laying haphazardly on the chair and ottoman. A scattering of mugs and plates on the coffee table.

Annie's heart hammered against her chest as she watched his mind working the puzzle.

Oh God, help me.

Max piled the logs in the fireplace and took the poker from his mother's hand. He stabbed at the glowing embers, stirring them to flames that licked the waiting logs. Finally, he turned to face her. "Mom?" he asked quietly. "What's going on?"

Annie looked across the room to Doc for help. Her eyes roamed the kitchen where she assumed Michael was still hidden behind the bank of cabinets. Doc nodded ever so slightly acknowledging the silent communication, then walked toward the kitchen.

"Max, there's so much I need to tell you," she began. "But before I say anything else, I want you to promise me you'll listen. Let me explain everything before you jump to any conclusions. Do I have your word?"

"Mom?" The frightened plea in his voice unsettled her.

She took a deep breath and wrung her hands. "Max, I came here to have some time to myself. I'm sure Dad told you. But a couple days after I got here, someone else showed up. I had no idea, of course . . . I mean, he just happened to come up here. The cabin belongs to Christine, an old friend of mine from college. And it turns out that *another* friend . . . well, actually a mutual friend, I suppose . . . he shows up here too, and he's in some kind of trouble and he was hurt and . . . well, I couldn't turn him away, could I?"

"Him?" Max searched her face.

A moan from the kitchen interrupted them. Annie watched as Doc lifted Michael from the floor, keenly aware that her son watched as well.

"If you'll excuse us, I need to attend to my patient." Max stared at Michael as Doc helped him out of the room.

Max pivoted. "Mom? What's going on here? Who is that?"

"That's what I'm trying to tell you, honey. I came up here to be alone, but it didn't turn out that way."

"Who's that guy?"

"His name is Michael Dean. He had no idea *I* was here, of course. He expected Christine to be here. He came here because he had nowhere else to go. He'd been shot and he was being followed and he—Max, I found him outside on the driveway. He had passed out in the snow. I didn't even know who it was until I was able to pull him inside here. And then . . ."

She started to pace, her words tripping over themselves in rapid succession. "Honey, I was so shocked! I couldn't believe it! I hadn't seen Michael in years, you see. And you can imagine my surprise—I thought he was dying! So, I called Doc Wilkins and he came up and he operated on Michael. Doc saved his life, Max."

He hung on her every word, despite the uneasiness she saw on his face. "Go on."

"Well, that's really all there is to tell. Except that the power went out and the phones went down and . . . well, he's in some very serious trouble, honey. Someone is trying to kill him. I know it must sound crazy. It's all very complicated."

He looked away.

"Max, I know it's an awkward situation. *Believe* me, I know. I've never been in such a strange mess in all my life."

"How did you know him in the first place?"

"Well, that's a long story, sweetheart."

"I came all the way up here to find you. Don't you think you should tell me?"

His tone tightened the knot in her stomach. "Michael and I go way back. We were in college together. That's how we both knew Christine."

"But he wasn't like a boyfriend or anything, was he?"

She rubbed her hands together. "Um, yes. Yes, he was. But honey, that was a long, *long* time ago."

His eyes bore through her. She couldn't bear the questions reflected in them. "Max, I told you not to jump to conclusions, and I meant it. There is nothing going on here beyond what I just explained to you."

He rolled his neck, both sides, then sat down on the hearth, planting his elbows on his knees. "I'm just so tired. I don't know *what* to think."

Suddenly, the overhead lights came on accompanied by a series of beeps from the microwave and the security system. Doc appeared at the utility room door. "Now that's more like it. Annie, how about making us all a pot of coffee?"

She clapped her hands together. "Good idea. Max, would you like some coffee? Are you hungry? Can I get you something to eat?"

"Coffee sounds good." He didn't bother looking at her.

She stood, reaching out to brush the bangs off his forehead. He flinched at her touch. A lump lodged in her throat. She pressed her lips together and headed for the kitchen.

"There really is so much I want to tell you, but first I want to hear about home. Is Dad okay?"

Max stretched out his legs, arching his back. "I suppose so. He's been really upset about you leaving and all." He stood up again, turning his back to her to stare into the fire. "I couldn't stand seeing him suffer like that. And Nana made a big scene and got her picture in the paper."

"Whatever for?" she asked, holding the empty carafe.

"You know Nana—it doesn't take much. She got all hot and bothered that no one knew where you were and went to the newspaper about it. Made it sound like you'd been kidnapped or something."

She set the carafe in the sink. "Oh Max. Please tell me you're joking."

"Front page. Big story. Big picture."

"Oh no. Poor David. How did he—"

"It was bad, Mom." He tossed a quick look at her over his shoulder. "I don't really want to talk about it right now."

An involuntary groan escaped her lips. She pushed the carafe under the faucet, filling it with frigid, clear water. She made the coffee, going through the motions on autopilot, then slowly walked over to the hearth and sat down.

"Max, I'm so sorry. I had no idea. I never meant to hurt anybody. I just needed a chance to think. Everything was closing in on me and—" Max sat down beside her and put his arm around her. She leaned into him, inhaling her son's musky scent. "I'm so sorry, honey."

"Mom, I didn't mean to make you cry."

"Annie?"

Mother and son looked up. Michael stood in the doorway from the hall, leaning heavily on Doc.

Oh Lord, give me strength.

"Uh . . . Max, this is the unexpected house guest I was telling you about." She cringed at the high pitch of her voice.

No one said anything. Doc proceeded to help his patient move to the sofa across from them, seating him there. "I think I'll go check on that coffee."

Michael lifted his head and looked into the distrusting eyes of her son. Annie watched as he took in everything—the eyes, the hair, the slant of her son's nose. She watched his eyes trace the line of Max's jaw, identical to his own. And she watched as Michael struggled to swallow his emotion.

"What are you looking at?" Max challenged.

Michael shifted his eyes to Annie. "Did you tell him?"

She pressed her eyes shut, furious he would ask at a moment like this. "No, Michael. Not now," she whispered.

"Tell me what?" Max narrowed his eyes at Michael. "Don't treat me like I'm a child. I want to know what's going on here. Did she tell me what?"

Michael cleared his throat. "Max, we haven't been introduced yet. My name is Michael Dean."

"Yeah, so? I know who you are. Mom just told me."

"She did?" Michael's surprise crossed his face. "Oh, you mean about us being friends from way back when."

"That's exactly what she told me."

Michael started to say something then closed his mouth.

He raised his eyebrows at Annie. "What else did you tell him?"

Annie buried her face in her hands. "Michael, please don't."

Max jumped up. She looked up in time to see white-hot rage rip across his face. He moved away from them, yelling at them, "Oh, now I get. I see what's going on here. You lied to me, Mom! You said there was nothing between the two of you but now I can see that was a lie!"

"Settle down. It's not what you think," Michael said.

"*You* . . . you shut up!"

Annie started after her son. "No, Max. He's right. It isn't at all what you're thinking. Please, calm down and listen to me!"

Max held up his hands, shielding himself from her. "Stay away from me. I don't want to hear this! I don't want to hear *any* of this."

He turned, rushing toward the front door.

"Max, I'm your father!"

They froze, paralyzed by the raw shock of the words still hanging in the air.

Max stood bolted where he was, his hand on the doorknob. "What did you say?"

"I said I'm your father," Michael answered. "But you don't understand any of this. Please, come back and let us explain it all. It's time you knew."

Annie took a step toward her son. "Honey, please, if you'll just—"

"No! I've heard enough. You think I'm some kind of idiot that I don't see what's gone on here? Geez, Mom. Give me some credit."

"Max, no!" she sobbed. "You don't—"

"Sure I do! But y'know what? I don't WANT to know. I'm not gonna stay here and listen to a pack of lies from this guy. I'm outta here."

❧

Max threw open the door and flew across the porch then down the stairs. He stumbled, falling onto the snowy driveway. His breath came in heaving gasps as he grappled to get back on his feet.

Suddenly, a strong hand pulled him to his feet. "Wha—"

"Well, look what we have here!"

"Let me go!"

Max fought the unseen person who held him. He heard a car door open and looked up, realizing a huge black Hummer was parked just down the driveway. Out of the back seat on the other side, a stranger emerged in a dark coat with a fedora pulled down low. The hat tipped slightly, signaling Max's captor to drag him to the other side of the car. Another passenger climbed out of the front seat.

"Marcus, you need some help?"

"Who are you?" Max shouted. "What do you want?"

"Nothing that concerns you, young man," the man in the hat said. "But, then again, maybe you can help us out."

Max struggled again, glaring at the stranger.

"Just who are you, young fella?"

"I'm not telling you anything. Let me go!"

"MAX!" his mother screamed from the porch. "Get your hands off my son!"

The accomplice grabbed Max's other arm in a death-grip.

The man in the hat looked up at Annie. "My, my, my. Isn't this nice? Quite a little gathering we have here, don't we?"

"Who *are* you? What do you want with my son!"

"Now, now, don't get upset. I'm sure we can all sort this out. We'll just come up and have a little chat inside where it's nice and warm."

"Stay where you are and tell them to let go of my son!"

"Let him go, Elliot." Michael limped onto the porch with Doc supporting him.

"Ah, yes. I was wondering when you'd show your face. Michael, you don't look so good!" the man chuckled.

"Let the boy go, Elliot. He has nothing to do with this. Just nice and easy, let him go." Michael had made his way slowly to Annie's side and grabbed hold of the railing. Doc stepped back away.

Max watched the man called Elliot take off his fedora, tapping it against his coat as he looked around the clearing. He brushed a few flakes of snow from his coat collar then walked leisurely toward the front of his large vehicle.

"The way I see it, Michael, this boy here is my insurance card. I'll be more than happy to hand him over if you'll just get inside the car. That's all. What could be easier?"

"Forget it. I've already passed along a whole packet of evidence implicating you in the murder of Christopher

Jordan. By now it's in the hands of the Attorney General."

Elliot laughed as he placed his hat back on his head. "Oh, I doubt that seriously."

"There's a document that spells it all out. Every word of it. My written testimony will put you and Duke away forever."

Max watched as the other back door of the Hummer opened. A tall, lanky man unfolded from the car's interior, holding up a packet in his gloved hand.

"You mean this?"

⁓

Grady!" Michael gasped. His knees started to buckle. Annie grabbed him, helping him stay on his feet. "Wha—what are you doing?"

Grady kept his head down, refusing to look him in the eye. "Michael, Michael . . . you just never know when you'll run into an old friend, now do you?"

"What? I don't understand! Why are you—"

"Oh, it's really kind of amusing. Elliot here has been my *mentor*, I guess you could say." Grady looked at the Congressman who nodded, noticeably pleased at the compliment. "He's been a tremendous help to me for a long time, pal. In fact, I have you to thank for introducing us."

Grady finally raised his eyes to meet Michael's. "I met Elliot at your wedding. It wasn't long after that I found myself in a rather nasty fix with a savings and loan company. If it hadn't been for Congressman Thomas I would be in prison today."

Grady made his way over to Elliot's side. "But he was gracious enough to make a few phone calls and before I knew it, the whole thing just disappeared." He cocked his head to look at Elliot. "After that, he took me under his wing. Helped me get back on my feet. Now and then he gave me an assignment or two, and I was always more than happy to comply."

"Like the son I never had." Elliot laughed, tossing a glance toward Michael.

"Amazing, actually," Grady continued. "I've lived a good life, had a successful career. Then you showed up in Tulsa, spilling your guts about your mysterious 'dilemma.' I may not be a rocket scientist, but I figured it out almost immediately. I knew it had to be Elliot who was putting the screws to you. Nobody else ever intimidated you except for him. And hey, for the record, I felt for you, big guy. But you want to know something? Believe it or not, I've never been a member of the Michael Dean Fan Club.

"You always got all the breaks. From the day I met you, you always had it easy. With grades, with women, with baseball . . . My *whole life*—even since I was a little snot-nosed kid—all I ever wanted to do was play professional baseball. It was all I ever dreamed of. But when the scouts came to our games, they never saw *me* play. Why? Because their eyes were always glued to you. They fell all over themselves to get a piece of the mighty Michael Dean. I sat on the bench and watched my dreams vaporize."

"But Grady—"

"—and then you married Amelia and it got even easier for you, didn't it?" Grady droned on, strolling to lean against the front of the Hummer. "Big baseball celebrity marries wealthy Congressman's daughter. But poor Amelia—she was just a pawn in your little game plan, wasn't she? Like everyone else who ever crossed your path. And then your precious Sports Page empire came along. Never mind that it was handed to you on a silver platter. See what I mean? It was just one break after another, your whole entire life! And you know what? With all those breaks, with all those doors that kept swinging wide open for you, you never gave *anybody* else so much as a thought. You never cared about anything or anyone other than yourself. It never mattered *who* you trampled over, did it?"

"Grady—"

"How very interesting to find you here with Annie, of all people. Who knew? After you ripped her heart out and stomped all over it way back when, she's the *last* person I'd expect you to be shacked up with here in your hideaway love nest."

Grady turned his gaze to Annie. "You were such a fool for him, Annie. All those years I stood by and watched you. How could you be so stupid? Couldn't you see that you were just another one of his conquests?"

"Stop it, Grady!" She looked helplessly at Max. He refused to look at her.

Grady burst into laughter. "Why? Am I embarrassing you in front of your kid? It didn't *used* to embarrass you, now did it? You *lived* with this scum bag, Annie. And everybody knew it! Not exactly the image of a good little preacher's wife, now is it?"

"SHUT UP! I beg you, Grady. For God's sake, this is my son!"

A smirk drawn across on his face, he cocked his head at Max. "I bet you didn't know your mother was a tramp, did you?"

An explosion ripped through the air. The windshield of the Hummer shattered. Standing in the doorway with a rifle aimed at the intruders, Doc Wilkins yelled at Michael and Annie. "Get in here! Hurry!"

Below them, Max wasted no time. With uncommon strength, he reared his elbows into the stomachs of his surprised captors, knocking the wind out of them. He was up the stairs before they knew what happened.

Michael and Annie pulled him into the cabin with them, slamming the door and bolting it.

Through the door they could hear Elliot shouting. "Stop them! Surround the cabin! Don't let them get away!"

Michael panted. "We have to get out of here. We've got to get away from them!"

"Annie, go open the door to the utility room," Doc ordered, handing the rifle to Max. "Max, get the flashlight over there on the counter. Hurry!"

Annie opened the door as Doc burrowed Michael under his good arm, hurrying him toward the back of the cabin. "I think I know a way out. Follow me! Hurry!"

They rushed through the utility room and opened the inside door to the garage.

"We can't drive out of here!" Michael blasted. "They'll kill us before we even back out!"

"We're not driving out," Doc answered. "Max, hold him up for me."

Max stared hard at Doc before moving to take his place under Michael's arm. The doctor rushed toward the side of the garage where a large worktable stood on an old braided rug. "Annie, help me get this moved." They shoved the table off the rug, clay pots and garden tools clanging off onto the floor. Doc threw back the rug, revealing a large trap door.

"What is this?" Annie cried.

Doc lifted the door. "It's an old mine shaft. The garage was built over it. Christine's dad and I used to hunt together years ago and we used this shaft to get out into the woods instead of climbing down the mountain. Max, hand your mother the flashlight. Annie, you go ahead and we'll send Michael down next. Let's go, let's go!"

They awkwardly made the descent into the dark hole below them. Before following the rest of them, Doc reached for a shovel leaning in the corner of the garage. He swung it above him, knocking the overhead light bulb out of its socket. Satisfied with the pitch black cover of darkness, he slipped into the shaft, pulling the door shut above him.

❧

Whatever you do, don't let Michael get away," Elliot stormed. "I don't care about the others. We'll take care of them later. Just bring me Michael!"

Still wheezing, Gus popped open the back of the Hummer. A large narrow box held a small arsenal of rifles.

Marcus shoved a rifle at Grady. "Take one. They're all loaded. Should be plenty of ammunition in these babies. You go around that way. Gus, you go the other way. Mr. Thomas and I will check out the house."

Gus and Grady took off in separate directions, circling the cabin. Marcus led the way as he and the congressman carefully rushed up the stairs, their guns aimed dead ahead. They backed up against the rough logs on either side of the front door. Marcus signaled his intent to kick the door open. Elliot moved away, inching along the wall.

Marcus shoved his foot against the door with all his might, screaming out in pain as it held intact. He moved back against the wall wincing from the pain shooting through his leg.

Elliot pushed him aside. "Can't you do anything right?" he growled while aiming his shotgun at the door. He fired a single shot, splintering the entire handle off the door.

They moved inside, their rifles sweeping the scope of the room for any movement. Nothing. Marcus tiptoed toward the hall. Elliot headed past the kitchen toward the back of the house. With each step he grew angrier. He would not accept the possibility that his prey had escaped. He passed through the utility room, opening the door that led into the garage. He fumbled with the switch, cursing when no light came on. He stepped into the windowless garage, seeing only the dim outline of Michael's Escalade. Yet, he was sure they had somehow slipped away. He stepped back, scanning the utility room. He pulled open a closet in search of a flashlight. Reaching for the mag light, he flicked the switch. Nothing.

He cursed again, hurling the heavy flashlight at Michael's windshield and turned back.

"Marcus! Where are you?"

"In here, boss. There's no one here."

"They must have escaped outside somehow. There—" He pointed to the French doors opening out onto the large balcony. "Look out there!"

They scrambled to unlock the doors then thrust them open. The biting wind blew the doors wide open. They peered over the balcony but saw nothing but the bright mountain landscape and the sharp decline beneath them, a winter wonderland masking trees and brush in a blinding white mass.

محو

Annie stepped onto the cold damp ground, careful to light their descent with her flashlight. At the bottom of the stairs an open landing spread around her. She reached up to help Michael off the last step feeling his gasping breaths against her hair. Max hopped down, helping her set Michael on the ground. Doc moved quickly, reaching for a lantern hanging from a hook in the rough log beam on the low ceiling above them. He dug in his pocket for matches and lit the wick. A soft glow mushroomed through their hideout.

"There. At least we can see where we are." He rubbed his hands together and looked around.

"Will we be safe here, Doc?" Annie whispered.

"Only for a moment. If they find that door up top, we'll be sitting ducks. Can't risk it. We'll take a moment to catch our breath then keep moving." He knelt beside Michael. "You okay?"

Michael shuddered, still trying to catch his breath. He nodded. "Where does this lead? We can't just waltz out in the open, y'know."

Doc turned around and pointed down a dark tunnel. "That leads on down the side of the mountain. Empties out onto an open cave that's tucked under a sizable overhang. It's well covered so they won't find it right away."

Annie moved close to Max and tried to put her arm around him. He avoided her embrace by bending over to stretch out his legs.

"We better get moving," he muttered.

"Max, how about you carry that lantern for us," Doc asked. "I'll bring up the rear with the flashlight."

"Sure." Max swapped the flashlight for the dusty old lantern. They followed his lead down the gradually descending slope of the tunnel.

Annie breathed a silent prayer. *Oh God, please help us. Protect us from those men. And from Grady.*

Though it seemed like an eternity, their journey through the tunnel ended in less than twenty minutes. Doc brushed away the cobwebs and debris from the rustic door and tried to unlock it. The stubborn latch held tight.

Max moved closer. "Here, let me try." He handed the lantern to Doc and gave the latch a shove. No luck. Max took a deep breath and tried again. This time the rickety old handle broke free. He turned around to face the others. "Now what?"

"Let me take a look." Doc handed the lantern back to Max. He leaned against the door pressuring it slightly to open. The blast of cold air took his breath away. Annie stood behind him, watching as he stepped out to observe the landscape outside. The echo of a distance voice froze them in place. No way to tell which direction it came from.

He pulled back inside. "I think they're still a good distance above us," he whispered. "But once we're outside, no talking." He motioned for them to follow, holding his index finger against his lips warning them again to keep silent.

One by one they stepped out of the tunnel into the open cavern. The wind whipped through the exposed cave, sending tremors up Annie's back.

Doc motioned for them to sit down. Max hunkered down in a corner, wrapping his jacket tighter around him. Annie helped Michael inch down the earthen wall. The overgrown brush hid them safely from sight. She stood close to Doc, wishing his courage would somehow rub off on her.

Minutes passed. The frigid air pressed down on them like strangling fingers. Annie couldn't stop shivering. She was freezing and miserable, but nothing could compare to the dagger she felt in her heart. Would this be how it ended? Would their enemies find them frozen to death on the side of this mountain? Would she never have the chance to explain everything to Max?

She found a spot and sat down, burying her face in her arms. She pulled her knees up tight and tried to stay calm. When she thought she couldn't bear the cold and the heartache a second more, she felt someone move in beside her. Max wrapped his arms around her just as she raised her head.

"We'll be warmer if we stay close together," he whispered, his cheeks flushed from the bitter cold. She saw a flicker of compassion in his eyes, if only for a moment. With a guarded smile, she snuggled closer to him, burying her face against his strong shoulder.

Her silent prayers continued in the agonizing minutes that crept by. After an eternity, she felt Max tense his muscles. She looked up. Doc held up a hand in warning, his head cocked at a strange angle as he listened for something in the wind.

Suddenly the air split with the distinct crack of a rifle locking into position.

"Drop the rifle, old man. Nice and easy."

❧

They followed the sound of Grady's strangely calm and commanding voice until they spotted him behind the barrel of a shotgun. His towering frame hovered only a few yards away just to the right of their hollow. Annie and Max stood together in one motion. Doc backed up to stand in front of them, his arms extending back to protect them. Michael remained seated, unable to stand.

"Grady, don't do this," he shouted.

"Sorry, man. It's too late to turn back now."

"It doesn't have to be. We can work something out. Just help us get away from Elliot and I swear—we'll leave you out of this completely."

"No way."

"You're not like him! You could never be as evil as Elliot! He's using you! Can't you see that?"

"You're wrong, Michael. By eliminating you from the picture, I return a huge favor to Elliot, and get rid of a life-long bur under my saddle—*you.* Killing two birds with one stone, you could say. Now, one more time, old man. Drop the gun."

Doc lowered his rifle to the ground, rising back up with hands uplifted.

"That's better."

Michael raised his good arm toward Max. "Help me up, Max, okay?" With great effort, Max helped lift Michael to his feet.

"Michael, I'll only warn you once. Don't do anything stupid," Grady cautioned in a slow, menacing cadence.

Michael nodded in compliance. "Listen to me, Brewster. Think about what you're doing. There's no way you'll come out of this clean and you know it. Tell me, man—what's Shari gonna think when she finds out your dirty little secrets? Huh? And what about Molly and Jason? Oh, they'll be *real* proud to tell their friends about their jailbird daddy—"

"Shut up!"

"Nice work, Grady." The smug compliment interrupted them as Elliot stepped into view, his own rifle now aimed at them alongside Grady's. "I never doubted for a moment that I could count on you."

Michael's eyes tracked back to Grady. Cautiously ignoring his father-in-law, he tried again to appeal to his life-long friend, hoping somehow to get under his skin. "You can't possibly want to bring this kind of shame to your family. Think of them, man! You'll break Shari's heart—"

"I said shut up!"

"All that stuff you said about me—it was true," he pressed on. "I know it now. But you've got it all wrong. *You're* the one who had it all. In the end, you came out on top. Don't you see? You have a wife who loves you. You have two kids—Grady, you're their hero! Think about them. Think about what you're doing! What will happen to them when this all goes down. What will they think of you then?"

"Shut up, Michael!"

"Don't throw it all away! Don't ruin their lives with this ridiculous attempt at revenge—"

"I said SHUT UP!"

"Shari will leave you. You know she will. She'll never put up with—"

"LEAVE HER OUT OF THIS!"

"Don't be an idiot, Brewster!" Michael yelled.

"I SAID SHUT UP!" A string of expletives followed his final warning before Grady snapped his shotgun straight up into the air and fired a shot. The blast echoed against the mountains, bouncing in deathly repetition.

He narrowed his eyes in contempt, lowering his weapon

back at Michael, aiming it right between his eyes. "The next one has your name on it."

"I think it's about time we put an end to this little soiree once and for all," Elliot announced as if ending some boring business meeting.

At first, it sounded like an amplified, prolonged ripping . . .

"What was that?" an unseen voice shouted above.

"Shhhh!" another hissed in response, from the lip of the ridge above them. "Listen!"

The ripping grew louder and louder until it roared all around them. Elliot and Grady lifted their faces, their eyes widening in terrified symmetry. Michael and Doc looked at each other in confusion. Annie clung to Max as the strange noise filled them with compounded fear.

"AVALANCHE!"

Like a runaway freight train careening off its track, the furious mountain broke off a wild, enormous slice of ice and snow. No doubt angered by the unwelcome assault of the shotgun blast, it spewed a raging landslide of white thunder from above.

Tucked beneath the protective overhang of the mountain shelter, Doc's entourage flattened themselves against the wall of the carved-out refuge. They watched in horror as the massive wedge of blinding snow bore down before them. Marcus and Grady flew past them like a couple of rag dolls, their arms and legs flailing in futile motion, their cries buried in the roar. The momentum lifted Grady and Elliot off their feet, flinging them out of sight into the wall of white.

The avalanche rumbled on and on, cutting a path of destruction and uprooting frozen trees like so many matchsticks.

The four of them grasped onto each other, holding on with every ounce of strength as the barrage continued around them.

And then—silence. They stood, stunned in the aftermath of what they'd just witnessed.

"Michael! This is part of your miracle!" Annie turned, grabbing his arm. "Remember how you said it would take a miracle to get out of your mess? Well, God did it—again! He gave you another miracle, don't you see?" Tears of joy streamed down her face. "He *saved* you! He saved all of us!"

She pulled back, turning to her son. "Max? Oh, sweetheart!" She cried in the arms of her son whose own tears slipped down his reddened cheeks.

"I know, Mom. I know."

An eerie silence slipped around them. The calm after the storm. No more threats. No more gun fire. No more explosions cascading down this mountain. The rush of nature's fury now rested.

God's little remnant of survivors held onto each other once more as the reality of their survival sunk in. Doc looked over his shoulder at the newly rearranged landscape. His lips parted as he tried to speak, then clamped shut, his chin trembling. He sniffed, obviously embarrassed by his emotion even as gratitude wrinkled his brow.

Max, too, found it difficult to speak. Annie knew a long list of unanswered questions still pounded at his heart's door, smothered in the wake of this moment. She watched as he stole glances at Michael. His *father.*

Moments passed. Then Michael blinked away tears as he smiled at her. "You're right, Annie. Except your count is off. The way I see, it, we've experienced *three* miracles here today." He briefly turned misty eyes toward the young man clinging to his side, then winked at her.

"Three miracles," she marveled, shaking her head. "Such amazing grace."

Epilogue

Weber Creek, Colorado

The seductive aroma of Mary Jean Williamson's fresh-baked cinnamon rolls wafted through the general store now crowded with a horde of welcomed guests. She and Bob hosted each and every one of them with beaming smiles, hot drinks and plates full of the piping hot confections.

David remained close at his wife's side, his arms wrapped tightly around her as they enjoyed the warmth from the stone fireplace. Annie relaxed, nestled snugly against him, thanking God to be back where she belonged—secure in her husband's arms.

She hugged him hard. "I love you, David. I'll never leave you again. I promise."

He kissed the top of her head. "Good. I just hope you

still say that a year from now. I've decided to take the next twelve months off. We are now officially on sabbatical. You and I are going to travel and spend a *whole* lot of time together. A fresh start, Annie. We'll learn from our mistakes and figure out how to do a far better job of this life we've chosen. How does that sound?"

She turned to face him, hardly believing the words she'd just heard. Then, with a burst of laughter, she jumped into his embrace, showering him with tears of love.

The questions, heartaches, and doubts that first led her to this remote mountain stayed tucked away in her heart as the healing process began. Reassured through the startling events of the past several days, Annie kept laughing, basking in the sweet relief of God's faithful sovereignty in her life. The whys and hows seemed insignificant now. In their place, God's strength upheld her with His promises. He had delivered her safely back to David, reminding her once again of His eternal hedge of protection.

When Sheriff Patterson, his deputy, and a small posse of the locals rescued them from their oasis, Annie was overcome with joy to find David waiting anxiously for her at the top of the cabin steps. He explained that Pete Nardozzi had persuaded a fellow officer—a former Navy combat pilot—to fly them to Colorado in his private jet despite the weather conditions. They arrived in Weber Creek just as Patterson and his crew were heading up to Eagle's Nest. Before they could piece together the apparent drama that preceded their arrival, a shotgun blast boomed through the winter sky. They rushed to the cabin's balcony just as the avalanche slid down the mountain beneath them.

In the aftermath, the lifeless bodies of Congressman Elliot Thomas and Grady Brewster were eventually dug out from the fallen debris covered by a shroud of snow. Their accomplices, Gus Rainey and Marcus Simmons, survived the avalanche. They were transported by ambulance to the nearest hospital some thirty miles away under heavy guard of Colorado State Patrolmen.

Now, as the group recovered in the safe haven of Williamson's General Store, Max and Michael talked quietly together, their rocking chairs pulled away from everyone else. Michael, his wounds freshly dressed at Doc's office, had refused an ambulance ride to the hospital. He needed to be here now. Still stunned by the wonders so graciously bequeathed to him, he also yearned for a chance to get acquainted with his son.

Then would come the long-overdue explanation of Max's lineage. Here, with the security of Annie and David so close by, Max agreed to hear the truth at last; the initial shock that sent him bolting out of the cabin, all but forgotten. Unbridled fear has a way of leveling out the playing field of emotions.

"Glory! I can't *ever* remember having so much commotion in our quiet little town!" Mary Jean handed Doc a fresh mug of coffee. "I feel like we've been through the grinder. At least four or five times! Don't you, George?"

Doc gave her a weary smile. He accepted the mug into his still trembling hands. "Yes, MJ, I do at that."

"How can I ever thank you? *All* of you?" Annie asked, her voice husky.

Bob draped his arm over Mary Jean's shoulder. He waved off Annie's gratitude, but his blush acknowledged her appreciation. Mary Jean simply smiled, happy as a mother hen with all her baby chicks safe and sound.

The bell on the front door clanged again as a gust of cold air whipped through the store, announcing another arrival. They all turned to see who it was. The newcomer entered, pulling off a red knit cap. Long blond tresses fell downward, spilling over a navy wool coat. Shaking the hair out of her face without looking up, she called out, "Mary Jean! Bob! It's me, Christine!"

Shuffling her way to the back of the store, Christine made her way to the swarm of people all frozen in their tracks staring at her. Her smile slowly faded as she took in the cast of characters. One by one, she looked at them, her blue eyes widening in recognition of each face. Then, at last, her eyes turned to the two rocking chairs off to the side. She gasped, her gloved hands covering her mouth.

Max stood up, holding out his hand to help Michael to his feet. Michael wrapped his good arm around the shoulders of his son. They broke into smiles before looking back at Christine.

As the silence grew unbearable, Annie whispered a moan. "I think I need a vacation . . ."

"NO!" David and Max shouted in perfect unison.

Perplexed for a split second, Annie began to laugh, the

roll of her laughter contagious as it swept through the small crowd.

Nose to nose, forehead to forehead, David warned his wife. "No more vacations, Annie McGregor. At least, not without me!"

THE END

ABOUT THE AUTHOR

Born in Texas and raised in Oklahoma, Diane Hale Moody is a graduate of Oklahoma State University. She lives with her husband Ken in the rolling hills just outside of Nashville. They are the proud parents of two grown and extraordinary children, Hannah and Ben.

Just after moving to Tennessee in 1999, Diane felt the tug of a long-neglected passion to write again. Since then, she's written a column for her local newspaper, feature articles for various magazines and curriculum, and several novels with a dozen more stories eagerly vying for her attention.

When she's not reading or writing, Diane enjoys an eclectic taste in music and movies, great coffee, the company of good friends, and the adoration of a peculiar little pooch named Darby.

Visit Diane's website at **dianemoody.net** and her blog, "just sayin'" at **dianemoody.blogspot.com**

Other Books by Diane Moody

Confessions of a Prayer Slacker (Non Fiction)

Blue Christmas (The Moody Blue Trilogy Book One)

Blue Like Elvis (The Moody Blue Trilogy Book Two)

Tea with Emma (The Tea Cup Novellas Book One)

Strike the Match (The Tea Cup Novellas Book Two)

3208711R00255

Made in the USA
San Bernardino, CA
16 July 2013